PRAISE FOR

Jean Johnson and Her Novels

"Terrific—fast, sexy, charming, and utterly engaging. I loved it!"
— Jayne Ann Krentz, *New York Times* bestselling author

"The magical land Johnson creates is a whimsical treat, and the brothers are a joy to behold. Readers will look forward to more in the Sons of Destiny series." *—Booklist*

"A fresh new voice in fantasy romance."
—Robin D. Owens, RITA Award–winning author

"A must read . . . Jean Johnson can't write them fast enough for me!"
—The Best Reviews

"Enchantments, amusement, eight hunks, and one bewitching woman make for a fun romantic fantasy." *—Midwest Book Review*

"An intriguing world . . . an enjoyable hero . . . an enjoyable showcase for an inventive new author. Jean Johnson brings a welcome voice to the romance genre, and she's assured of a warm welcome." *—The Romance Reader*

"Jean Johnson has created a mystical world . . . very much like the great folktales we love to hear over and over . . . Delightful entertainment."
—Romance Junkies

"The writing is sharp and witty and the story is charming. [Johnson] . . . has created an enchanting situation . . . She tells her story with a lively zest that transports a reader." *—Romance Reviews Today*

"A fun story." *—The Eternal Night*

"An intriguing and entertaining tale of another dimension." *—Fresh Fiction*

Bedtime
STORIES

A Collection of Erotic Fairy Tales

JEAN JOHNSON

HEAT
New York

THE BERKLEY PUBLISHING GROUP
Published by the Penguin Group
Penguin Group (USA) Inc.
375 Hudson Street, New York, New York 10014, USA
Penguin Group (Canada), 90 Eglinton Avenue East, Suite 700, Toronto, Ontario M4P 2Y3, Canada
(a division of Pearson Penguin Canada Inc.)
Penguin Books Ltd., 80 Strand, London WC2R 0RL, England
Penguin Group Ireland, 25 St. Stephen's Green, Dublin 2, Ireland (a division of Penguin Books Ltd.)
Penguin Group (Australia), 250 Camberwell Road, Camberwell, Victoria 3124, Australia
(a division of Pearson Australia Group Pty. Ltd.)
Penguin Books India Pvt. Ltd., 11 Community Centre, Panchsheel Park, New Delhi—110 017, India
Penguin Group (NZ), 67 Apollo Drive, Rosedale, North Shore 0632, New Zealand
(a division of Pearson New Zealand Ltd.)
Penguin Books (South Africa) (Pty.) Ltd., 24 Sturdee Avenue, Rosebank, Johannesburg 2196,
South Africa

Penguin Books Ltd., Registered Offices: 80 Strand, London WC2R 0RL, England

This book is an original publication of The Berkley Publishing Group.

This is a work of fiction. Names, characters, places, and incidents either are the product of the author's imagination or are used fictitiously, and any resemblance to actual persons, living or dead, business establishments, events, or locales is entirely coincidental. The publisher does not have any control over and does not assume any responsibility for author or third-party websites or their content.

PRINTING HISTORY
Heat trade paperback edition / April 2010

Library of Congress Cataloging-in-Publication Data

Johnson, Jean, 1972–
    Bedtime stories / Jean Johnson. — Heat trade pbk. ed.
        p. cm.
    ISBN 978-0-425-23257-6 (trade pbk.)
    1. Erotic stories, American. 2. Fairy tales—Adaptations. I. Title.
    PS3610.O355B43 2010
    813'.6—dc22
                                    2009043811

PRINTED IN THE UNITED STATES OF AMERICA

10 9 8 7 6 5 4 3 2 1

Acknowledgments

I really have the coolest job in the world . . . and the best readers. You have all been very kind in taking the time to contact me and let me know what you liked, and even what you didn't like, about my stories. (Yes, I include the didn't-like stuff, because it can still be helpful in shaping my future works, particularly when phrased politely and thoughtfully.) So thank you very, very much.

Also, I'd like to extend a thank-you to all the editors and compilers of folklore, legends, and fairy tales everywhere, and to the many, many tellers of those tales over the centuries. I'm proud to be part of this long-standing tradition of entertaining people, and I'll do my best to keep it up.

~Jean

CONTENTS

The Frog Prince

Author's Note: Welcome, and I hope you'll enjoy my versions of erotically revised fairy tales. Revising them erotically isn't as strange as it might seem, either; I'll bet you didn't know that in the oldest German version of this story, the princess didn't own a golden ball so much as she owned a golden ballus . . . which was a local corruption of the Latin word phallus. Puts a whole new twist on this classic tale, doesn't it? In an effort to preserve the true spirit and meaning of this classic fairy tale, I feel it should be told in a way that honors that original, adult intent.

PRINCE Henrik was a frog. It wasn't his idea, but he was one. There were worse things he could have been enchanted into, of course. The flies he ate, for one; it was bad enough how the wings tickled on the way down into his gullet, but to actually *be* a fly would have been horrible. A disturbingly short life span and an unnatural attraction to animal droppings were not at all on his list of must-have experiences.

Still, there was the mud between one's toes; that wasn't as bad as it could have been. At least, not on a warm summer's day like today. It was soft and squelchy, and satisfying in a way he hadn't felt since he was a lad. The only problem was, he wasn't a lad, and feeling like a lad was what had gotten him into this predicament.

Prince Henrik was doomed to remain a frog, unless he either married the Fairy Tilda—who was more than twice his age, and Henrik just couldn't bring himself to marry a woman who had been born before even his own mother—or found a young woman willing to fulfill the fairy's codicils.

I shouldn't have said to her face that I didn't need a "second mother." That wasn't well done of me. Nor did it help when my father's chief counselor pointed out she was surely in the last gasp of her childbearing years and thus unlikely to bear a suitable heir . . . and I definitely should not have agreed, let alone concurred so wholeheartedly.

I also should have paid more attention to my geography lessons as a lad . . .

Part of the Fairy Tilda's curse had been to translocate Henrik to a foreign land. Instead of the birch trees he was familiar with, this forest boasted a plethora of broad-trunked oaks. The only tolerable things about it were the mild weather and the large, tasty flies. One full month of life as a frog had taught him the different flavors of a variety of insects from spiders to gnats, and the fat, fuzzy, flies were the best. Except they tickled when they went down. Tasty, but disturbing at the same time.

If ever a frog could pray to the ears of the angels in Heaven, Henrik certainly tried. Every single meal, he offered up a prayer for deliverance. Every single mouthful, he worried he would never again be a man.

A strange, beautiful sound tickled his ears, or what passed for them. For a moment, the transformed prince wondered if he was hearing angels laughing. It was coming from the far bank of the river he had been deposited by, the river which was his temporary home. The near bank had a gentle slope to it, green and mossy, with the occasional thicket of bracken ferns. The far side was steep and clifflike; had he been a man, it would have been taller than his head, counting from the rippling surface of the water.

The noise echoed across the little valley again; his wide, blinking eyes swiveled and focused as three pastel-clad figures came into view. One of the three maidens—for they seemed to be young and lithe and full of laughter, though he couldn't be completely sure at this distance—was holding aloft in one hand something gold and glinting. She twisted and turned in her attempts to dodge as the other two leaped and grabbed, trying to wrest it from her grasp.

Cries of "No, it's mine!" and "Oh, please!" and "I just want to hold it!" echoed across the water, along with a particularly odd, almost lasciviously voiced, "Just hold it? *I* want to *try* it!"

Intrigued, but unable to make sense of what the golden thing was, Henrik cursed his amphibian eyes. They were good enough for seeing things clearly within a few yards, but not so good for viewing things at a far distance. Hopping along the edge of the water—he never went far from the water, as his skin seemed to prefer being moist—he twisted his eyes this way and that, trying to focus on the object in the dark-haired maiden's hands.

The three of them dodged and grasped, laughed and shrieked, begged and protested, until an accidental bump and an unexpected trip sent the owner of the gilded whatever tumbling to her hands and knees. The gleaming object, flung free of her grasp, tumbled over the edge of the low cliff and *splopped* into the river.

The other two girls, with their brown hair and their giggles, caught themselves before they also fell. Huddled together, they gaped at the water, dark with the thick mud coating the river bottom. From the disappointed, rueful looks on their faces, he guessed they couldn't see whatever had been dropped. The way they sheepishly backed up as the other maiden struggled to her feet told Henrik they weren't about to help the girl look for her fallen treasure, either.

"Wonderful. Just wonderful!" the grass-stained maiden muttered as she dusted off her gown. "Well, don't just stand there. Help me get down the bank!"

The other two girls warily eyed the muddy edge of the cliff and backed up. Henrik heard them muttering something about "chores" and "embroidery" as they shook their heads. Without further ado, they hiked their skirts and ran up the slope, heading deeper into the woods. The young woman they left behind dropped to her knees and stared glumly at the river below.

Mindful of the terms of his enchanted imprisonment, Henrik hopped into the river. Whatever the girl had lost, if he could help her find it, she might consider herself indebted to him. It was a slim chance, but the only one he had. All he had to do was find a golden, metallic object in the mud of the riverbed.

It didn't take long to find it, since logic dictated the object had fallen straight in, given the heavy splash it had made. Though it hadn't been swayed more than an inch or two from its trajectory by the river's current—geometry had been one of Henrik's favorite classes as a lad with his tutors—the bottom was very muddy at that point, giving him only a glimpse of polished gold. Orienting himself underwater, Henrik made sure he could find the spot again, then stroked up toward the surface.

His wide-swiveling eyes spotted the maiden gingerly picking her way down to the river's edge several yards away. Letting the current carry him toward her, he watched her test the water with a hand, flinching at the chilly temperature. He was used to it, as it was one of the hazards of amphibious life, but she was clearly dubious about getting wet in search of her lost treasure. Leaping onto a head-sized rock at the water's edge, Henrik cleared his throat.

"*Ahem.* Good afternoon to you, fair maiden!" he called out.

Startled, she lifted her gaze from the water. This close, Henrik could finally make out the details of her features, since as a frog he was woefully shortsighted. She had lovely light blue eyes and curly brown hair, a slightly turned-up nose, and a hint of freckles on her otherwise creamy complexion.

"Who . . . Who's there? Who spoke?" she demanded, twisting to look up and down the bank.

"Down here, on the rock. The frog," Henrik clarified. She turned and peered his way.

"The . . . *what?*"

Executing a courtly bow wasn't easy in an amphibious form, but Henrik did his best. "Greetings, fair maiden. I am, as you see, an enchanted frog, capable of speech, including intellectual discourse and helpful hints."

She blinked at him.

"I believe you have lost a golden object in the muddy depths of this river, yes?" he inquired politely.

"A . . . talking frog," she muttered.

"Yes," Henrik repeated patiently. "My name is Henrik. About a month ago, I said the wrong thing to a fairy—for which I am ever so sorry—and now I am stuck in the body of a frog. But I still have the wit and courage of a man. I noticed how you lost an item to the river, and I just happen to know exactly where to find it."

She blushed. It wasn't a shy, maidenly, becoming blush. It was a bright red, full-faced, all-the-way-down-onto-the-sternum blush, as revealed by the square neckline of her gown. Henrik wondered what could have embarrassed her so much.

"Would you like my assistance in recovering it?" When she said nothing, he prompted, "Or would you rather leave it in the mud and forget the expense of its fine gilding?"

She buried her face in her hands for a moment. "My mother is going to kill me . . . And a frog! A *frog* offers to help me!"

"A talking frog," Henrik reminded her. A gnat buzzed into range of his tongue. Gnats were tasty, if not very filling. He carefully ignored it so as not to upset this maiden with too much froggish behavior. "Do you want my help, or would you rather splash around in the cold water and squishy mud, trying to find your lost item on your own?"

Face still red, she lowered her hands and gave him a tight-lipped look. Hitching up her skirts, she gingerly waded into the water. Henrik stifled the urge to point out that the knee-deep section she was sloshing through was a good eight feet or more from where she needed to be wading. Instead, he mustered his patience and waited. She finally gave up after several more minutes, shivering as she crawled out of the water.

"Oohhh! It's no use! I've lost it forever!"

"No, you haven't," Henrik countered. At the sound of his croaking confidence, she started and glared at him.

"Haven't you gone away yet?" she asked, struggling to wring out her skirt without baring too much more of her lovely pale legs.

"My offer still stands . . . if with a small price," Henrik stated. "I know exactly where your lost item has fallen. In fact, it can be done in a mere handful of minutes, with the assistance of your belt. And I will gladly help you retrieve it . . . *if* . . ."

"If?" she asked warily.

"Well, first you should introduce yourself. I, as I have stated, am Henrik." He left off the part about being a prince. Such things would be impossible to prove unless and until he was restored to his human form. "What is your name?"

"Gisette." She lifted her chin a little, though her proud look was spoiled a little by her shivering. "Princess Gisette."

"A pleasure to meet you, Your Highness." Again he attempted a bow, though his stubby body wasn't exactly built for such things. "I would be willing to help you retrieve your fallen item, Princess Gisette . . . *if* you would be willing to help me recover my humanity. Suffering as I do from an enchantment, I require your assistance to break the fairy's spell that traps me in this form. You want your lost valuable, and I want to be a man once again. Swear you will assist me, and I will assist you."

Abandoning her hem, she rubbed her upper arms. "What . . . what sort of assistance?"

"That you take me home with you. That you treat me as your closest companion. That you let me eat off your plate and drink from your cup. That you let me spend an entire month as your constant, closest companion," he clarified. "And . . . that you let me sleep in your bed with you."

"Oh! Oh, how dare you! I am a princess, not some village trollop!" Gisette immediately protested. "I am an unmarried maiden of genteel birth, and I will not—"

"My lady, I am a *frog*. I can hardly endanger your chastity in this form," Henrik said, chiding her dryly. "Now, you can either acquiesce to this simple enough request, or you can risk freezing yourself in this chilly, muddy river looking for something you haven't the first clue how to find."

She eyed him dubiously.

"I assure you I can be an entertaining, delightful companion," he added. "You won't regret it."

"How will my belt help you retrieve my lost . . . item?" Princess Gisette inquired warily.

"I will take the end of it into the river with me, wrap it around the item, and allow you to draw it out without getting wet. At least, any more wet than you already are," he added. "Once you have it back, you and I can travel back to your home where I shall be your companion for the next month. We shall eat together, sleep together, laugh together, and play together. Hopefully somewhere in there I shall be released from my enchanted state, whereupon I will go merrily on my way back home, and you shall be able to rest contentedly, knowing you have done a good deed in aiding me. Just as I will have done a good deed in aiding you . . . Are we agreed?"

Sighing heavily, Princess Gisette unbuckled the long belt wrapped three times around her hips and waist. "We are agreed . . . I suppose."

Lifting his foreleg, Henrik gestured her closer. She inched toward him and he patiently beckoned, until she was almost standing upon him, the long strip of leather trailing from her hand. Taking the end of the belt in his mouth, he dove into the water. The golden object still glinted in the mud right where he had found it.

Frog paws weren't the kind most suited for digging, but the mud was soft. Kicking up clouds of thick silt, he managed to work enough of the oblong object free and wrapped the belt around it. Tying the knot was a bit complicated, but he managed something that looked like it would hold.

A kick of his hind legs popped him back up to the surface. "Pull it up gently!" he warned the princess. "I have no thumbs, so I wasn't able to secure it as tightly as I'd wish."

Nodding, she gingerly tugged on the belt. The leather went taut after a moment, then angled itself through the water as she dragged the object up out of the mud. Stooping, Gisette picked it up. Despite the mud and the leather wrapped around it, Henrik could see it was longish, somewhat lumpy, and not just gilded, but plated in gold, or perhaps even crafted from solid gold. She turned from him as she picked off the leather, then stooped and swished it in the river, but he caught a glimpse of its true shape all the same. Henrik gaped.

"It's a *phallus*?" he croaked, as much from surprise as from his enchanted state. "You dropped a gilded *phallus*?"

"Oh! You . . . you . . . horrible beast!" Flushed with embarrassment, Princess Gisette hiked up her skirts and fled.

"Wait! Wait—our bargain! Please, wait?" Grimacing as she sprinted away, Henrik stared glumly after her. So much for fulfiling Tilda's demands on how to break his unlucky enchantment. About to consign himself to spending the rest of his life as a frog, he spotted a glint of gold with his swiveling eyes. It was from the buckle of her belt, abandoned on the ground when she had freed her rather naughty toy.

Peering up at the hillside, Henrik made up his mind to follow her. He tucked the leather of the belt into his mouth, letting its ends trail after him like two flat, brown snakes, and started hopping in the direction she and the other two maidens had gone. It might take him all day to hop his way after her, but he doubted she had wandered overly far with her amusing, symbolic prize.

With her muddied belt in his possession as proof of their bargain, he just might have the means of enforcing that bargain, and thus have a chance at ending his enchantment. *If* he could find where she had gone.

Nothing like a long hike, a difficult quest, and an uncertain chance of success to make a man-turned-frog feel humble, he thought. *Well, that and stubborn. I will* not *let Fairy Tilda win. I will* break her curse. Somehow.

THE knock at the door disrupted supper. It wasn't often the royal family came to this hunting lodge, but when they did, King Henri preferred not to be disturbed. Dinner, the midday meal, was the time for requests and interruptions, but not the evening meal. The guards knew this, and it was a hesitant knight who poked his helmed head through the doorway.

"What is it?" King Henri inquired, his attention deliberately focused on cutting into his lamb chop. Queen Jeanne eyed her husband, then the guard, waiting to hear his excuse for disturbing their tranquillity. Princess Gisette picked up her goblet and sipped at the freshly squeezed grape juice it contained, unconcerned by the interruption.

"Um . . . sire . . . there is a . . . well . . . a talking frog outside," the guardsman said apologetically.

Gisette choked.

Her father stilled the movements of his fork and knife. "A what?"

"A talking frog, sire. He claims he assisted Her Highness with a certain task earlier, in exchange for a certain set of privileges and, erm, has even returned with Her Highness's belt as proof of their lawfully made barter, in order to claim those privileges."

Henri rested his wrists on the edge of the table. He studied his blushing, throat-clearing daughter. "I take it from your reaction that this . . . talking frog . . . has a truthful claim?"

Embarrassed, Gisette nodded glumly. There was no way out of this, though she'd hoped she had left the memory of her humiliation and that frog far behind this morning. *If it's not to be, the only thing I can do is control any possible damage. I hope.* Cheeks hot, she watched as the guard ducked out again, no doubt to fetch the talking frog she had met. *My best hope is to make sure he doesn't mention* what *he helped me retrieve.*

She snuck a glance at her father, but he had gone back to carving up his meat. A glance at her mother showed Queen Jeanne's blue eyes studying her daughter. Her mother said nothing, though. Not quite hungry anymore, Gisette waited for the guardsman to return.

When he did, the knight entered with the green and yellow frog balanced on his chain-mail-clad hands. Her belt was caught in the frog's mouth and draped over the knight's wrists, visibly damp and muddy. The golden buckle had little tufts of grass caught along its hinge, a testament to the long journey the frog had undertaken, hopping from the riverbank almost half a mile away.

Guilt seeped into her thoughts, mixing with her embarrassment. *He's so small, and it's such a long way from the river . . .*

"This is the talking frog?" her father asked, skepticism coloring his voice.

The frog removed the belt from his mouth. "Greetings, Your Majesty. I am Henrik, and I do apologize for disturbing your meal, but I have business with Her Highness. Earlier today, I helped your sweet, kind daughter fetch her lost possession from the mud of the river, in exchange for a certain promise, which she now needs to fulfill."

"Lost possession?" King Henri repeated, glancing at his daughter. "What did you lose in the river, Gisette?"

"My ball!" she blurted quickly, flushing with the fear the frog might answer for her. "The wooden one you gave me when I was twelve, the one that was gilded? I took it down by the river to play with it—you know how I love to play with my ball . . ."

Her father gave her an indulgent smile. "That's my little girl . . . Now, what is this about a bargain you made with this frog?"

"It's quite simple. Your daughter tripped and accidentally dropped her . . . ball . . . in the river. I offered to help her fetch it from the river in exchange for finding out what it would be like to live as your daughter does. To eat off the same fine plates as she does every day, to sleep on the same fine sheets as she does every night—to live in the lap of luxury, as it were, rather than on the banks of a cold, muddy river."

"A frog who wishes to live like a princess?" Queen Jeanne questioned. "A *male* frog?"

"More to the point, a male frog who wishes to sleep in the same bed as *my little daughter*?" King Henri growled.

Gisette wished she could crawl under the table and hide without making matters worse.

"As much as I am willing to respect Your Majesty's rank and title," the frog explained calmly, "such an accusation is patently absurd. *I am a frog*, sire. Logistics alone render impossible any threat to your daughter's virtue. Never mind that she isn't a fellow amphibian, and thus isn't terribly appealing—I'm certain she's quite lovely by your human standards," he croaked in an aside, "but her skin would have to be considerably more moist and green for me to look twice at her in such a manner.

"Your daughter gave her word that she would treat me as her dearest friend for the next month, in exchange for my assistance in fetching her . . . ball. I have upheld my part of our bargain, and have even fetched home the belt we used to fish the . . . ball . . . out of the river, which she left behind in her haste to return home. Now I am here, awaiting the upholding of her end of the matter. It is a matter of honor that I am here. Your little girl's word of honor, in specific."

"I see." Turning once more to his daughter, King Henri asked, "Gisette, did you indeed swear you would treat him as your closest companion for a full month?"

"Well, yes, but . . ." Gisette wanted to protest that the whole idea was absurd, but she'd heard those slight hesitations over the word *ball*. Henrik was not only a talking frog, he was an *intelligent* talking frog. That subtle pause told her he wouldn't hesitate to say what she had *really* lost in the river.

"Then you should have brought him home with you," her father chided her, surprising Gisette. "When a princess gives her word, she needs to uphold it. You'll never grow up to be a good queen one day if you don't behave like one from the start. Guardsman, bring the frog to the table, and set him by Her Highness."

Gisette sat there in misery as the knight settled Henrik the Frog next to her plate. She accepted her muddied belt, barely managing to murmur a "Thanks."

Her mother cleared her throat, managing a cordial smile. "Well. I must say we don't often entertain such . . . unusual visitors. Particularly during one of our private family retreats. But is there, erm, something we can have the servants fetch for you? I'm not sure if our chef knows how to cook, er, flies and things, but I'm certain he'd be willing to try," Queen Jeanne offered politely.

"A bowl of tepid water would be deeply appreciated, if it isn't too much trouble," Henrik stated. "It was a very long hop from the river, and I'm quite thirsty. Not to mention I wasn't exactly given the time or the means to make myself more presentable. Otherwise, whatever you're having smells divine. Just be so kind as to cut it up into very small portions, and I should have no trouble at all, I think."

Queen Jeanne gestured, and the knight bowed and took himself out of the room, no doubt to fetch the requested bowl of water. "You have a remarkable air about you, Sir Frog," the queen added as she turned back to their unexpected guest. "Are all frogs so dignified?"

"When one is merely a frog, dignity is often all that one has," Henrik pointed out. "Dignity and good manners, that is. I thank you for being willing to share your meal with me."

Wishing she had never shown her two handmaidens that naughty birthing-day gift from her mother, Gisette carefully cut up some of her own lamb. She nudged it to the very edge of her silver plate, hoping she didn't have to actually feed it to the frog next to her. That would involve *touching* the frog. Gisette had never been the sort of girl to go around catching and holding frogs, snakes, and other such woodland creatures.

She jumped when his tongue shot out, snagging one of the little bits of lamb. He flicked it out again, snagging one of the chickpeas as well. A hum escaped the frog.

"Oh, my, that's better-tasting than a horse fly! Whatever did your chef fry that in?" Henrik asked her.

"Er . . . bacon drippings, I think?" Gisette offered.

"Very tasty. My compliments to your chef."

Her mother smiled. "I'll pass that along. Ah, here comes your water, erm . . . Sir Frog."

"Henrik, please; as your daughter's new companion, I would hope we could dispense with formality. At least, when not in a formal setting," Henrik added.

"I wouldn't think frogs would have much use for formal settings," King Henri observed.

Climbing into the bowl the knight set on the table, Henrik paused to thank the man, then addressed the king's comment. "Normally we don't, I will admit. As I said, most of the others lack sufficient intellect. But the fairies do visit all manner of creatures, granting some of us unusual abilities . . . and it does not pay to insult or slight a fairy, as many of us have learned through the years. Thus, polite manners are preferred nearly everywhere one goes."

His tongue darted out again as he clung to the edge of the silver bowl, snagging another piece of meat. It was a remarkably graceful move, for he neither lost the targeted chunk of lamb nor disturbed any of the others on the edge of her plate. He was also charming, erudite, dignified, and a remarkably good conversationalist as the meal progressed. Gisette almost forgot Henrik was a frog, particularly when he related an amusing tale involving a trio of forgetful fairies who were supposed to be watching a young prince one summer day.

But every time she glanced his way, she could see his diminutive form, his glistening green-and-gold skin and his bulging, independently moving eyes. She not only had to feed him, she had to keep him by her side . . . and let him sleep in her bed.

When the meal ended, Gisette rose and curtsied, more than ready to escape. A *ribbitty* clearing of Henrik's throat reminded her of her next painful duty. To take the frog back to her quarters with her. From the dubious looks on the faces of the maidservants clearing the table, they weren't about to offer to carry him for her. Even her own father slanted her an expectant look. And her mother . . . well, Gisette blamed her mother for starting this whole mess.

Sighing roughly, she held out her hand and tried not to flinch too much as Henrik climbed onto her palm. His skin was cool and wet, though not quite as slimy as she had imagined it would be. In fact, picking up the long, muddy leather of her belt felt worse than the frog did. Gingerly holding on to both, Gisette retreated upstairs to her bedchamber.

The royal hunting lodge was actually a modest keep. It had six bedchambers above the great hall and a large garden within its stout stone walls. Her chamber was one of the ones overlooking the garden. With the window open to the cooling breezes of the late summer night, she could hear the sounds of a pair of minstrels playing for the entertainment of the residents down in the garden, and the delicate singing of Annette, one of her wayward handmaidens.

If Annette hadn't tried to grab my present out of my hands, I would've seen that root or rock or whatever, and I wouldn't have tripped. I wouldn't have had to make a bargain with a toad to get it back from the mud, and I wouldn't be stuck with a reptile for a roommate. In fact, I would be down there *right now, having fun with the others, now that our private supper is finished . . .*

Henrik's deep voice interrupted her petulant thoughts. "If you would be kind enough to provide another bowl with fresh water, I would appreciate it."

"Are you so interested in being clean?" Gisette retorted. "At least you have the sense to know when you are slimy, and therefore unwanted."

Henrik twisted both of his eyes to focus on her at the same time. "Frogs drink through our *skin*, Your Highness. Depriving me of water to bathe in is literally depriving me of the liquid I need to survive. I may be merely a frog at the moment, but to slay me with thirst would still be murder."

Gritting her teeth, Gisette set him gently on her writing desk and fetched her washbasin. She rinsed out the bowl, in case he objected to soap in his precious water, then filled it from the pitcher and set the broad bowl next to him. "Your water, Sir Frog. Now, if you are quite comfortable, you can bathe in privacy all you like. I am going to go down to the garden to listen to the minstrels."

"Right *now*, you and I are going to have a little talk," he countered, ignoring the bowl at his side. "Or would you like me to hop downstairs and apologize to your father for lying about what I *really* helped you fetch from the river?"

She narrowed her eyes. "You wouldn't."

"I *would.*"

"Fine. You can come with me to hear the minstrels." She reached for him, but he scooted back.

"Not so fast, Princess. As I said, you and I need to talk first," Henrik corrected. "The first thing we need to discuss is *why* you lied to your father."

Guessing he wasn't going to let the subject go, Gisette sat down in the chair at her writing desk. "Fine. I lied because my father still thinks of me as a little girl. I just turned twenty years of age, yet he still thinks of me as if I were twelve! Do you know what he gave me for a present?" she asked, folding her arms defensively across her breasts. "A *doll.* A lovely porcelain-headed doll, imported all the way from the East, but nonetheless a doll! I haven't played with dolls since I was fifteen! He refuses to accept that I have grown up!"

Henrik croaked. It was a soft, low, surprisingly sympathetic sound. "No wonder you didn't want the phallus mentioned in his presence . . ."

She blushed. "It was a gift from my mother, given to me in private. *She* knows that I'm a woman grown, even if *he* won't admit it."

Henrik scratched his head with a hind foot. "I suppose it is a good gift for a grown woman, but . . . why would your own mother give you one?"

"Ever since I turned sixteen, princes and noblemen have been asking Father for my hand in marriage, and Father has been turning them down. He constantly insists I am far too young to wed. Even Mother thinks he's getting ridiculous about it. She's warned him that I just might elope one of these days, should I ever find a young man worthy of me, but no, he is as blind as an owl in the daylight.

"I do confess I have been tempted, simply so that I can finally be treated as an adult . . . but I'd rather not run away with just anyone. Most of the young men Father allows to be around me are *too* young, and rather featherbrained. Handsome enough of face, but dull-witted of mind. Mother thought I should have a . . . *you know* . . . so that I can at least temper the *urges* I get, as a fully grown woman," Gisette confessed, glad Henrik was a frog and not a human. It just seemed easier to confess these embarrassing things to a mere frog. "She says it's better to use a safe substitute than to let myself be swayed by a momentary lust into doing something stupid."

"Your mother is a wise woman," Henrik praised.

"Yes, and I'm a fool for showing my handmaidens what she gave me," Gisette muttered.

Through the open window, the sounds of singing and playing came to an end. The listeners in the garden applauded, and requests were called out for another performance. Gisette glanced longingly at the window.

"Patience, Gisette," the frog on her writing desk stated. "We still have more to discuss. Now, I'll presume if your father knew you had a phallus, he would grow enraged?"

"Absolutely," she agreed glumly. "Not even Mother can make him see sense. I'd have to be married and pregnant before he'd admit I'm *capable* of becoming pregnant, and even then . . ."

"Well, I know it's terribly ungentlemanly of me to make this demand, but . . . if you do not assist me with *my* problem . . . I shall have no choice but to worsen *your* problem."

That caught her attention. Narrowing her eyes, Gisette stared at the frog on her desk. "What do you mean by that?"

"I mean, if you do not do as I say, your father is going to learn about your mother's secret gift."

She fumed at his implication. "I cannot believe I'm being blackmailed by a *frog!*"

"If my own situation were not so dire, I wouldn't dare. My parents did raise me to be a gentleman. Unfortunately, I have little choice. Luckily for you, the sooner you cooperate, the sooner I'll be out of your life."

"I can endure a month of your presence," Gisette asserted. "It's only a month."

"It could be sooner, if . . ." He let the offer trail out.

"If, what?" she asked, suspicious.

"You are trapped by your father's belief that you are still a little girl. My situation is not too dissimilar, in that I am trapped in the shape of a frog by an enchantment. If you help me break the enchantment, I will be free to leave. Otherwise I will have to stay at your side."

"Eating off my plate and sleeping on my pillow will help you break the enchantment?" Gisette asked, confused.

"Unfortunately, no. I have to . . . uh, that is . . ."

She peered at his broad, elliptical face. "Are you . . . blushing?"

He cleared his throat with a croak. "I have to give you a climax."

Gisette blinked. "You . . . *what?*"

"The Fairy Tilda stated that, as a punishment for refusing to accept her offer of marriage, I am cursed to remain an ugly, unwanted creature until a beautiful woman demonstrates beyond a doubt that she associates me with pleasure. In other words, I must seduce, assist, or otherwise be associated with a woman as she climaxes."

She stared for a moment in horror, then grimaced. "Eww!"

"If you don't want your father to find out about your golden phallus . . . you will have to *use* it in my presence. Under my direction, following my suggestions."

Shoving out of her chair, Gisette whirled away. "I'm not listening to this!"

"I'll give you a week to get used to the idea— Where are you going?" Henrik croaked as she headed for the door.

"Down to the garden, to listen to something more pleasant!"

"Not without *me*. I go wherever *you* go, remember?" he reminded her. "Or would you rather I had a word with your father?"

Gritting her teeth, Gisette walked back to her writing desk. "I suppose once the enchantment breaks, you turn back into a *toad*?"

"Hardly. I was born a human prince. Second son, to be exact, and not the heir apparent," he added as he crawled onto her grudgingly offered palm, "but a prince nonetheless. And I *would* be a gentleman and not press the matter . . . but in order to *be* a gentleman, I'd first have to be a *man*, wouldn't I? Don't squeeze me quite so tight," he ordered as she curled her fingers around his fist-sized body. "I'm hardly going to escape, now am I?"

"On that much, we can agree," Gisette quipped, heading once more for the door. "You, sir, are no gentleman!"

Henrik didn't press the matter. At least, not the matter of breaking his enchantment.

He did press the matter when it came to being poked, prodded, and even insulted by the others in the small court that had come with Their Majesties to the royal hunting lodge. His dignity, charm, and wit—if supplied in the form of a mere frog—managed to quell even the rudest of young men and most importunate of young women who associated with Princess Gisette. Though it did take a few pointed, swivel-eyed looks at Annette and the other handmaiden, Jacqueline, to get them to stop snickering whenever Gisette's "golden ball" was mentioned.

As the days progressed, he strove to be as charming and entertaining and friendly as he could manage, until the princess no longer flinched whenever she had to pick him up, and no longer wrinkled her nose even the slightest bit when she glanced his way. When the first week of their month was up, as promised, only then did Henrik strike.

Having changed behind a screen into a lace-edged linen nightdress, Gisette sat by the window, brushing out her long brown curls. Seated on the window ledge beside her, Henrik snapped his tongue at a mosquito—tangy and bitter—which was threatening to bite her, and composed himself for his plan of attack.

"Gisette . . ."

"Yes, Henrik?" Gisette asked, her attention more on working out a stubborn snarl with her brush than on the frog on her windowsill.

"May I tell you a bedtime story?"

That caught her attention. Blinking, she focused on him. "A bedtime story? What, like a child would hear?"

"Hardly," he snorted. Or rather, croaked. Being a frog meant it was difficult to make suitable scoffing noises. "I think we've long since established that you are an adult woman. No . . . I'd like to, if I may, tell you a bedtime story of the sort suitable for an adult woman to hear. I'm in the mood to tell one, you see, and I'd like to think I can tell an entertaining tale."

She smiled in remembrance. "That story you told about the donkey two days ago . . . I've never seen my father laugh so hard as he did over that one."

"I aim to please," Henrik agreed, bobbing his body in his best approximation of a bow. "So. If I may . . . I would like to tell you the tale of 'The Courtship of Wali Daad.' I learned it from a book of tales brought from the East, and I think you will like it."

"'The Courtship of Wali Daad'?" Gisette repeated. Finished with brushing out her locks, she drew up her knees and wrapped her arms around them. "All right, it sounds interesting. I take it this is a tale of romance?"

"Indeed," Henrik chuckled, "though not quite the romance you might expect."

Launching into it, he did his best to enthrall her with the story, gesturing with his forefeet for emphasis and making full use of his deep amphibian voice to heighten the drama. At first she smiled and laughed as the amusing tale progressed. But when he mentioned the phallus, she gasped and glared at him, blushing.

Henrik wasn't deterred. If anything, he emphasized the lascivious parts all the more strongly, until she was all but covering her ears, her skin as red as a summer strawberry. Bringing the tale to its conclusion, he smirked. Frog mouths, being extra wide, were well suited to smirking.

Face flaming, Gisette glared at him. "I can't believe you said all those things!"

"Would you rather I treated you like your father does, and restrict my tales to those suitable for a little girl? The kind of little girl who only ever plays with a gilded wooden ball?" Henrik offered. "Before you protest how this story is 'beyond the pale' . . . consider the stories I *could* tell, if I weren't concerned about your delicate sensibilities."

From the curious, if wary, look she gave him, Henrik knew she was hooked.

"Oh, yes. Tales of love and lust, of passion and pleasure, of adventure and romance. Stories of seduction, stories of instruction . . ."

"Instruction?" Gisette couldn't help ask. "Isn't it just . . . Don't you just *do* it?"

Henrik croaked with laughter. "Hardly! Assuming you automatically know how to make love is like assuming you automatically know how to hitch a horse to a plow. The farmer knows how because he has been taught from an early age, but hand a city-dweller a harness and he's as likely to hang himself by the straps as get them on the horse the right way around."

The image his words conjured amused Gisette, soothing away her embarrassment. Chuckling, she rested her chin on her forearms. "All right. Let's say you *do* know how to make love so that one doesn't get all tangled around. What makes you think telling *me* about it is all that appropriate?"

"I told you. It's part of the conditions holding me captive in the body of a frog," he reminded her. Swiveling his eyes, he snapped his tongue at another mosquito hovering near her shoulder. "Bleh. Tangy, but not exactly tasty . . . As I said, I am not inclined to remain this way for the rest of my life. Thankfully, I happen to know a fair amount about sensuality and seduction."

"*Do* you, now?" Gisette challenged him. "And how is it you come to know all of these things, hmm?"

"Well, I did have to learn all the various ways to manage a state 'just in case' . . . but my older brother Gustav is as healthy as a horse and quite competent as a ruler-to-be, so I haven't been pressured to study the dry, boring bits extra hard. Thus I have been left with a decent amount of time for studying, shall we say, extracurricular materials?"

"I'll bet," Gisette snorted. Still, her curiosity got the better of her after a moment. "So . . . what exactly did you learn?"

"That men and women are different. That women take longer to find their pleasure than men, but when a man learns properly how to help her find it, it's far more delightful for both of them." His tongue snapped out again, catching another mosquito. One of the wings snagged on his throat, making Henrik cough. "Bleh . . . Could you carry me to the water bowl, please? I think I'm getting a little dried out."

"Certainly." Scooping him up, Gisette left the bench under the window and carried him to her nightstand and the silver dish filled with cool water. Once he was in the basin and splashing around, sighing happily, she returned to the window to close the shutters and fetch her brush. As she turned back toward the bed, her gaze fell on the inlaid chest sitting in the corner. "Henrik . . ."

"Yes, Gisette?" Hooking his forelimbs over the edge of the basin, he swiveled both eyes in her direction.

"Could you, erm . . . *can* you . . . well . . . teach me?" She blushed as she asked it, but she didn't take it back.

Henrik struggled manfully—or rather, frogfully—not to smirk too much. *Finally, she's in the mood to cooperate with my needs. Which means I must take extra care to attend to hers . . . however limited in usefulness this form may be for such things.* "Of course I can. It would be my honor to guide you in exploring your adult sense of pleasure."

Her lips twisted ruefully. "Not to mention the means to release you from your enchantment?"

Henrik coughed, hastily raising a forepaw to his broad mouth. "Well, that is a bonus, to be sure . . ."

Gisette blushed, but moved toward the chest. Unlocking it, she dug through the cloth, down to the cool, hard lump of metal hidden beneath the layers of her best dresses. Once the gilded phallus was exposed, however, she started having doubts. Henrik was a frog, yes, but if he was indeed an enchanted frog, then he was also a man underneath his damp green and yellow skin. *Whereas I am a maid, and so shouldn't be thinking such thoughts . . .*

"Come along now," Henrik croaked, cajoling her. "No need to be shy. I may not have one at the moment, but I do know what it looks like, so it won't shock me to see it."

Somehow the thought of a man being shocked at the sight of a phallus struck her as funny. Giggling, Gisette bit her lip and faced him. Her face was hot with embarrassment, but she still managed to meet at least one of his swiveling eyes without flinching. Much. Moving back over to the bed, she perched herself on the edge, facing the nightstand and its amphibian-occupied bowl. She lifted the oblong object and cleared her throat.

"Um . . . what's this part?" she asked, pointing to the knobby bit at one end.

"Those are the bollocks. If you respect a particular man, treat them very gently and he will enjoy it. However, if the man tries to disrespect you, and particularly if he tries to maul you in some unwelcome manner, hit them as hard as you can," Henrik advised her. "But we'll presume this is a man who respects you, and a man whom you like, so touch them gently. Obviously they will be made of flesh and not metal, so there will be some warmth and some give, but you can stroke, pet, and very, very gently knead them."

"I see." Blushing a little, Gisette petted the rounded bulbs, then trailed her fingers up to the shaft. "And this part?"

"That is called the shaft, or the rod. It can be grasped more firmly than the bollocks, but the best way to treat it is to encircle it with the fingers . . . or one's lips, or other body parts," Henrik allowed as she gingerly stroked the gleaming metal, "and rub it up and down. Men can get excited just by looking at a beautiful woman such as yourself, but if you rub a man's rod, he'll definitely get excited, making it turn stiff and ready for copulation."

"Like . . . this?" she asked, following his instructions. The metal was slowly warming under her touch, but it was also beginning to stick to her skin a little, thanks to the way her embarrassed blushing made her palms a little damp. She grimaced as her hand bumped unevenly up the shaft of the phallus. "How do I keep my hand from dragging on it, like that?"

"Lubrication. Moisture. One can use a salve . . . or one can simply use one's spit."

"Eww." She wrinkled her nose, eyeing the dildo, then the frog. "That sounds messy."

"Sex, when properly done, *is* messy," Henrik croaked. "When a man is excited and his rod stiffens, moisture will leak out of that little dimple at the top. Just as when a woman is excited, her slit will leak fluids of its own—don't wrinkle your nose at me. The moisture is perfectly natural, and makes everything work together a lot more easily than if everything remained dry. It's also a lot more pleasurable when things are moist, and if you deliberately make them so, it helps. Nature doesn't always provide sufficient liquid for the job."

"Why not?" Gisette asked, curious.

"Think of it this way. If you haven't had enough to drink in a while, does your mouth get dry?" he asked.

"Of course it does. But all I have to do is find something to drink and it's moist again . . . Oh. Right. Of course. But women don't look like this," she pointed out, lifting the phallus in her hand. "Not that I've exactly peered at everything down there, but I don't have one of these. How do I get moist down there?"

A pity this is only an abstract exercise for me, Henrik sighed silently. *Stuck in this form, I literally am unable to get aroused, at least one presumes not outside of mating season . . . which I hope to Heaven I won't have to experience as a frog.* Clearing his throat, he explained briefly.

"You have various folds of flesh between your legs. Some project outward a little, and feel marvelous when gently rubbed—or so I have been told by women, since I am not a female myself—and you have other bits where it's like a pocket of flesh. That is your womb. A man pushes his rod into that pocket, rubbing it in and out, which feels good for both of you, until you both shudder with pleasure, and that is the point when the seed for a baby is planted. If the man pulls out before that point and spills his seed on the bed or the ground, it isn't as likely for a baby to be planted.

"But for now, we're talking about how to pleasure a man. The bollocks are where the rod is rooted to the front of the man's hips. At the tip is that little offset ridge. There are three parts to that end which you should know about."

"Yes?" she asked, tilting the phallus so she could examine the indicated end.

"The first, the ridge itself, feels nice when it is rubbed, licked, or otherwise stimulated. On a real one, there is also a little sleeve of skin which often covers the head before the rod is fully stiffened. Once it does stiffen out, that cowl-sleeve gets stretched and pulled out of the way. The second one is the little slit at the top and the soft skin in front. These two spots feel good when touched, if in a different way. You can stroke them, rub them, knead them, kiss them, suckle them, and even flick them with something soft and moist, such as your tongue. All of that will feel good to the man."

"And the third spot?" she wondered.

"Where the ridge sweeps up into a little point. On some men it is more blatantly visible, and on other men it is less noticeable, but all men have this spot," Henrik told her. "This is what I like to call the Dear Sweet Heaven spot, and if you stroke it just right, you will have a man begging to do anything you please, so long as you keep stroking it until he squirts his seed."

"Really? This little spot here?" Gisette asked, touching the arrow-like section of dimpled metal. "It's so small . . ."

"Yes, that spot there. Stroke that just right, whether it's with your fingers, your lips and tongue, or even the moist folds of your womb, and you will make a man very, very happy. And if you combine all the spots I've mentioned into one, you will put him into Heaven while he's still alive."

She pouted a little. "Well, that's not very fair. I know I don't have anything shaped like that on *my* body. Why should a man get to have a spot that makes him think of Heaven, but a woman doesn't?"

"Trust me, you have your own special spots," Henrik said, chuckling.

"Really? Where?" Gisette demanded.

"First, you'll have to set down your golden *ball*," he teased. "Then fetch out that little hand mirror you have. And you'll want to sit on the bed so that the light from the candles falls on your body. You'll have to be able to see yourself, since we don't have a gilded substitute on hand."

Tucking the phallus under her pillow, Gisette fetched her silver mirror. Seating herself on the bed so she faced the candles, which meant facing Henrik in his bowl, she eyed the frog on her nightstand. "Now what?"

"Now you'll have to be very brave, and lift up the hem of your nightgown. All the way up to your waist," he added in clarification.

Staring at the green and yellow frog, with his swiveling eyes, broad mouth, and moist skin, Gisette hesitated. "Erm . . ."

"I'm a frog," Henrik reminded her. "Unless you are green and warty, you will not be able to arouse me physically. The only part of me which is still a man is my mind, and as such, I will only be able to enjoy the view in an abstract, intellectual way at best . . . which makes it all the more imperative I regain my human form. Now, don't be shy; I'm hardly going to tell anyone about this. Even a frog could be arrested if word got out I was tutoring you in such matters."

"Father's dungeons are damp, but not *that* damp," Gisette agreed. "You wouldn't like them very much."

"Exactly. Go on," he encouraged her.

Biting her lower lip, she gathered her courage and worked the material of her nightdress up above her knees. Up until now, she had taken care to dress and undress behind the carved wooden screen in the corner of her chamber. Now she bared her calves and her knees, blushing as she did so. Beneath the finespun linen, she wasn't wearing underdrawers. The rising hem hesitated and halted near the tops of her thighs.

"Go on," Henrik encouraged her. "You need to bare your loins, part your thighs, and position the mirror so that you can see what lies between them. Once you see what you have down there, I can explain to you how you and whatever man you choose can have fun with it. You *do* want to have fun, don't you? Adult fun?"

"Well . . . yes," Gisette admitted. She firmed her conviction, nodding. "Yes, I do." Bunching up the front of her nightgown, she lifted one foot onto the frame of the bed and lowered the mirror, angling both it and herself so that no shadows obscured the reflected view. "Um . . . now what?"

"Use your free hand to part your folds. At the top, you'll see a triangular bump of flesh. That is *your* Dear Sweet Heaven spot. You can touch it, stroke it, tickle it, rub it, and even lightly pinch it, and if you try several different things, you'll figure out what touches are most enjoyable for you. As with everything," Henrik lectured, eyes swiveling as he followed the movements of her free hand, "pleasure varies from person to person, so it is best to experiment.

"Some things will be similar, others will be different. Some men prefer a firm stroke upon their rod right from the start, while others prefer to start with a feathery touch. The same goes for women—you might find that easier if you lick your finger to moisten it, so that it glides rather than drags."

"Right." Trying to ignore the fact she was taking orders from an amphibian, Gisette squirmed farther onto the bed, curled up one leg so she could brace the hand mirror against it, rested her other foot on the edge of the bed frame so she could keep everything exposed for viewing, and stuck her finger in her mouth to moisten it. With her left hand now free, she held open her folds and gently petted the little peak of flesh with her right forefinger.

It felt very good. Surprisingly good. She had cleaned down there when taking baths, but that had been a perfunctory touch, with no expectation of pleasure and no association with pleasure. This was an exploratory one, seeking that elusive Dear Sweet Heaven spot her friend Henrik had mentioned. *Goodness . . . it seems he's right! That does feel like a bit of Heaven. Particularly when I circle it, and . . . and rub a little harder on the downstroke than on the upstroke . . . Oh, yes . . .*

Feeling dry, Henrik ducked briefly under the surface of the water, but only briefly. While it was true his body wasn't the least bit aroused by what his eyes were viewing, his brain remembered the sympathetic delights he had felt before when viewing a maidservant doing the same thing under his tutelage. The interest, the fascination, and the arousal. The delight of watching a woman find the path to her pleasure, and the desire to be a part of it, helping her to achieve her bliss.

Gisette tossed back her head, making one of his eyes twitch up and focus on her face, while the other kept itself fixed on her loins. Her eyes had strained shut and her lips had parted, allowing her to pant a little as she rubbed and flicked. Speaking softly in his deep amphibian's voice, Henrik praised her.

"Yes . . . just like that. There is nothing more beautiful in this world than a woman seeking her Heaven-bestowed passions. Embrace the feelings," he murmured, trying not to croak ignominiously. Right now he needed to speak as smoothly as he could, so as not to jar her out of her sensations. "Feel the pleasure. Dip your finger a little lower, into the deeper folds of your womb. Circle it, touch it, and stroke the pinnacle that stands guard over your pleasure. Yesss, like that . . ."

Gisette sucked in a surprised breath; dipping her finger into her flesh felt good. There was an odd, hollow sensation rising low in her belly, but touching herself like that felt good. Plus it was quite warm, and rather wet. Enough that when she slid her finger back up to the peak to rub it again, the moisture made everything feel better, more sensitive, more responsive to her touch.

"Oh, yes . . . oh, yes! More! Tell me more! Where else does it feel good?"

"Both men and women like their chests caressed. Their breasts, their nipples—rub one of your nipples like you're rubbing that little peak," he instructed.

Movement at the edge of his vision made his left eye swivel to the side. A moth had fluttered into the room. As much as his transfigured body longed to snap it up for a late-night snack—they were fuzzy and tickled going down, but were sweeter than mosquitoes—Henrik refrained. The last thing he wanted to do right now was remind Gisette of the frog in her boudoir.

A gasp from Gisette drew his attention back to her. The fingers of her right hand were rubbing madly between her thighs, and the fingers of her left hand were plucking at her nipples, alternating between one and the other. There was no mistaking her targets, either; they pushed against the age-softened linen of her nightshift, taut and ready for the attention she was rapidly learning to give them.

Her back arched and her muscles strained. "Oh . . . oh! Oh! Oh, yes! More! I need *more* . . ."

"Gisette . . . fetch out the dildo," Henrik coaxed. "Fetch your golden phallus and rub it between your lips."

She twisted awkwardly, halfway falling onto her right elbow as she reached for it with her left hand, and managed to fish the gilded icon out from under her pillow. Squirming onto her back, knees splaying wantonly, she licked the rod with her tongue. Henrik coughed, mentally stimulated despite the amphibious calm of his flesh. The sight of her sucking it into her mouth would have broken him, had he been a man. As it was, only the fact that he was a frog kept him in his bowl at a safe, gentlemanly distance.

"I meant your *other* lips. Rub it up and down your folds until it is coated all over. Rub it and roll it against your peak," he directed her. *So much passion,* he thought, enjoying the way she dragged it through her femininity, using her right hand so that her left could go back to playing with her breasts. *I really hope this works . . .*

"Mmm . . . it's still not enough!" she complained, breathing heavily.

"Then dip it into your womb," Henrik ordered smoothly, making use of his deep frog's voice.

Gisette strained, twisting the phallus in her grip. She prodded herself with the tip and wrinkled her nose. "It's cold!"

"If it were me, it would be deliciously hot," he murmured. "Just soft enough to give and warm enough to soothe. But think of it as me anyway, because if I were a man, I'd want to rub our parts together. Because deep inside of you, there is a spot which only the head of a man's rod can touch, a spot every bit as good as that Dear Sweet Heaven spot at the top of your folds. Push it inside," Henrik urged. "Push it in a little ways, then pull it out again, and think of how I could truly pleasure you if I were a man. Think of my hands on your skin, of me pulling off your dress, of my lips kissing your beautiful breasts . . . Yessss, like that. Exactly like that."

It stung a little, but the girth of the rod wasn't overly large. Her mother had explained in private that it shouldn't be made as large as a man, so that she wouldn't ruin her maidenhead by stretching it out too far, but Gisette didn't care. The stretchy feel faded quickly as her wrist and fingers found the right angle to push and pull on the bollocks, plunging the metal rod into her flesh, over and over, deeper and deeper.

She wasn't quite sure where that spot Henrik mentioned was, but the murmur of his deep voice continued, encouraging her efforts. His words wrapped around her senses. At his suggestion, she abandoned her breasts, switching the movement of the phallus to her left hand so that she could use her right one to play with her peak. All the pleasurable sensations building within her flesh swirled together, tightening her muscles.

"Oh, Henrik—Henrik! Oh, Henrik! Oh! I'm going to . . . I'm going to fly apart!"

"Leap! Leap into your bliss!" Henrik croaked, clinging to the edge of his bowl.

"I'm leaping! I'm—*leaping*! *Hen . . . rik*! Ohhhh . . ." Shudders swept through her muscles as the combination of thrusting rod and swirling fingertips shattered her composure. Her fingers lost their grip on the phallus, and the tension in her body caused it to slide out of her depths, but even that was a pleasure. Slowing the touch of her fingers, she panted heavily, drifting down from her leap of passion. "Oh, Henrik . . . *thank* you . . ."

Energy sizzled across his body, burning his nerves. Henrik croaked, twitching from the pain of it—and suddenly expanded. The bowl tipped, the nightstand wobbled, and he pitched awkwardly off the suddenly too-small piece of furniture. Gisette yelped as he landed partly on her; Henrik grunted as the rest of him landed partly on the bed and partly on the floor. The candelabra wobbled on the nightstand, making the golden light cast by its flames dance around the room, but the candles didn't tip over, thankfully.

Left thigh bruised from the bed frame, right shin stinging from clipping the edge of the nightstand, booted feet thumping onto the floor, he scrabbled to keep from falling completely off the bed. Once again he was a man, clad in the green velvet, gold-trimmed doublet and breeches he had been wearing when he had been enchanted into an amphibian. Twisting, trying to find his balance, Henrik found himself with his left hand braced on the feather-stuffed mattress and his right hand clasping a deliciously soft, warm, linen-covered breast. His eyes—both of them brown instead of yellow, and both of them firmly focused forward—met her startled blue gaze.

Clearing his throat, Henrik carefully eased back, gingerly shifting his weight off of her body. "Uh . . . *thank* you. Thank you very much, Your Highness. I, uh, apologize for the, uh, intrusion."

The feel of his fingers leaving her breast disappointed Gisette. His hand was warm and dry, his touch evoking more of the same feelings she had just experienced. Losing it now was unthinkable. Catching his wrist, she gently tugged his palm back to her flesh. She blushed as she did so, but she did it. He blushed, too, she noticed, and that made her smile. He was good-looking without it, but the gentlemanly blush made him look particularly cute.

"Umm . . . care to show me how you'd touch me in person?" she asked, wondering if she was being too bold.

Henrik parted his lips, ready to reply . . . and felt another tingle of magic against his skin. Being enchanted for a month seemed to have made him sensitive to it. Bolting up from the bed, he whirled to look for this new menace to his dignity, and spotted a sparkle of light.

So did Gisette. Squeaking, she snapped her thighs together and yanked down the hem of her nightgown, sitting up quickly. The lump of her phallus dug into the underside of her left thigh, but at least it was hidden by her thigh. Grabbing the edge of the blanket, she dragged it up over herself as the sparkling light coalesced into a glowing silhouette, before solidifying into a matronly figure. One with several strands of silver streaking her sable hair.

Blushing hotly, Henrik positioned himself between Princess Gisette and their unexpected guest. Clearing his throat, he addressed the older woman respectfully. "Fairy Tilda . . . this is an unexpected . . . honor. If you've come to accept my apology for offending you, I'm more than ready to give it, with heartfelt remorse."

Hands planted on her blue-clad hips, Tilda eyed the re-formed prince. "Are you willing to marry me?"

Henrik cleared his throat again. "I think it best that a youth as young and callow as myself should not sully your chances for happiness. You deserve a man of maturity, thoughtfulness, and far greater intelligence than I possess. And I do apologize profusely for the insult and pain my thoughtless, careless words caused you. I'm quite certain that somewhere out there awaits a far better husband for you than I could ever be, and I know with all my heart that you deserve such a man in your life."

Green eyes gleaming with humor, the fairy quirked up the corner of her mouth. "Indeed. Your apology is accepted, Prince Henrik. You *are* a callow youth, and I do deserve better. As for *you*, young lady . . . you are rather brave, to be so willing to kiss a slimy little frog."

Kiss? Henrik thought, startled by the fairy's words. *She thinks we kissed? All we* had *to do was kiss?*

"But your compassion for even an unlovely creature such as Prince Henrik was shall not go unrewarded. Would you like me to whisk him back to his family before your virtue could possibly be compromised by this cad?"

Blushing, confused by the older woman's words, Gisette glanced at Henrik. His face was a little blotchy, half-red with embarrassment, half-pale with startlement. Her mind whirled, filled with the thoughts of how dignified he had been as a frog, and how genteel his manners . . . given what he had *thought* were the conditions to release his enchanted state. Her body still hummed with pleasure, but there was more between the two of them than what they had just done together. Sort of done together.

It's not just him teaching me how to find pleasure, she realized. *It's him making me laugh, and entertaining me, and charming everyone in Father's court with his dignity and his good manners. It's how intelligent he is, and how likeable, and how he enjoyed listening to me. It's how we shared ideas and laughter so freely. And how much I* don't *want him to go away . . .*

"If it's, erm, all right with you, Lady Fairy," she said as politely as she could manage, "I would rather he stayed. We are both young, and no doubt somewhat immature, but, well . . . We do get along very well together. I've come to think of him as a friend as well as a frog. Not that I want to keep him as a frog, since he'd be much happier as a man once again, but . . ."

Gisette let her words trail out, not quite sure how she wanted to put it.

Tilda folded her arms across her chest and rubbed a finger thoughtfully along the edge of her jaw. "So . . . you want to keep him as your companion, but *not* as a frog?"

"Yes, milady," Gisette agreed.

"Princesses usually do not get to *keep* young men as companions. Even if he is a prince," Tilda allowed. "I'm afraid the only way you could keep him is if you were to marry him."

"I could do that," the younger woman agreed, giving it only a moment of thought. "I just, um . . . It's my father, you see. He thinks of me as a little girl. I'm not sure how he'd take the sudden appearance of a man in my bedchamber, never mind a prince. Poor Henrik has already suffered enough, and I'd hate to see him clapped in irons."

"I suppose I could smooth things over with your father," the fairy graciously allowed. "Since His Highness seems to have learned his lesson." Lifting her hand, she snapped her fingers. Prince Henrik vanished, making Gisette gasp.

"What—what did you do with him?" she asked, pulling the blanket more fully over her nightdress-clad frame.

"You needn't worry, my dear; I merely dropped him off at the front gate with a suitable entourage, a coffer filled with sufficient funds for a dowry, and a generous peace treaty between his nation and yours. Your father will find all of it irresistible, particularly as your two lands share a border along the mountains to the northeast," Fairy Tilda explained. She smirked a little. "Almost as irresistible as you found his instructions just now."

Gisette didn't think her face could get any hotter from embarrassment without bursting into actual flame. "Er . . ."

"Don't worry, your secret is safe with me. May the two of you live happily ever after." A flick of her hand, and the fairy vanished, her figure dissolving in a swirl of golden sparks.

Biting her lower lip, Gisette grinned. Beyond the shutters of her window, she could hear noises from the castle gates. Setting aside her blanket, she rose and fetched her clothes. As late as it was, she knew her father would still be up, and she wanted to be on hand when he received their "unexpected" guest.

There were far worse things one could have besides a rather charming, educated, handsome former frog for a suitor.

The Courtship of
Wali Daad

Author's Note: This tale was simply too charming not to tell. At one point during the editing process, my friend Alexandra likened these stories to a box of assorted chocolates, each of a different kind and flavor; if so, this one probably would be the maple-walnut crème, sweet and wonderful. I simply could not pass up the chance to share this adorable, funny little romance—obscure though it may be for a fairy tale—with the rest of the world. Here's hoping you'll enjoy my version of it . . .

THE trapdoor would not shut.

Lifting the panel back up again, the owner of the small cottage poked at the contents piled into the hidden space. Normally his table sat over the door, hiding the trapdoor from casual view. Normally, it looked like just another piece of his floor, age-worn boards polished more by the passage of time and a scrubbing brush than by artistry and oils. But not today. Not even when he tried rearranging the cluttered mass of metal discs yet again, as he had carefully done for the last few months.

The trapdoor would not shut.

Sitting back from the opening, Wali Daad sighed and scratched his head. For sixty-seven years, he had lived in this house, and the lid of the hidden cache had always closed flat. That was part and parcel of how it remained hidden.

There is no use for it, the aging man thought, shrugging his shoulders helplessly. *I suppose I have too many coins.*

A look around his cottage—which only qualified as a cottage because it had a wooden floor, otherwise it would have been a mere hut—showed there was nowhere else for the coins to go. Smoked meat and onions hung from the rafters, a barrel of rice for his morning porridge stood in the corner by the hearth, and there were a couple of shelves to hold his pots and a half-eaten loaf of wheat bread. He had two chairs at his table, for himself and a guest, and his bed sat in the corner across from the hearth, a simple, grass-stuffed pallet covered with linen and wool. On the wall by the door hung two scythes; below them sat a grinding wheel, while just outside sat his wooden wheelbarrow, sheltered by the thatching of his roof.

Everything was exactly where he wanted it and where he liked it, for Wali Daad was a simple man with a simple life and simple needs. Not simple in the sense of being a fool, but simple in the sense of being content with his life. Except the trapdoor would not shut. He had too many coins.

One wouldn't think a simple grass cutter would have too many coins, but Wali Daad had never married, had no offspring to feed, and no relatives dependent upon his income. His parents had perished in a flood some fifty years before, leaving him their mud-caked home and a few surviving tools with which to make his living. It was a good living, too.

His home lay near the junction of three roads and three kingdoms, one to the east, one to the west, and one to the north, with several green fields leading down to the river, which lay to the south. Merchants traveled up and down those roads all year round, bringing caravans of hungry, laden camels and horses past Wali Daad's home. Plus there was a well in the yard between the house and the three roads, a deep well filled with fresh, sweet water. Wali Daad charged the merchants a penny for every troughful of hay, which took three to four wheelbarrow loads to fill, but he did not charge anything for the water, no matter how many times he pulled the bucket up from its depths, or how many horses and camels and men wanted a drink.

These things made his home a popular resting point for many a caravan, though there wasn't much of anything else here to entice people to settle this far from a town. No orchards, no gardens, just the river, the grass, the house, and the well. But he had enough customers to pay for his simple needs, and enough left over to tuck his unspent pennies into the cache in the floor.

Which would not shut.

"Too many pennies," Wali Daad muttered aloud. "I have too many pennies. I don't even need them! I just kept putting them in there because that was what Mother and Father would do. What am I to do with them?"

He tried closing the door one more time, but it jutted up a tiny bit, enough to be noticeable. It wasn't that he needed the money, but he didn't want some passing traveler to notice the uneven floorboards and think to attack and rob him. He liked his simple life, but he was no fool. Sighing, Wali Daad took out the coins he had just put in, plus a few more, and closed the trapdoor. Once it was flush with the floor, he dragged the table back into place, rearranged the chairs just so, and took the coins over to the barrel of rice. Lifting the lid, he dropped the pennies onto the grains, sighed at the copper brown blotches they made on the tan and white kernels, and sealed the barrel again.

Something had to be done with his money. *Something good*, Wali Daad thought. *Something . . . well, not something for me, but something*

for someone else. The only questions are what should I do, and for whom?
Wali Daad stared around his simple home, with its simple needs, and couldn't think of a thing.

Noise in the distance made him discard his thought. Noise meant travelers, and travelers usually meant a need for water and hay. Sighing again, the grass cutter stepped outside. Coming up the road from the West Kingdom was a caravan of twenty horses and fifty camels. Their leader was a man with a blue-dyed turban wrapped around his head and a green and white striped aba, the loose but comfortable traveling robe of the Westerners.

"Ah! Hassim! *Hassim!* Welcome back, Hassim!" Clapping his hands together in delight, Wali Daad lifted and shook them over his head in acknowledgment that he saw his Northern-born merchant friend coming, then hurried to fetch his wheelbarrow and head for the hay shed. He loaded up his barrow with several bundles of grass, then brought them out to the long wooden troughs that served his caravan customers as mangers. By the time he had brought half a dozen loads of grass to the troughs, the caravan handlers had already sorted out their charges and were pulling water up from the well, pouring it by the bucketful into the long stone troughs for both man and beast to have a drink.

"Good evening, Wali Daad, and good fortune to you!" Hassim called out, hurrying to clasp arms with the grass cutter.

His robes weren't plain linen, but fine cotton from the Eastern lands, which were further trimmed with bits of silk from the Western ones, proof of how his merchanting travels had allowed him to prosper. He had bracelets on his wrists and brooches on his riding boots, and a necklace of rare red coral strung around his throat. Even his beard was waxed and perfumed, forming a curly point as was currently popular in the Eastern lands. But for all of his finery, Hassim greeted the simply clad Wali Daad as an equal and a friend, for he had long been a merchant who visited the grass cutter's resting point.

"Good fortune indeed," Wali Daad agreed as they clasped forearms, thinking briefly of his collection of too many pennies, "and better fortune still to you! Come, drink, eat, and feed your animals my finest, fresh-culled grass!"

"A delight, as always," the merchant master replied, grinning at his old friend. "No journey from west to east or from east to west is ever complete without a visit to your house. How have you been, this last month and a half?"

"Quite good; the sun has not been too hot, the rain has not been too heavy . . ." By chance, Wali Daad's gaze fell upon one of his friend's bracelets. It was crafted from bronze with inlays of silver, and quite lovely. Tucking his arm around the merchant's shoulders, Wali Daad guided him toward the cottage. "Hassim, my dear friend . . . I have a request to make of you. Would you accept the hospitality of my humble home, and hear of my problem?"

"It would be my honor to listen, and my privilege if there is anything I can do to help you," Hassim agreed readily. Pausing just long enough to give his caravan handlers their instructions, Hassim left them to feed and water their beasts. Accompanying Wali Daad into his home, he accepted the mug of water Wali Daad offered, and the bit of bread with a little pot of *ghi* for dipping. Once the matter of hospitality had been attended to, Hassim spoke again. "So, my old friend. What troubles you?"

"You are an honest merchant, my friend. Every caravan master from the East to the West, and even to the mountains in the North, speaks of how honest and honorable you are. I consider myself privileged to be considered your friend," Wali Daad stated.

"And that you are," Hassim agreed, bowing his turbaned head. "Your praise humbles me, coming from a man as honorable and wise as yourself. How can I assist you?"

"It is because of your honesty that I wish to ask a great favor of you," Wali Daad stated.

"Name it, and if it is in my power, I shall do it," Hassim agreed immediately. "What is this favor?"

Wali Daad rose and approached his rice barrel. Opening the lid, he reached inside and extracted the pennies he had dropped in there earlier. "It is a simple thing. You see, I have too many pennies."

Hassim eyed the eight or nine small coins in the older man's work-callused hand and blinked. "I'm not sure I understand."

"I have a hiding place," Wali Daad explained, returning to his seat at the table. "And I have too many pennies to fit into it. These are the ones that would not fit. I live a simple life, with simple needs, and simple expenses. I do not need so many pennies as I have saved over the years, and I would like to do something with them. But I did not know what, until I saw you."

"What did you have in mind?" Hassim asked, intrigued.

"I would like you to take my pennies to a jeweler. The best of the ones you know," Wali Daad stated. "I want you to take my pennies to this jeweler and have him make the most beautiful bracelet he can, given the money he will receive—and for your trouble, I would like you to keep a hundred pennies for yourself," Wali Daad added. "Would you be willing to do this task for me, my friend?"

"I had thought when you first asked that I would be given a difficult task," Hassim said, chuckling. "But this! This is an *easy* thing. There is a very fine jeweler I know in the East; in fact, he is the royal jeweler to Prince Kavi himself. As I am already headed eastward, your request is a simple enough matter. I will take your pennies to him, let him create whatever he may while I carry out my business, then pick it up again when it is time for me to come back. So! Tonight we shall count out your pennies and put them in my strongest coffers, and I shall treat you to the cooking of my best chef, and we shall pay for several more bundles of your best grass, to start replacing what you are about to spend. Or would you prefer to add them to your order?"

Wali Daad chuckled and shook his head. "I should probably keep a few, in case my grinding stone should break, or I should need a new fishing hook, or one of my scythes should break. But only a few, as my needs are simple, and my life is quite happy for it."

"Then we shall save out a few, and tomorrow I shall take the rest of your too many pennies with me to the Kingdom of the East, along with your request for the finest bracelet the jeweler Pramesh can possibly make. Are we agreed?" Hassim asked, holding out his palm.

"We are agreed," Wali Daad said, clasping hands with his merchant friend. "Come, let us move the table," he added quietly, "and I shall show you my problem of too many pennies."

Hassim raised his brows, but obligingly moved his chair out of the way and helped shift the modest table. His brows rose a second time when Wali Daad lifted up a section of floor . . . and rose so high they all but disappeared under the edge of his turban the moment he saw the large opening stuffed full of copper coins. "I *see* . . . You *do* have too many pennies, my friend. I shall have a struggle to find enough room in my coffers to carry even half of this wealth."

"Well, I cannot keep it here any longer. I am left putting pennies into my rice, and I should not like to mistake coin for corn in my porridge on the wrong sleepy morning. This jeweler, Pramesh, will have a very fine commission headed his way," Wali Daad agreed, closing the trapdoor. "And I want every single penny I send with you to be spent on this bracelet he is to make. The finest bracelet my pennies could possibly buy."

"I will consult with him personally on the matter," Hassim promised, "and I shall not return until the bracelet is perfection itself."

THREE months later, when the summer sun blazed very hot and high in the sky, when the grass which had been so green just a season before was now yellow and brittle, Wali Daad spotted the green and white aba of his merchant friend at the head of the caravan coming up along the eastern road. The deep blue cloth coiled around Hassim's head had been replaced with a pale blue one, soaked with water as well as sweat in the effort to keep its wearer cool.

This time, Wali Daad hurried to lift buckets of water into the stone troughs first, for man and beast were undoubtedly parched. Though the river in the distance was low from the lack of rain, the well had been dug down deep and provided cool, clean water for his visitors to drink. This time, the caravan handlers unpacked their tents for much-needed shade as the very first thing, setting them up before the grass cutter had finished distributing dry but still green grass into the wooden troughs.

This time, when Hassim followed Wali Daad to his small cottage, the merchant was carrying a stout, iron-bound box. Once the door was shut and bread and water had been shared, Hassim centered the box on the table, unlocked it with a key from his pouch, and turned it to face his grass cutter friend.

"Here it is, my friend. You not only had a handful more pennies than you could fit into your hiding hole, you had a handful more pennies than a single horse could comfortably carry. So when I brought them all to Pramesh the jeweler, he made not one bracelet, but *two*. As perfectly matched as he could make," Hassim related, nodding at the casket. "You will not find better outside of a royal palace, I'll wager."

When Wali Daad just sat there, Hassim gestured at the lid.

"Well? Go on! Open it and see what all your hard labor and careful savings have bought you. Every penny has been accounted for, I assure you. Even the hundred you would have given me has gone to buy this casket to help keep them further safe for you. Open it, and wear your new bracelets in good health and great fortune!"

Wali Daad lifted the lid and stared at the contents for a long, long moment. Then he smiled and shook his head slowly, carefully closing the lid again. "Your generosity and friendship warms me more than any hearth fire could during the coldest of monsoons, my friend. But I did not buy these bracelets for myself. I thank you deeply for the trouble you have gone to on my behalf . . . but I must task your generosity with one more request."

Puzzled, Hassim scratched the side of his waxed and pointed beard. "Another request? I would be pleased to fulfill it, if again it is within my power but . . . What request?"

"Bracelets of such incomparable beauty are not meant for a man like me. I live a simple life, and I am blessed with deep contentment by it, as you know," Wali Daad told his friend. "When I saw your bracelets on your last visit, I knew what I could do with my money . . . but it wasn't really *my* money, for I had no use for it. Do you see?"

"Well, no . . . but you and I have different things in our lives which give us satisfaction. For you, it is living a simple life, watering and feeding the caravans who pass by your house day after day, year after year," Hassim said. "For me, it is bringing news and new items to distant lands, to delight, entertain, brighten, and ease the lives of others. I love to travel, and I love to make a good bargain. Though I would not care to live your life, I do respect it, for it brings you happiness. So if you say this is so, I shall believe it for you, though it is not something I would believe for myself."

Wali Daad bowed his head. "Thank you. As I said, since I did not need it, I felt the money was not mine, so how could bracelets made with that money also be mine? No, my friend . . . as you *do* travel so extensively, and meet so many people, what I need now from you is a name. In specific, the name of a woman of incomparable intellect and virtue, a woman of great wisdom and compassion. A woman as beautiful in her mind and soul as these bracelets clearly are."

Hassim blinked. He hadn't expected that question. *While it is true that Wali Daad is an elderly man, of an age where most men are grandfathers,* he thought, *I suppose even a man who lives a simple life could be interested in courting a woman . . .*

"Uh . . . the greatest woman who comes to my mind is the Princess Ananya, she who rules the West Kingdom. She is young—young enough to be your granddaughter—but her youth is tempered by a great maturity of mind, and a youthful wife is a good thing, if the man is still healthy. If your, er, sap can still rise to bedew her flower, I *suppose* she, or a woman like her, could bear your . . . You are blushing?"

Wali Daad quickly shook his head, lifting his hands for emphasis. "No! No, no . . . I am healthy, yes, but I do not wish to take a wife! What woman of great learning and wisdom would want to live as a mere grass cutter's wife? No, her knowledge and her compassion are best used where they are, serving the people she rules. I simply wish you to take these beautiful bracelets and give them to her as a gift. Tell her they come from an admirer for her wisdom and her worthiness, and that she should be adorned on her outside in a manner befitting her inside.

"I am a simple man," Wali Daad repeated, touching the unbleached linen covering his chest, faintly stained by years of wear and toil. "I wear simple clothes, for they are suitable to my life. But you are a fine merchant, and wear fine things to reassure people of your prosperity, which speaks in silent eloquence of the good deals you have to offer. How much more should a woman of incomparable virtue and enlightenment be adorned? Please, take these bracelets to Her Highness with my compliments and my purely *spiritual* admiration. I am too old and my life too content for anything more."

Nodding, not quite understanding but getting a glimpse of what his friend meant, Hassim turned the casket around, locked it again, and promised to take it to the capital of the West Kingdom, since that was conveniently where he was headed next.

BOWING low with every step, Hassim entered the audience chamber of Her Royal Highness Princess Ananya, Flower of the Land and Light of the West. Such obsequience was more than what protocol demanded, but he could not help himself. Next to the opulence and riches of this palace, the visual delights of the carvings and the paintings, the gilding and draperies, the aural delights of songbirds and sweetly placed string instruments, the olfactory nirvana of a thousand flowers in riotous bloom, he felt as if his life were as simple as Wali Daad's.

"Hassim the Trader, caravan master of the Northlands," the master of ceremonies announced, rapping his staff on one of the sections of pattern-tiled marble floor not covered in thick, ornately woven rugs. "Hassim comes before Your Highness with a gift of admiration and esteem."

Hassim, so busy bowing and bobbing, was startled by a soft, feminine chuckle as gentle as water babbling down a brook.

"Come and rise, good trader," the woman bid him. He lifted his head cautiously and found himself staring at a youngish woman clad in cloth of gold embroidered in bright hues and stitched with precious jewels. Her dark hair was draped with creamy gold pearls, and her dark eyes gleamed with good humor. The curve of her lips was a graceful, friendly curve, like a hunter's bow that had been strung but not nocked with an arrow. "I would not have a traveler such as yourself lose his way in an excess of politeness, nor allow him to trip and injure himself. Lift your head and be the man you are, and honor me by it."

Blushing at her praise, embarrassed by his overwhelmed awkwardness, Hassim straightened, gave one last hasty bow, and lifted the casket that had been tucked under his arm, presenting it to her.

"I . . . Your Highness is most gracious to receive a humble merchant such as myself. I come on behalf of Wali Daad, who wishes for me to present to you this gift of beauty, which until now I thought was incomparable. But now that I have met you in person, I know that it *is* comparable, and I am afraid it now seems flawed . . ." Aware he was babbling—for while her nose was ever so slightly crooked, the warmth of her spirit made her look like a deva-angel to him—Hassim struggled to remember his message. "Wali Daad sends you this gift, which was made by the hands of Prince Kavi of the East Kingdom himself—I mean, by the *royal jeweler* of Prince Kavi, by the jeweler Pramesh, he who crafts all the adornments of His Highness's court. It was made by His Highness's jeweler."

Princess Ananya blinked. "It . . . was made by the jeweler who serves Prince Kavi of the East?"

"Yes," Hassim agreed, relieved he hadn't made too much a fool of himself.

"The name of the jeweler is Pramesh?" she asked.

"Yes, Your Highness," he confirmed.

"Then who is this Wali Daad?" Princess Ananya inquired.

"The wisest man I know," Hassim told her. Then he quickly bowed, in case his bluntness was offensive. He fumbled for the key to the casket and unlocked it as he spoke. "It was requested that these be given to the most wonderful woman in the world. A woman of high intellect and compassion, of noble virtue and great wisdom. We immediately thought of you, Your Highness—Wali Daad said that only a woman whose inner beauty exceeded all outer expectations could possibly be worthy of these bracelets, commissioned and crafted by the royal jeweler's own hands. Indeed, Prince Kavi himself could not have owned a more beautiful pair, and so he wanted *you* to have them."

Opening the lid, he displayed the bracelets. Her Highness drew in a sharp, startled breath. Hassim blushed, but this time with pride, not fumbled embarrassment. Even the guards and servants attending Her Highness stared wonderingly at the contents. Wrought from the finest filigree gold, the finger-length cuffs had been encrusted with tiny pearls, each no bigger than a lentil in size and all carefully matched in color so that they formed zigzagging bands of pale blue and pale pink, creamy gold and silvery gray. Each cuff mirrored the other, so that one could tell left from right, but such was the selection and the craftsmanship that it was the only discernible difference between the two bracelets.

"Ohhh . . . these *are* beautiful," Princess Ananya whispered. Gently removing them from the silk-lined casket, she turned them over and over, examining them reverently. "You say His Highness wishes them to go to a woman as beautiful on the inside as these are on the outside?"

"Uh . . ." Not quite sure how to correct the ruler of a nation, Hassim shrugged helplessly. "After consulting with Wali Daad—who is the wisest man I know—he said they should go to a woman as beautiful on the inside as these gems are on the outside. Without any doubt, that woman is you, Your Highness. Your people sing your praises more about your compassion and your skillful management of this land than they do of your face. Having seen you for myself, I can say that you have the face of a deva on earth, yet it still cannot match all the good things for which you are renowned."

Gently caressing the pearls, Ananya smiled. She even blushed, her tanned cheeks taking on a charming rosy hue. "Such a beautiful compliment should not go unanswered . . . Chamberlain?"

"Yes, Your Highness?" a man clad in crimson silks asked, stepping forward from the side of the chamber and giving her a deep bow.

"Give this good merchant a camel to take back with him to his patron, a camel laden with the finest weavings of the West. Silks, brocades, and even a length of our best cloth-of-gold, all of it from the looms of our royal weavers. As a token of esteem for this wisest man in the world, that he should name *me* the most beautiful woman solely for what lies within, not merely what is seen without. Good merchant, pass along my gift to this Wali Daad, along with my thanks to His Highness, and His Highness's jeweler, for the crafting of these bracelets," Princess Ananya added formally. "When I wear them, I shall think fondly of the men of the East, and the great skill and wisdom they possess."

Bowing deeply, knowing when he was dismissed, Hassim bobbed his way back out of her audience chamber. *I have been to the palace of the West, and I have seen the most beautiful woman in the world . . . and I shall live to tell the tale!*

A thought crossed his mind as he straightened outside the chamber and let the guards who had escorted him into the hall of the princess now return him to the main courtyard. *But . . . if Wali Daad did not want all of those pennies, and he did not want those beautiful bracelets . . . what will he think of a camel laden with the finest silks and brocades that are woven in the Western lands?*

WALI Daad stared at the camel. He stared at the bolts of fabric being unloaded by the caravan handlers, silks in more brightly dyed shades than a rainbow had hues, fancifully woven fabrics, and even a carefully folded length of cloth-of-gold. All of it contrasted against the sturdy linens and cottons worn by most of the caravan crew, who were busy with the task of watering and feeding their animals. The monsoon rains had come over a month ago, leaving today a cloudy day, but enough light shone through the clouds overhead to make that cloth-of-gold gleam.

Wali Daad stared in utter dismay, until his eyes stung from staring too much.

"What am I going to do with all of *this*?" he finally demanded, his voice cracking as it had not done for the last five decades. "I thank you most deeply, friend Hassim, for delivering the bracelets along with my admiration . . . but what am I going to do with all of *this*? Do *you* want it?"

Hassim blushed. "As much as part of me would like to say yes . . .

after having seen the palace of the West and all of its wonders, I feel I have far more in common with you and your simple life, Wali Daad. Such riches are not meant for me."

"It would be payment for your many troubles on my behalf these last several months," the grass cutter pointed out.

Hassim shook his head. "No. What I do for you, I do for friendship. I am content with that. And it has not been a trouble, nor really out of my way."

"Well, if *I* do not want it, and *you* do not want it . . ." Covering his chin with a callused hand, Wali Daad thought for a long moment. Finally, an idea struck him and he snapped his fingers. "Hassim, my friend, I have another request of you, if I may . . . ?"

The merchant stifled a groan, guessing what he was about to be asked. "As before, if it is within my power, I will gladly do it for you, Wali Daad."

"This is another easy one, my good, well-traveled friend. What," Wali Daad asked, his sun-burnished face crinkling with humor, "is the name of the wisest, bravest, smartest man in the world? A man of such virtue and honor, his exterior should be swathed in the finest cloth of the West, which is renowned for the undeniable skill of its weavers?"

Hassim didn't bother to stifle his groan. He even chuckled a moment later. "That, my friend, is an easy request to fulfill . . . as I suspect will be your following request. The bravest, wisest, most spiritually exalted man in the world is Prince Kavi, ruler and champion of the East."

Wali Daad touched the tip of his nose with the edge of his finger, grinning at his friend. "You have guessed my mind, O wise merchant. Pack up the camel when you leave, and take its contents to His Royal Highness, Champion of the East, and whatever else he may be. You may keep the camel for yourself as payment for your troubles, if you like."

Hassim nodded. "I think I shall this time, as I did not keep the hundred pennies I turned into a casket for the bracelets. A hundred pennies is as nothing to a well-traveled caravan master such as myself, but a camel . . . well, a *camel* is worth its weight in gold!"

Both men laughed, and the caravan handlers sighed and started reloading the bolts of precious cloth back onto the placidly chewing beast.

THIS time, the merchant wasn't quite as overwhelmed by the lushly painted and carved halls of the royal palace of the East. They were equal in their magnificence to the halls in the palace of the West, if different in the artworks and layout, but having seen one, Hassim was now prepared for the other. He still bowed deeply as he was brought into the receiving room of His Royal Highness Prince Kavi, Champion of the East and Defender of Justice.

"Rise, good merchant," Prince Kavi ordered him before Hassim had finished kowtowing halfway across the hall. "You are no subject of mine, but a man of the North; you honor me with your bows, but they are not that necessary. Moreover, merchants share news and peace even as they share goods and coins with all the people they may encounter, and I would honor that side of your trade. Come, clasp hands with me!"

Flushing, Hassim clasped forearms with the prince, once again finding himself as tongue-tied as before. "Your Highness honors me. You are indeed as great a man as Her Highness . . . er, I mean as great a *person*—I come on behalf of Wali Daad, the wisest man I know, who wishes to honor you for all of your magnificent internal qualities. The honors and virtues, the courage and compassion you hold within your heart are matched only by the wisdom and grace of Her Highness of the West."

"Your praises warm my ears, good merchant," Prince Kavi told him. "But come, you said you bring gifts?"

"Yes, Your Highness." Gesturing, Hassim motioned his five best caravan handlers forward. As he had done, they had dressed themselves in their finest robes, though their garments only made the rich bundles of fabric they brought look all the more exalted in comparison. "Wali Daad wishes to pass these fabrics along to you, which come straight from the looms of the royal weavers of Princess Ananya, Flower of the West. I bring you bolts of silk, yards of brocade, and even a length of cloth-of-gold. Wali Daad thinks that a man of such innate nobility as yourself should dress his outside to match his inside, and can think of no one better to wear the finest weavings of the West than you."

Setting out the bolts, Hassim's caravaners draped the fabric over the low-backed chairs and cushions in the prince's receiving hall. Though the materials covering those cushions were already high in quality, they were from the looms of the Eastern Kingdom. The weavings of the Western lands were discernibly better.

"This is an incomparable wealth you bring me, Merchant Hassim," Prince Kavi said in praise. His dark brown eyes flicked from bolt to bolt. "A gift this fine is usually not given without expectation of a return."

"Wali Daad is not a man to ask for anything in return," Hassim asserted, glad he was able to speak the truth with utter conviction. "He insists that these materials, the finest the royal weavers of Princess Ananya can produce, be brought to the wisest, most courageous, most just and capable leader in the world. Outside of Her Highness, of course, who is your equal in all ways. Knowing how much the two of you have in common, Wali Daad could think of no one better than you to be clothed in the softest silks and most intricate brocades woven in both lands. They are a gift given straight from her hands to my friend Wali Daad, and Wali Daad wishes for you in turn to benefit from them."

"He does, does he?" the prince mused.

"He insists your outsides should match your insides, Your Highness," Hassim asserted. "Her Highness gave this cloth to Wali Daad to do with as he saw fit, and he saw fit to have me bring it straight to you. The only other person Wali Daad and I know who could possibly be worthy of such beauty would be Her Highness, but as they came as a gift from her hand, they could hardly be returned to her, now could they?" He shrugged eloquently.

Prince Kavi chuckled. "Indeed. A gift given with no expectation other than the honoring of one whom someone admires is indeed a true honoring. But though it comes with no expectation, I cannot let the generosity of this Wali Daad pass unanswered. You shall spend the night as a guest in my palace, and in the morning, I shall send twelve of my finest horses back with you, as a gift for this Wali Daad. A man so wise and so generous deserves equal praise and presentation. Come!" Prince Kavi added, gesturing at one of his attendants, "My valet will introduce you and your men to the delights of my bathhouse, with its steam room, its talented masseurs, and the sweetest scented anointing oils from the four corners of the world . . ."

"Twelve horses."

"Yes, my friend."

"Twelve horses . . . for *me*."

"Yes, my friend."

"Hassim, I *feed* horses!" Wali Daad protested, throwing up his hands. "I do not *own* them! *What* am I going to do with two magnificent, royally bred stallions and ten equally marvelous mares? Horses need exercising and tending and . . . and being put to work, either before a plow or beneath a saddle! What am *I* going to do with them? I cut grass all day!"

Eyeing his men, who were grinning as they went about their tasks of watering and grooming the horses and camels of the caravan, Hassim coughed delicately into his hand. "Well . . . you *could* always make another request . . ."

"And just have you pass them along to Her Highness with more of my compliments?" Wali Daad finished for him, his tone as wry as the twist of his lips. Hassim grinned, and the grass cutter sighed. "Fine! Pass them along to Her Highness with both my *and* His Highness's compliments! She undoubtedly has far more need of such fine beasts than I ever would. *I* cut grass for horses. I do not stable and breed them—keep a horse for yourself, if you like," he added, wanting to share such generosity. "For though you may travel that way anyway, you still have gone to great lengths for me in all of this."

Laughing, Hassim shook his head. "No, no, my friend; a camel is worth its weight in what it can carry, but horses as fine as these are meant for warriors and queens to ride, not mere humble merchants such as myself. I shall not insult the royal breeding stock of the East by demanding they carry baggage. As I am headed to the West, I shall deliver these fine animals to Her Highness personally, exactly as you request."

"Thank you," Wali Daad replied. "You are a truly worthy friend, Hassim."

"As are you, Wali Daad," the merchant agreed.

This time, after the gift of the horses were presented and a few questions were answered, Her Highness requested that the merchant Hassim enjoy the delights of her fruit garden while she consulted with her advisors on a suitable reply to this newest gift.

Her grand vizier, an old friend of her father's and a particularly wise nobleman, stroked his beard as they sat in council. "This is a *very* impressive gift. While our textiles may be accounted the finest, the royal stables of the West have nothing quite as good as these Eastern stallions and mares. And to send *two* stallions, with the potential to breed them to many more mares as well as the ten fine, four-legged ladies you have been given, Your Highness . . . this is a wealth above and beyond all expectation."

"It is, indeed," Princess Ananya agreed. "I cannot help but wonder at the motivation."

"The esteemed merchant was very insistent that this was a gift of admiration, not of expectation," the princess's lady of the exchequery stated. Matronly but still something of a beauty, she deigned to wrinkle her nose in distaste. "But as it is such a generous gift, it does carry an obligation. Your Highness is right; we must wonder at his motivation."

"If there were more ties between the West and the East, such generosity would be less fraught with worry over His Highness's motivation," the chamberlain pointed out. "We are not at war with them by any means, but, well, our dealings with the East have been cordial and polite at best for the last few generations. For His Highness to send these horses . . . !"

"Technically, he sent them to this Wali Daad," the lady of the exchequery pointed out.

"Who in turn sent them on to us," the grand vizier argued. "As he sent the bracelets, crafted by Prince Kavi's own royal jeweler. Is this a prelude to a stronger treaty of trade and peace between our lands?"

"Priceless bracelets and royal steeds?" the chief enchantress snorted. She was originally from the North Kingdom, where wizards and enchanters were found and trained. She was also a plainspoken woman. "They sound more like courting gifts to me! On the eastern edge of the kingdom, where the grasslands stretch long and wide, it is not unusual for a would-be groom to gift the family of a prospective bride with a fine horse. If it is a custom so close to the border on our side, it may be a custom close to the border on their side as well, and His Highness may be trying to subtly capitalize upon such a similarity."

The general of the armies spoke up, joining the argument. "But we do not *know* if this is the case." He did not speak often, but when he did, his points were salient. All of the men and women in the room gave him the courtesy of their attention. "Your Highness," he stated, addressing Princess Ananya, "we must ascertain what his motives are. But we must be cautious in doing so and not give offense. As wonderful as these gifts are, we must treat these things carefully."

"My thoughts exactly," Ananya agreed. "If we ask outright if this is a courtship gift and he says no, this could be a point of embarrassment between us, and thus a point of tension between our lands. If it is a courtship gift, and we do not treat it with the respect such an offer deserves at the very least, again we may cause offense. Thus we must probe subtly at His Highness's intentions."

"Do you have an idea, Your Highness?" the grand vizier asked.

"Yes. If this is a prelude to a closer political relationship, it would behoove us to exchange more information about our own cultures. I will therefore send back several gifts: some will be trade goods such as we get from lands beyond our far borders, some will be the finest goods from within our territory, and some shall be books of the history and customs of the West. Among these books, I shall include a few tomes that are my personal favorites. *If* this is a prelude to a marriage offer more than a mere treaty," the princess stated, "I would like to know from the onset whether or not His Highness will respect my passion for knowledge and respect my tastes in reading material."

The others mulled over her choice, and one by one they nodded, coming to an agreement. The lady of the exchequer summed it up neatly. "The books in Your Highness's personal library are the finest in penmanship, illustration, and crafting I have ever seen. They are rare and costly, and would be valuable even to someone who does not read. I suggest you add a personal note or two in some of these books, notes requesting His Highness's opinion of those of custom and history, and opinions of some of your favorites. Or at least a letter suggesting the opening of a personal dialogue between the two of you."

"An excellent suggestion," the chamberlain agreed. "If this is a prelude to a treaty, he will speak of matters of state more than of personal ones. If this is a prelude to a, well, a more intimate level of relationship, he will speak more of personal matters than of national ones."

"It is subtle and strategic. I think this is good," the general approved.

"Plus you will gain insight into the way how he thinks, by studying what he chooses to think about," the chief enchantress added firmly.

"I shall consider carefully what to write in these notes soliciting Prince Kavi's opinions," Princess Ananya stated. "In the meantime, Chamberlain, please arrange for Merchant Hassim and his caravan to enjoy the delights of the palace. If he and this Wali Daad are the intermediaries between us and the Prince of the East, we should treat the messengers of His Highness with as much courtesy and hospitality as we would show His Highness himself."

"You are indeed as wise as this Wali Daad has proclaimed," the chamberlain murmured, rising and bowing to his liege lady. "It is an honor to serve and obey you."

"Ah, Hassim! Come and break your thirst at my well!" Wali Daad called out as the caravan approached along the road from the West. "I have fresh-cut grass for your steeds and some fresh-caught river fish for your friends! I was going to smoke it for preserving, but I can always catch more tomorrow."

"Your hospitality is always a delight, and your offer of dinner shall not be turned down, my friend," Hassim called back, reining in his horse so that he could dismount by the stone troughs.

Wali Daad craned his neck, peering at the strings of horses and camels, of baggage and handlers, before he returned his attention to filling the watering troughs. "You have no gifts for me this time?"

"Oh, the usual . . . but this time it is only a fraction for you. Do you wish to see any of it?" he asked.

"Oh, no," Wali Daad demurred. "I am happy exactly as I am. Please send all of it to His Highness, save only for what you would like to keep for yourself from among the bits reserved for me. But what do you mean only a fraction of it is meant for me? I am curious."

"It is an amusing thing," the merchant informed him. "Her Highness seems to have the impression that these gifts you have been sending her are originally Prince Kavi's idea, as a prelude to strengthening the ties between these two lands . . . and I have decided not to disillusion her. Now, as you are the wisest of men in all the world—or so I have proclaimed to the rulers of both lands—can you tell me why?"

Wali Daad thought about it as his callused hands hauled on the rope again and again. He hadn't quite finished filling the six watering troughs radiating out from the well when the answer came to him. "Peace and prosperity! You think these exchanges of gifts are good for both lands, Hassim, for it makes each ruler think fondly of the other. Am I right?"

Hassim chuckled and clasped Wali Daad on the shoulder. "That is *exactly* right, my friend. I feel as much like an ambassador of peace as a man of business these days. I have been hosted very well by both Highnesses, and while I am very content with my life on the road, it is a delight to see I am spreading a joyful new friendship and a deeper understanding between these two nations, as well as bringing each side the finest goods the other has to offer. Only good can come of this, Wali Daad. Only the best of good!"

Equally happy, Wali Daad nodded his age-grayed head and made sure the last of the stone troughs was properly filled.

∽

It wasn't until almost a full month after Merchant Hassim's departure that Princess Ananya discovered the book.

She only discovered it because it was raining lightly and she wanted some solitude in which to think. That meant leaving her ladies-in-waiting behind to enjoy the much drier, indoor delights of the palace while she wandered the garden. Demurring to the need for an umbrella boy, she protected herself from the light pattering of rain with the end of her sari held over her head while she moved from gazebo to gazebo, lost in thought. Not until she reached the far pavilion did she find the book, and only because the rain was starting to come down heavier than the silk of her garment could easily have withstood if she'd tried to return at that moment.

Seating herself on one of the cushions to rest and think, she found herself sitting on something hard and lumpy. Puzzled, Ananya dug under the cushions and pulled out a jewel-crusted tome. A familiar jewel-crusted tome, with a cover worked in age-darkened silver, amethysts, and rubies. It was one of her favorite books of heroic tales, some of them based on historical fact and others embellished beyond all recognition of any kernel of an authentic origin.

It was also one of the books she had shipped off to His Highness.

This cannot be right; this is the book I tucked my letter into, inviting His Highness to consider discussing the contents of my personal favorites! I know I ordered this one packed. She looked out at the increasing rain beyond the carved stone and wood walls of the broad gazebo, and debated risking the hissing downpour it was becoming. The thought of the book in her hands—even if it was the wrong book—stopped her from leaving just yet. Books were too valuable to risk getting wet.

Which makes me even madder that someone should hide it here, of all places. Covered by a pillow, yes, but otherwise exposed to the weather. But . . . who would do such a thing? And why? . . . And where is my letter? she thought suddenly. Without the letter, Prince Kavi wouldn't know these books were not just a personal gift from her, but a chance to open a dialogue between the two of them, to hopefully draw the two rulers closer in understanding and perhaps even into a friendship. Peace between their lands was good, but peace was always fragile without more ties than just a treaty or two to strengthen it.

By the time the downpour had eased, Princess Ananya was confident the letter was not in the pavilion. She had turned everything upside down that could be turned upside down, moved everything from one side to the other and back, and worked up quite a sweat in the process. The exertion was good, since it kept her warm in the rain-cooled air, but it left her disheveled rather than composed. Doing her best to repair her appearance, she straightened the folds of her sari. Lacking a mirror, she was checking her neatly braided and bejeweled hair with her fingertips when the chamberlain approached, two umbrella boys in tow: one to shelter himself and the other clearly for her.

"Your Highness," he said in greeting, bowing along with the teenaged boys. "I would not disturb your meditations, but it is nearly time for the afternoon petitions to be heard."

"Yes, of course," she agreed, doing her best to shift her mind from the mystery of the book to the needs of her people. Except she couldn't quite let it go. "I have a task for you. This is one of the books that *should* have gone east with the merchant Hassim, the one acting on behalf of Wali Daad and Prince Kavi of the East. It was the book that had my letter of correspondence hopes tucked within it, yet I cannot find the letter, and I should not have this book in my hands here and now. Would you please find out what happened for me while I attend to the requests of our people?"

"Of course, Your Highness—I am as puzzled as you," he added, "for I thought I saw this very book being placed into the chest when I checked on the maids, which was just as they finished their packing."

"I will trust you to be thorough in the investigation and to bring all of your findings to me," Ananya instructed him, smoothing a wayward wisp of dark brown hair behind her ear. Her maidservants would tell her if she needed a moment more to look presentable, but if the chamberlain had come personally to fetch her, then the hour of petitions was very near. "We will hold off any punishments until we know why this has happened, as well as how. Right now, mostly I want to know *how*."

THE truth was revealed shortly after supper. Bowing himself into her presence as Her Highness sat in consultation on a point of taxes with her lady of the exchequer, the chamberlain brought with him Princess Ananya's cousin, Pritikana. He pushed the younger woman to her knees before Her Highness with a heavy hand upon her shoulder.

"*This* is the one who took the book, Your Highness."

Pritikana tried a smile on her cousin. She was not nearly as wise or as learned as her cousin, but she was sweet by nature. "I meant no harm by it, dear cousin. It was just a book! And I made sure to put another book in its place. I even tucked your letter into it, because I figured you wouldn't want that to be left behind."

Feeling the beginnings of a headache coming on, Princess Ananya frowned at her cousin. "Why would you take a book—one which I had personally selected for His Highness to read—and keep it for yourself?"

"Because I hadn't finished reading it, of course! But it's all right, for I just put in another book of tales," Pritikana offered. "You were going to give one book of tales, so I figured another one would be acceptable. And I made sure it also had a cover of silver and rubies, so it would be just as pretty.'"

Sitting back, Ananya calculated which of her books of tales were bedecked with silver and ruby gems. There weren't many on the list, but there were enough to need it narrowed down a bit more. "Do you remember *which* book of tales it was?"

"It was the one I didn't like, but which you did," Pritikana replied blithely. Her smile slipped a little as her royal cousin frowned. "Er . . . the one about the very strange people. With the story of the princess on the glass hill? Only it wasn't a glass hill, but the moon, and they were talking about many strange and boring things which I couldn't understand."

In the entire of the Her Highness's collection there was only one book with a tale about a woman who lived on the moon . . . and yes, it was a book that she did indeed like. A lot. Ananya was glad she was already seated, for she would have fallen down from shock as all the blood left her head in horrified realization. Dizzy, she felt the lady of the exchequery patting her face and bathing her wrists with water from one of the goblets on the table.

"Highness, Highness, please. Surely it isn't that bad?" the lady of the exchequery asked her as she roused out of her half swoon. "Is your cousin wrong? Is it a book you hated?"

"No," Ananya croaked, throat dry with trepidation. She reached for her own goblet and had to steady it with both hands in order to take a drink. "No . . . that *isn't* the case. I liked that book for *other reasons*. My fool of a cousin never got past the first few pages and never read the rest of each story. Did you?"

Pritikana shook her head, her brown eyes wide with confusion. "It was full of strange words and concepts—you know, the sort of thing *you* like to read about. With strange sciences and wild speculations, and a very bizarre way of life. I didn't like it at all. But I thought that, if you liked it, and you're very smart, then His Highness might like it, for he also is reputed to be smart. And I knew you wanted to send him books that you yourself liked, to see if the two of you had anything in common. I also knew you really like reading that book at the end of a long day, for I've heard the maids mention how they've found it on your bedside table many a time in the mornings."

Ananya felt the blood rushing back into her face. "Pritikana . . . you should not have been named for 'a little bit of love'—you should have been named Piki after the *cuckoo* bird! That was a book of *erotic* tales! *Very erotic* tales!"

"Oh, my!" the lady of the exchequer gasped, paling.

The chamberlain clutched at his silk-clad chest. "Gods in Heaven, preserve us!"

Ananya set the goblet back on the table before her hands could shake out its remaining contents. "If His Highness wasn't contemplating the thought of anything more than peace and prosperity between our two lands before this point . . . he will be *now*! Particularly since my *thoughtless*, *selfish* cousin put into *that* particular book the very letter inviting him to *discuss its contents with me*!"

Pritikana buried her face in her hands, hiding from Princess Ananya's glare.

"It has been too many days to send anyone after that caravan, even at the pace of heavily laden horses and camels," the chamberlain murmured, still rubbing at his tunic-clad chest. "We cannot stop the book from arriving . . . but maybe we can have our chief enchantress contact his chief wizard? Maybe he hasn't received the book yet?"

Ananya found herself shaking her head before her thoughts caught up with her subconscious instincts.

"No . . . no, we will not mention this unless *he* mentions this," the ruler of the West explained, reasoning it out aloud. "If His Highness *is* interested in a marriage possibility, to deny the book we sent him would be seen as a discouragement and possibly an insult. If he is offended that it was sent at all . . . *how* he reacts in his offense will tell us much about his character and reveal much about how any deeper treaties between our two lands will be handled. And if he *is* offended, we will plead our ignorance that it was sent, explain how it came to be sent at all, and apologize profusely at that time. Not before.

"No, this is a monsoon we will simply have to endure." Her gaze sharpened, focusing on her kinswoman, who was still hiding her face. "In the meantime, *cousin* . . . I shall have to punish you. Your selfish act of bad karma, wanting to keep and read a book which I had specifically set aside for someone else, will have to be balanced. You are hereby assigned to the city hospice, where you will report to the sisters of the goddess of compassion. Under their orders and instruction, you will bathe and feed and tend to the needs of the crippled and the ill, and you will spend your days comforting the dying, until such time as we know the fallout from this trouble you have caused.

"If I did not know you are a sweet creature at heart as well as a *silly* one, I would have had you locked in the dungeons. But I would rather find a better use for you. Be gone from my sight!" Flicking her hands, which were bedecked at the wrist with the same pearl-encrusted bracelets the wise man Wali Daad had first sent, Ananya dismissed her cousin.

Sinking back in her chair, Her Highness prayed that Heaven had given Prince Kavi of the East a high tolerance for honest mistakes, and a very healthy sense of humor.

PRINCE Kavi was so aroused, he couldn't stand. Which made it a good thing he had decided to save reading this book—after skimming its pages and realizing its true content—until the end of the day. Lying on his side in his bed, with one hand propping up his head and the other fondling his loins, he reread the first of the stories contained in this astounding tome sent to him by the equally astonishing Princess Ananya of the West.

Some of the trade goods this time around had been spices and fruits, some of them minerals and gems. Rare oils and perfumes from far-off lands. Included with such mundane items had been a collection of books on various aspects of Western life and land. Some of the tomes on religion and custom, history and law had contained notes penned by Her Highness, offerings to discuss any differences and similarities between their two nations in the effort to "get to know our dear Eastern neighbors that much better, in order to cultivate a greater peace and understanding, and to emphasize the many things we have in common as fellow human beings." A smaller number within the proffered selection consisted of books which Princess Ananya apparently enjoyed reading for pleasure and relaxation, not merely for information.

This book, one of the books in the chest designated for Her Highness's personal favorites, had contained a note as well. An invitation for the two rulers of the East and the West to "get to know each other on a personal level, to see how much we might ourselves have in common as two fellow intelligent, learned humans having renowned interest in exploring the many facets of thought and understanding, from the factual to the fanciful. I hope you find yourself enjoying this particular book as thoroughly as I myself do. After all, at the end of each day, we are human beings as well as rulers of mighty nations . . ."

Well, I certainly fancy her *way of thinking,* Kavi thought, eyeing the sensual descriptions of the lovers enjoying an intimate interlude in their strange, science-heavy universe. *Too many noblewomen think they must be prim in order to be proper, and this throttling of natural feelings leads them to be stiff and formal in their private lives as well as their public ones.*

That was one of the leading reasons why he hadn't married yet.

Kavi wanted a wife who was his intellectual equal, who understood the burdens of leadership, who could share those burdens, yes to all of that. But he also wanted a wife who could *be* a wife as well as a queen, as he wanted to be a husband in addition to being a king. Women who were prudish because they thought it was the proper thing to do weren't going to make the kind of wife he wanted, and women who were passionate weren't always capable of being proper in public. On top of these considerations, he needed a woman with the level of education necessary to be his equal.

I will not settle for anything less than an equal, unless I have no other choice, he repeated silently, enjoying the stroking of his fingers. A smile curled up the corner of his mouth. *It seems as if Heaven is smiling upon me, for here is a woman whom all report to be as cultured as she is wise . . . yet she clearly has a passionate nature deep inside . . . and a requirement for the same in me, to have asked me to discuss her favorite book of tales with her . . .*

My suspicions have been confirmed, he thought, satisfied mentally, if not yet physically. *She* does *want to discuss a marriage as well as a treaty. From everything I've heard, she'd make any man a magnificent wife. A marriage between us would unite our lands and bring greater prosperity for all . . . but she could have selected a worthy enough man from her own realm, rather than run the risk of possibly being rejected by the lord of a rival nation. Even though I rule the East and could have any woman within the boundaries of my own kingdom . . . I am flattered she has chosen to send all these gifts to me, of all possible men . . .*

The thought of the gifts she had sent, and this book in particular, made him frown in sudden thought. He would have to consult with his cabinet of advisors on what else to send: spices and herbs from his own lands and the realms of lands farther east, pashmina goats for their wool, and rare woods meant for carving, and of course books on the history and customs of the East, with annotated letters of his own pointing out whatever similarities he might find. *And of course the*

*good merchant Hassim shall have to enjoy my hospitality for a few more
days as I quickly devote my time to* finding *those similarities, so that I can
take her more publicly proper requests as seriously as they deserve . . . but
answering* this *book requires a very personal touch.*

*I shall have to think . . . heh . . . long and hard about what to send
back to her personally when I send all the other goods.* Smirking, Prince
Kavi rolled onto his back and finished sating himself with both hands,
thinking about all the things he might send to share with Her Highness his own opinions on such important, intimate matters. *It can't
just be another book, though I think I shall send her one of my own favorite erotic tomes, in the hope she will like it as much as I like this one. No,
I should send her something extraordinary on top of all the other gifts, to
reassure her of my appreciation of her passionate nature . . . and soothe any
hesitancies she may have had over sending such a bold, personal, and . . .
mmm . . . intimate gift . . .*

THIS time, Hassim rode a full hour ahead of his caravan. His current
mission troubled him, and the nature of it had prompted him to rise
early, saddle his mare, and instruct the members of his caravan to take
their time in following him, giving them an admonishment to keep
their lips sealed as to the location and the nature of Wali Daad.

His solitary approach caused the weather-browned face of the aging
grass cutter to wrinkle further. Wali Daad hurried to meet him, calling
out as he approached, "Hassim, my friend! Have you lost your caravan? What ill fortune has fallen upon you? Tell me the gods have not
turned their back upon *you*, of all people?"

"No, no, my old friend. I come alone only because I come ahead
of my camels and men," Hassim reassured him. "They are on their
way."

He let Wali Daad lead his horse by the reins to the troughs, where the grass cutter left him to fetch the first bundle of hay. Hassim dismounted and started drawing the water from the well to satisfy his mare's thirst. Once the animal was comfortable, with her tack removed so that it could air dry as she rested, the two men retreated to the shade cast by the eaves of the thatched roof and a bench Wali Daad had thoughtfully bought with his meager hoard of saved pennies.

"If you come early, you must have a strong reason to leave your men to follow," Wali Daad reminded him, pouring water into a cup for the merchant.

Hassim nodded, sipping at the liquid. It was a plain pottery cup, not the fine blown-glass goblets he had drunk from at the palaces of the West and the East, but the taste of Wali Daad's simple well water was just as fine as any of the wines he had sampled. "I come because there are not just goods in this caravan. There is also a contingent of guards, and a woman."

Wali Daad frowned, scratched his head in puzzlement, and frowned again. "She isn't a gift for *me*, is she?"

"No, no. You have been sent the usual—fruits and spices and carvings from the East," Hassim said dismissively. "No, the woman and the soldiers guard a casket said to come from the hands of Prince Kavi himself, the contents of which are to go into the hands of Princess Ananya herself, and no other. And the woman who rides with us, she is the mistress of the chambers!"

Hassim said it with awe in his voice. Wali Daad blinked. "What does that mean?"

The merchant flushed behind his beard, then grinned. "The mistress of the chambers—I believe the West has a master of the chambers as well, though I am not completely sure—is the person who instructed His Highness in the courtly art of *passion*."

Wali Daad blinked again. "Forgive me my friend, but . . ." He flopped his hands loosely on his linen-covered lap. "Well, I do not understand. Why would His Highness send his lover to Her Highness, if all this going back and forth—which we started—is now happening because they are seeking to unite their two kingdoms in marriage?"

"It is because of the gift she brings, which she brings as a reassurance that though it must not be placed into anyone's hands but Princess Ananya's, it will not harm Her Highness," Hassim explained. "I was told all of this so that I, too, would know what would happen. She will kneel with her head under a sword blade while Her Highness accepts this mysterious gift, and willingly offer up her life in punishment if it harms the Flower of the West even by the tiniest bit."

Wali Daad sat back against the stone and plaster wall of his hut, absorbing this extraordinary news. Hassim sipped at his water, then smiled.

"She told me herself how she volunteered for the job also to personally reassure Her Highness that His Highness was *properly* instructed in how to please a woman, as is the custom of the Eastern lands. Since it seems His Highness *is* very much interested in pursuing the possibility of these two rulers and their two lands wedding together as one."

The grass cutter rubbed at his age-salted hair and finally shrugged. "The ways of the highest ranks in both lands escapes me . . . but I will hope Her Highness is not insulted by this visit, and pray she sees this as a good thing. I am a simple man, and I lead a simple life. Perhaps I missed out on passion, but I find my joy in other things, and I am content. Who am I to question the ways of those with more complex lives?"

"Yes, well, it is because of this woman and the guards who accompany her that I have come early to meet with you, my friend," Hassim cautioned him. "I have not said who you are, other than the wisest, most generous man I know. Or rather, I have not mentioned how you live and what you do for your living. I did not do so out of shame— you have taught me by example that the man who is content with his life is the happiest, healthiest, and wealthiest of men, and there is no shame in that, only something worthy of honor in my eyes—but I kept silent because I did not know how *you* would feel to have yourself revealed.

"You are as you say you are, a simple man who leads a simple life," Hassim said, gesturing at the cottage, the well, the troughs, and the hay shed. "To reveal this simplicity to others might complicate matters beyond what you might find comfortable. So I have come ahead of my caravan to ask you if we should reveal who you are, or keep your identity private."

Wali Daad blinked and sat in thoughtful silence, absorbing his merchant friend's words. He sat for so long that the line formed by Hassim's caravan came into view in the distance, rising up out of the rippling stalks of grass as they followed the road from the East Kingdom. Hassim did not pressure Wali Daad for an answer, but did rise with the intent of filling the rest of the stone troughs with water for his animals and men.

Sighing heavily, Wali Daad rose to follow him. "I think it best to keep my identity a secret. I may have started this because I could not shut my trapdoor on all the pennies I had collected, but this has become far greater than you or I, my friend. We have played our parts in the start of it, but the blessings of Heaven have taken over. It would be presumptuous to claim anything more."

Hassim nodded. "I thought you might feel that way. So. You shall simply be the grass cutter with the well and the sweet hay at this stop along our journey. Though I ask that you do not hesitate to greet the mistress of the chambers; I wish your opinion of her . . . since if Prince Kavi and Princess Ananya wed, she will need some other occupation. It may be presumptuous of me to say this, and I may be reaching beyond the stars themselves . . . but she and I have been getting along very well on this journey. Her name is Bhanuni, and she seems to me at least half as wise and beautiful as Her Highness. A jewel who might be out of my reach . . . but one for which I feel I must strive."

Wali Daad nodded at his wheelbarrow. "Then I shall fetch the sweet hay and collect my pennies for it as usual, and give the kindest of greetings to the mistress of the chambers for your sake, my friend."

∽

IT was in the closest semblance to privacy possible that Princess Ananya was presented with the contents of the fiercely guarded casket.

That semblance included five of her personal guards and her chief enchantress, the merchant Hassim as bond for his fellow travelers, the noble Lady Bhanuni, and the lady's three guards, one of whom bore the small casket literally manacled to his arms by stout iron chains. The meeting for this personal presentation had also been arranged to take place after sunset. The guard with the casket knelt and bowed his head, lifting the metal lockbox in presentation. Lady Bhanuni offered Her Highness the key and a list of instructions on its contents.

"The item within this casket is an enchanted item, Your Highness," the noblewoman offered, bowing deeply. "It is, by its enchanted nature, the most precious possession His Highness could possibly offer to you. Aside from his very self, of course. The nature of the enchantment cannot harm you, and as a reassurance it cannot, I have volunteered to kneel under a drawn sword while you receive it. Should it harm you in any way, my head is willingly forfeit."

"And your head, of all the heads in the Eastern lands, is forfeit because . . . ?" Princess Ananya asked, looking between the key in her hand and the lovely middle-aged woman lowering herself gracefully to her knees.

Lady Bhanuni lifted her head and smiled. "Because I am the mistress of the chambers for His Highness, and I am also here to give explanations and reassurances for any questions you may have about my liege's abilities in matters of love and marriage. The proposed merger of two kingdoms is a matter for rulers and their advisors to discern, but the merger of two people is a different matter."

"*I* would rather you explained a bit more about this enchantment," the chief enchantress interjected as Princess Ananya blushed. "What does it do?"

"It, erm, *links* His Highness to this prized possession. The nature of the enchantment is to key it to the touch of one hand alone, the first hand to touch it since the moment it was enchanted. And once it is keyed, it is enspelled to *animate* the object when that hand alone is touching it," the mistress of the chambers explained. "It has been declared a death sentence by Eastern law for any hand but yours to be the first one to touch the item His Highness has sent. It is also realized that this is not the kingdom of the East, but it is hoped that you will give due consideration and honor to Prince Kavi's wishes in this matter."

"We would not insult a gift of such esteem by ignoring His Highness's requested precautions, though I do not think you will need to bow your head to a drawn sword," Ananya returned politely. She lifted the key, then nodded at the wizardess at her side. "My chief enchantress will keep an eye upon this Eastern magic, of course, but I will put my trust in Prince Kavi's words, and in his desire for this alliance."

Lady Bhanuni chuckled, making Her Highness aware of her choice of words. Blushing a little, Ananya unlocked the casket still being held aloft by the Eastern soldier. She lifted the lid, peered at the contents . . . and blushed a lot. Dropping the lid, she covered her face with her hands for a moment, trying to cool the heat burning in her cheeks, then lowered them slowly. Princess Ananya had to be sure she had seen what she thought she had seen, so she lifted the lid a second time.

The contents were the same at a second glance as they had been at the first: nestled in soft red and gold brocade—some of the very same red and gold brocade she had sent to Wali Daad, who had apparently passed it along to the Prince of the East—was a golden phallus. Every ripple, every wrinkle, every vein had been carefully crafted, making it the most realistic metal penis she had ever seen. From the dimpled slit at the tip to the bulbous bollocks of its sack, it was a proud curve of crafted manhood.

"Er . . . and . . . I'm . . . supposed to pick this up?" she managed to ask politely, finding her voice.

"Yes, Your Highness. Once you do, it will respond to no other touch. His Highness requests that if you refuse this gift, it must be locked and returned to him utterly untouched by any other hand, for he offers this enchanted opportunity solely to you." Lady Bhanuni paused, then smiled again, though this time the smile was more puzzled than warm. "He did not say exactly why, but he did mention something about the two of you having similar tastes in many subjects, including . . . bedtime stories. I am afraid I did not understand his meaning, and he did not explain."

Blushing again, Ananya nodded. "I do understand myself, and that is enough; you need not ask why. I do accept this gift," she stated, reaching into the casket and curling her fingers around the metal, which warmed rapidly, "and thank His Highness for the great trust he displays in offering it. I shall do . . . Oh! It moved!"

Lady Bhanuni smiled. "As I said, it is enchanted." She gestured and the soldier holding the casket lowered it, offering it to the mistress of the chambers. Reaching in, the older woman plucked out the phallus. "You can see for yourself how in my hands it is nothing more than a bit of sculpted metal."

Knocking it on the side of the casket made both the iron and the gold *clank* loudly as they were struck together. All of the men in the room winced in sympathy. Unfazed, the mistress of the chambers held out the phallus to Princess Ananya, continuing her explanations.

"Even when we both touch it . . . see?" she said as Ananya reached for the proffered phallus. "It is still nothing more than metal. But the moment I let go . . . it becomes as one with its progenitor—you cannot harm him by it, of course, not even if you were to place it upon an anvil and strike it with a hammer under the force of your own hands," Lady Bhanuni added in caution, "but every touch that inspires pleasure and passion will be transmitted to him. And every response he feels through your pleasurable touches shall be displayed in return for you.

"To this end, it is *strongly* requested by His Highness that you refrain from touching it at any point during the hours of daylight. He does have a kingdom to run, and it would not be good to startle him when you did not know he was, oh, descending a long flight of stairs, perhaps. Or sitting in judgment on a petition brought to him by his people."

"Of course, of course," Princess Ananya hastily agreed, still a bit embarrassed by this presentation.

She wasn't an innocent; members of the royal house were instructed in passion as thoroughly as they were instructed in geography or riding. Her embarrassment was more on Prince Kavi's behalf, to have had his manhood displayed before her watchful guards and her magical advisor, even if only through a metallic proxy. Treating it gently, she set it back into its padded casket and closed the lid. One of the other soldiers came forward with a second key, which he used to unlock the first soldier's shackles.

Ananya gestured at the box as it was set at her feet. "This is indeed a gift beyond all . . . beyond all *imagining*. I find myself overwhelmed by His Highness's generosity and his, er, thoughtfulness."

She hesitated, then looked at her chief enchantress, who leaned in and whispered in her ear. Nodding, Ananya addressed the others.

"You may all go—and a suitable reply shall be formulated for you to return with to His Highness on our behalf, noble merchant," she told Hassim. "In the meantime, you are invited to once again enjoy all the delights of our palace. The same hospitality shall be extended for you as well, good soldiers of the East. Lady Bhanuni . . . if it would not be too much trouble, would you care to stay and answer a few more questions for me? I realize it is late, and you have traveled a long way to get here."

All of the others, save for one Western guard, bowed themselves out of the private salon serving as their audience chamber. Lady Bhanuni remained on her knees, ignoring the lingering bodyguard. "I would be honored, Your Highness. His Highness has been increasingly interested in your overtures of courtship, and—"

"*My* overtures of courtship?" Ananya raised her voice, catching the others as the last of them filed out of the room. "Merchant Hassim! Come back in here!"

The merchant came back promptly at her sharp command, along with another one of the Western bodyguards as an escort. He bowed his way up to her and knelt. "Yes, Your Highness? You wish something of me?"

"Did you, or did you not, bring *these* bracelets to me on behalf of Prince Kavi?" Ananya asked, lifting her wrists.

Hassim blushed, scratched briefly at his beard, and finally shrugged. "Not exactly, Your Highness . . ."

"Not exactly?" Princess Ananya repeated, arching one dark brow. "What does that mean? Were these bracelets not made by Prince Kavi's own royal jeweler, as you have claimed?"

Hassim bowed his head, choosing his words carefully. "I brought them to you, as I said, at the behest of Wali Daad. He decided in his wisdom that you deserved them, and he requested they be made by the finest jewel crafter I knew . . . which happened to be the artisan Pramesh, who was appointed royal jewel crafter to the Prince of the East just over two years ago."

"So these came from Wali Daad, and no other. *Not* in any way or shape from His Highness of the East. And the silks and brocades and the cloth-of-gold I sent back to him?" she asked, flipping open the lid of the casket at her feet. Hassim glanced at the contents of the box out of reflex, then quickly looked away, flushing. "This very same gold-woven silk was among the bolts I sent back with you to this Wali Daad as a thank-you gift for the generosity and thoughtfulness of these bracelets I wear. How did this cloth come to be in the possession of the Prince of the East?"

Hassim shrugged. "Wali Daad decreed they were too fine for himself to wear, and selected Prince Kavi as the most suitable recipient. Just as he felt you should be adorned so that your outsides match your insides, he thought such fine cloth should adorn such a fine man."

"And the horses?" she asked.

"They were a gift from Prince Kavi to Wali Daad as a thank-you for his generosity for sending such fine fabrics to him," Hassim admitted.

"But were they a gift meant for Wali Daad or a gift meant for me?" Ananya quizzed him.

"They were a gift meant for Wali Daad," Hassim confessed. "But in his wisdom—"

Ananya held up her palms, cutting him off mid-explanation. "Yes, yes; I am beginning to see his machinations. It is not His Highness who started this offer of negotiations between our two lands and this . . . this *courtship* between our two selves, but this Wali Daad who instigated it instead. This is *his* courtship decision and not His Highness's idea."

Hassim, very nervous inside, daringly offered her a smile. "Well, yes, Your Highness. But isn't it a most wonderful idea? There have been no wars between the East and the West for three generations. Just a long span of peace intermixed with some prosperity. Yet there haven't been many changes in the treaties of the two lands to make the peoples of both realms move closer toward friendship and understanding. And there Wali Daad sat, straddling the crossroads of the border, thinking nothing of himself and only of bringing delight and happiness to all others.

"He saw the possibility of bringing you delight and happiness, Your

Highness, as a reward for all the good you have done, and he seized upon the opportunity it presented," the merchant added coaxingly as she listened to him. "It is he who saw the possibility of passing along further delight and happiness to His Highness as a more worthy recipient of your generosity . . . only to find the admirations and delights blossoming further like a flower under the spring sun. Is it such a terrible thing he has done, in passing along these things between yourself and the Prince of the East? Or is it a good thing which even the gods in Heaven would praise and honor?"

"Not to mention, in the meantime, he has made himself a fortune off our generous replies," Ananya muttered darkly.

"Oh, no! He has not kept a single penny of any of it," Hassim quickly reassured her. "Not in all of these exchanges he has facilitated. In fact, he gave up his own pennies to have those bracelets made, a veritable fortune willingly traded away for nothing more and nothing less than the satisfaction of knowing he honored a person as worthy of it as yourself."

"Well, what of yourself? Have you not kept any of it?" Princess Ananya asked, eyeing him warily.

Hassim flushed and rubbed at the back of his neck. "Well . . . none of the fabrics, and none of the horses, and none of the spices and such . . . but I did keep the original camel you gifted to him, the one which bore the original shipment of cloth. At Wali Daad's insistence."

"The camel," she repeated. She spotted the smile on the face of Lady Bhanuni, half-forgotten to the side. Ananya began to see not just the absurdity of this situation, but its humor as well.

"Yes. Because I am a merchant, and it *is* a camel," Hassim said, shrugging. "And because Wali Daad insisted I should take it. But all else has gone into the making of your bracelets, and the transporting of the cloth, and the herding of the horses, and the . . . the rest of it. So on and so forth. Erm . . . if you are offended, Your Highness, I *could* give you the camel back, I suppose?"

Unable to help herself, Ananya sat back in her chair and chuckled. It became a laugh, which she half-muffled as she turned her head and rested it in her palm, elbow propped on the armrest of her makeshift throne. "A camel . . . And a wise man who saw the wisdom in leading His Highness and me by the flattered nose to an arranged marriage."

Relieved by the way it looked like he wasn't going to be beheaded, Hassim daringly said, "If I may be so bold, Your Highness, Wali Daad merely opened the path to the *possibility* of a marriage, just as I merely carried out his requests, as a good friend should. The two of *you* decided it was a path worth walking upon. You are both wise, benevolent rulers who wish only what is best for your people, as well as yourselves. You decided to do this much more on your own."

Princess Ananya chuckled again, unable to refute his honest assessment. "That we did, good merchant . . . that we did. You may go. And you may still enjoy the delights of my palace. Sleep well, Hassim. You have earned it."

A flick of her pearl-and-gold-clad wrist banished him and his escort from her presence. Ananya sighed and stooped. Scooping up the casket, she rose and offered her hand to the kneeling mistress of the chambers. The bodyguard, a stoutly muscled woman handpicked and trained from early youth to be able to guard a member of the Western royal family, came to attention and followed them out as Her Highness led the way.

"Come, milady," she said. "You and I shall retire to my private chambers, where you shall instruct me in all the touches His Highness likes best. And though I do not think my chief enchantress has the skill to replicate anything of an equivalent nature, I will send my master of the chambers back with you when it is time for you to return, so that he may reassure His Highness that I have had equal instruction in such matters myself."

Lady Bhanuni chuckled. "Trust me, Your Highness. If I am to teach you all that I know, His Highness will know exactly how skillful you are. Remember, if *I* touch it, he will feel nothing at all. The same will not be true for you. He will feel everything you do . . . which is why I am here to help instruct you."

Blushing, Princess Ananya carefully carried the casket to her rooms.

THE first touch came as he was enjoying a performance in the palace theater. The feel of warm, soft fingers encircling his shaft startled him. They shifted and squeezed a little, and it felt so real, he couldn't help but glance down. No one had a hand in his lap, though he could still feel the sensation. The phantom touches paused for a few moments, then came back as the invisible hand held him once again, then finally stopped.

Blinking, Prince Kavi returned his attention to the words and actions of the actors on the platform. Thankfully, they were in the final act of the drama. Unfortunately, they were only partway into it. No sooner had the second of three scenes begun than he felt the phantom touch of a woman's hand again. At first it was just a grasping sensation, almost like she was carrying him. Then he felt her circling his shaft with her fingertips, exploring his skin. She stroked his glans and trailed her fingers down to his sack, gently weighing each of the soft globes tucked within.

Her random explorations aroused him. He felt her sliding his foreskin back from the tip of his rod, and wondered if it really was being physically slid back. Another glance at his trousers showed his flesh beginning to strain against the brocaded fabric. Realization struck; he nudged his grand vizier, whispering for the older man to pass the word that he wanted to speak with his chief wizard.

Rising, the Northern-born man moved along the row of chairs in the royal viewing box and crouched in front of his liege, whispering, "You wished to see me, Your Highness?"

Leaning forward—grateful that he still could—Kavi whispered in his ear. "Your special spell is working *very* well. Too well. Now you will do something about it."

"I beg your pardon?" the chief wizard whispered back. "Do you wish me to end the enchantment, Your Highness?"

"No." The feel of the hand of Princess Ananya—given the instructions he had sent with his envoys, it could be no other—was too seductive to give up just yet. "I need you to cast an illusion upon my clothes so that I may stand up at the end of this play with my dignity still intact."

"Ah." Mouth curling up in amusement, the chief wizard bowed his head. "Of course, Your Highness. And tomorrow, I should have an amulet ready for you to wear which will keep the illusion going. Even if I have to work all night to enspell it."

"Thank you." Keeping his chin up, Kavi watched the play as the mage chanted quietly over his lap. A slight tingle was the only proof the magic had worked. The chief wizard bowed and returned quietly to his seat, leaving Prince Kavi to enjoy the rest of the play. Or at least the appearance he was enjoying the play.

It wasn't the daring flash of swordplay between the hero and the villain in the historical drama that made him suck in a sharp breath. It happened because he felt a soft pair of lips press themselves to his skin, followed by the lapping of a warm, damp tongue. A glance down at his trousers showed them in their normal, slightly loose fit, but he knew his shaft was engorged enough to rise from his lap. He could even feel the fabric straining with the pressure of his arousal. But most of all, he could feel her lips and her tongue, and the slightest, lightest scrape of her teeth.

The one thing that helped him keep his sanity was how sometimes his shaft would go numb to sensations, and other times it would be tapped and prodded and touched gently, without much in the way of pleasure . . . only to be followed shortly by more deliberately experimental touches. *I do believe Lady Bhanuni is giving Her Highness . . . Ah! Exquisite instruction*, he thought. Sweat seeped onto his brow, making him grateful there weren't any oil lamps lit beyond the ones focused on the stage. *If I didn't have a public image to maintain, and didn't want to disappoint or insult the performers, I would leave . . . Oh, Heaven! Oh, Heaven help me . . .*

She was sucking on his sack. His own had a thick dusting of dark hairs, but his phallus did not, allowing the soft, mobile lips of the Flower of the West to draw upon first one, then the other of his royal jewels without impediment. *Oh, Goddess . . . I finally see a reason to shave down there . . . OH!*

A ripple of her fingers on his shaft, coupled with those lips, coaxed the milk of his loins up and out unexpectedly. Fingers clenching the armrests of his chair, throat locked tight against the need to shout, Kavi endured his climax in silence. He wanted to relax as the euphoria ebbed, but she was still *touching* him with her unseen hands, still keeping him aroused.

The play came to its end, but Prince Kavi didn't hear or see it. Only the applause of his court woke him to the fact that something had happened. Sweating, aware that he had to stand up and walk away, he glanced quickly at his lap before putting his hands together. Everything *seemed* normal, thankfully.

That was good, because he felt more like he had been fitted with the bowsprit of a sailing ship. Rising, he managed to make a few comments about the play being good and being willing to see it again another time. Such as when he wasn't hypersensitive to the fact that

Her Highness was now rubbing the tip of his phallus between her soft, wet, crinkly-haired netherlips.

Somehow, he got to his feet. Somehow, he walked serenely—if stiffly—out of the performance hall. Somehow, he made it all the way back to his private chambers, where a curt order and a flick of his hand dismissed everyone from his presence. And somehow, he walked all the way to his bed, which he couldn't really see, and dropped onto it. Faceup, of course, because there was no way in Heaven or Hell that he was going to break the spell-hidden shaft Her Highness was now enthusiastically sliding in and out of her slick, enchantment-distanced heat.

She was torturing him and didn't even know it. Unable to control her touches, to guide her and advise her, Kavi was rendered helpless by her enthusiastic exploration of whatever pleased *her*. Because it pleased him too much, to the point where his body wanted release, but his brain longed too much for more of her unwitting torments.

Her thrusts became more rapid, more erratic. He felt her flesh constricting around his shaft, then felt the pulses of her pleasure as she shuddered. Only then did he, too, shudder, letting his body loose itself like an arrow from a bow. In the privacy of his quarters, Prince Kavi let himself tense and release without restraint, panting and groaning openly with satisfaction. As his own pleasure ebbed, he felt her tongue flicking along his shaft and draped an arm over his eyes.

Part of him wondered if he should call the creator of his enchanted phallus into his chambers to end the spell. He didn't know how much more of this he could take. After a moment, he realized that he was now being rubbed by her fingers and what felt like a warm, damp cloth. A few moments after that, blessed numbness came back as he felt her replace his phallus in its strongbox, leaving him with only the tangible, real sensation of his exhausted shaft nested on his belly, cocooned in a pool of its own juices and the silk of the trousers clinging because of it.

Arm still draped over his eyes, Kavi wondered if he was insane, because the larger part of him *didn't* want to end the enchantment. Mouth quirking at his own perverseness, he set his mind to the task of merging their two kingdoms quickly, so that he could merge their two bodies all the sooner—the rest of their two bodies, to be specific.

NEVER had Wali Daad seen so many couriers riding back and forth between the road to the East and the road to the West. For three months, couriers and messengers and officials of all sorts rode back and forth, carrying with them all number of proposed laws, ordinances, and suggestions for comingling the customs, beliefs, and traditions of the East and the West. And the word from the caravans that passed back and forth said that the people of both nations were quite happy with the proposed merger.

A part of him was pleased he had started all of this, but the aging grass cutter was also kept very busy. The dry season was coming, and with so many more animals being sent back and forth by their riders and handlers, it was all he could do to keep up with the demands of each day and still store enough hay for the long wait for the rains of the next monsoon season.

Indeed, he had taken to leaving a sign, scratched on a scrap of wood with a nail, for people to help themselves to the hay he laid out in the troughs twice and three times a day, and to leave pennies in the jar under the sign. He had no choice; he needed to spend most of his time out in the fields, cutting and bundling the long stalks of grass, rather than trotting back and forth to tend to the various couriers. His visitors were generous, often leaving him more pennies than the hay was worth, but that was all right. Wali Daad had plenty of empty space beneath his trapdoor.

It was late when he returned one day to his little thatched cottage, with the sun beginning to set in the west. Wali Daad found an exhausted horse nibbling tiredly at the hay left in one of the wooden troughs, with the mare's tack resting on the ground and no sign of her owner. Confused, the grass cutter pulled on the latch-string of his door, only to find his home already occupied by a very frazzled, shadowed, worried-looking Hassim.

Wali Daad immediately fetched his cups and the pitcher of well water waiting for him. "Please sit, my friend. It must be a very grave concern to have brought you all this way in such a great hurry. Is something wrong with your caravan?"

"No! No . . . Business is . . . business . . . Oh, Wali Daad, a terrible thing is about to happen! I ran away from Her Highness, and I suppose from His Highness, too—and they will be *here* in just a day or two!" Hassim babbled, wringing his hands together. "Oh, Wali Daad, what are we going to do?"

Blinking, Wali Daad took his pacing friend by the elbow and guided him into a chair. "Please, sit. If I am to understand what has happened, you must calm yourself. Sit and drink. Eat, my friend," he added, fetching the loaf of bread waiting for his supper, along with some strips of dried fish and slices of dried fruit. "You must rest, then you will think more clearly."

"Yes . . . yes . . ." Seated, the merchant nibbled on the offered food, his brown eyes still a bit wide and a little unfocused. Only after Wali Daad had refilled his cup did he focus them again. "They want," he announced with a disturbing solemnity, "to hold the marriage . . . *here*."

Wali Daad blinked again, unsure he had heard his friend correctly. "Here? At the crossroads?"

"In the home of the inestimable Wali Daad," Hassim corrected gravely. "They are on their way *here*, right now. I let it slip that you lived at the crossroads here at the border, but they think you live a little ways off, perhaps a little to the north." He flung up the hand not holding on to his cup in a wordless gesture of disbelief. "I was to guide Her Highness there—here—with all of her entourage, and then go east and meet up with His Highness and all of *his* entourage, and bring them all to the home of the wisest man in the world, the great Wali Daad! They are expecting a man who lives in a mansion, and they wish to be married in your magnificent gardens!"

"And so you ran away?" Wali Daad asked, wanting clarification on that point. He could barely think about the rest of his friend's news as it was.

"I escaped two nights ago on the road, just took my mare and left, riding as fast as I could to warn you. They want to meet you—they *insist* that they meet you," Hassim corrected himself, "and they want *your* blessing upon the union of their two lands and the union of their two selves! Her Highness knows now that it was *your* idea, not His Highness's idea, to send the bracelets one way and then the silks the other.

"I do not know if she told His Highness or not, but the one thing I have *not* revealed is that you are a grass cutter and that you live in a hut! Well, a cottage," he amended, dazed and distractible in his distress. "It does have a floor . . . I do not know what we are going to do, my friend. I honestly do not know!"

Silence stretched between them. Outside, Wali Daad heard the mare nickering softly. He rose from his seat and patted his friend on the shoulder. "I will tend to your mare. You rest and continue to eat. Somehow, we will figure out what to do. If they truly want my blessing, then they will have it, *if* they still want it once we have met . . . though they may only have my fields of half-mown hay for their wedding garden."

Hassim covered the grass cutter's hand with one of his own for a moment, then dropped his forehead into his palm. Leaving the merchant inside, Wali Daad filled a bucket with water and led the mare to his hay shed, already three-quarters full with dusty, sweet-smelling bundles of grass. He found an old currying brush and stroked the mare's hide, trying to think of what to do about the approaching wedding parties.

I am a simple man . . . I know nothing of pleasure gardens, nor did I ever think I should want to, he thought as he groomed the tired animal. *And yet that is what these people are expecting to find.* Stars were beginning to glimmer in the darkening sky. Wali Daad looked up at the jewels they made, and prayed.

Heaven . . . all of Heaven . . . if there is any way to give these people what they want, show me the path to it and I will walk it for them. But I am a simple man. I cannot craft miracles like a God! All I can ask is that You open the hearts of these women and men so that they *see the beauty that I see whenever I wander through my home . . . and soften their hearts so that they do not take offense at being match-made and kingdom-wed by a lowly grass cutter.*

All I wanted was to do something nice, *to give a gift to someone who deserved it,* he thought wearily.

He gave the mare one last pat and made sure she had the bucket of water close at hand, before leaving her tied up for the night. Having fetched her tack on the way back to the house, Wali Daad carried it inside. He would offer Hassim his own pallet for the night, since his friend had ridden off without a bedroll, and Wali Daad would sleep on the floor. It would make him stiff, since he was in his late sixties, but not much more so than these long days of cutting enough hay already made him feel.

"MASTER Wali Daad . . . It is time for you to awaken, Master. Oh, Wali Daad . . ."

Snuggling deeper into the cloudlike softness of his bed, Wali Daad grumbled and tried to ignore the quiet, lilting voice bothering him.

The touch of a soft, cool palm against his cheek snapped his eyes open . . . and the sight of the arm and body attached to that hand did more to banish the urge to sleep than lighting a fire under his chin would have. That hand, and that arm, belonged to the body of a slender woman wrapped in a bright blue and purple sari studded with more than enough silver to match the ornate jewelry woven into her neatly braided hair.

"Good morning, Master Wali Daad! You have awakened just in time," the young woman—well, in her late twenties, which was quite young compared to him—told him as he sat up. "Your bath has been readied and your clothing laid out. Once you are dressed and have dined on your breakfast, you will be ready to receive Their Highness-es's outriders."

Wali Daad was too busy staring at the opulent splendor of the chamber surrounding him to make much sense of her words. Carved marble had replaced the ordinary river stone of his cottage, and exotic woods now occupied the simple lumber beams which had once defined his home. Not to mention silk curtains, embroidered cushions, gilded paintings, and brightly colored bits of glass lining the five—*five*—windows to north. Five stained-glass windows showing a view of the crossroads from higher up than he had ever seen before, when he normally had just one, simple, wooden-shuttered opening down on a solitary, single floor.

"I . . . I do not understand. Where am I?" he asked as the young woman coaxed him out of bed by the hand, revealing how someone had clad him in soft, white silk garments instead of his age-stained, familiar linens. "What has happened to my home?"

The woman smiled, releasing his hand. Pressing her palms together, she bowed to him. "I am a deva, Wali Daad. Heaven has heard the prayer of your heart and granted you a home worthy of it."

An angel of the gods! Wali Daad stared at her. *Am I . . . Am I dead?*

She straightened and grinned. "No, you are not dead, Wali Daad—

Master Wali Daad, rather. And yes, I am an angel of the gods. You may call me Desna. This is the truth of what has just happened: You, Wali Daad, are honored by Heaven. Nothing more than that . . . and nothing *less*." Sweeping her hands at the palatial chamber around them, she repeated herself. "Heaven has peered into your heart and remolded your home overnight to match it."

"But . . . why?" Wali Daad asked. Part of him was a little frightened that she could read his thoughts, though she wasn't frightening in the least. He felt as if he should know her, though he knew he had never seen her before. Everything was confusion, and he didn't know what to make of these sudden changes in his life.

Tucking her arm in his, she guided him toward an archway hung with strands of precious pearls for its beaded curtain. "Because you are worthy. And because you gave a true gift, expecting and wanting nothing in return, and *continued* to give and give with no expectations. And because there are two mighty nations, both of whom honor Heaven, who are expecting to see what you have always seen. But . . . their eyes are busy thinking that wealth is equal to beauty." Her smile slipped into a moment of sobriety. "It is sometimes easier for Heaven to transform a simple cottage into a magnificent palace than it is to open the eyes of the people to the natural wonders of the world."

"So . . . this will only be here for the length of the wedding?" he asked, gesturing vaguely at his unfamiliar, opulent surroundings.

Smiling, she drew him into the next room, where several more youths, some of them men and some of them women, awaited with towels and anointing oils, with the promised bath and finely woven clothes to follow it. "It will be here for as long as you wish it, Wali Daad. For as long as your heart is true."

Bemused and wordless, Wali Daad allowed himself to be bathed and readied for the day.

⌬

She was every bit as beautiful as her letters had proclaimed. Not in a listing of her features, which were indeed fine, but in the way she had written, full of wit, charm, humor, and intelligence. Her brown eyes gleamed with amusement, her mouth curved with kindness, and her cheeks blushed with awareness when Prince Kavi, Champion of the East, requested a moment alone with her in one of the palatial rooms in the home of the kind, quiet-spoken, slightly befuddled-looking Wali Daad. In a palace that his couriers and border guards, one and all, had sworn *hadn't* been there just the day before. But the prince could not focus on that peculiar fact just yet.

Dismissing even the last of his bodyguards, he waited until Princess Ananya, Flower of the West, had reassured and sent on her way the last of her own guardswomen. Closing the door carefully, Kavi turned back to her. She looked like a painting from Heaven in her beautiful sari and pearls. A living deva. His wife-to-be.

"What did you wish to discuss in private, Your Highness?" she asked him politely.

"No." Leaving the door, he lifted his finger between them. "Right now, there is no 'Highness' between us. No prince, no princess, and no nations. We will not have this chance to be alone again until late tonight, long after we have become the joint rulers of our lands . . . but right here, right now," Kavi coaxed her, taking her hands in his, "there is just a wonderful woman and a very grateful man."

Her smile widened and her blush deepened. "It is I who should be grateful. I had no plans for anything other than a marriage of state, but your letters . . ."

He lifted her fingers to his lips, deeply grateful he could finally touch them. "And yours," he agreed. Drawing her closer, he placed her palms against his chest. He smiled and closed his hands as she flattened and spread her fingers. "Yes . . . touch me. Touch *all* of me.

Did you know you have been driving me insane with passion nearly every night?"

Ananya smirked and stepped closer, brushing their bodies together. "Lady Bhanuni gave me some ideas to start out with, but most of it has been inspired all from my own imaginings. But this, touching the rest of *you* . . . this is better than mere imaginings."

Cupping her face in his hands, Kavi kissed her. He kissed her deeply, thrilled when she returned each nip and suckle with her own lips. Aware of the passing of time, aware that they could not stand there and kiss each other forever—however much he longed for it—he reluctantly broke their kiss. Resting his forehead against hers, ignoring the slight scratch of her hair ornaments, Kavi spoke from his heart.

"Marry me. Marry me and make me happy, and teach me to be wise, and help me to be a good father and a good ruler, and continue to share with me all your excellent advice. Rule with me, so that all of our people may prosper, both West and East. Please?"

She grinned. "I was about to ask you something similar. I am honored to accept, Kavi. My Kavi . . ." Her fingers shifted a little, finding the hard beads of flesh beneath his ornately embroidered tunic. Deepening her smile, she rubbed them a little. "Do you think . . . ?"

Kavi groaned. "With your hands finally on the rest of me, *how* can I think?"

"I believe you can think about *this*," she murmured, exploring further with increasingly bold fingertips which wandered southward down his chest. "Do you think . . . we have enough time . . . for a quick . . . ?"

Groaning, Kavi kissed her again, plundering her for everything implicit in that invitation. Their courtiers would have to wait, the palace servants would have to wait, and the inestimable, kindhearted, *brilliant* Wali Daad, the wisest man in the world, would have to wait.

Heaven itself would just have to wait, though Heaven itself would surely agree why.

"You have a truly beautiful home, Wali Daad," Queen Ananya said, praising her quiet, almost bashful host. She looked down the terraced slope of the gardens toward the river in the distance, lit more by colorful lanterns, made of dyed paper in the Eastern tradition, than by the last, glorious hues of the fading sunset. Nestled as she was in the curve of her new husband's arms, she let loose a sigh that sounded somewhere between happy and wistful. "I wish we could stay here forever."

"As do I," King Kavi agreed.

Wali Daad looked at his transformed home. He looked at the gardens, at the walls, at the windows and the stables and the milling guests of two nations joined happily into one mighty land. All he wanted to see was his grassy fields and his little cottage, barely more than a hut with a wooden floor. But everyone was happy here, as they would not have been happy in his simple grass cutter's home. He could not spoil their happiness at the expense of his own.

A glance to his side showed the attentive deva still hovering near his elbow, as she had lingered for most of the day. The name she had given for herself was Desna, which he thought was very appropriate, for it meant *offering*. He had been offered this palace for as long as he wished it. *For as long as my heart is true . . . and my heart is saying I must do this.*

Can you hear my thoughts, Desna? he wondered. *The ones in my heart?*

She smiled and nodded, giving him a single, graceful bow of her head. A bow of permission.

Pleased and relieved, Wali Daad turned to Their Majesties. "Then if you admire it so much . . . it is yours. I give you this palace and all of its delights to be your new home—it is well placed between the two arms of your new land, and the well has never gone dry, even in the deepest of droughts. But, as in *all* things in life, you must give generously of its water to all who come to visit, however long or brief, so that its generosity will never have cause to dry out."

"No, we couldn't accept your home," His Majesty demurred.

"I insist. Heaven itself insists—and who are we to argue with Heaven?" Wali Daad added, lifting his hands in surrender, though he smiled as he did so.

Her Majesty touched him with one of her gentle hands, her wrists still adorned with the bracelets he had ordered made. "Then you *must* stay with us and honor us with your presence."

Wali Daad glanced between her and the deva and smiled sadly, shaking his head. "I may come back for a visit, but my work here is done. This is your home now, and your life. Mine lies elsewhere."

Bowing as gracefully as he could, Wali Daad escorted Desna away.

"That was a generous, true-hearted thing which you have done, Wali Daad," the deva murmured in his ear.

Wali Daad nodded to his friend Hassim, who had taken his sudden change in households with a blink and a smile, and a prayer of thanks for Heaven having saved both of them.

"It was the *right* thing to do. But now . . . Now I must find a new home, and a new field or two, and new customers for whose horses I can cut grass. Would you know of any crossroads in need of an aging but very good grass cutter?" he asked her.

Desna leaned back a little, her pose coquettish. "Why yes, actually. The gods just happen to need a good grass cutter at the borderlands between the mortal realms and Heaven. They send Their devas back and forth several times a day, and though we are devas, our horses still need to drink sweet water and dine on the finest hay. If you accept, we will have a cottage with a wooden floor and a big field of grass waiting for you within the hour. It is a simple life, with simple rewards and simple pleasures, but I think it would suit you. *If* that is what you want, Wali Daad."

"It would," he agreed, relieved. "And it is. Thank you."

"No, Wali Daad," the deva corrected softly, kissing him on his age-weathered cheek. "Thank *you*."

The Princess
on the Glass Hill

Author's Note: This was one of my favorite stories as a young girl. Though I can't really put my finger on why it was a favorite, I have decided to put my own twist on the story. Since my three favorite genres are fantasy, romance, and science fiction (in no particular order, though I do enjoy combining romance with the other two), this time I'm going to rewrite the tale with a sci-fi twist. My deepest thanks go to my friend Iulia for sharing her great knowledge of chemistry with me; she was the professional, thus any mistakes or oddities are entirely my own.

Victor Amariei, captain of the *Închiriat*, knew his cousin had a dare for him when Ston swaggered onto the bridge. Sighing, the muscular captain sat back in his chair, temporarily abandoning his search for the next round of cargos to deliver. Most of the time he was good at lining up business, ferrying supplies and goods from space station to spaceport throughout the solar system and usually doing so in a profitable chain of connected locations. But in the last five runs, his luck had run out.

He didn't want to dip into their savings fund, since that money was earmarked for ship upgrades. So it was either take on disparate runs, which would send his ship bouncing around the system with no intermediary stops, wasting time and money, or sit in port until a good string came along. If necessary, he'd take a single, high-paying run that would get him into a better position to set up a new chain of runs. But that meant sitting here and staring at the trade channels, looking for work. He didn't have time for more pleasurable things.

Unlike Ston, who had vanished for five hours onto the local space station, *Liberty VII*, no doubt to drink and carouse. The last thing Victor wanted to do was go onto the space station in search of relaxation. Mining outposts like this one had a peculiar sense of what was acceptable behavior and what was not. What a "local boy" could get away with was not the same thing as what an outsider such as the two of them could . . . though it looked like Ston had come back unharmed.

His cousin's unabashed, smug grin did not bode well. Nor did the way he lounged insolently against the navigation console.

"You look like the cat that swallowed a whole rabbit," Victor muttered, folding his arms across his chest. The movement made the metallic fabric of his shirt gleam in several shades of red.

"Maybe I did," Ston agreed.

"Spit it out, cousin," he ordered. "What trouble are you trying to get me into this time?"

"It's a contract, not trouble. And it's worth half a *million* credits . . . *if* you take on the additional, mmm . . . side-quest, shall we say?" Ston offered, rubbing at the short, neat beard darkening his chin.

Even though they were sixty/forty partners and had been working together for years, Victor didn't trust his cousin implicitly. "What is the regular contract worth, without the side-quest?"

"Eighty thousand," Ston admitted, shrugging carelessly. The amount wasn't bad, but the jump to half a million made the younger man's words suspect.

Like his cousin and captain, he wore a metallic shirt—currently the fashion of choice back home on their family's portion of Earth—though Ston's shirt was a dark metallic blue, making him look more enigmatic. Deliberately, no doubt. Victor narrowed his eyes, and Ston pressed his hand to his heart.

"There you go again, making with the fox-eyes. You're about to ask me what's illegal about the rest of it, aren't you? Well, there is *nothing* illegal about it. My word of honor as your cousin."

Victor sighed. "You may be a pain in the asteroid, but you are an honest pain in the asteroid. What is the cargo, what is the side-quest, and why is the side-quest worth so much more than the main contract?"

"The cargo is a rare isotope of bismuth 209. Normally they mine it on Earth and Mars and the inner asteroid ring, but not in very large quantities. The miners here at *Liberty VII* have found a substantial deposit of it, and they've been working to refine it into a pure metal.

"The side-quest involves a certain special lady whom the isotope needs to be delivered to. *Hand*-delivered, to be specific," his cousin clarified. "Her name is Dr. Evanna Motska, chief researcher at LUCI, the Lunar Ceramics Institute. If you accept the contract for the cargo, you will have handcuffed to your wrist a case about the size of your head that can only be unlocked by a combination of a personal code, which you yourself will enter, and by Dr. Motska's personal security thumbprint as well—I have been reassured the isotope is not dangerous, just very, very rare and very, very expensive, leading to these security precautions."

"And the side-quest?" Victor asked, still skeptical. Part of his mind was already leaping through the trade channel information he had been perusing, trying to line up at least one other cargo toward either Earth or its sole natural satellite, or to one of the stations orbiting Saturn, which was sort of on the way to Earth. "What about it and this lady make it worth nearly half a million?"

Ston grinned. "You have to kiss her, for a start."

"A *kiss* is worth nearly half a million? Who pays that kind of money for a simple kiss?" Victor demanded, scowling at the insulting thought. "You just *do* it!"

"According to the friends I made, the friends who are offering this contract . . . fifteen miners here at the station, twelve previous couriers of various other supplies and goods, forty-three chemistry lab workers, seventeen ceramics engineers, thirty-seven . . . no, thirty-six former lab assistants, and twenty-seven relatives and friends of the good doctor," Ston recited, lifting his gaze toward the low ceiling of the bridge as he recalled the count. He smirked. "It seems they have all pooled their betting money together as a reward for the man—or even the woman—who can make the Ice Princess melt."

That made more sense, though it still disgusted him a little. Victor folded his arms across his chest. "I only kiss willing women. Or anything else, for that matter. What if she doesn't *want* to be kissed?"

"That's the problem. According to her coworkers and her family members, she's *never* been kissed," Ston related, shifting to drop into the navigator's seat. Swiveling the chair, he stretched out his legs, crossing his ankles. "It's not Dr. Motska, you see. It's the Lunar Ceramics Institute, and the group she belongs to, the Lunar Intelligence Trust. They had the largest hand in raising her since she was about seven or eight, from what I was told . . . and they have been so determined to keep their greatest 'brains' isolated in their 'brain trust' that they have very carefully raised their little geniuses to have zero interest in 'biological activities.'"

"Zero interest?" Victor asked, curious in spite of himself. "How is that even possible? She *is* a Human, isn't she?"

"Basically, the Ice Princess has never been kissed because she has never been *given* the opportunity to be kissed. Everyone who goes to work with her must sign a non-intimacy clause, swearing they will keep their interactions with the members of the Lunar Intelligence Trust to 'an efficient, impersonal level of workmanship, with a neutral level of interpersonality' or some such space-rot." Ston scratched his beard again. "So far, Security has stopped all attempts to defy this clause by the workers employed at LUCI, even among non-Trust members. Which is why her friends and relatives, coworkers, and even the miners here, have pooled their resources to reward the lucky, handsome prince who will melt the ice from their brainy princess.

"When my drinking buddies mentioned how they needed a prince to rescue their fair maiden, naturally I thought of *you*." Giving Victor an expressive shrug, Ston tucked his hands behind his head and studied his cousin, coworker, and captain with a lighthearted look. "So . . . are you going to take the bet?"

Victor eyed his cousin, sorely tempted. Bets involving women were one of his few weaknesses, though in the last year he had gotten a lot better at resisting the temptations presented by the wilder ones. *Still . . . a very intelligent woman, so intelligent she's been sheltered from passion all her life . . . no doubt from some silly belief that sex detracts from one's intelligence . . .* He knew that wasn't true. It *was* a distraction, undeniably yes, but in his experience, the more a person embraced all the various aspects of life, the more likely that person was to think of innovative new ways of tackling life and all of its inherent problems.

But to be paid to kiss a woman . . .

The money was very, very tempting. With half a million added to his savings, he could upgrade the in-system thrusters for their ship to those new, fast FTL engines, increasing their speed by a thousandfold. *No more having to worry about conservation of mass if we go to FTL. We can start lining up cargos for outside the home system—even if we stayed in-system, people would pay all the more for fast delivery of their goods, and Ston and I do have a good, strong customer base right here in the heart of Terran space . . .*

But to kiss a woman just for profit and some ship upgrades?

His conscience dwelled a little longer on that part, chewing on it, until the weakest corner of his mind piped up. *If she's never been kissed before, then isn't this Lunar Intelligence Trust* robbing *her of one of her most basic rights as a Human being? To kiss and be kissed, to hold and be held, to love and be loved? You* would *be rescuing the princess from her imprisonment-by-ignorance if you tried . . . thereby making the attempt the* right *thing to do.*

It was a very compelling argument.

His cousin flashed a grin. "You're taking the bet. The last time I saw *that* fire in your fox-colored eyes was when you agreed to spank the lithe and lovely Melissa Mtaube in public. Have the monks forgiven you for disrupting their prayer services yet?"

Victor gave Ston a dirty look. "I *haven't* decided yet. And I've promised never to return to that part of New Mumbai, so it doesn't matter if the monks forgive me. Now, what would constitute solid, bet-winning proof of this kiss?"

Ston rubbed his beard once more, making Victor wonder why his cousin didn't just shave it off if it kept itching so much. The younger man shrugged. "According to what I heard . . . there are security cameras everywhere. Some of the lab workers have connections in Security and would be able to watch everything you did while you are at the institute. But . . . they also say that seeing her learn the importance of a kiss isn't enough, though it might be the right way to thaw her initial resistance, if done properly. Which I know you can do."

"They say that, do they?" Victor repeated, his skeptical side vindicated that there was indeed a catch.

"Someone else—one of the former chemistry lab workers—tried to kiss another member of the LIT group," Ston told him. "Apparently she was fired for the 'audacity' of it. Which is why she's willing to pool most of her savings on this project and why they've come up with the idea of getting the miners in on it, so they can give the job to the isotope courier. The courier is *not* bound by the rules imposed on everyone else by LIT and LUCI, you see . . . so *you* cannot be fired."

"No, I cannot be. But for trying I could be blackballed, at least from picking up similar contracts, though since I haven't heard of this Lunar Ceramics Institute before now, I doubt they have the power to shut down our shipping business entirely. And I'm still waiting for the rest of the catch." Victor clasped his hands across his stomach, studying his cousin and shipmate. "What is so important about teaching this doctor the value of sex that all these people are willing to pay half a million for someone to pull it off?"

"Well, there is one other thing, cousin," Ston added, uncrossing his ankles and lowering his hands so that he could sit forward, elbows braced on his knees. "Dr. Motska is *the* top researcher at LUCI, and *the* biggest brain in the Lunar Intelligence Trust. Whatever Dr. Motska wants, Dr. Motska gets. She is a modern-day princess as far as the management at LUCI is concerned. If she puts her foot down on a project she is associated with, all work on it stops until her conditions are met.

"If *she* can be convinced that passion and personal interaction are worthwhile . . . then that means the *other* people caught up in LIT's control of LUCI can finally date each other. They can have personal lives in the same place where they work and live. As things stand, only those who are allowed to go out to one of the civilian domes, or down to Earth, or to one of the other colony worlds or space stations out there can have a personal life, and only while they're away from the Lunar Ceramics Institute. So you would not only be doing the Ice Princess a favor by melting her with a kiss, you would be freeing many others trapped in their own glass prisons by the Trust's anti-interpersonal policies. Stupid policies, if you ask me . . . but that's the object of the bet. Kiss the good doctor, get her to demand the anti-interpersonal policies be revoked from all contracts, and win half a million dollars as a grateful thank-you from everyone involved."

"They *are* stupid policies," Victor agreed, thinking about it. "You say her family is in on this bet?"

"Yes." Ston held himself still, no doubt giving his cousin room to think.

"Then I want information," Victor stated, making up his mind. "I want to know what her life was like before she was sent to this brain trust she's with. Plus information on what her life is like now. Anything she may have let slip to her friends and family of a personal nature. Dreams, wishes, hobbies, longings, everything she may have mentioned that they can recall, particularly anything to connect the woman she is now with the girl she used to be. Be sure you tell them in advance I will make no guarantee of success . . . but that I will try. In my own way, at my own pace, and only after I have sufficient insight into her past and her mind.

"While you're at it, Ston, ask if they have any other, less encumbered cargo they want us to deliver to the vicinity of Saturn, Earth, or the Moon. Eighty thousand will pay for the return trip to the inner system, plus some of our operating expenses," Victor admitted, "but the rest of that half million isn't guaranteed. I'd rather rebuild ourselves a good cargo chain that will be guaranteed."

"I'll look into it, but like you said, there's no guarantee of success," Ston warned lightly. Standing, he stretched, spreading his arms to either side to avoid smacking his hands against the overhead controls. "Well, I should get to bed."

"It's supposed to be *your* duty shift, remember?" Victor pointed out.

Ston shrugged and scratched his beard. "I took an anti-intoxicant before heading for the bar. I'm not stupid, and I knew I'd want a clear head if I drank while on the station. But it's going to come crashing down on my system for about two hours in just a little bit. Considering how much I drank, I'll want a nap when it does—I'll owe you one, right?"

"You certainly will. You can have the eighty thousand and I'll take the rest of that half million, if I can rescue this Lunar princess from durance vile," Victor muttered. "You'd better hope this doesn't backfire as badly as that bet over those twins from the Ganymede settlement— and you still owe me for three pulled muscles and the red tape over the spacelane violation, you know."

Ston made a face, but left the bridge anyway. His cousin returned his attention to the commodities channel displaying various goods, prices, and destinations on two of his viewscreens. A moment later, he shifted and called up a browsing service on a tertiary screen.

Whoever this Dr. Evanna Motska is, she's bound to have her image posted somewhere. And maybe some trade papers published. I need to get into her head. If this LIT group has brainwashed her into thinking life is meant to be all work and no play, I'll need some sort of leverage to get her to open herself up to new possibilities.

*B*UT *what if the annealings were done at 14 mils instead of 17, to lighten the mass of the hull? Would that affect the shearing forces adversely?*

"Dr. Motska?"

Her left hand rotated the microscopic view of the ceramic alloy projected by her headset glasses. Flicking her right finger, she applied several direct blows to the simulation, observing the results. *It would still harden the plating from a direct hit, yes . . . but I think it might chip the panels with a glancing blow. That would be unacceptable for combat applications in spite of the increased in-system maneuverability due to the overall lower ship mass . . .*

"Dr. Motska?"

What I need is a way to stop those shears from stripping off chunks of the plating, without adding significantly to the mass of the—

"Dr. Motska!"

Irritated, Evanna clenched her fists to end the connection between her hands and the program, and stripped off her glasses. She glared at her assistant. "*What?* I *told* you I needed time alone to concentrate on this project!"

Amanda Heatherfield gave her a patient look. "You *also* told me to tell you the moment the new diamagnetic isotope for bismuth came in, and that the delivery was very important to *this* work."

"Oh. Right." Evanna felt her cheeks growing warm. "Sorry."

Her assistant sighed and rolled her eyes. "It's all right. You have a lot on your mind. You're in charge of a lot of projects, most of which are of importance to the Terran military. You don't have time for social niceties. The work is what is important."

Normally, Evanna would have taken comfort in those frequently repeated words. She *was* important to the ceramics industry, and she *did* create superior armor plating for the ships of the Terran United Planets Space Force. Lives literally depended on her work, and she took pride in her careful considerations. But the way Amanda rolled her eyes and the stiff, rote tone in her voice spoke more of impatience with such things.

Like maybe she doesn't think this project is important? That's not like her, but what else could it be? Evanna narrowed her eyes. "Are you belittling the work we're doing? We *are* in the business of saving lives, you know."

Amanda met her gaze straight on, her impatience replaced with sobriety. "My brother is serving on board a TUPSF-Navy starship, remember? I *know* we're in the business of saving others' lives. But I think you should take a look at your own life, too."

That made no sense. Evanna frowned again. "What do you mean by that?"

The other woman flicked her gaze briefly up at the corner of the room, to the black bubble on the ceiling that housed the security camera. "Nothing. Nothing at all. The courier needs your thumbprint scan to unlock the canister of bismuth, Doctor. He's waiting in the upper conference room."

"Not the lower one?" Evanna asked. The upper conference room, with its bay windows overlooking the craters of Clavius sitting below the installation and the upside-down visage of the Earth hanging in the sky overhead, was usually reserved for visiting dignitaries. Even if the new isotope held the potential for promise, delivery personnel were usually shown to an interior conference room, one which was closer to the docking hangar. She herself didn't visit it as often as she would have liked, but then she was often preoccupied with her work.

"He insisted on waiting in a room with a view." Stepping back, Amanda gave her space to exit the holographic lab.

As she walked along the clean white and pale gray corridors of the institute, Evanna focused her thoughts on the isotope sample she had ordered. *If Dr. Farberjiin's calculations are correct on the heightened diamagnetic properties of the isotope when combined in his experimental compound, it could be possible to mitigate the impact of incoming projectile attacks. The only problem will be synthesizing sufficiently large enough quantities for practical applications in military hull plating, never mind the civilian sector.*

Of course, bismuth isn't the only diamagnetic element, she acknowledged, silently cataloguing substitute materials as she and Amanda rode the nearest lift to the upper levels of the complex. *Dmitrium has four times the opposing polarity qualities, albeit with a half-life of a fraction of a second, which makes using the 115th element highly impractical. And bismuth has a certain thermic sensitivity, making it difficult to incorporate into the ceristeel matrix during the manufacturing process. Which means I'd need to come up with a mineral additive to bind and stabilize it with so it would not be affected by temperature or time.*

Maybe if I bound the isotopic compound within nanocages and injected it into the foam as it cools during the annealing process? That could *work if I picked the right matrice for the cage, though I may have to figure out how to activate the compound without requiring that it be a catalyst,* Evanna thought, picturing it in her head half as clearly as the holographics programs in her workroom could project it. The lab required several terahertz of computational matrices to calculate molecular changes on both the micro- and macro-scales, but it required the spark of an idea to combine the right materials in the right patterns. *But I still don't have a solution for the shearing potential. And I'd have to have some means of regulating the placement of the isotope in its copper cages . . . Wait . . . copper?*

Copper was the color of the courier's clothes. She was supposed to be thinking about *carbon*, not copper, but the moment she entered the conference room, it was hard to think about anything else. Not when he wore tight-fitted leather pants that looked like they had been dipped in liquified copper and a sleeveless tank shirt which looked like the remaining metallic paint had been poured down his shoulders and chest. His muscular, lean chest.

Evanna couldn't remember when she had last seen a body that well defined. Everyone at the Lunar Ceramics Institute kept themselves in good shape, of course; despite the acquisition of artificial gravity technology fifty years before, allowing comfortable, normal-gravitied life, it was still imperative that anyone living in space exercise to ensure optimum health and motility. But no one exercised so hard that even their minor muscle groups could be discerned and identified at a glance. Usually, they had too much work to do to waste their time on such frivolous pursuits.

Even his skin was somewhat tan, either naturally or enhanced by solar treatments. The courier made a colorful, eye-catching statement, surrounded as he was by the shades of gray carpeting, black table, matching chairs, and white-enameled walls framing the equally monochromatic view behind him. That view should have been arresting, given its stark, black, star-studded sky, the sliver of the Earth currently illuminated by the sun gleaming off to the left, and the white-gray-black landscape of the airless Moon. But no, the man captured her gaze first and foremost.

Normally, she liked looking out this window. The landscape was crisp and clean. It reminded her of her work, straightforward and methodical. Neat and tidy. She had asked once, a handful of years ago, if the marks left by the institute's construction crews could be covered up. Someone had cobbled together a grit-scattering machine, powdering over and filling in the boot prints and tire treads that had spoiled the view. But now, all she could see was a man with dark brown hair, light brown eyes, and copper-painted clothes. He didn't look like a member of any courier company she was familiar with, not in that outfit.

"Captain Amariei, this is Dr. Evanna Motska, who ordered the bismuth isotope. Dr. Motska, this is Captain Victor Amariei of the *Închiriat*, who is here on behalf of the Liberty Mining Corporation," Amanda said to introduce them. Then—uncharacteristically—Evanna's chief assistant retreated. The pneumatic door hissed quietly shut behind her, leaving the two of them alone.

Evanna wasn't used to being left alone with outsiders. She was always surrounded by people whenever strangers were present, whether it was assistants, lab workers, support services, or security personnel. *I suppose Amanda has something to do*, she allowed, lifting her chin a little as she moved forward. *And Security will send someone here shortly, I'm sure. Besides, this is just a delivery. As soon as he hands over the isotope, I can have someone from Accounting pay him for his trouble.*

She almost hadn't spotted the package; it was white and gray, and tucked into the curve of his left arm, blending into the rest of the room and its view of the Moon. An odd, sudden thought wafted across her thoughts. *I think I'm getting tired of everything being soothing, pastel shades of white and gray. I think I want more color in my life . . .*

But isn't color a distraction? Distractions were discouraged, because distractions weren't productive. Evanna had been given the opportunity to explore her intellect; she knew she had an obligation to pay back all that the Lunar Intelligence Trust had done for her. *So. No more wit-wandering.*

Pulling her wayward thoughts back into order, Evanna lifted her chin a little more. "Thank you for delivering the isotope, Captain. If you'll hold out the container, I'll release you from the security cuff, and you can be on your way."

His light brown eyes warmed with what looked like humor. They were very alive, flicking down over her plain white lab coat and the gray slacks visible beneath its mid-thigh hem. The rest of him looked like a molten copper statue, sculpted and still, but those eyes moved. So did his lips. "No."

That checked her mid-stride. Fumbling to a stop, Evanna stared at him. Not only had her assistant deviated from procedure, leaving her alone with this courier who didn't look like a courier should, he had . . . he had said *no* to her. No one said *no* to her. Not when she was in charge! "What do you mean, no? I ordered the isotope, I am paying for the isotope, and I shall receive the isotope. Hold out the security cuff so I may receive the goods I am purchasing."

He shifted the arm cupping the oblong container, hitching it a little higher against his waist. Not protectively, just pointedly. "No."

She stared back in confusion. "Why not? You can't go around forever with my purchase shackled to your wrist. It's mine!"

"No, I can't. And no, I won't. You *will* receive your goods," he stated, his eyes flicking up over her hair, which she had pulled into its usual knot on the top of her head. A knot which she realized was coming loose, thanks to the unruly nature of the fine blonde strands. The corner of Captain Amariei's mouth curved up. "In due time."

Like her hair, this situation felt like it was coming loose when it should be neat and tidy. Evanna frowned at him. "Nonsense. You have no control over whether or not I receive my goods. I hold the personal access code, and the thumbprint to unlock it from your wrist."

"Your delicate hand holds the lovely thumb meant for the scanner to read, yes . . . but the miners gave *me* the correct access code," he corrected, smiling.

"Nonsense," Evanna repeated. "Why would they do that?"

"Can I show you something?" the copper-clad man asked, gesturing with his free hand at the bank of triple-paned plexi windows.

Bemused by the non sequitur, Evanna moved across the conference room. He made room for her to pass by the end of the table, stepping up behind her as she faced the windows. This close, she could feel the chill of space seeping through the layers of tough, transparent material, despite the narrow vents blowing warm air up from the edge of the carpeting and the stark glow of the sunlight slanting in from the left. It reminded her of how fragile and precarious her existence was, how dependent she was upon the stout, sheltering, atmosphere-sealed walls of the compound for her survival.

The strange copper-clad man stepped up close behind her, forcing her to edge closer to the windows, until it was either risk chilling herself on the white-enameled grid framing the view or let him touch her. As it was, she could feel the heat of his body warming hers. Warmer than the sun, and more enveloping than the air of the vents toying with the loosened wisps of her hair.

"What . . . what exactly are you trying to show me?" Evanna asked, firming her voice so that she could retake control of the situation. "That you come from a culture that has no appreciation for the boundaries of personal space?"

She felt him lean in closer, felt his body brushing against the back of her lab coat. Felt the soft heat of his cheek barely brushing against hers. "I'm trying to show you a heavenly body."

His right arm slid around her waist, fingers splaying lightly over her belly. Evanna sucked in a sharp breath, startled by the uninvited, unexpected touch. No one touched her there. The hand, the shoulder, those places yes, but not her stomach. She backed up instinctively, but that bumped her spine against his chest, and her backside against his thighs. He wasn't that much taller than her, and a corner of her mind catalogued the way their torsos fit together. An odd comparison flitted across her mind. *Like two complementary electron orbits bonding chemically together . . .*

Don't be silly! This is a distraction, she reminded herself sharply. *Distractions detract from all the good I can do— Ooh . . .*

Somehow, without dropping the oval container from the crook of his elbow, Captain Amariei had managed to cup the fingers of his hand around her left hip bone, pulling them closer together. Those fingertips had managed to find nerve endings Evanna hadn't known about. She certainly didn't expect the sympathetic tingling that zinged out to her navel and dropped straight to the bottom of her pelvic girdle, making her clamp her thighs together. The action didn't contain the feeling, but rather enhanced it somehow.

The feel of his right hand lifting, gliding up, and brushing against her white-draped breasts distracted her further. His arm didn't linger— she might have had cause to protest if it had—but instead moved to gesture at the shades of gray before them.

"Every single day of your life is surrounded by the dullest rocks of the Moon," he murmured. "Barren. Dead. Lifeless. Black and white. You have been told over and over by your colleagues that your mind needs to be equally black and white, focused solely upon your work. In fact, you have been told this so much and so often since being handed over to the Lunar Intelligence Trust that you have come to believe them. You have been told over and over that there are only black, white, and shades of gray, to the point where you now refuse to believe in colors like red and green, gold and blue . . . things they don't want for you. Every single day, you are told how important your work is, and how you don't dare let anything distract you. Isn't this true?"

Evanna craned her neck, pulling away just far enough so she could frown at him. "How did you . . . ?"

"How did I know? Ask me instead, how do I know what your favorite story was as a child, back when you were still allowed to live a life full of color and potential?" he murmured. His light brown eyes glowed with an almost copper warmth. "Do you remember *why* you liked that story? Do you even remember *what* story you liked best? Or has everything you ever liked in your young life been shoved and exiled so far away, it's now farther away than the Earth itself in that empty, barren sky?"

His questions were confusing her. Evanna blinked and tried to gather her scattered thoughts. She wanted to demand the release of the isotope, knew she should demand it, but his questions about her childhood disrupted her thoughts. So did the return of his right arm, which he wrapped around her ribs just below her breasts. Old memories surfaced, making her blink and look out at the barren stretch of powdered grit and sun-bleached stone.

My favorite childhood tale . . . I haven't thought of childhood tales in . . . in twenty years. I haven't had time *to think of such foolish things,* she told herself, shaking her head. Or rather, she tried to shake her head. Captain Victor Amariei pressed his cheek against hers, stilling her denial even as he soothed her distress with his next words.

"Your mother told me which one was your favorite. *Snow White and the Seven Dwarves*. She read it to you every night when you were little. You used to have fifteen different books of it, too—*real* books, with illustrations painted on their pages in the fullest of colors."

Out of the corner of her eye, she could see his mouth quirk in a smile.

"She said your favorite part was when Snow White was lost in the forest. You always stated that Snow White should have been happy to be among all those trees, not frightened . . . remember? Do you remember why you thought she should be happy?"

Overwhelmed by his odd embrace—by the first embrace she could remember since she was a child—Evanna licked her lips. "I . . . wanted to *be* Snow White. I wanted to . . . to walk among a whole forest of trees. To go to the Motherworld and see and hear and . . . smell everything."

All she could see was barren lunar rocks, and all she could smell was . . . No, not all she could smell was the same slightly dusty, recycled scent of the ventilated air. Evanna realized she could also smell something warm, something slightly soapy and a little musky. The scent of the copper-clad man holding her. Unless it was a chemical that she needed to pay attention to in the labs, or the food on her plate, Evanna couldn't remember the last time she had paid attention to smells. Certainly not how a particular man smelled.

"I see that even then, you were a very smart little girl," the courier who wasn't a courier murmured. "Books and videos and holograms aren't the same as the real thing . . . and books and videos and holograms are all too easily shoved aside and locked away by the people who try to control you."

"They're not controlling me," she countered, feeling the need to assert that fact. "I am here of my own free will."

"I read your employment contract."

That wasn't expected, either. Puzzled by the change in topic, Evanna twisted to look at Captain Amariei. The movement caused the canister to drop, since it dragged his fingertips along with the twisting of her hip. As the canister dangled on its security chain, she ignored the bouncing of the lump against her thigh, in favor of demanding, "You read my contract? Why? And how?"

"By Terran law, you are legally entitled to a minimum of three weeks of paid vacation every single year . . . and yet according to the work logs of this lovely little prison . . . you haven't once left the Lunar Ceramics Institute." His eyes, alive as they were, pinned her in place. "Not in the ten years you have worked here. You earn more in a single year than I can earn hauling cargo around the solar system in five, even with the best of cargos . . . but not once have you bought a shuttle ticket, or booked a hotel room, or traveled to see in person the forests you longed to visit as a child. And I'll bet you every single atom in this can of bismuth that your colleagues and superiors in the

Lunar Intelligence Trust were the ones who convinced you that you didn't need to go anywhere."

Evanna flushed at his words. "It's not that I don't need or want to go elsewhere. It's that I'm needed *here*. And I'll have that can of bismuth from you, or I'll—"

"You'll what, have me thrown off the Moon? With your precious can still attached?" he said mockingly. "You know as well as I do that *you* specified the isotope should be delivered in a catalytically encrypted container. If it is removed from my wrist by force, or by anything but the right code as well as your thumbprint—a code which you do not have—then according to what I was told, the liquid bismuth in this can gets mixed with the compressed oxygen in the outer shell, turning this stuff into a very expensive version of a fire-starter. Until you can separate out the pure metal again, it won't be good for anything involving the extremely high temperatures of the ceristeel ceramics manufacturing process your LUCI requires it to endure."

Evanna stared at him. "You're just a courier! How do you know all this chemistry?"

"You don't have to be the pawn of a brain trust to have the brains to spare, *Doctor*," he drawled. "I just did a little research in my free time before I came here. My point is, *you* designed the security system to avoid risking the sample being contaminated by industrial espionage, but the miners gave *me* the correct access code. That means I can make whatever demands I like, and either you fulfill them, or you wait another eight months before they can mine and refine enough of the ore under their current production methods to send your way again."

"You're trying to *blackmail* me?" she demanded. She craned her neck again, this time peering at the black bubbles in the ceiling. *Why isn't Security here yet? Why haven't they leaped in here to rescue me from this . . . this . . .*

"Actually, I prefer to think of it as 'rescuing' you." Cupping her cheek with his free hand, he brushed his thumb over her lips, stilling her next protest. "I want three things from you, in exchange for the correct release code. Three simple things."

"What do you want?" Evanna asked warily, wondering why his thumb should be causing the same electrified feelings his fingers had on her hip bone.

Warm brown eyes gleaming, he murmured, "The first is a kiss, here and now."

Disgusted that he was interested in something she had been told over and over was nothing more than simple, crass, useless biology, Evanna wrinkled her nose. She *did* want that isotope, and she didn't want to have to wait eight months to get it. But she also didn't want to commit herself until she knew the full extent of this blackmailer's demands. "And the second thing?"

"Oh, no. First, the kiss. Nothing less will unseal these lips," he murmured, smiling.

His thumb brushed her lips again, confusing her. *Oh, come on.* Evanna chided herself. *It's not like you haven't kissed anyone in the past. The very* distant *past.* She vaguely remembered kissing her mother at the end of each bedtime story, though it had been a good twenty years. Sighing, she puckered her lips and leaned in, bumping them against his cheek. "There. Your kiss. And you're a blackmailer, not a rescuer, Captain Amariei. If you *are* a captain."

His mouth quirked up at the corner. "I *am* a captain, but that is *not* a kiss. And I will rescue you, as you will see."

"Rescue me from what?" Evanna demanded.

"This place. This is like that other fairy tale, the one about the princess whose father dumped her on the top of a glass hill. Your father said you didn't like that one so much, though your little sister asked for it often enough . . . You've been isolated from everything and everyone for too many years, Evanna," he told her. "Including that forest you used to long for."

A nudge turned her around to face the stark, lifeless moonscape beyond the triple-thick windows.

"Trees don't grow on glass hills. Nothing grows up here, because life needs color instead of black-and-white. Life needs freedom and fresh air. Life needs everything you don't have . . . because you've been told over and over that you need to stay on your precious glass hill. Entirely alone, up here."

One moment she was all but wrapped in the warmth of his unorthodox, uninvited embrace. The next, he stepped back, abandoning her to the cold, impersonal air of the conference room. She couldn't feel the warmth in the air puffing up from the vents, or the heat of the sunlight streaming in from the left, an unrelenting part of the weeks-long lunar day. All Evanna could feel was alone, just as he claimed. Alone and bereft. An electron torn from its rightful path and sent careening without control through the interstitial void between atomic orbits.

That is a silly piece of mental imagery, she scolded herself after a moment, striving to collect her dignity. *You are not a free radical! Free radicals are dangerous! They cause trouble, and . . . and . . .*

The view of the crater, stark and lifeless, mocked her. Barren. Lifeless. A glass hill on which nothing could grow. She remembered that fairy tale, too, as well as her favorite. Evanna hadn't liked it because she had always thought the father of the princess had been unnecessarily cruel, abandoning her on top of that hill with nothing but three apples for company.

She had always liked this view, since it was the largest section of windows in the complex, but the transparency of the tough plexi sheltering her from the vacuum of space was too glasslike now for comfort. Worse, this not-a-courier captain was right, now that she thought of it. Every time she had made a comment about taking a vacation elsewhere over the past ten years—no, the past *twenty* years, Evanna realized—the others in the Intelligence Trust had convinced her out of it, often coming up with a solid, logical, school- or work-related reason why she should stay.

I do love my work, she admitted silently. *I didn't mind staying . . . after a while,* honesty prompted her to add. *And I did use my holo-projection programs to simulate being in a forest . . . but I did long to see a forest for real.*

I still do. *Now more than ever, now that I've been reminded of everything I've been missing . . .*

Turning, she half expected the copper-clad captain to be gone. He was only a couple meters away, lounging against the side of the long, black conference table like a sober statue. His hand cradled the canister of bismuth against his hip, silently reminding her of why he was still there. For one wild, irresponsible moment, she was tempted to toss aside her quest to explore the potentials of adding diamagnetic repulsion properties to military starship hulls. Only for a moment.

I'm not abandoning my work, she asserted silently, staring at him. *I'm not! But . . . I* am *going to take a vacation. A real one. On Earth, no less. And soon. I'll do it very soon.*

He hefted the canister, balancing it on his palm. "Care to try again? Or do you not want this after all?"

"I already kissed you once, Captain Amariei," Evanna pointed out, flustered. "Is that your second demand?"

"That wasn't a real kiss. You'll have to give me a real one to know what my second request is . . . and you should call me Victor. You are about to kiss me, after all," he added. His somber appearance seemed to melt away as he smiled. The copper statue was alive once more, and though he wasn't even within arm's length of her, she felt warm again. Warm all over.

She regathered her wits and moved closer. She even put her hands on her hips in an attempt to assert some authority over the situation. "Well, if that wasn't a real kiss, then what is, by your definition?"

Pushing off the edge of the table, he lifted his free hand to her chin. Tilting her head slightly, he tipped his the other way and brought their faces so close, she had to shut her eyes to keep from crossing them. His lips brushed against hers, lingered, and lifted a fraction away. Then they came back, pressed a little more, and nibbled. Just a little.

It was an intriguing feeling, rather than the disgusting one she had been told it was. Curious, Evanna moved her own lips. He nibbled a little more, encouraging her to respond, and startled her by licking her bottom lip. The moment her mouth parted in exclamation, he swept in and claimed it fully. It would have been unnerving in a bad way, if part of what unnerved her wasn't more of that strange twisting in her nerves. This time, instead of connecting a short, understandable distance, it speared from her mouth all the way down through her groin to her toes. Neither of which were near anything he was actually touching.

Her knees buckled. Victor let go of her chin, though not her mouth, wrapping his free arm around her back. That snugged their bodies together, once more giving her the feeling that the two of them together formed some unknown, exciting, yet somehow stable compound. The kind rife with possibilities. She just had no clue what those possibilities were, other than that he was now sucking on her lower lip and her hands were exploring the warmth of his throat and the texture of his short-cropped hair.

Her nerves were buzzing like an unstable element when he finally ended the kiss. Evanna felt like half of her life was suddenly going into decay, transforming her into something unexpected. She tried to frown at that. *Another silly mental image. I'm supposed to be focusing on my . . . Ooh, his thumb again . . .*

This time, with the moisture of their kiss still on her lips, his thumb tickled her as it glided across her flesh. *"That,"* Victor Amariei murmured, "is what I'd call a kiss."

She blinked, feeling a worrisome urge to lick the pad of his thumb. It was entirely unlike her to think of such things.

Victor smiled. "So . . . are you going to give me one? I've given you a good example of a real kiss, but *I* gave it to *you*. I want one from you to me, of your own free will."

Evanna blinked. Not only was he demanding a kiss from her, he was demanding several of them, in a sneaky way. "I'm not sure this is such a good idea . . ."

"Why not? It's perfectly normal, and perfectly natural, and perfectly *not* what that brain trust wants you to do. And why not?" Victor asked rhetorically, shrugging as he leaned back against the edge of the table. "Because they want to control you. They want to *enslave* you. They want every last iota of your life plugged into this institute, so they can suck it out of you. There's only one problem. You're not a machine. You're a Human. And Humans *are* allowed to have fun. We are *supposed* to interact in personal ways.

"Anyone who tells you otherwise, who *demands* that you give up your humanity 'for the good of humanity' . . . well, I'd say they're not Human, but that runs the risk of comparing them to the other races in the Alliance. Even the aliens don't believe in sucking the joy out of their lives, whatever their versions of joy may be."

That distracted her. "Have you met an alien?" Evanna asked. "The Lunar Ceramics Institute does a lot of research for the Terran military, so visits from foreign races have always been discouraged for security reasons . . ."

"Have *I* met an alien?" the copper-clad captain repeated, touching his chest. "Every time I go to Earth, I run across aliens! They're all over the spaceports! Gatsugi scientists, Solarican ship crews . . . even the occasional K'katta tourist or two. They're also at Ganymede, and the domes on Mars, and plenty of other places.

"There aren't *many* of them, I'll admit, but they do visit this system." Victor shook his head slowly, giving her a pitying look. "All those weeks of vacation you were never allowed to take, you could have been rubbing elbows with the other sentient races. You could have been conversing with their scientists. Being inspired by outside ideas as well as your own, bouncing potential theories off of colleagues who have different life experiences and thus different perspectives on a suggested problem.

"But no. Instead, you're stuck here. A princess on a glass hill, isolated and alone." He hefted the container manacled to his wrist and twisted his mouth. "According to what I read of that fairy tale, that poor princess wasn't even allowed to eat her three apples, was she?"

That made Evanna fold her arms across her chest. "No, she wasn't. She was forced to give up all three of them to whoever could reach her."

"She wasn't forced, when one finally did reach out to her. She gave two of them as a gift," he pointed out.

"And got nothing in return for it," Evanna pointed out.

Victor shook his head. "She gained something far more precious than mere apples. She gained her freedom."

"Well, that's where your analogy breaks down, Captain." Flipping her hand at him, Evanna indicated his clothes. "You come here all dressed in copper, which if I remember right was the color of the first suit of armor, and you're asking me to give you my three apples. But a canister of liquid bismuth *isn't* equivalent to my freedom. And I'm not buying it for three kisses. Two of which you've already had from me."

"I never said it was the equivalent. And I never said I wanted three kisses from you. Just the one. But it has to be of your own free will; given, not taken or demonstrated. Give me that one kiss and I'll tell you what the second apple is," he bartered, tucking the canister under his elbow once more. "And not for a mere can of metal, however rare, but for your freedom from this barren glass hill."

Amanda's words came back to her. *I know we're in the business of saving others' lives. But I think you should take a look at your own life, too . . .*

At your own *life . . .*

Did she mean . . . ? If this man is right, then logic dictates I'm not the only person constricted by LIT's policies of discouraging "personal distractions" in its members and, by correlation, LUCI's employees. Evanna frowned in thought. *Wait, wasn't there that scandal about a year ago of some lab worker over in Dr. Priznell's lab behaving in an unprofessional manner, of her being dismissed and then trying to sue the institute? I wondered about that, because she'd always seemed like such a competent lab assistant . . .*

Looking up at the author of her disquiet, she found him once again waiting with silent, statue-like patience. The only things that moved about him were the slow rise and fall of his chest as he breathed and those tawny brown eyes flicking down over her lab-coat-clad body and back up to her face. Until he licked his lips. The simple act of moistening them, the subtle glide of the tip of his tongue, reminded her of his demonstration kiss.

She wasn't even touching him, yet she could feel that tingling once again inside her skin. It defied logic and the explanations of science . . . and yet it *was* chemistry.

Acting on impulse, Evanna swayed forward. She hesitated as their bodies almost brushed together, then daringly closed the fractional gap between their lips. At first, she just pressed her mouth to his. When he didn't move, she tried an experimental nibble, followed by a tentative lick. He responded by opening his lips just a little and nibbling back. It was encouragement enough to make her try a bolder touch. A deeper taste. An angling of their mouths and a burrowing of her fingers in his crisp, wavy, dark brown hair, until his tongue met hers, helping her to repeat the same excitement as before.

This time, both of his arms wrapped around her, pulling her breathtakingly close. That left the canister dangling awkwardly against her backside, but she didn't care. All she could do was agree. *This* was a kiss. It was delicious, it was invigorating, and it was exciting. Full of any number of unknown variables just waiting to be catalogued and explored.

Researcher at heart that she was, Evanna wanted to explore every possible permutation. Unfortunately, the door hissed open. Alarmed by the noise, she pulled back, blushing furiously at having been caught in a very nonprofessional act. It was only Amanda, but the sober look her chief assistant gave her unnerved Evanna.

"I'm sorry, but you've run out of time. You have about a minute, maybe two at most, if you're lucky."

Frowning, Evanna looked from her assistant to her . . . well, kisser, for lack of a better word. He definitely wasn't a courier, despite the isotope chained to his wrist. Victor grimaced. "Damn. Okay. Here's the second request. Come with me to Earth. Right now. Take a leave of absence, go on vacation, and walk on the Motherworld. Walk in a *real* forest, not in a holographic one. Visit the beach. Gawk at some aliens. But go *now*. No excuses, no waiting, no prevaricating, and *no* letting anyone else convince you that your work here is so vital you cannot leave it for a week."

"He's right, Doctor. Every project you currently have going *can* be put on hold for a while," Amanda agreed. She started to say more, then touched her ear with one hand and held up the finger of the other. Evanna believed her assistant must be listening to the same sort of earbud comm piece that Security used. When Amanda rolled her fingers in a hurry-up motion, Evanna knew her guess was right.

"A simple yes or no," the courier who wasn't a courier urged her. "Make up your mind. I would have worn silver for this next part, but you haven't much time."

Evanna looked between him and Amanda, grasping the conspiracy they had formed. "You have everything all figured out, don't you? Except, how do I know I can trust you?"

He shrugged. "Your family does. Your assistant does." Victor paused, smiled, and hefted the canister chained to his left hand. "And your bismuth does."

The absurdity of that made her laugh. The reaction wasn't at all what she would have expected, but even more jolting was the realization that she *liked* laughing at an absurdity. She sobered as she tried to recall the last time someone had joked about her work in her presence, and had to silently confess it had been at least three years.

Because jokes are inappropriate in a serious workplace, she thought, parroting all that she had been told. *He's right. They* have *stolen my humanity from me.* Lifting her chin, Dr. Evanna Motska gave him her reply. "Yes. I'll need to go back to my quarters first—"

"It's all taken care of," her assistant interjected, enduring Evanna's startled look. She flicked her gaze up toward the dark bubbles of the security cameras in the ceiling, a pointed look much like the one she had given earlier in the holographic lab, and nodded. "If you'll leave the canister with me, I'll see that it gets to the lab while Captain Amariei shows you those astro-survey charts of the regions containing the bismuth isotope, so you'll know the scope of what can be extracted in a potential larger scale production in the future."

"Yes, I'd bring them into the complex, but they're proprietary charts," Victor added smoothly, not showing any sign that the abrupt change in subject had fazed him. "The Liberty Mining Guild has only loaned them to me temporarily. They insist I can't even take the data-pad storing them off of my ship. . . .which I took the liberty to mean my shuttle, which is parked in your hangar," Victor added.

Evanna caught on to her assistant's smooth babble of words, and the captain's equally smooth reply. *She's giving us a cover, an excuse for me to go to his ship.* Nodding, she headed toward the door, only to hear him clearing his throat behind her.

"Your thumbprint, Doctor?" he asked, lifting his oval, white burden.

Returning to him, she flipped open the little door covering the sensor panel and pressed her thumb to the scanner. A second panel slid open, revealing a grid of buttons. He punched in the combination . . . which looked like the code she would have used herself. A sharp glance at his face showed his eyes all but gleaming with a lively sense of humor.

"And the third apple?" she couldn't help but ask under her breath.

"All in good time, Doctor." Tossing the canister at her assistant, who hastily caught it, Victor rubbed at the reddish marks circling his wrist. "That feels really good."

"What, lobbing a can of priceless bismuth 209 at my assistant like it was a sofa cushion?" Evanna demanded.

"Freeing myself of a cumbersome, unnecessary restriction. You should try it sometime," he added, gesturing for her to join him in heading toward the door. "This way to the mineral charts, Doctor."

Aware that they were being watched by Security—though she would have to interrogate her assistant at a later date as to why she *hadn't* been watched before now—Evanna managed a cool, professional nod. "Thank you, Captain. I appreciate the troubles you are taking on my behalf."

"I hope you do," he muttered, escorting her out of the conference room.

VICTOR worried about the security guard who had insisted on accompanying them into the shuttle, unsure how to get rid of the other man. It was true he couldn't be fired for kissing their genius chemist—and what a kisser she was—and he *was* the captain of this shuttle, but they were still on Lunar Ceramics Institute turf. There was only so much he could do without getting into trouble.

He didn't have to worry for long. After the third time the man tried to wedge himself between Victor and Dr. Motska, trying to get a closer look at the datapad she was perusing, the good doctor lost her patience.

"Enough!" she snapped, shoving back on the elbow that had intruded yet again on her shoulder. The sudden, hard act knocked both men back, but she didn't apologize. Instead, she surged to her feet out of the copilot's seat and glared at the gray-uniformed man. "Get out!"

"Excuse me?" the guard asked, blinking as he righted himself.

"I said, get out! There isn't enough room in here for all three of us, and your presence is *not* necessary!"

"But I'm here for your safety!" the man protested.

"Captain Amariei is *not* going to do anything to me which I do not wish him to do—isn't that right, Captain?" Evanna asked.

There was only one safe reply he could make to that. Touching his chest, Victor promised, "You have my word of honor, I will do whatever you wish me to do. All you have to do is tell me."

"Really? Good. Throw him out." She kept her hazel eyes on Victor's face as the security guard spluttered. "I want him *off* this shuttle, and as you are the captain of this craft and I am his superior, *he* has no right to object to my wishes, or to your carrying them out in the course of your duties. Will you comply?"

"Whatever you wish, Doctor." Grabbing the other man by the elbow and the collar, Victor shoved him out of the small confines of the cockpit. The guard struggled, but the captain out-massed him by several kilos of solid muscle. Manhandling him around the corner to the access hatch located between cockpit and cargo hold, Victor shoved the still protesting man through the opening, then blocked it with his own body, folding his arms over his chest.

"You can't do this! I'll have a security detail here immediately, and I'll have you arrested for . . . for . . ."

"For what? Kidnapping? I could hardly be accused of such when Dr. Motska is on board my ship entirely of her own free will," Victor pointed out. "For throwing a disruptive element off my ship? While on board a ship, *all* passengers are subject to the decrees of its captain and/or pilot by Terran law. And I happen to concur with Dr. Motska. Your presence is unnecessary and unwanted."

The thinner man scoffed. "Unwanted?"

"Captain, I cannot concentrate on these mineral charts with all that noise outside! Please seal off the ship against all *unwanted* intrusions."

Victor smirked as the guard spluttered again. "You heard the lady. Your presence is most definitely *unwanted*."

Jabbing the buttons on the control panel, he closed the hatch, then locked it with a scan of his thumb. Returning to the cockpit, he found her seated once more at the copilot's station, nibbling on her lower lip and staring out the viewports rather than perusing the datapad in her hands. "Are you all right?"

She looked down at the pad, then up at him. "I've never done that before—I've had, well, tantrum fits from time to time, but . . . that was work-related. This . . ."

"You're having second thoughts," Victor summarized. "You've always been a good girl, always done what you were told."

"Well, of course! It was logical. This is . . . this is impulsive, and irrational. Maybe I should—"

Blocking her with a hand on her shoulder as she started to rise, Victor pressed her back down into the well-padded chair. "Read what's on the datapad, and tell me if leaving really is as irrational as they wanted you to believe. Go to the data menu and look at the other folders, the ones *not* involving astrogeology. I think you'll find the eighth one down the most interesting."

Thumbing the controls, she scrolled through the menu choices, and frowned. "Depositions of known instances involving breaches of contract?"

"Read," he urged, settling into the pilot's chair on the left.

She did so, frowning and thumbing through the paragraphs. A couple of times she paled at what she read; other times, she flushed red, brow furrowing in a mixture of shame and aggravation. When she came to the end, Evanna set the datapad in the flat depression of the mid-console projecting out partway between their seats.

"Well. I *have* been manipulated, haven't I?" Her tone was flat, somewhere between bleak and angry. "All these people *knew* my employers were deliberately blocking any interest I might develop in leaving the institute . . . and they *never* spoke up."

"I'm sure they thought they had the best of reasons. Such as, your superiors believed most of those reasons involved the bottom line and whatever they could milk out of you, and your inferiors believed if they did speak up, they would lose their jobs and be blacklisted out of the industry. The *real* point, Doctor, is that you have legal leverage in your hands now, with those gathered depositions," Victor stated. She glanced over at him and he nodded at the pad. "They have breached their contract with you, violating the Terran United Planets ordinances governing the limit of how many hours *any* company may work its employees in a single year, whether it is private, public, or government-run.

"Worse, they have isolated you from your friends and family, and from *making* friends and family. They have robbed you of your right to have a private life . . . and with the same contractual obligations they have forced upon you with those clauses about 'maintaining a strictly professional atmosphere at all times,' they have forced these unnatural, restrictive viewpoints upon everyone *else* who works with you." Victor knew he was playing with fire by admitting his own role so bluntly, but something within him prompted him to be honest with her. "Your friends, family, and colleagues all know that *you* are a force to be reckoned with at the institute. They asked *me* to 'wake you up' to your situation and everything you've missed knowing as a result."

"Including being kissed?" she asked, giving him a suspicious look. "Was that really necessary, Captain?"

He met her gaze steadily. "As necessary as breathing. At least, to me. You're still learning the possibilities of what it could mean for you."

His honesty took her aback. "Really?"

"Really. I will admit I've been dared into doing any number of things involving women," he added, that same inner urge prompting him into possible verbal suicide. "But I was only asked to wake you up to all the things you've been denied by your captors. Including the fact that you are a real person and not the creative little robot the Lunar Intelligence Trust has tried to make of you.

"I have done that, as requested. You are aware of your glass hill prison, and you have met me at least halfway, which means you are halfway to your freedom. Whatever I do from this point onward, I do of my own free will. Not because of a bet, or a dare, or a contract, but because I honestly want to do it." Pausing to let her absorb his words, Victor smiled slowly at her. "Would you like to know what I want to do next?"

He watched her nibble on her lower lip a moment, then lift her chin. "Why not? What do you want to do next, Captain?"

"Well, first, I'd like to be able to call you Evanna instead of Doctor, and hear you call me Victor instead of Captain," he told her. "Titles distance you from people. Yes, they induce a certain respect which can be needed, but they also rob you of emotional intimacy. After that, Evanna . . . I'd like to shuttle you over to Earth, to a place called Sol Duc. It's in a rich, lush, evergreen forest on the North American continent, and it has a series of mineral hot springs, a hotel with several private cabins, some restaurants, and all the peace and privacy and *reality* a woman desperately in need of a vacation could want.

"Once we're down there and have rented a cabin for a few days, I would like to change into a *silver* outfit," he teased, referencing the fairy tale, "and take you hiking in the woods, since I've been there a few times before. I want to take you somewhere far away from your glass hill, somewhere colorful and filled with an excess of life. Or if you prefer a mix of civilization with your wilderness, we can go to visit some forested land my family owns near Bucureşti. There aren't quite as many trees, since the land is a bit more developed in that region, but you could see how a normal family lives."

"What about my own family? Why shouldn't I visit them first?" Evanna inquired.

"Because they still live on the Moon, and that's far too close to the influence of your precious Intelligence Trust to risk," Victor reminded her. "You can visit them after you've had a taste of real life, which you will only find far from this lunar glass hill. I'll take you myself, if you like. To Sol Duc, to Bucureşti, and even to your family, but the latter only after you have visited at least one of the others."

"Only after I walk among real trees . . ." she murmured. "You keep referencing the story of the princess on the glass hill, but what about Snow White and her seven friends? Are you going to take me to meet six other men in these woods of yours?"

Hesitating, Victor shrugged and gave her the truth. "I suppose I could scrounge up six more men, between my brothers and cousins and their friends . . . but I'd rather spend my time with you figuring out just how quickly you can master the art of kissing. After all, you can only kiss one person at a time. You're very good at it, for someone who has never been properly kissed before. A natural, even. But . . . there is still plenty of room for improvement."

"Is there really that much more to learn, then?" Evanna asked.

"Quite a lot left to learn." He started to say more, but the comm beeped, warning him the Lunar Ceramics Institute was attempting to contact them. "I believe you are being paged by your overeager, earnest, well-meaning captors, Doctor. Would you care to reply?"

Picking up the datapad, she thumbed a few commands into it, studied what came up, and nodded. "Yes, I would. And I'd like to go see that forest you recommended. The first one, with the hotel and the hot springs. And then I'd like to see the second one, where your family lives. After that, I want to visit my own family. And after *that* . . . we will see. Because my contract does *not* specify I have to use each year's vacation time solely within that year. With twenty years of vacation accrued, I could take off for a whole year and then some, if I wanted to.

"I'm not *sure* if I want to, just yet, but I do want to get away. With your help, Captain," she allowed, giving him a courteous nod. "Erm . . . Victor."

Plucking her nearest hand free from the datapad, Victor lifted it to his lips for a kiss. "I am pleased to be of any service you desire, Evanna."

With his other hand, he flicked on the comm unit, connecting her with the image of one of the institute's administrators.

"A webwork! That's what I need!"

The exclamation made Victor blink. Evanna pointed with her free hand at a spiderweb glistening with dew from the fog misting the forest. He dutifully peered at it, though he didn't know why. "What about it?"

"Right before you arrived, I was working on a problem with lightening the mass of the ceristeel hull platings for the military. The problem is annealing the thermal layers of the ceristeel for strength and durability while still permitting sensor integration," Evanna explained, her attention more on the orb spider and its web than on him.

She was also smiling, which she hadn't stopped doing since arriving at this resort last night, with its damp, mossy rain forest waiting to be explored. Still, she had a lifetime of thinking about work as a habit, and this was an important idea to explore. *And to think, it's because I'm here that I thought of this solution to my problem.*

"If I patterned the foam with a webwork of intercrossed annealings—*vertical* ones as well as horizontal," she stressed, "it would mitigate the shearing stresses of a glancing impact while cutting the overall mass of the thermal tiles. Not by as much as I'd hoped, but it would be enough to . . . I'm boring you, aren't I?"

"Not by that much," Victor teased. "I do fly a spaceship, so the protective factors of its ceristeel plating *are* important to me. Besides, wouldn't long lines of annealment cause the potential for parallel stress fractures? If the manufacturing process can be pattern-worked as you suggest, wouldn't a honeycomb be more efficient? There aren't any long straight lines in a honeycomb pattern, so any potential fracture would find itself blocked after fissuring only a short distance."

"Of course—why didn't I think of that?" she murmured, hazel eyes gazing somewhere beyond the boundaries of the trail they were following. They weren't far from the two-bedroom cabin they had rented, having just begun the morning's walk in the woods. "It's an incredibly simple solution to the problem, so why didn't I see it earlier?"

Victor wrinkled his nose. "Because you've been isolated from life too much?"

Facing him, Evanna smiled. "That I have. Care to de-isolate me again, Capt— Victor?"

Happy to oblige, he shifted closer and met her upturned lips with his own. If kisses were apples, he had shared a basketful with her so far, never mind a mere three.

Evanna sighed happily, returning each touch and taste. As the kiss progressed, her arms ended up looped around his silver-clad shoulders, and his wrapped around her flower-printed waist. Colorful, patterned clothes were among the first things she had bought after arriving on Earth. She had yet to find a supplier of the same metallic shirts he preferred, but that was all right; she had discovered the allure of nature, and liked how her flowery shirts and dresses reminded her of the real world. This world.

Laughter from a couple of kids broke them apart. The kids were at that age where they weren't really children anymore but not quite teenagers, and they pushed at each other, racing to be the first one up the trail. Behind them, their parents followed at a more sedate pace. The indulgent look the adults gave Victor and Evanna made her blush, because it was the kind of look that said the two of them just had to be a couple, given their intimate closeness.

She might not know much about interpersonal relationships yet, but she was learning, and she was learning that she liked the idea of being a couple. Looking up into the light brown eyes of her host, she found them moving over her face with that same penetrating sense of life. "You know what?"

"What?" Victor asked, distracted by the sight of her hair, left down this morning. Last night they had shopped, dined, talked—and kissed— and parted to their separate rooms to sleep. This morning, she was a different woman, much more approachable than the crisp, impersonal, lab-coat-wearing scientist she had been yesterday. Now she was as soft and silky as her hair looked, and he was the one who seemed colorless by comparison, clad in a silver shirt and matching pants today. He didn't feel colorless inside, though; just watching her delight in these new experiences refreshed his own view of their birthworld.

"I have just realized I can research microannealing patterns and the integration of bismuth isotopes into ceristeel compounds any old day. Today, I am on vacation, and I am on vacation with *you*. And *you* promised to teach me more about kissing. You . . ." She broke off as a large drop of water *plopped* onto her forehead. It was accompanied by the pattering of several more starting to fall around them. Glancing up through the trees, she wrinkled her nose. "I see that a real forest has real drawbacks. Holographic ones don't get you *wet*."

"They also don't have bugs. But we can get an umbrella and better coats, and the rain will chase away the bugs," he offered. "You didn't get much of a walk in the woods last night when we arrived."

"I'd rather not overdo it on my first day, and the forest will still be here in a few hours, when the rain has hopefully faded. Why don't we go back to our cabin, and you can show me all the different ways someone can kiss?" Evanna asked, flinching as more drops pattered down through the trees, cold and wet. "We can do that indoors, where it's nice and *dry*."

"If that is what you wish." Victor wanted her full cooperation before he went as far as a kiss could be taken. He just wasn't sure she knew what that meant yet. Walking faster and faster as the rain started falling in earnest, they reached their cabin quite damp, though not actually soaked. Shutting the door on the now hissing drops, Victor turned to face her, only to find himself crowded against the door. Startled, he eyed her warily.

"I did some research, you know," Evanna murmured, rubbing her hands over the slippery, damp fabric of his silver shirt. "Last night, while you were sleeping, I crept out here and used the workstation to look up all manner of kissing techniques. Some of them were . . . *very* personal."

One of her hands slid down his chest to his stomach as she spoke, and slipped a little lower still. Victor sucked in a sharp breath. He caught her wrist. "Evanna . . . are you *sure* about this?"

She looked down at his silver-clad chest for a few moments, then shrugged. Her free hand rubbed gently over the material as she spoke. "Well, as I said, I did some research. The descriptions for the things I'm feeling apparently fall under the category of adult interpersonal interactions. I find you an attractive specimen of male humankind, I admire your wit, I am aroused by the way you kiss me, and I am intrigued by the passion you invoke in me."

Her other fingers fluttered slightly, making him stiffen. Evanna smirked.

"Judging from your reactions, you find me equally arousing, and my intelligence hasn't scared you away. At least, as far as I have been able to tell. Given that we are attracted to each other, it makes perfect sense to pair up as research partners. After all, the things you've said and done suggest you do have some empirical experience in researching passion between men and women, which would make you an exemplary assistant in this matter. You do, don't you?"

Nodding, he released her wrist, allowing her the opportunity to cup him fully. "I'm sure I could instruct you. I, ah . . . nice . . . In fact, the first lesson is all about hands-on research, which I see you're already eager to explore."

"Hands-on?" Evanna repeated, lifting her brows. "I thought this was supposed to be lips-on."

"Hands-on first," Victor corrected her. Catching her hands, he tugged them up to the top button of his shirt. "In order to kiss your research partner *everywhere*, you first need to remove any and all impediments to your lips, and that usually involves using your hands."

Nodding, she began unfastening his shirt. "Yes, I see you're right. I also understand that the best research environment—or at least the most comfortable—is a bed. Do you have a preference for which one?"

Lifting his fingers to the buttons of her own dress, Victor started removing it. "I think the nearest one will do."

She looked up at that. "I read that a sofa also works, if you really want the nearest comfortable surface."

"I think we should stick to traditional comforts the first few times," Victor countered wryly, amused by her pragmatic approach to passion. *Sweet scientist-lady, you have a lot to learn, don't you?*

She was staring at his chest with a bemused look. "Victor . . . if I may ask, why do you have all these muscles? Surely you don't use primitive, brute force to haul around all those cargos you carry?"

"No, my cousin and I use exosuits and hydrolifters, just like any other crew. But we fly an in-system ship, so we can literally go days and weeks between destinations— Please move your arms like . . . that, yes, thank you," he murmured, navigating her shoulders and elbows out of the constraints of her garment. "As a result, hauling cargo gets rather boring at times. There are only so many hours one can spend watching netshows, so I bought some fitness equipment a couple of years ago and have used it ever since."

"You must get bored quite a lot, to have developed all of this," Evanna observed, shoving his shirt off his shoulders so that it joined her dress on the floor. She skimmed her palms over his chest until her fingers reached his waist and began figuring out the intricacies of his trousers. Then she stopped and shook her head. "I almost forgot a step. We have to remove our shoes, then I can take off your pants and you can remove my underthings. After that, I have to give you a 'blow' or whatever it's called, and then . . . what?"

Wincing, Victor shook his head. "You do not *have* to give me one, Evanna."

She frowned at that. "Why not? Admittedly I didn't research the topic of sex exhaustively, but the preliminary research I did suggested it's best to satisfy the man first, so that he'll last longer the second time. It also suggested that a male should take extra time preparing a virgin female so that the pain is minimized and the experience overall is as enjoyable as possible. Logic suggests that if men are so quick on the first round as all that, then the man *should* be satisfied first. And the best way to satisfy a man the first time around is to blow him."

He stared at her a moment, then rubbed his palm over his face. "I can't believe you're turning me on with a dry, clinical recital of what we *should* do . . . Regardless, I'm afraid your research is incomplete."

"It is? But I read seventeen articles and watched twenty-three vids," Evanna pointed out. "That should be a sufficiently large enough sampling for preliminary instruction, at the very least."

"Passion is *not* meant to be treated like mixing up a batch of chemicals, even if it's been compared with chemistry for centuries," Victor corrected her, amused. *She really does throw herself into her research projects, doesn't she?* "And I don't *need* to be satisfied immediately. Such things are more for men who haven't bothered to put in a lot of research on self-control, which I have done. Besides, until you know what real passion is, how will you know if you're giving it adequately?"

Evanna tilted her head, thinking about that. "You mean I have to empirically experience passion in a practical application before I can grasp the theory correctly for future usage?"

"Exactly. Real life isn't a hologram, or a set of formulas on a screen," he agreed. Before she could react, Victor scooped her off her feet, hefting her into his arms. She was average in height and average in weight, and not too difficult to carry the few meters across the sitting room of their cabin to the nearest of the bedrooms. Once there, he laid her on the bed, knelt beside it, removed her shoes and socks, and pulled her undergarments down her legs.

Squirming up onto her elbows, Evanna watched him toss her clothing aside and remove his own shoes, though he left his silver trousers on.

His eyes, which she had heard his cousin call "fox eyes" during their brief meeting on the trip from the Moon to the Earth, flicked from her face to her pelvis. She could see why his cousin had said that, for while the rest of the man kneeling before her parted legs was controlled and methodical, those light brown eyes were as free as a wild animal, roving all over her. The mixture of control and freedom fascinated her; Evanna realized that the dichotomy between the two made her want to make his body just as free as his eyes. *I wonder what he'd be like if he unleashed some of that physical control . . .*

Curiosity prompted to her to ask, "Now what?"

"Now I kiss you."

Evanna watched avidly as he shifted to match actions to words. He didn't start with the obvious, though. Instead of going straight for her mouth or her loins, he lifted her right leg and pressed his lips to her ankle. Pressed slow, succulent kisses up the inside of her calf. Lingered at her knee and licked her inner thigh. Just as she started to squirm in anticipation, he retreated and caught her other ankle, beginning his salutations all over again.

By the time he finally claimed her lower lips, Evanna wondered why the hell she'd ever thought anyone at the logical, passionless, work-only Lunar Intelligence Trust was a genius. Particularly for throwing passion out of life. Yes, it disrupted her concentration. Yes, it destroyed her ability to think. But *this* was worthwhile, even if it never spared a single ship in combat. Her colleagues and so-called superiors were all idiots. Every last one of them.

More than that, this man was the right man with which to research all the things she'd missed so far in life. Evanna was sure of it. He was just like her: dedicated, methodical, and thorough. Knowledgeable, skillful—a veritable genius. Particularly as he gently inserted his finger, working it into her in a way that taught her hips—or perhaps just reminded them—a movement she instinctively knew was as old as life. Every touch of his hands, his tongue, and his lips drew her deeper into the mysteries of her own body, and she wanted more of it.

He was certainly good enough to turn that twisting feeling of pleasure inside of her into an explosion of bliss. Particularly when he eased a second finger inside, curled both of them up, and fluttered against *something* that sent her mind reeling with explosions of pleasure. Nor did he seem to mind when she grabbed at his head, alternately tugging and pushing and pulling, encouraging the swirling flicks of his tongue. A tiny, somewhat still rational corner of her mind worried that the shouts and cries he evoked from her were going to disrupt the other vacationers, but the rest of her did not care. In fact, part of her hoped they could hear her all the way back on the Moon, enjoying her freedom to its fullest and then some.

It helped that Victor kept at it until her belly was a cramped, trembling knot. Only when she was panting and flushed, soaked with her own sweat, did he climb onto the bed and stretch out beside her. Smiling, he soothed her flesh with gentle strokes of his left hand. The other, she noted when she pried open her eyes, propped up his dark-haired head. As her panting eased, she could hear the pattering of the rain outside and the slow, steady breathing of the man lounging smugly at her side. Once again, he looked controlled and calm, save for the wild life visible in those golden brown eyes . . . and the lump in his pants now prodding at the side of her hip.

Her mind, briefly quieted by passion, leaped into action. By the time her breathing had calmed and her abdomen no longer spasmed, she had picked through several possible choices. Evanna drew in a deep breath and let it out as a deep sigh.

Victor quirked one of his brows. "Well? Do you like being kissed that way?"

Evanna snorted. "Even an idiot would like that, and I'm no idiot."

"No, you're not," Victor agreed. His left hand stroked up from her stomach to her breasts, gently cupping one, then the other.

As pleasant as that was, Evanna focused on a more rational thought than passion. It wasn't easy with his thumb circling her nipple, but it was necessary. "But . . . I do need to know something."

"Ask," he prompted, wondering what she had on her mind. And wondering if his touch was effective enough if she could still think so much while he was caressing her.

"How much time are you willing to spare toward researching passion with me?" she asked. His smile broadened, making her frown defensively. "I'm serious, Victor! I'm asking you because I tried kissing your cousin yesterday, while he was showing me where the restroom facilities were on board your ship."

Victor stilled. He did *not* like the sound of that, and wondered at the strength of his reaction.

"As obliging and skillful as he was, I didn't like kissing him," Evanna stated. She watched him relax slightly, glad she had made the attempt, since it had helped secure preliminary confirmation of a hypothesis she was currently pondering. "It was *much* more enjoyable with you. I therefore see no reason to search farther afield when it's clear you and I interact very well. Which leads me to wonder if you feel the same way."

"I do." He flushed a little at the words, recognizing their significance, but otherwise didn't let himself react to the idea forming in his mind.

"Good. So, if we're both agreeable . . . would you be willing to extend our research association? I mean, beyond this visit in the woods?" she asked.

"Of course." He didn't have to think about it. He already knew that he wanted to spend more time with her. Giving the future a moment of thought, he shrugged. "I suppose I could let my cousin buy out my share of the ship and maybe find a job ferrying supplies locally to and from the institute . . . presuming they'll forgive me for helping you escape."

Evanna blinked. "The institute? I was going to ask if I could have one of the spare crew cabins on your ship converted into a hologram lab."

That made him blink and stop his gentle caresses on her abdomen. "A hologram lab?"

"Yes, a hologram lab," she repeated. "Most of my work is done in the hologram lab."

"But . . . what about the bismuth isotope?" Victor asked.

"Well, I *do* follow up holographic theory with hands-on applications, since even the best of computers can synthesize chemical reactions only so far. Real chemical interactions have an element of unpredictability . . . for all that that particular element isn't found on the periodic table," she quipped, pleased when his mouth curled up, enjoying her joke. "But that only happens for a few days a month, and usually it consists of me handing off projects to various lab workers, and overseeing a repeat of the occasional promising result.

"I'd need one or two crew quarters on board the *Închiriat* to install the processors and projectors into—and of course a mini hydrogenerator to power them, to keep from draining the ship's energy needs—but you do have four empty crew quarters, and your cousin said it was rare for you to take on passengers, so it's not like you actually *need* them." She paused as he thought about it, then asked, "Or am I presuming too much about our future interactions?"

"No, no," he reassured her. "You're not presuming too much. I wouldn't object to that plan in the least. Particularly since I know you'd get to have a real life outside of your work that way. I'd guarantee it personally . . . though I think I'd have to change the name of the ship if you joined me on it." He slid his hand back down to her stomach, teasing her navel with the edge of his thumb. "No, I'm just wondering what your employers would think of you moving all that industry-sensitive information out of their control."

"They can stuff it down the nearest black hole if they do have a problem with it," Evanna told him bluntly. "I am *not* going back to living my life on a glass hill. You've ridden up its slopes to rescue me, and I am suitably thankful . . . and I'll thank you even more if you'll continue to help me learn all the things I've missed out on. But I'm not going back to a prison. If they want my genius to give them their technological advances, they'll have to deal with *my* terms from now on. Those depositions you gave me will ensure it, one way or another."

Pleased his princess was determined to retain and enjoy her freedom, Victor leaned down and kissed her. To his surprise, she pushed him back. At his puzzled look, Evanna smiled and switched from pressing on his chest to caressing it with her palm.

"My turn. And I must point out that you are inappropriately attired for our little research endeavor." Sliding her hand down, she explored the placket of his silver pants. The corner of her mouth quirked up. "As a lifelong, dedicated scientist, I must insist on following the established procedures and protocols. At least, for the initial experiments. Which means the last of your silver armor must go."

Grinning, Victor complied. *I see I'll have to teach her how to speak sexily instead of scientifically, but the way she's approaching this so far is enthusiastic enough to be amusing.*

No sooner had he shucked his pants and undergarments than she tugged him down onto the bed on his back. Pleased by his compliance, Evanna leaned over him and kissed his chest. Some of the vids she had watched hadn't covered this, but some of the literature had. He also smelled too good not to wonder what he tasted like.

Mmm, salty, and musky . . . and warm. I like it. Lapping her tongue across his pectoral muscles, she blinked as he shuddered and sighed. *What was . . . ? Ah, the nipple. If he liked that, would he like . . . this?*

Flicking her tongue across the tiny little bud made him groan and bury his hands in her upswept hair. Somewhere between him cupping her head and her sucking on his flesh, circling each nipple with her tongue, he managed to pluck out her hairpins, scattering her locks across his chest. Victor stroked her hair back from her face, allowing her to switch to his other areola. His moans faded, until all she could hear was the sound of the rain pattering on the roof of their rented cabin.

A glance upward showed why he was now so quiet. His lower lip was caught between his teeth, his face taut with silent strain. She peppered kisses down to his ribs, then licked those. His lip popped free with a chuckle, then with a squirm. The hands cupping her scalp pushed gently away, silent warning that he wouldn't tolerate being tickled for much longer. Grinning, Evanna kissed lower, enjoying the way his stomach tightened, defining each muscle group.

His muscles weren't the only firm thing about him. Up close, she saw that his shaft wasn't particularly long, but it was thick, and it had a slight curve. Wrapping her fingers around it proved it was warm and satin-soft on the surface, with a firmness that belied its earlier, softer state. She knew she would have to look into the physiological reasons for the change—out of pure curiosity—but that would happen later.

For now, empirical research, the hands-on, direct sort of exploration, was her main goal.

Except she hadn't ever done this before. Seeking reassurance, Evanna glanced up. Most of his face showed signs she was pleasing him, in the flush of his cheeks, the curve of his lips, but it was his eyes that really glowed. Not quite wild, but definitely alive. Rippling her fingers, she experimented until he groaned and bit his lower lip again, head dropping back onto the bedding.

I wonder . . . Bracing herself on her side, she cupped his shaft in her hand and leaned down over his chest. A swirling lick of her tongue made him growl and shudder. One of the hands caressing her hair flopped down onto the mattress, fingers clenching and crumpling the covers.

That was interesting. Ever the researcher at heart, Evanna decided to switch position. Squirming on the bed, she shifted her head to his groin and her other hand to his chest. Except the dusting of dark hairs on his legs demanded to be explored, so she slipped her fingertips down onto his thighs and played with the different textures, soft skin, crisp curls, and warm flesh. Very warm, in certain places.

Her explorations made him shift and part his legs, made him moan softly and caress her own thighs, until he shifted onto his side and lifted her knee, making room for his head between her thighs. Confronted with the change in their positions, and the shaft prominently, conveniently placed, Evanna tentatively licked him. He groaned louder and kissed her fervently, encouraging her to do more.

Giving in to this new hunger, Evanna gave and received as much pleasure as instinct could provide, with scent and sound, taste and touch combining until she was rendered helpless with bliss. Shuddering, she slumped on the bed. She tried to return the pleasure but wasn't sure if she was doing it right, until he cupped her hand in his and showed her the best ways to rub and stroke. It was close to what she had done, but she knew she had a lot more to learn.

With her lower body freed from his distracting attentions, Evanna shifted position so that he could lie back and she could watch their combined hands manipulating his shaft. When she dipped down and kissed the tip of him again, he growled and arched his back. Barely warned in time, she pulled back, watching him climax, from the trembling tension in his muscles to the wetness spilling over her fingers, to the way his hips bucked up into her touch. His fingers coaxed hers into gentling their grip, until with a last, mutual stroke, he tugged her palm free.

Bringing her damp knuckles up to his lips, Victor saluted them with a kiss. His breathing was still deep and unsteady, but the gleam in his eyes was both lively and calm. "Absolutely brilliant. You did that very well. I think you have a natural aptitude for passion."

"You have a natural aptitude for teaching it," Evanna replied. Squirming again, she righted herself in relation to him and eyed her damp hand. He grinned and helped her wipe it on his chest.

"Don't worry about it," he said dismissively as she started to protest. "In fact, if you do it right, lovemaking can be *quite* messy."

"I'll defer to the expert," she conceded. "You're quite talented, you know. And brilliant yourself. I wouldn't settle for anything less in a research partner. I, um . . . hope you're willing to help me research all manner of things," she added. "Not just passion, but other aspects of social interaction. Like how do men and women live together, and which side of the bed do we each sleep on, and things like that."

He grinned. She was definitely enjoying her freedom and definitely enjoying it with him. "I'd be honored. I do have one request, though."

"Oh?" Evanna asked, curious.

"Yes. Could you . . . well, dare me to love you?" he asked, flushing as he did so, but forging on anyway. "I can't resist a good dare when it involves a beautiful, fascinating, compelling woman."

Blushing herself, Evanna grinned. "All right . . . but I won't dare you to love me. I'll dare you to love me *forever*. If it'll help, I'll take that dare, too, regarding you. Or at least give it a try."

Victor grinned. Moving the hand resting on her stomach, he slid it up to her small breasts, cupping the far one. "I'll take that bet with you. But first . . . we still have a lot more to research in the realm of hands-on passion. Quite a lot more. These things must progress in their proper order, after all."

"I'll defer the progression of these particular lab experiments to the expert," she granted airily. Then she glanced down his chest to his legs and the flesh she had enjoyed. "I do have one question, though."

"Only one?" Victor teased.

She rolled her eyes. "Only one *for now*, if you insist on my being accurate. No, sorry, *two* questions."

"A good researcher always strives for accuracy. So, what are your questions?" Victor prompted as she twisted onto her side, propping her own head on her hand, mirroring his pose.

"The first one is, if that was how you kissed my lips while you were wearing copper, and this is how you kiss my loins when wearing silver, what kind of a kiss will you give me when you're wearing your suit of gold?"

He smiled slowly. Wickedly and yet warmly, too. "I think I'll save *that* particular kiss for our wedding day."

Her breath caught and her heart felt like it stopped, if only for a moment. Leaning in close, he kissed her, restarting it. Wrapping her free arm around his ribs, Evanna kissed him back with everything she had. Not until she was flat on her back, panting with re-aroused passion and squirming with desire for more, did he release her lips.

"And the other question?" Victor asked, barely remembering it in time. What he wanted to do was part her thighs with his own and finish introducing her to all the delights of researching passion. But her question was important to her, which made it important to him.

"Hmm? Oh! Yes. The other question. You said if I joined you to live on board the *Închiriat,* you'd have to change its name. Why, and what to?" she asked, curious.

"Well, *Închiriat* means *Rented* in Romanian," he explained. "I own the ship sixty-forty with my cousin Ston. I'm the one who picks which cargos we will carry around the system, and I have the right to name it. But with you on board, you would own *me,* as well as being my most precious cargo on board . . . and that means it should be re-named *Vandute.*"

Hands straying down to his buttocks, Evanna prompted, "And that word means . . . ?"

He leaned down and kissed her lips in a soft, brief salute. *"Sold."*

Snow White
and the Seven Dwarves

Author's Note: Okay, I did it. I apologize, but yes, I deliberately lied to my readers and withheld information. I told everyone that I didn't have any plans to revisit the Isle of Nightfall and its eight famous brothers; I did it to avoid people pestering me for "sneak peeks" at what I was writing next. But as you can see, I did have plans, muahahahaa! All right, technically this isn't the Isle of Nightfall . . . but it does take place about half a year after the events at the end of the Sons of Destiny series. Don't go looking for a lot of action from the Corvis boys and their wives, though; their story is done, and we have tales of new heroes and heroines to focus upon and explore. (I just wish I'd had more room than this to explore the city of Menomon and its culture!)

T HEY were at it again. Being unabashedly *frothy*. She could hear them through the balcony doors.

Well, not all of them, Nevada acknowledged with a sigh. *Dar-shem is asleep in the back bedroom because he's on the night shift, and Rogen is late getting back from his work on the day shift at the desalinator site . . . but there go Cotter and Baubin . . . No, wait, those are Kristh and Tal-*

laden. Talladen always does that little wail thing whenever he realizes he's getting loud. Mainly because it embarrasses him to think of anyone overhearing them . . .

She grinned, thinking of her sixth husband. He was rather cute when he blushed. Actually, they were all reasonably good-looking. *Unfortunately,* she sighed, looking out over the stained glass waters of the city, *they're all besotted with each other. Not with me. The only man I know who I'm pretty sure likes me in that way . . . doesn't even live in this city.*

Other women might give her arch, knowing looks and sly little winks whenever she went out from the house, but Nevada was envious of *them*. They had husbands who loved their wives. Nevada—on the advice of her "co-father" Sierran—had taken husbands who were only interested in one another.

Because, "It wouldn't do for the heir-presumptive of Althinac to marry for the wrong reasons, or to the wrong persons," she thought, silently mocking her mentor. *Even though I had to get married.*

Unlike the four lovebirds, paired off in two of the tenement's handful of bedrooms, the author of that piece of advice was sound asleep in the overstuffed chair by the radiant block prominently placed in the center of the parlor. Life under the ocean meant living with perpetual dampness, and her mentor's aging joints needed frequent doses of soothing heat.

Nevada loved him all the same; Sierran had literally rescued her from death at the hands of the insurgents. *His* hands, for he had been the one assigned to kill her and bring her family's rule to a resolute, final end. Instead of killing her, he had fled with her, escaping across the vast, treacherous waters in a stolen under-wave ship. He had told her that he couldn't bring himself to kill an innocent young girl just because she had been born a Naccaran.

He had also told her the facts of her family, how her next-mother's greed and influence on her father had caused the city regent to impose

increasingly harsh taxes on the people. Other laws had gradually op-
pressed their rights, and building projects to "beautify" the city had
instead spoiled formerly pristine views. Particularly as some of the
land for those building projects had been seized on the flimsiest of
excuses, infuriating their rightful owners to the point of fomenting a
rebellion.

Moving from the partially underwater city of Althinac to the fully
underwater city of Menomon had been a calculated move on his part,
or so Sierran had explained. Nevada needed to know what life in an
oceanic city was like, since at the time they had left, loyalists were
fighting back against the rebels . . . and in the twelve years she had
been gone, there were still reports of fighting going on. Until Althinac
was politically stable, she had to remain in a safe place. But on the off
chance that the loyalists won, she had to remain capable of returning
to the city, which meant maintaining no permanent ties to Menomon.
And on the off chance that the rebels won, but wanted to make peace
with the loyalists, she had to remain politically available for negotiations of one sort or another.

But in the meantime, she had to live in Menomon, under Menomonite customs and traditions. Since she had no magical or medical
reason to counter the local customs, the City Council decreed that
Nevada still had to get married after she turned eighteen and have
three husbands by the time she turned twenty-five, the same as any
other woman.

*. . . Aaand there goes Baubin. He does that growling thing whenever he
and Cotter go at it. Then again, Cotter's a good lover; he certainly made
Rogen happy, at least for a while.* She smiled again. First she had picked
Cotter for her husband, then Rogen, because she had been best friends
with Cotter, and he and Rogen had been lovers. Since she wasn't interested in Cotter sexually, it made sense to pick a second husband who
would keep Cotter happy.

But then Rogen had met the handsome Dar-shem and fallen in love, which meant Nevada had ended up marrying him, too, and cheerful, easygoing Cotter had hooked up with Kristh, who had become husband number four. Only Cotter had met Baubin a year later and decided he was much better off with the short, blond land-butcher than with the tall, redheaded leatherworker. The two were still silly over each other, though it had been two years since they had fallen in love. It was cute. Kristh had wanted to get a divorce after being dropped by Cotter for someone else, but had met Dar-shem's friend Talladen, who had secretly fallen for him back when he was still with Cotter . . . and there went another heart caught up in the maelstrom of masculine romances filling Nevada's life.

Dar-shem used to have a thing for Talladen, which makes Rogen irritable from jealousy, she thought, counting out the pairings on her fingers. As their wife, it was her legal responsibility to keep abreast of potential family tensions, so she made a point of reminding herself each day of her marriage's dynamics. *Particularly since they're on split shifts over at the desalinator and don't get to see each other as much as they used to. I really should talk to the Aquamancy Guild about getting them reassigned to the same shift. Even if they are really good coral masons, and really good coral masons are rare, they'll be happier and thus work better if they're paired together.*

Three explosive sneezes made her grin. *And there goes Kristh, with his allergies. I always know when* he's *having fun . . .*

Her smile slipped a little. *She* didn't know if she had any little quirks during lovemaking, like Talladen with his shy wailing, or Kristh with his sneezing, or Baubin with his growling. Cotter had gladly shared all manner of secrets with her about the mysteries of what men liked and wanted; they had met in primary school, being the same age, and had made friends with each other as they grew. Cotter worked in the Mage Guild as a generalist enchanter like her, albeit a few ranks lower. But being told what men liked wasn't the same as being shown what *she* liked. In that much, Nevada envied her husbands.

A shadow loomed on the horizon, distracting her. Not a figurative one, either; a large ship had drifted into view while she had leaned on the railing of her tenement balcony and listened to four of her six husbands making love back in their bedrooms. It took her a few moments to realize why it looked so strange and yet so vaguely familiar; it wasn't an oblong, fish-shaped *udrejhong*, the kind with the raisable fin-sails preferred by the Menomonites around her. No, the long, triangular-hulled ship was starkly Althinac in its design.

Alarmed, Nevada peered through the rippling green-glass light of the ocean, beyond the layers of hydrostatic barriers separating the city from the sea. The sight of several smaller, fish-shaped vessels surrounding the foreign ship reassured her a little. *Good . . . the Wavescouts are up there, giving it escort. And . . . yes, they're docking it at the new Flame Tower. Sheren's apprentices will be the first ones to examine the newcomers for any potential threat to the city.*

Craning her neck, she looked back at the white-haired figure sleeping peacefully in his overstuffed chair. Sierran had negotiated asylum for the two of them twelve years ago; the final word on whether or not their request was accepted had come from the lips of the Guardian of Menomon herself. Even after having studied with the redoubtable woman, Nevada was still a little in awe of the elderly but imposing, formidable Guardian Sheren. She also respected the guardian's new, official apprentices, but she was more in envy of them than in awe.

Sometimes it seems like all the world is happily married, except for me . . . Talladen wailed a second time and Kristh sneezed twice, then twice again. She smiled wistfully. *Even if some of them are supposed to be married to me. If the boys haven't woken up Dar-shem yet with their fun, I should go wake him up anyway. He'll have to eat and get ready to go to work soon. Which means I'll have to start getting dinner ready, since it's my turn to cook.*

I'd better wake up Sierran and let him know an Althinac under-wave ship has arrived. A particularly large one. She gave the large, prism-shaped vessel one last, worried look before moving inside. *Normally we get our news from Althinac via mirror-scryings. Something big must have happened to have prompted them into traveling halfway across the Western Ocean without warning. Something most likely involving Sierran and me.*

ROGEN came swimming home in time for supper. Pausing only long enough to run one of the suction wands that hung along the balcony wall over his leather clothes in order to eradicate stray drips, he headed for the kitchen and kissed Nevada on the cheek. Then he kissed Darshem on the lips and dragged his co-husband away from prepping the rice rolls, hauling the taller, darker-skinned man by the hand to the refreshing room to "help" him rinse off the saltwater that had soaked his skin for half the day.

He banged on the bedroom doors of the other four as he went, ordering them to help set the table, making Nevada smile. Cotter might have been her best friend and first choice in the face of Menomonite custom, but Rogen made the best lead husband.

The long tile table was set in rapid order, the last of the rice rolls fixed by Baubin, and the dishes carried out to the table by Talladen and Cotter. Kristh fetched and poured the drinks, shielding the occasional, lingering sneeze into his shoulder. Once everything was ready, the seven men in Nevada's life took their seats around the long table, with Nevada at one end and Sierran at the other.

Just as she took her first bite of butter-fried dulse, the reddish brown seaweed cooked the special way Cotter's mother had shown her shortly after her first marriage, someone rang the bell-chime. Mouth full, Nevada glanced around the table. It wasn't unusual for such a large family to have visitors, though usually friends and family visited later in the day. The look in Sierran's eyes echoed her worry that their unexpected visitor had something to do with the two of them.

Rogen set down his fork with a scowl. "It's probably for me. Yet another problem with wedding the coral seed stock to the base granite, no doubt."

Dar-shem smothered a yawn and rose at the same time his co-husband did, unfolding his tall, dark brown body from his chair. "I'd better listen in. If it's something a coral mason has to fix, it'll be done on my watch, after all."

Swallowing her mouthful of seaweed, Nevada cut into her pepper-and-onion-smothered halibut. Baubin could and did get them choice cuts of land meat from time to time, since he worked as a butcher and that was one of the perks of his job, but feeding eight people took a lot, and fish was a cheaper protein to cultivate under the sea than birds or beef. Land animals required a lot of feed, and that took a lot of space from the harvest caverns deep below the city.

It was no good. She couldn't distract herself with thoughts of food. Setting down knife and fork, she strained to hear any actual words coming from the front hall. The only things audible over the sounds of the others eating were the low rumble of Rogen's voice, the slightly lighter one of Dar-shem, and at least one other, unfamiliar male.

She didn't have to strain for long. She heard Rogen speaking firmly as they came toward the dining room. "But she'll finish her meal first, and take the time to properly dress. In the meantime . . . I offer you the hospitality of our family; you may dine with us if you wish."

"No, thank you," the gray-uniformed man following between him and Dar-shem stated as he entered the room. Though the upper half of his face was hidden by his guardsman's helm, the wavescout's eyes could be seen taking in the number of men at the table. He faced Nevada after a moment and gave her a polite bow. "Good evening, mistress; I am Wavescout Tiels. May I presume you are Nevada of the family Naccara, born in the city-state of Althinac?"

"That is correct," she agreed, glad she had given up on the pretense of eating, leaving her mouth clear for speech. "What can I do for you, Wavescout Tiels?"

"A delegation from the city of Althinac has been sent to the city of Menomon to speak with you regarding the means to bring an end to the last of its civil war. The Guardian of Menomon and her apprentices have interviewed the delegates and believe it is safe for you to meet with them under their supervision. The city council has generously offered the use of its facilities for hosting this meeting."

"No doubt they hope to wrest some sort of trade advantage out of this from the Althinac," Talladen murmured. "Now that they're finally getting their heads out of the sump pump about keeping in contact with outsiders."

"Keep a civil tongue in your head, Talladen," Rogen chastised him.

"I'm a bard; I'm *supposed* to speak the truth," Talladen shot back, though he blushed as he said it.

"Gentlemen," Nevada said soothingly, lifting her hand slightly. That was all she needed to do; both of her co-husbands settled back down.

One of the few reasons Sierran had been in *favor* of her marrying so many men—for all he had discouraged her from marrying any of the ones interested in her romantically—had to do with the hands-on teaching it would give her in how to manage disparate personalities. Although he had merely been the equivalent of a wavescout lieutenant back in Althinac, the aging man had paid attention to city politics. Nevada had to agree; she had learned quite a lot about how to manage people just from managing her personal life.

The wavescout waited for her reply. Nodding her head, Nevada complied. "I would be honored to accept the council's generous offer. My lead husband is correct, however; I really should eat and change into something more suitable first. You are welcome to join us, as he offered."

"Thank you, but it isn't necessary, mistress," the wavescout replied politely, giving her another bow. "I ate before coming on duty. I'm willing to wait while you get ready, and will be your escort to the Congregation Halls. Guardian Sheren has sent her personal gourami vessel for your use, to make sure you arrive safe and dry. In the meantime, the Althinac delegation has been invited to enjoy the delights of the Aviary."

Cotter rose from his seat, giving Nevada a half bow as he did so. "I'll show him to the parlor, mistress."

"Thank you, Husband," she murmured. Rogen and Dar-shem sat back down as Cotter led the wavescout out of the room. Nevada concentrated on cutting into her halibut. Her appetite had vanished from nervousness, but she knew she would need the energy to deal with this sudden visit from Althinac.

A few seconds after they were alone again, Baubin *snerked*, shoulders trembling with the effort to keep his laughter quiet. "Did you see the look in his eyes? He was clearly wondering what our wife had that his didn't!"

Rogen jerked in his seat, as did Kristh a moment later; Nevada heard a *thump* from under the table. She didn't have to peer under the furniture to know the chain of discipline was being passed from nan to man. As she watched, Kristh twisted and smacked Baubin on the back of his head. "Keep a civil tongue in your head regarding *our* wife. She's the one who gave us this lifestyle."

"That's enough," Nevada told both of them. She kept her tone light and was pleased when they settled down. It hadn't always been this easy, particularly when her co-husbands' relationships had been breaking apart like a crumbling reef, but she had earned their respect over time. Particularly since all six of them were now very happy with their choice of mates.

"You will wear the blue dress, won't you?" Baubin asked her. "The one with the bits of lace? The dye in the scales really brings out the color of your eyes."

"She's meeting with people who, from the sound of it, are from the other faction in the Althinac civil war," Rogen pointed out. "Not going off to marry husband number seven. She should wear black, so she'll look intimidating."

"Then she should wear a bold red, so she'll look like a force to be reckoned with," Talladen countered.

"Black is more intimidating," Rogen countered back. "With her black hair and a black dress, she'll look like someone who cannot be easily threatened."

"Gentlemen," Sierran interjected, "if this *is* a chance for reconciliation and an end to civil strife, then she shouldn't be trying to frighten them out of it. If anything, she should look like a princess, since that *is* what she is. She should wear gold, to remind them of her heritage."

"*Gold?*" both Kristh and Baubin protested. Kristh continued for both of them. "Gold doesn't go with her eyes. I agree she shouldn't look quite as beautiful as she does in the blue dress with the lace, but too much gold would make the dress more visible than her."

"He has a point," Talladen agreed. "Perhaps a compromise?"

"How about her long gold skirt and one of her blue tops?" Darshem offered.

Talladen and Rogen both winced, and Baubin wrinkled his nose. Cotter, coming back from showing the wavescout to the parlor and its balcony view of the city, rolled his eyes. Nevada stepped in verbally before they could continue.

"Your suggestions all have merit . . . but I'll wear black pants and a gold top for this first meeting. It'll give an impression that I still have access to wealth and thus power, yet cannot be easily intimidated."

"Pants? Why pants?" Sierran asked as the others nodded in agreement. "You know as well as I do that noblewomen in Althinac wore skirts, as a sign of their status. Commoner women who had to work for a living wore pants. I'm sure nothing has changed *that* drastically fashion-wise in the last twelve years."

"Because it's a compromise. My good black leather skirt is barramundi leather, and my good gold blouse is stingray. The two scale patterns clash. Not to mention I seem to remember Althinac having a lot more access to land leathers *and* actual fabrics," Nevada pointed out. "If I walk into this meeting wearing blatantly fish-scaled leathers, I'll look more like a Menomonite than an Althinac. I have a pair of trousers made from manta, which is close enough to stingray that it'll match the blouse. And the blue dress, lovely though it may be, was made from parrotfish hide. It matches the salvaged lace for the trim, but otherwise it looks too Menomonite."

"Never mind what she's wearing," Cotter said dismissively, cutting into his own steak now that he was seated again. "We need to figure out what *we* are wearing."

"You?" Sierran scoffed. "This is an Althinac matter, not a Menomonite one."

"We're still her husbands," Dar-shem reminded him. "If these delegates came with an entourage to impress people with their importance, then we'll need to provide her with one, too . . . or rather, *you* will. I'll have to head to work in half a glow."

Nevada glanced at the clock out of habit. Like the clocks in the other rooms of their tenement, it was crafted from nodes of suncrystal similar to the ones embedded in the ceiling. Unlike the overhead crystals, the clocks weren't turned off by a switch; instead, spells caused them to light up and dim twice a day on a twelve-hour, twelve-spoked cycle, shining brightest and fullest at noon and midnight. Measuring time was important when one couldn't always see the actual sun and moons sliding across the rippling waters of the Menomonite sky.

It was her guild, the Mage's Guild, that enchanted and maintained such things. Her guild that grew the suncrystal towers which brought blessed, necessary sunlight from the wave-tossed surface all the way down to the plants and animals growing in the harvesting caverns at the base of the reef-ringed city. Her guild that had graciously done its best to maintain contact, however sporadic, with Althinac . . . and her guild that hadn't warned her that a delegation from that distant city was on its way.

Why didn't we know? Why didn't Althinac warn us they were coming? Picking at her food, Nevada worried over that point. *Even if I don't have the seniority of some of the others, I'm the one our "informant" has been talking with these last few years. Nor would the others go behind my back; I'm among the top ten highest ranked mages in the guild. I would have known about it even if the message had come during my off hours!*

So why didn't *they say they were coming?*

THE moment she entered the Aviary, one of the best meeting rooms in the council Congregation Halls, Nevada knew why nothing had been said. Mouth gaping, she stared at the most important man in the room. Only peripherally did she notice the quartet of men and the one woman who accompanied him, distinct in their fabric clothes from the Menomonites in their sea leathers. Mastering her shock, Nevada struggled to adopt a pleasant expression instead of a stunned one as she approached, flanked by her husbands and her honorary co-father.

That approach was masked by the chirps and twitters of the song-birds flitting from tree to tree. Breathable space for animals and plants as well as humans was at a premium, but the Aviary was one of the oldest and fanciest public venues in Menomon. Normally it was only available during daylight hours; with the sun having set during supper, only the residual light lurking in the crystals of the sun towers and the occasional passing of a luminous fish could illuminate the pitch-black depths of the city. Agitated by the extended span of crystal-wrought light, the birds flitted from bush to tree, almost as colorful as the fish residing in the city's many reefs, and certainly noisier.

Althinac was a city partly on the surface and partly beneath the

sea, built as it was around a pearl necklace of coral atolls much older
and taller than the reefs sheltering Menomon. They were undoubtedly used to seeing non-edible birds flying about freely, but Nevada
could tell the visitors were still impressed. Particularly that one central
figure, who was craning his neck so he could peer at the bright yellow
and green budgerigar that had boldly landed on his shoulder. The bird
finished cleaning its beak with a talon and fluttered off, allowing its
human perch to finally notice Nevada's approach.

The smile he gave her was big, friendly, and unabashed. It made his
teeth look very white in his suntanned face. He emphasized his pleasure by breaking away from the others, hand outstretched in greeting
as he crossed the brick-tiled courtyard being used as their meeting
space. "Nevada! I'm very glad to finally meet you in person."

"Migel," Nevada returned, smiling back as she clasped hands with
him.

She couldn't help smiling; for a man raised on the rebel side of the
civil war, he had always been very nice toward both her and Sierran.
Of course, Migel's insistence on staying neutral all these years and
focusing on expanding his knowledge of training through his contacts
in various cities hadn't hurt. It had given them a non-hostile contact to
talk with back home. Now, in person, that warmth in his personality
transmitted itself in the warmth of his hand. Part of her just wanted
to wrap herself up in his hand. Part of her wanted to wrap herself up
in the rest of his embrace.

With the remainder, she managed a coherent question. "It is indeed
a great pleasure to meet you in person, instead of via the mirrors . . .
but *why* are you here? They made you the Guardian of Althinac last
year, at the start of the truce. Why would they let the Guardian of the
City go anywhere?"

"They 'let' me because they don't know I've left. They think I'm
undertaking a purification ritual in strict isolation; otherwise I would
have told you I was coming. Unfortunately, there are still a few radi-

cals on both sides who would not only violently protest my leaving the city, but also the reason why I came here at all." His eyes, the same cerulean shade of blue as hers, flicked to the faces of the men spreading out to flank her. "Are these your fellow guild members?"

"Only Cotter is part of the Mage Guild. Migel, this is my first husband Cotter, a generalist mage of the fourth rank; Cotter, this is Migel, Guardian of Althinac." Nevada turned slightly to her other side, ready to introduce the next man in her entourage, but the stunned, crumbling look on the Guardian of Althinac's suntanned face stopped her. "Is something wrong?"

He shook his head, but not in reply. "This isn't going to work . . . I came all the way here with what I thought was a brilliant idea, and it's not going to work."

Getting the feeling she was missing out on something, Nevada tilted her head. "Mind telling me what's wrong? And what your idea was?"

"It's the Convocation of the Gods," Migel explained. "The priestess picked to represent Althinac during the Summoning of Althea presented both sides of our civil war to Her and asked if there was a simple, workable solution to our ongoing civil war. The Goddess of Waves answered with the statement 'When the two houses are rendered one, the war will end.' Or words to that effect.

"Most of the radicals on both sides took that to mean a resumption of hostilities and tried to break the truce. I stopped it . . . barely . . . and said I would meditate on its meaning. But I thought at the time the meaning was very clear. To render doesn't mean to destroy—that's to *rend*—but rather, to render means things like to conform, submit, and represent. So I thought it meant we should make the two ruling houses of the loyalists and the rebels join as one," he explained. "The loyalists won't accept anyone but a Naccaran leading the city.

"You're the last one, unless you count a few embittered, distant cousins among the extremists who have been keeping the loyalist faction firmly alive. The majority of loyalists don't want an extremist on the city seat, though. They'd rather take their chances on an exiled princess. On the other side of the matter, the rebels won't accept anyone but an Althec paving the way to a new and better future, because of the excesses of your father and next-mother.

"I'm a first cousin to the idiots who started this mess. Plus I'm the guardian of the city, the only one both sides felt was calm enough to take up the position and enforce the truce. That gives me a certain level of authority to . . . well, to have imposed my will, making everyone accept a marriage of alliance between us." He paused and shook his head, the ends of his dark brown hair flicking over his shoulders with the quick, negative movement. "But if you're already married, it wouldn't work."

"Why wouldn't it work?" Cotter asked, giving the Althinac male a puzzled look.

Migel glanced at him. "Because she's *already* married?"

"What has that to do with anything?" Rogen asked, folding his arms across his chest. "She's already got six husbands. One more at this point won't matter that much."

Nevada took in Migel's shocked look and blushed, remembering why he was so upset. *It's just proof of how well I've adapted to the Menomonite way of looking at things that I totally forgot about this.* "Migel, I'm only married because, under Menomonite law, I had no legal reason *not* to be married. The law in *this* city is that unless a woman is willing to pay a very stiff fine, or has a medical or magical reason to sidestep the law, *all* women have to have at least three husbands by the time they turn twenty-five.

"Given how I'm twenty-four, I've never had a great deal of wealth, and I had no clue whatsoever that this solution for ending the war was going to be presented to you before my time limit was up, I went ahead and married my best friend, Cotter, five years ago and then picked out a few more. This is Rogen, who is my second and lead husband," she added, introducing the two of them. She gestured at the others as well. "I'm also wed to Kristh, Baubin, and Talladen here, as well as to Dar-shem, though he's not here."

"Dar-shem had to go off to work the night shift instead of accompanying us to meet your delegation; he's helping to construct our own desalinator, based on the blueprints of the one on Nightfall Isle, the place which hosted the Convocation of the Gods," Cotter explained for her.

Nevada gestured at the last of the men in her entourage. "And of course you know Sierran, who is my honorary co-father, since he helped raise me once we settled here. And he did have the wit and the compassion to spare my life as an innocent child."

Migel nodded politely to each man, but there was still a lurking level of dismay in his deep, Althinac blue gaze. At least it wasn't quite as strong as the expressions of distaste in the four men behind him listening to their conversation, though the one woman in his entourage was still smiling politely enough at Nevada. The Guardian of Althinac gestured with his hand. "The laws in Althinac are very different from Menomon. We have a one woman, one man policy. Plus there's the whole question of . . . of paternity, since in order to make the merger successful, we'd have to . . ."

He trailed off when Nevada gaped at him. She laughed as soon as she could catch her breath; a glance to either side showed her husbands sharing her sense of humor. "You think I'm *sleeping* with them? I'll admit I'm the envy of any number of Menomonite women for the sheer number of men I've managed to fit into my life, but trust me, it's not at all what you'd think. *Ours*," she said, gesturing to include her five present husbands along with herself, "is a true marriage of convenience. I needed to obey the laws and rules of Menomon, and they were willing to oblige that need in return for all the legal advantages of being married. Which *they* could not obtain any other way . . . because each and every one of my husbands is paired off with one of the others."

"Paired off?" Migel repeated, flicking his gaze to the faces of the men flanking her.

"Yes. They're *frothy*," she explained. At his blank look, she realized she had used another Menomonite term. "It means they're only interested in other men, sexually?"

Migel's lips parted, but for a moment no sound came out. He finally settled on a simple "Ah."

"Her marriages have simply been a political move," Sierran offered, speaking up from his position behind the others, drawing the full attention of his fellow Althinacs. "I reasoned that an offer like this might happen someday, among many other possibilities . . . but I also knew we had to be model Menomonite citizens in return for being given asylum here for so many years. I counseled Nevada to take on husbands who were only interested in sexual relations with other men, which would protect her from any questions of paternity in an alliance match with someone from Althinac."

Cotter wrapped his right arm around Nevada's shoulders, giving her a little squeeze. "Trust us, she's more like a sister than a wife, in that regard. Not that she doesn't know what to do; she got high marks in her sexual education courses, plus I've filled her in on a few more things about men since then."

From the rolling eyes and hastily averted gazes of the men behind Migel, Nevada guessed these Althinacs still didn't grasp Menomonite culture. And still the one woman in their group continued to smile benignly at her. Migel caught the line of her gaze and introduced them.

"These are Fedor and Ismail of the loyalist faction—I should say rather, two of the levelest-headed members of the loyalist faction I could find to bring as witnesses to my plan. These are Carmen and Lajos of the rebel faction, also the calmest and most trustworthy witnesses I could find. And this," he added, gesturing for the woman in their group to come forward, "is my cousin Socorro, who is the witness for the Althec family. I, ah, would have sought someone of the Naccaran family to be your witness . . . but you're the only one left of sufficiently strong enough blood ties. The remaining three cousins . . . they might accept you as a co-leader, but they'd protest the 'co-' part, particularly when instigated by the rebel side."

Nevada lifted her hand, dismissing his subtle apologies for the things his kin had done to hers. The two of them had long since covered such things via their occasional mirror-scried conversations. "That's all right. My husbands can stand witness."

Migel blinked. "They *can* stand witness? Not *could*? Have you made up your mind that quickly?"

"Not entirely," Nevada told him, smiling. "But since I already know *you*—as much as we could know each other through a pair of mirrors—you're not the part of this marriage alliance idea I'd object to. What I need to know now is how this marriage of our two houses will be translated into the governance of Althinac."

"Why don't we all sit down while we hash out such details?" Talladen offered, playing the diplomat. He gestured at the expensive, wrought-iron chairs clustered to one side of the cobblestone-paved courtyard.

Nevada knew the chairs wouldn't be comfortable for any real length of time, but she figured that might help speed up the preliminaries. Letting Talladen hold her chair for her, she sat down at one of the smaller grate-topped tables. It was a power move, for it allowed only enough room for Migel to sit across from her and forced both sides to spread out, finding seats a short distance away.

If she had been dealing with Menomonites, she would have picked the largest of the three different sizes of tables offered by the Aviary furniture, but she wasn't dealing with a committee-minded people.

Althinacs were used to being led by a single leader who was supported by a selection of advisors. That meant these negotiations were between herself and Migel.

The table was small enough that when Migel adjusted his position in his chair, their feet bumped together briefly. Migel dropped his gaze to her sandal-clad feet, visible below the soft, sueded, black rayskin of her pants, then pulled his focus back up to her face. "As you may recall, Althinac is ruled in a pyramid fashion; the higher up you go in the ranks of authority, the fewer people you'll find. At the top are two positions: the guardian and the prince or princess.

"Right now, the city is technically ruled by Prince Alvan, a mutual uncle of Socorro's and mine. But it's a precarious perch, because while he's popular among the rebel faction, he's a bit too staunchly an Althec for the loyalists to fully accept him. I have more of the effective power, if not the rank, because I have been careful not to offend the loyalist side. Nor have I offended my kin overly much.

"Unfortunately, the Althecs would not accept me as the next prince because I'm the strongest mage in the city. They want me to be the guardian," Migel explained. "They want both positions to stay as they are, filled by members of the rebel faction, but the loyalists disagree. Because of this, the truce is an uneasy one, held in place more by my agreeability and the threat of my power against both sides than by Uncle Alvan's leadership abilities."

Nevada shifted in her seat. That caused their feet to bump together again. It distracted her briefly from the hard, unyielding metal supporting her backside. Migel cleared his throat.

"On the other hand, if you were to take over as princess while I remained guardian, the rebel side would object to having a Naccaran in power over them once again."

That made her tilt her head. "So . . . are you suggesting that you step up as the prince, and that, what . . . I take over your position as guardian of Althinac? I'm a strong mage, but I'm not *that* strong. I'm not even strong enough to have been considered a suitable replacement for Guardian Sheren here in Menomon."

"Not exactly—actually, it's your own city guardian's situation that made me think of this solution," Migel confessed, nodding at the pair of redheads who had taken seats at the edge of the group, watching the proceedings quietly but intently. The man was somewhat tall and slightly exotic, being a foreigner, while the woman was rather short and quite familiar to Nevada. "Her apprentices are weaker individually than they are when they pool their powers together. Together, they will rule Menomon as its joint guardian whenever Guardian Sheren steps down.

"You and I couldn't pool our magics on nearly the same scale that they apparently can, but we *could* pool our authority," Migel explained. "Instead of having a prince *or* princess at the top, followed by the guardian of the city as their champion and protector, we combine the two offices. We can't make ourselves a ruling king and queen, since that's not in our covenant with Althea, but we can make ourselves a ruling prince and princess. Equals, with equal share of the power and equal share of the responsibility. And to make it unshakable, we should probably marry before we return to Althinac. I know it's rushed, but this way we'd have several days of travel to get used to working together. Except . . . you're already married."

His own foot shifted against hers. It shifted and lingered, in fact. Nevada didn't realize for a few moments what he was up to, until she shifted her foot aside a little and his followed hers. His boot was leather, waxed somewhat stiff, but he still managed to caress her ankle gently with the edge of its toe. A blatant caress. Quirking the corner of her mouth, Nevada lifted her toes a little, returning the foot play.

"That . . . sounds like it'd take a lot of work to implement. Though I suppose I do have more of an advantage than you in that I've grown up used to the Menomonite mind-set of committees for this and councils for that." Bracing one elbow on the table, she rested her chin on her hand, toes rubbing gently against the lower part of his calf. Touching him just felt too good to pass up the opportunity. "But it will still take work on both our parts. Not only will it take work for the people on both sides to accept our joint authority, it will probably take some time for both of us to learn how to trust each other's judgment enough to honestly share all the powers, privileges, duties, and responsibilities.

"I'm used to sharing power because that's the way Menomon is run, ruled by layers of committees, guilds, and teams. Can you handle that?" she asked, wriggling her toes subtly behind his calf. The birds were still agitated from the extended light, and they were being watched by the Menomonites and Althinacs around them, but she was fairly sure Migel was aware of her subtext: *Can you handle me?*

Migel smiled in a way that said he was taking a moment to tactfully phrase his reply. "As part of a team ruling the city, yes, I believe I can handle that. As part of a team married to you . . . *Frothy* or not, I think I would have to insist that you divorce your husbands before you married me. I'm not inclined to share you."

"She can't do that," Cotter stated. At Migel's sharp look, he shrugged. "If you want her to get married here, she has to do it by Menomonite law, and there are a handful of indemnity clauses involved. If she divorces us, she is forbidden by law to marry anyone for a full year, plus she must pay us in marriage equity for the loss of access to a wife and all the privileges that entails. If *we* divorce her, she would be free to marry again, but we cannot marry anyone for three years, and we would lose our marriage privileges."

"I'm missing something," Migel murmured, glancing at the other husbands. "You're *frothy* men. Why would losing marital privileges be an issue?"

"Not marital privileges, *marriage* privileges," Baubin corrected. "Under Menomon law, a woman is allowed larger and better quarters dependent upon the number of her husbands, plus a tax break, rental discounts, and even a larger food budget. With six husbands, Mistress Nevada has one of the best tenements in the upper East Reef zone. Menomon also has a slight housing problem at the moment. We'd have to move out of her nice, large tenement and cram ourselves into three sets of tiny quarters at the base of the city."

"We can't expand by very much in size until we have the desalinator up and running, taking from our city protections much of the burden of filtering out freshwater to drink," Rogen stated, folding his arms across his black-leather-clad chest. "At that point, the magics allocated toward drinkable water can be shifted toward expanding the city's limits, easing the housing pressures. Until that point in time . . . we are disinclined to divorce our wife."

Migel looked at Rogen and his co-husbands, then at Nevada. Finally, he nodded his head. "I can understand your point. But we won't be living here; we'll be living in Althinac, where polyandrous and polygamous marriages aren't accepted. I have, however, spotted a loophole."

His foot moved under the table, sliding partway up Nevada's calf. She raised her brows as much from suppressing the urge to shiver as from polite inquiry. "And that loophole is . . . ?"

"You and I marry, and *then* you divorce your husbands." He turned to the husbands. "Her marriage equity can then give you all the right to maintain your current housing status and location . . . and Althinac will foot the bill in paying for the tenement for the next three years, giving Menomon plenty of time to build your desalinator and begin expanding the city's housing limits. After that," he said, spreading his hands slightly, "you're on your own."

"Six years," Talladen counteroffered. "With the provision that we— the six of us—remain housed in the tenement, no more and no less. Or seven, if you care to stay, Sierran?"

"I'd have to think about that. I'm not as young as I used to be," the former Althinac stated. "My mind is fine, but relocating into a tense political situation is something for younger, swifter reflexes."

"I do owe you my life, Sierran; you'll always have a co-father's rights with me, and a warm welcome in my home. I'll have to hash out these ideas with the city council," Nevada warned Migel as she turned her attention back to him, "but I think there's a precedent for co-husbands getting to keep their upgraded housing for at least a year, and I'm sure we can extend it to three at the very least. Particularly if I point out that they'd be getting friendlier trade relations with Althinac if I'm allowed to divorce with their legal blessing toward the terms. But it may take a few days before they make up their minds, since this isn't a life-or-death crisis."

"Hopefully they won't take forever in reaching a decision. I can fake appearing to still be in Althinac only for so long," he warned her, and gave her ankle one last caress with his own before rising. "In the meantime, would you be willing to show me—us—more of this city? I'm told it's just as beautiful at night, lit up by suncrystals and bioluminous plants and animals, as it looked to be by day."

Rising, Nevada smiled. "I'd be delighted. That is, if you don't mind getting wet? It's best seen from above when swimming through the towers outside the main air dome."

"I don't mind getting wet . . . if you don't mind me making you wet," he murmured, taking her hand and tucking it into the crook of his elbow. "But as I am a mage, I'll just cast a spell to keep our *clothing* dry."

The masculine warmth in his rich blue eyes, coupled with that phrase, made her blush with pleasure. From the moment they had first met via mirror, Nevada had liked Migel. But it had just been liking until now; they lived too far apart and the political situation was too unstable for imagining anything more. But from the moment their hands had first met . . . Nevada could definitely picture more.

"I wouldn't mind at all," she promised him, smiling as she guided him out of the Aviary Hall.

◈

"AND then the bladder wrack broke free, but instead of making things better, the long strands got all tangled up in the propellers and I *still* couldn't get anywhere!" Migel confessed humorously, gesturing expressively with a hand before returning it to hers.

Nevada laughed and squeezed his fingers. "Menomonites use jets for propulsion more often than propellers, but I've been thwarted by clogged intake chutes a time or two. Which reminds me of this time when I—"

"Ohhh, for the love of Menos!" Seated off to the side, on one of the balcony's padded lounging chairs, Cotter gave the two of them a glare worthy of his lead co-husband. His demand woke up Baubin and one of the Althinac men, Lajos, who had been dozing on two of the other couches. "It's almost an hour past midnight, and the two of you won't *shut up*! Some of us *do* have to work in the morning, you know—for reefs' sake, *go to bed* already!"

Visibly reluctant, Migel sighed and lifted Nevada's fingers to his lips. He kissed them lightly and gave her a wistful smile. "I guess I'll have to hear your next story tomorrow morning . . . unless you have to work first?"

Cotter made a rude noise and hauled himself to his feet. "Not *separate* beds, *her* bed. Left-hand hall, first door on the left, you can't miss it. And *do* remember you'll have six of her best friends to answer to if you don't make sure she enjoys it. You are more than welcome to enjoy the hospitality of our home and anything else she wants you to enjoy."

"Lajos . . ." Pausing to yawn, Baubin scratched his short-cropped head and nodded politely at the remaining member of Migel's entourage. "It's a bit late to try and find your way back to your ship in a foreign city. You're welcome to stay here. The couch in the parlor is more than comfortable enough for napping, so you should be able to sleep comfortably on it. I'll get you some blankets and a pillow as soon as these two clear out."

Blushing, Nevada rose from the end of the lounging chair she was sharing with Migel. Cotter snagged her around the shoulders as she started to pass him. He smacked a kiss on her cheek and murmured in her ear before she could move on.

"Just remember all that I told you about men, and you'll do fine," he encouraged her beneath his breath. "But don't use all of it at once, or you'll kill him."

Nevada laughed and hugged him back. Slipping free, she caught Migel's hand and led him to her bedchamber. *Finally! My turn to make the others roll their eyes at the noise we'll be making. I hope.* She didn't want to get this wrong. A glance at the Guardian of Althinac showed his tanned cheeks were a little pink, but he was smiling just as much as she was. *Good. He's not objecting in the least.*

She couldn't remember even half of what Cotter had told her. All her senses were wrapped up in the excitement of finally getting to make love with a man she liked, respected, and found attractive. Touching the crystals just inside the door, she lit up her bedroom and moved to the side, giving Migel room to enter. As soon as he stepped inside, she shut the door and twisted the lock.

Migel lifted one of his dark brows at that, but didn't protest. Instead, he glanced around her chamber, taking in the mix of colors from the chests, bookshelves, paintings, and scrap-quilts adorning the walls. His gaze fell upon her large bed, and he frowned in puzzlement. "Are those . . . *leather* sheets? Are all Menomonites obsessed with leather?"

"Hardly. We just don't have the room to grow fibers for cloth, whether from plants or from animals. Fabric is too rare and costly to waste it on bedding materials, so we usually piece together long strips of eelskin," Nevada told him. "It's very soft and supple, and the sueding process helps keep it from sticking to sweaty skin. Or so I'm told. This will be my first chance to find out."

He looked at her and smiled. "Then I'm honored to help you get . . . wet."

Grinning, she lifted her hands to his face. He wasn't too much taller than her, and it didn't take much effort to tip his head just so and draw his mouth down to hers. His willingness to be drawn into a kiss helped, as did the way he slipped his arms around her waist, pulling their bodies together. With their mouths mating, she tempered her eagerness with a thorough exploration of what kissing was all about.

He detoured after a little while to the side of her throat, nibbling gently with teeth and lips. Nevada reveled in the soft texture of his fabric shirt as he feasted. It was warmer than leather, though not as warm as the skin of his throat. And supple; when she slid her hands to his chest, she could feel the small beads of his nipples beneath it. His own hands played with the fitted leather of her golden rayskin shirt, but the leather was too tough to shift easily, for all that its beaded texture was soft enough to wear.

Taking her turn, Nevada nibbled on his ear, brushing back the exotic, shoulder-length strands of his dark brown hair. It was very unlike hers, which had been cut short in a scale-tooth pattern, with most of her black strands no longer than the width of two fingers. At least he didn't seem to be offended by the shortness of her hair. Nevada knew that a lot of outsiders didn't care for women with short hair, but the Menomonite lifestyle demanded it.

Last year, the rage had been stripes of brightly dyed color; this year, some people were attempting to grow their hair long, following the surface-dwelling fashion preferred by the Pyromancer now living in their midst. The rest had gone back to pattern cuts. Since her soot black hair didn't bleach well and thus didn't dye well, Nevada had rarely bothered with coloring it. She was glad she hadn't done so this time around; she didn't want to scare off the man in her arms. Reclaiming his mouth, she kissed him as best she could.

I'll have to get used to thinking like an Althinac again, she acknowledged, helping him find the cuttlebone buttons holding her blouse in place as their tongues meshed. *I . . . Ooh. Wow. I didn't know he could make my whole body shiver like that, just from touching my bare skin . . .*

Migel broke off from their kiss, pulling back far enough to give her bra a bemused look. "Even your *underwear* is leather?"

"Salmonskin. It functions as a swim outfit, in case I have to go into the water while I'm on the job but don't want to get the rest of my clothes wet. Salmon leather doesn't stretch out of shape when wet, like other leathers usually do," she explained. "Rogen and Dar-shem wear a lot of it, since they're coral masons."

He winced a little at that. "Can we leave the subject of your husbands on the other side of that door?"

She nodded. He kissed her and drew her hands to the ties of his shirt. As much as she enjoyed the feel of all that cloth under her hands, Nevada wanted to touch him when he was naked and eager, too.

Somehow they managed to get from standing by the door to the side of the bed, shedding clothes and footwear with a minimum of fumbling. Nevada didn't know if he or she was the one responsible for getting them onto the bed, just that they were still kissing and touching when they lay on their sides, legs and arms and lips interlaced.

Migel finally eased back with a humming sigh, his hand caressing the curve of her hip. "You are very beautiful, both inside and out, Nevada," he murmured, rubbing his thumb gently along her hip bone, making her shiver. "Even if expediency didn't demand it, I'd still consider marrying you. I'm glad I thought of it . . . if you don't mind my being practical enough to combine both reasons."

Nevada smiled. "Believe me, I understand practicality. And I'd marry you, too, I think, under different circumstances. More romantic ones."

"I think I can make things romantic enough," he murmured, leaning in for another kiss. Shifting the hand on her hip, he tickled her thighs apart. Brushing against her nethercurls, he eased his way into her folds with soft, slow sweeps of his fingertips.

Her breath caught in her throat when he rubbed her peak with the pad of his index finger. It caught again when that same finger dipped into her opening. She liked it, and sucked on his tongue to show her enthusiasm, since it wasn't as if she could say anything in the midst of his kiss. He chuckled and shifted his thumb into play, teasing her clitoris in time with the gentle in-and-out pumping of his finger. Unable to stay still, she let her hips move with the feelings he stirred in her, rocking into his touch.

The urge to reciprocate had her brushing her palms over his skin, exploring the crisp hairs on his chest and the muscles lying beneath. She discovered he was ticklish on his lower abdomen; he sucked in a breath when she teased her fingertips around the dimple of his navel. And that he really liked it when she brushed her knuckles lightly against his shaft, so she did it again, then wrapped her fingers around him and stroked slowly. He was already warm and firm, but under her touch his flesh grew hot and hard.

Migel kissed her harder and added a second finger to the first. It was a tight fit, but he didn't rush, easing his way into her depths. Thumb circling steadily, he kissed his way from her mouth down to her shoulder, then onto one breast. When his tongue flicked out and circled her nipple, matching the movement of his fingers, Nevada cried out. It wasn't a loud cry like Cotter's, and it didn't quite match the bashful wail her bard co-husband gave, but she understood the bone-deep sentiment behind both. Having her breast licked felt just as overwhelming as being shocked by a lightning eel, if one could be shocked in a deliciously pleasant way. Beyond pleasant.

Shifting lower on her body meant shifting out of her grip. Nevada moaned in disappointment, her palms missing the satiny-smooth feel of her new toy. Migel soothed her with little kisses sprinkled across her stomach and nudged at her legs, making room for himself between her thighs. Catching on to what he wanted, she parted her limbs and lifted her knees a little to make the new position more comfortable for both of them.

Murmuring his approval, Migel nibbled on her thighs, licking between nips. His thumb never stopped stroking her flesh. Unable to lie still, needing an outlet, Nevada moaned again. Her fingers fisted in the soft, silvery gray leather sheets, then stroked up her ribs to cup her breasts. The moment he replaced his thumb with his tongue, she cried out, arching into his touch.

Her flesh stung again when he added a third finger. Distracting her with swirling, lapping flicks, Migel coaxed her into arching and moaning more. When he fluttered his fingers deep inside, she squeaked, throat locking in shock at just how *good* that felt—then cried out when he fluttered and suckled at the same time. Blinded by bliss, she drowned in sensation as he did it again and again until she was weak and trembling.

Warm flesh covered her torso. Prying open her eyes, Nevada met Migel's gaze just moments before his hair curtained her from the light and his lips blotted out further thoughts. She could smell and taste herself on him, essence of woman mingling with musk of man. Stroking his hair back from his face, she kissed him enthusiastically despite her passion-sated state.

After a few minutes, he rested his forehead on hers while he shifted his weight, bracing most of it on his forearm and knees. With his free hand, he gently prodded his shaft against her flesh, rubbing it through the moisture still seeping free. Nevada smiled at him, pleased he was taking his time with her.

"Do you want me to reciprocate, first?" she asked. Most of him stilled at her question, though a certain part of him *twitched* against her as he contemplated her offer.

"Later," Migel decided. A shift of his hips, an adjustment with his hand, and he pressed the tip of himself into her. Her body resisted, making her suck in a sharp breath, but he tucked his thumb between them and gently rubbed. Pleased by his care, she tempered her own touches, soothing him with gentle strokes of her hands on his skin rather than trying to excite him.

Between his soft kisses and his gentle touches, his slow entry into her untried flesh took a while, but it didn't hurt too much. By the time he was fully inside, Nevada wanted more than this gentle consideration. Cupping his face, she angled her mouth against his and suckled his tongue. He hummed in appreciation, but didn't move. She tugged gently on his hair. He stayed still inside of her, concentrating solely on their kiss. So she stroked her nails lightly down his back in that stimulating, scratching way her first husband had said most men liked—and he bucked at that. It stung, but it felt good, too.

"Gods!" Head flung back, Migel grimaced, visibly struggling for control. She did it again experimentally, and he swore, panting. "Dammit! Don't do that!"

"Why not?" Nevada asked. "Didn't you like it?"

"Too much," he rasped, shifting to grab her wrists one at a time.

Unable to evade his grasp—not without an actual struggle—she focused on convincing him via words instead. "Well, I liked it, too. Slow and gentle is a good way to start out, and I thank you for it, but I'm interested in something with a bit more vigor now."

"A bit more vigor?" Migel repeated. She shifted her knees, lifting them higher so that she could tilt her hips up into his a bit more, and nodded. So did he. "All right, a bit more vigor, then."

He pulled out partway, then sunk back in with a sigh. It stung and soothed at the same time, like scratching a persistent itch. Releasing her arms, Migel braced more of his weight on his elbows, allowing him to withdraw and thrust with a bit more control and speed. Nevada liked that. She liked the feel of their bodies joining and the sensation of his shaft stretching her flesh to accommodate him. She also liked the way he picked up his pace when she lightly scratched his back again, and really liked how a slightly higher hitch of her hips let him rub against that flutter-spot deep inside.

She liked it so much that when he paused to adjust his weight on elbows and knees, she dug in her nails in protest, not wanting the sensations to stop. Migel groaned and lifted her left leg higher, pulling it up with his hand. Weight braced on his other arm, he pistoned into her, thrusting over and over, faster and faster. Raking her nails from his shoulders to his thighs, she barely remembered to be gentle. The feelings built and built, until once more her eyes rolled up in blissful blindness.

Vaguely, she heard herself cry out; it was hard to hear when her whole body thrummed with pleasure. As she drifted down, he bucked against her raggedly, groaning and collapsing on her, though his hips still twitched a little, trying to press into her those last few times before his own climax deflated his ability to do so. As he sagged onto her, sated, she wrapped her arms around him, enjoying the sweat-sticky way their bodies clung to each other.

After a while, he kissed her softly, gently, then eased out of her and shifted to the side. Their skin clung a little, making the movement awkward, but it didn't matter after she twisted onto her side and cuddled against him. Holding her in the curve of his arm, Migel sighed deeply.

"That was wonderful . . . beyond wonderful. I'd figure out what word would qualify, exactly . . . but you seem to have melted my mind," he muttered.

Nevada chuckled. "Stupendous. Blissful. Definitely something to be repeated twice, and thrice, and a hundred times more, all over again. Especially since next time it won't hurt as much."

He craned his neck, peering at her. "I didn't *mean* to hurt you. I thought I was being careful."

"You were, but first times are inevitably difficult, for one reason or another. I'm glad I shared this one with you," she stated simply, and got squeezed in return. "So . . . how soon do you think we can try it again? Practice makes perfect and all that."

He laughed. "I'll need at least a few minutes more. Besides, he was right . . . uh, the one, Cotter. *Some* people do have to work tomorrow. I'm presuming that 'some people' includes you, so you'll need your sleep."

"Cotter and I work in the same guild. He can tell the others why I'm not coming into work for my next shift—the diplomatic reasons," Nevada clarified quickly, "not the personal ones."

"Good. I'd rather no one cast a giant, flashing illusion over the city blazing, *'Migel slept with Nevada!'* It's bad enough I'll have to share you with six other men, even if only for as long as it takes us to get married and for you to divorce them," he said.

"I'll miss them," she murmured. "They aren't husbands in the fullest sense of the word, but they are my friends."

"Once we get Althinac fully settled down and the people accepting our joint leadership, we'll be able to come back and visit them. Or they can come and visit us, which would be easier," he pointed out. "They obviously care about you, and I can't begrudge them that."

Pleased, Nevada cuddled closer. "Thank you. I know it's not your culture, and this one shouldn't have been mine, but it is a part of my life."

"I'm just sorry my relatives decided to be so brutal in their objections to your family's rulings. Your next-mother was a terrible influence on your father and his policies, and I think she got what she deserved for all the misery she caused, but they shouldn't have tried to kill *you*. Not when you were innocent of all wrongdoing."

"I think we should leave discussions of politics and history outside the bedroom," Nevada decided after a moment. "It sort of ruins the mood."

He chuckled and pulled her close enough to kiss the top of her head. "You're right. My apologies. We'll be all serious and sober to-morrow. Tonight, we make love."

"*Is* it love?" she heard herself ask, and flushed at her temerity.

Migel didn't prevaricate. "I think it is. One of its stages, at any rate. You are a very lovable woman, Nevada, and I do admire you. I have for a long time. This . . . just makes it all the better."

"I feel the same way. About you," she added, just in case he thought she was being narcissistic. Squirming up onto her elbow so that she could lean over him, Nevada started exploring the fine, dark hairs on his chest with her fingertips. "I also think it's about time I recipro-cated. Don't you?"

His grin was answer enough.

"NEVADA? I'm Socorro." The Althinac woman held out her hand in greeting as Nevada descended the steps of the Congregation Halls, having successfully petitioned the council for the terms of her im-pending divorce and relocation.

"Yes, I remember," Nevada admitted, clasping hands. "I didn't mean to ignore you yesterday. It was rather rude of me, the way Migel and I just kept talking . . ."

Socorro shook her head quickly, making her long, dark braid bounce a little. Dressed as she was in a fitted Althinac gown and corset, both made from fabric, she was drawing a lot of attention from the Menomo-nites passing them on the steps up to the halls. "No, you had a lot on your mind last night. And a lot in common with my cousin, it seems."

Nevada smiled. "Thank you. We'll try not to monopolize every-thing again."

"Well, if *I* could monopolize you for a little while," Socorro teased, "I have some gifts I promised to pass along to you. Most of them are from the loyalist faction, though a few come from the moderates among the rebels. A set of clothes in the Althinac style, some trinkets and jewelry, that sort of thing. When my cousin told me what he had planned, I didn't know what sort of culture you'd be living among, and figured you'd want some Althinac finery so you'd feel more like you'd fit in when you return with us. Men don't usually think of such things, you know."

"That's very kind of you. I'd like to see what you brought," Nevada agreed. "I've missed wearing skirts. They're not very practical here in Menomon, not when the fastest way from one point to another sometimes means literally swimming to get there. Are they on your ship or . . . ?"

"I brought everything down to my guest room in the Flame Tower earlier this morning. I'm told you didn't have anything like a hotel until recently, just a temporary housing hostel for newly arrived citizens," Socorro said.

Nevada demurred. "Menomon has had good reason for isolating itself over the years," she said, turning and heading toward the tower in question. "Which means we don't have a lot of outside visitors passing through."

"That's understandable. I trust you have the same sort of water-breathing spells enveloping your city environs that we do," Socorro added, gesturing at the hydrostatic dome sheltering the section of city they were in, separating the air-filled spaces of Menomon from the water-filled ones. A second dome was vaguely visible beyond the first, sheltering the city from the sheer weight of all that water overhead.

"Of course. Our water-breathing spells are rather extensive, in fact. This general section of the Sun's Belt Reefs is easier for ships to traverse than other sections, but easier isn't the same as easy. Every year, a couple of ships sink as they try to ply their trade routes between the Aian and Katani continents . . . which is why housing is at such a premium right now. This way to the Flame Tower," Nevada added as Socorro started to turn the wrong way.

"That way? But the tower is visible over this way," Socorro countered, pointing at the granite edifice on the far side of the plaza from the Congregation Halls.

"If you go that way, you'll have to pass through a hydrostatic barrier and swim for about fifty lengths," Nevada told her. "If you go this way, it only adds another hundred lengths to the walk and we'll stay perfectly dry—Menomon is a bit of a maze, I'm afraid."

"A bubble-filled maze," the Althinac woman agreed. "Over half the buildings, I wouldn't even know they *were* buildings, if it weren't for those silvery barriers keeping the water off the balconies. Even that new tower we docked at has coral growths on it, and I was told it was finished only a few months ago. Coral usually takes years to grow just a few finger-lengths."

"Normally, yes, but Menomonites have learned how to influence and enhance the growth patterns of marine life. A lot of the coral you see on the Flame Tower has actually been transplanted from elsewhere and literally cemented into place," Nevada told her. "They're having more of a problem doing so with the desalinator, since the intake tunnels have to be coral-free to allow maximum freshwater processing, yet the exterior of the building has to be merged with the appearance of the rest of the reef, as set down in the city's construction policies— Where exactly are your quarters? We'll need to pick the right turning, up ahead."

"The West Buttress," Socorro stated, pointing at one of the smaller support towers ringing the spire of the Flame Tower, visible now that they had taken the U-shaped detour of barrier-sheltered streets to get to it. "We couldn't even see the Flame Tower until we were almost on top of it, thanks to some sort of disguising spell, but now that we're here, it's quite gorgeous. Almost reminiscent of some of our Althinac towers."

"I remember them," Nevada agreed, smiling. "Just as I remember what it was like to wear a dress made of fabric. I was only a little girl when I left, but I do miss seeing the dresses."

"Then you'll definitely enjoy the clothes I brought. We'll have to gauge sizes, of course; just because you see someone in a mirror-scrying looking about your height doesn't mean the focal point of the mirror isn't magnifying the view." Catching Nevada's hand, Socorro smiled and led her into the West Buttress entrance. "We can leave the politics to the others for a few hours; for now, we're just a couple of women about to try on a bunch of clothes!"

Grinning, Nevada followed.

NEVADA politely smiled and waved to one of her tenement neighbors. The older woman was staring at her gown, a rippling concoction of light blue silk cinched by a black stomacher corset. The underbust construction emphasized her waistline, giving her figure more of an hourglass look than it usually possessed. The corset also made her look exotically foreign, compared to the other woman's sensible salmonskin vest and pants. Then again, everyone had stared at her on the way here, some people even following her a short distance, asking questions about her clothes.

"Lovely, isn't it?" Nevada asked, setting down her sack of new clothes and twirling yet again to display the gown. The sleeves were fitted down to her elbows, from where they flared out to the cuff in a fluttery, trumpetlike shape. The bodice fitted snugly to her breasts, thanks in part to the stomacher, and the skirt flared out from her hips, slightly longer in the back than in the front, allowing it to trail a little on the ground. Her brown stingray sandals didn't quite go with the look, but she did have a pair of black ones in her quarters.

"It's not very practical," her neighbor muttered, though envy was evident in both her gaze and her tone.

"It's Althinac. Half their city's on the surface. They don't have to worry as much about swimming to every place," Nevada pointed out. Actually, it was probably only a third of the city that existed on the surface, but it wasn't necessary to be accurate at the moment. Picking up her bag, she unlocked the door of her tenement and stepped inside.

The moment she shut the door, alone for the first time in several hours, she realized the corset was starting to feel a bit tight. *I guess I'm just not used to wearing the things. Not that I wore them this tight as a child,* she reminded herself, heading toward the parlor and the hallway to her bedroom. *But it's definitely beginning to get to me . . . I'd better get it off soon, and let my ribs breathe. But first, I just have to show it off. A pity everyone else is still at work at this hour . . .*

"Dar-shem?" she called out, checking the glow of the nearest wall clock. The constriction of her corset was really beginning to get to her. "Are you up yet? Dar-shem?"

Guessing he was still asleep, Nevada headed for her bedroom. Her ribs were beginning to ache now, making each breath a struggle. *I definitely have to get this thing off. I'll show it to everyone later. I— Ow!*

The corset constricted abruptly, startling and scaring her. *Oh, Menos! Ow! I can't—I can't breathe! The laces . . . I— OW!* Dropping the sack of clothes, she tried to reach the laces before the boned corset could crush her ribs . . . and *felt* them slither as they tightened further, entirely of their own volition. Gasping for breath, she stumbled against the wall just inside her bedroom door.

"Dar . . . Dar-shem . . ." Chest wracked with compressed pain and vision blurring at the edges from lack of air, Nevada went for the only thing that could help her. With the last of her strength, she stumbled to her vanity table and dragged it to the ground with her in a crashing, tumbling mess.

❧

"Easy . . . don't move just yet . . ."

Hearing Dar-shem's voice, low and soothing, Nevada relaxed into the soft bedding supporting her. Her chest ached abominably, but she could breathe freely. Prying open her eyes, she found both him and a purple-clad healer bent over her. The healer was swabbing something along her right side. "You . . . you heard me. Good."

"I'm glad I did. I thought you were an intruder when I woke up from the noise you made— Don't move," her dark-skinned co-husband said soothingly. "That thing that was throttling you broke seven of your ribs before I could get it off. I've mirror-called for the Mage Guild to send over a team to investigate it. Cotter's on his way, too. From the looks of it, there was some sort of spell woven into the cord of the lacings; I couldn't cut them with my knife, so I had to cut through the corset itself . . . so you also have a long gouge on your side. Sorry."

"It will heal scarlessly, *if* you lie still," the healer added pertly, dabbing on the last of whatever salve she was using. "And no vigorous activity for at least a full day, preferably two. I've set and spell-healed your ribs, but they'll still need time and a couple of bone-healing potions to finish strengthening."

Nodding, Nevada closed her eyes again. She knew she had almost been killed by the enchanted corset, yes, but she also knew she was safe. At least for now. At some point, she would have to find out who enchanted those laces and why. Socorro didn't have any magic, at least as far as Nevada had sensed. At the ninth rank, she was strong enough to sense the presence of a fellow mage. So it had to have been the work of someone else. *The question is, who?*

Besides, she was so nice to me . . . It had to have been someone who enchanted the clothing before handing it over to bring to me. One of the rebel faction.

She felt Dar-shem kiss her on the forehead, and let her questions go. Her ribs still ached, her side tingled from whatever salve the healer had applied, and she didn't have the strength to worry over what had just happened.

After my nap, Nevada decided. *I'll figure it all out after my nap . . .*

ALL six of her husbands rose when she finally entered the parlor. Seven, if she counted her husband-to-be. The eighth man was Sierran, and bodies nine and ten crowding her family's living room were the guardian apprentices Koranen of Nightfall and Danau of the Aquamancer Guild. After a restful, spell-enhanced nap, Nevada felt better about her ordeal, but the grim expressions on the men and woman in her home reminded her of how close she had come to being crushed to death.

Nodding politely to the apprentices, Nevada took the seat Migel offered to her. "Well. What have you found out?"

"The lacings were enchanted with a Fortunai pattern-woven spell," Apprentice Koranen stated. "I had to consult with my twin on it, since it's not too common in this half of the world, but the spell was literally woven into the lacings when they were made."

"They were set to trigger when the wearer was alone," Apprentice Danau added, her tone grim. The petite redhead had warmed up a bit—socially speaking—after her visit to Nightfall and subsequent marriage to her singular husband, but she was still cool and unflappable when on the job.

Nevada hadn't interacted with her overly much, since the Aquamancer Guild handled a completely different set of magical needs for the city, but neither had she shunned the other woman for being born different. It was a good thing, too; combined, Danau and Koranen were at least as powerful as Guardian Sheren. Together, the two of them had enough power and knowledge to dissect the magics involved in Nevada's brush with death.

She turned her attention to the cause of her suffering. The disenchanted tangle of black threads lay on a silver tray on the low drinks table between them. Next to them on the tray lay a jeweled silver hair comb. The comb was set with beautiful, gleaming rubies. Their red glow compared favorably with the bowl of apples sitting next to the tray, for all that most of the gems were barely a quarter the size of Nevada's littlest fingernail.

Talladen had brought the apples home with him the moment he had gotten word of what had happened. He was sweet like that, remembering even in the midst of a life-threatening crisis that Nevada liked apples. The hair comb had puzzled her from the moment she had been given it; her hair wasn't long enough to use it, but Socorro had insisted she accept the gift of it anyway. The comb was the kind that Nevada remembered Althinac women liked putting into their long hair for ornamentation whenever they pinned it up.

She *would* have tucked it into her hair if she'd had enough to hold it, but she didn't, so she hadn't even picked it up. Socorro had tucked it into her bag of things, along with her new fabric clothes. Now, as the shorter of the guardian apprentices continued, Nevada was glad she hadn't handled it.

"When we checked the bag of clothes for other dangers, we found that. The hair ornament was also tainted with magic. In specific, a spell-trapped poison, which like the corset was meant to be activated once you were completely alone," Danau explained, glancing briefly at her husband, Koranen, before returning her attention to Nevada. "Had your hair been long enough to tempt you into using it, either one could have killed you swiftly enough, but the combination of poison and constriction would have killed you before anyone could have saved you, even had they been in the next room waiting for it to happen."

Nevada shuddered. She felt Migel touching her shoulder. At the same time, Cotter reached over and touched her hand, both of them giving her comfort. Of all of them in the room, only Migel and Koranen had hair long enough to have pinned up, though Danau's hair was almost long enough. But Nevada did remember a time when she, too, had once possessed locks long enough to dress with ribbons, pins, and combs.

"Whoever planned this is a criminal under both Althinac and Menomonite law," Migel stated. He lifted his chin slightly. "Their opportunity to do so was in part my responsibility, for having had the idea to come here at all. I'll undergo any questioning you have by Truth Stone, and I'll command everyone who came with me to undergo it as well. Since the crime was committed in Menomonite territory, we will submit to Menomonite justice. All I ask is, if you're going to arrest me, let me make a mirror-call back to Althinac to let them know of my absence."

Strangely enough, it was the normally sober Danau who smiled. "I don't think arresting any of you would do our political ties any good. At least, not without solid proof first. Even the city council has been forced to admit that total isolation isn't good for us. But we *will* question everyone, including yourself. Starting with you, in fact. *Husband?*"

Nevada bit the inside of her lip. Danau still sounded a bit smug whenever she said that word, for all it had been months since their return from the distant island of Nightfall. The poor woman had suffered from an excessive affiliation with aquamancy, to the point where she literally had problems regulating her body temperature, making it impossible for her to be intimate with anyone. Her husband had suffered in the same way, only from his affinity for pyromancy, in the opposite direction from the chief aquamancer of Menomon. Together, they made the perfect couple, even if they were rather monogamous about it. Scandalously so, by Menomonite culture.

Fishing a white marble disc from the pouch at his waist, Apprentice Koranen tossed it at Migel. The Guardian of Althinac caught it with both hands. Missing his touch on her shoulder now that his hand was otherwise occupied, Nevada listened to him test the stone's enchantment.

"I am a shellfish." A quick check of the smooth-polished stone showed a blackened imprint where his fingers had pressed during his absurd statement. It faded within moments, and Migel nodded, gripping the stone again. "I am Migel of the family Althec, Guardian of Althinac, and I came here to convince Nevada of the family Naccara to wed me and help rule at my side, with the intent that the joining of our two families would convince our war-torn people to join back together. I did *not* come here with the intent to harm her in any way, nor would I have allowed anyone else to come for that purpose, had I known about it at any point."

Displaying the Truth Stone showed everyone it was white. His words were true. He handed the stone back to the pyromancer, who nodded and tucked it back into his pouch. "Right. One down, and almost a dozen more to go, including the crew of your ship. The first suspect is your cousin. I'll—"

The chimes for the front door rang, cutting him off. Kristh shrugged and rose, heading down the entry hall to the right to answer it. A murmur of voices lasted only a moment, then he closed the door and led their prime suspect into the parlor. Socorro greeted everyone with the same friendly smile she had sported from the beginning. "Hello, everyone! Did you get to see Nevada's new clothes?"

"More of them than we wanted," Cotter muttered, glaring at her.

"Here, hold this," Apprentice Koranen told her, pressing the disc into her hand before she could see what he was handing her.

She blinked down at it, then looked up at him. "What's this for?"

"The truth," Rogen growled. Like her other husbands, he was still incensed at how close Nevada had been brought to death. "Did you deliberately bring clothing which was enchanted to throttle its wearer? In specific, to choke our wife, Nevada?"

Socorro blinked, her smile wavering with puzzlement. "Why would I do that?"

"Answer the question, yes or no," Koranen directed her. "Wait, you're wearing rings. Take them off first."

"My rings?" Socorro asked, glancing down at the gemmed metal circling three of her fingers. "Why?"

"We had an incident on Nightfall involving rings that thwarted Truth Stone scryings. Migel wasn't wearing any when we questioned him, but you are. Take them off or be held in contempt of Menomonite law," Danau ordered.

Shrugging, Socorro complied. Setting her rings on the table, she gripped the truth stone. "I was not aware of any particular item which was enchanted to throttle or otherwise harm a particular wearer." Unfolding her fingers, she showed the unblemished marble to the others in the room. "Is that your only question?"

"Were you aware of a plot by anyone else to harm Princess Nevada Naccara?" Sierran asked.

Socorro gave him a sardonic look. "I'm an Althinac. We've been embroiled in a civil war for the last twelve years, and I'm a part of the family doing its best to overthrow the Naccaran bloodline. Of *course* I knew of plots to harm Nevada! I've been hearing of plots to try and find her and hopefully eradicate her for almost half of my life."

"I don't think we need to check the Truth Stone for the veracity of *that* statement," Koranen muttered dryly.

"Well, that's what most of them were. Just plots," Socorro pointed out tartly, setting down the admittedly unblemished stone and picking up her rings from the table. "I'm sure the rest of you have indulged in idle speculation a time or two. Any other questions? No? Mind if I put my rings back on?"

Yes, I have a question, Nevada thought, distracted by an ache in her gut that had nothing to do with having her ribs crushed by a silly garment. *When is dinner?*

Guessing that no one had started it while she napped, she sat forward to reach for an apple. Her ribs immediately protested, just as they had protested when she had tried slipping her bare feet into a pair of sandals before coming out of her bedroom. At least Dar-shem had done a thorough job of cleaning up the broken toiletry bottles she had knocked off of her vanity table, so that she didn't have to. And the healer had done a good job of reknitting and strengthening the bones, though her chest would still be tender for days to come. But she was hungry. She tried leaning forward again and sucked in a sharp breath, sinking back in her seat.

"What's wrong?" Migel asked her.

"Do you need the healer again?" Dar-shem offered.

"No, no; I'm fine. Or I will be. I was just hungry, and wanted an apple," Nevada muttered, sitting back.

Talladen got up to fetch her one, but Socorro was closer and faster. Plucking one from the bowl, she turned and offered it to Nevada. The suspicious stares from Nevada's husbands made her heave an exasperated sigh.

"It is *just* an apple. She wanted one, so I was going to fetch her one. But if you're worried that it's somehow poisoned—see?" Bringing the fruit to her lips, the Althinac woman took a large, crisp-cracking bite out of the ripe red fruit. Chewing, she displayed the fleshy white interior. "Af you can fee," she mumbled around her mouthful, "it'f perfectly fafe to eat."

Handing the bitten fruit to Nevada, Socorro folded her arms defiantly across her chest. Nevada eyed the apple warily, but not because she feared it was poisoned. Not after that demonstration. She just wasn't in the habit of eating fruit which someone else had bitten into. She turned the apple around to the unblemished side and bit into it, enjoying the sweet-tart smell.

Mere moments after she swallowed that first bite, the world went numb. It didn't hurt, like the corset had. But she was aware of a sudden inability to breathe, of the lax muscles of her arm which let her head loll back and the fruit drop from her fingers. Dimly, she heard her husbands shouting her name in alarm, felt Migel's hands touching her, scooping her out of her chair. She heard the sizzle and crackle of hastily applied spells, but she couldn't do anything, couldn't react, couldn't even see as her eyelids drooped shut under their own lax weight. Even time itself seemed muddied, bogged down by whatever spell or poison had her in its grip, until every second she lay there seemed to devour whole minutes of everyone else's time.

Am I dead? she wondered. *Or at least dying? Is that . . . Is someone crying?*

Lips touched her mouth, as did the salty wetness of tears. She recognized Migel's touch, though she had only known it for a single night, and she hadn't heard him sob before now. The world swayed and the noises went away, though she could still feel Migel's presence at her side.

Someone shouted something close by, startling her. She couldn't react, but the strong voice did pull at her consciousness, bringing back pain and life as it sucked the numbness out of her. Within a minute, she could draw a deep, rib-aching breath on her own, replenishing her air-starved lungs.

Cracking open her eyes, she found herself back on her own bed, with Migel holding on to her left hand and a stranger with long, light brown hair standing at her right side. A power crystal, of the usual egg-shaped sort used to collect and store magical energy, hovered in the air above his hands. But instead of the brighter hues of pure power she was used to seeing, the crystal was being filled with a sickly, greenish darkness, a darkness that the crystal sucked up out of her body as it slowly hovered its way down her legs. The faint glow of the clock crystals on the wall showed she had been drifting in her strange state of numbness for several hours.

Once the last of that darkness left her, Nevada felt disturbingly light-headed. The last time she had felt this way, she had spent too much of her magic on tasks for the Mage Guild, yet all she had done was lie here, almost dead. The stranger with the light brown hair and the oddly familiar features muttered something to end whatever spell he was using and fitted a thick-padded silk bag around the crystal, moving with deliberate care to avoid touching the hovering, malevolently dark green orb. Before she could summon the strength to ask him who he was and what was happening, he gave her and Migel a polite nod and left her bedroom.

She licked her lips. "What . . . ?"

"We thought you were dead at first. But the healers found traces of life still in your body. You were soul-sickened by a combination of poison and spell, one specifically targeted to the Naccaran bloodline," Migel told her. His voice was rough and his eyes red, his touch gentle but trembling as he caressed her cheek. He gave her a wavering smile. "The Guardian of Menomon discovered it was a poison meant to bind to your magic and suppress it, mimicking death. But you weren't *dead*, just very deeply asleep. Almost in stasis."

"Sounds . . . pleasant," Nevada murmured.

"You would have slept for a hundred years while the poison worked its way through your magic, if Menomon's Guardian hadn't remembered a description of something similar happening to another mage long ago, in some of the city archives, the story of a beautiful young woman being poisoned by an older rival and cursed to sleep for a hundred years. Guardian Sheren arranged for her apprentice's twin to come all the way out from Nightfall Isle and clean it from your system, since she isn't quite as confident of her powers as she used to be, and this other mage apparently has enough power and control to extract the poison without killing you or risking himself.

"But while this Morganen fellow did save your life, he had to drain you of all of your excess magic and a good portion of your life energy, too," Migel murmured. "I'm afraid you won't have any energy reserves for at least a week, if not longer."

"And I'll be . . . *ravenously* hungry," she managed, already feeling her body beginning to shake from hunger.

"Never fear, we have just the cure for that," a voice from the doorway proclaimed. Cotter came over to the bed, sitting down at her side, a bowl of what looked like mushed peas and other things cradled in his hands. "Raw vegetable pease-pottage, otherwise known as the ultimate in baby food for starving, power-exhausted mages. You're lucky that most of these fresh, ripe vegetables you'll be eating for the next three days were ones our kind mage guest brought. Otherwise they'd have cost me two weeks' pay, given they're outside the Menomonite harvesting cycle. Open up now, there's a good mistress . . ."

Too hungry to care what it tasted like, Nevada complied. The mush on the spoon was as messy in taste as it was in appearance, but her body recognized the nutrients it craved even as her tongue rebelled at the texture and flavor. Eating each spoonful her first husband fed to her, she listened as Migel cleared his throat and continued.

"It, ah . . . it turned out my cousin has been hiding the fact that she's a mage all this time. She had built up a false personality to wear like a shell, which allowed her to successfully lie while using the Truth Stone—as well as some very tight, camouflaging shields to disguise her aura—some of the Althec family mages discovered her aptitude as soon as it manifested, and chose to train her in secret, to hide her abilities so that they could have a hidden weapon in the civil war. Someone no one would suspect as a mage, because she'd never displayed her powers as a mage where anyone outside of a rare few in the family would see them."

Migel caught a bit of mush that had landed on the edge of her lips and gently scooped it inside. Nevada managed not only to accept it, but to nibble on his finger a little. He blushed, and Cotter cleared his throat.

"Now, now, children; she's not in any shape for such activities. And certainly not while I'm in the room, thank you. I may be married to her, but I'm not interested in ogling her charms. Time for a sip of water," he added.

Migel helped Nevada sit up a little more, allowing Cotter to bring a glass of water to her lips. The Althinac mage shook his head as Cotter resumed feeding her. "I shouldn't have come here. I shouldn't have put your life at risk . . . It was a stupid plan, and I'll not hold you to any of it."

He got up from the bed. With her mouth full of mush-laden spoon, Nevada couldn't speak. Mutely, she glared at her husband. Cotter nodded, understanding what she wanted.

"If you set one foot outside this bedroom, Guardian, I'll be forced to challenge you to an Arcane Duel," Cotter warned the other man just as he started to open the door.

Spinning on his heel, Migel eyed him askance. "*You?* Challenge *me?* Even adjusting for the differences between Althinac and Menomonite gauging standards, you're less than a third my rank!"

"Yes, and I'm barely even half of her rank," Cotter agreed, unperturbed. "But I *am* her husband, and since she's not in any shape to protest this asinine idea you have about leaving her—save your strength, dear," he warned Nevada as she swallowed, preparing to speak—"it's up to me to champion her and knock some sense into you. Especially since you were trying to make a unilateral decision about leaving her, when you came here to become one-half of a *team.* Besides, it's not *always* about sheer, raw, magical strength."

Migel snorted. "In an Arcane Duel, yes it is!"

"Not if you're a sneaky son-of-a-squid like me: I *cheat.*" Popping another spoonful into his wife's mouth, Cotter winked at her. "*And* I'd involve my co-husbands. Even if they aren't mages, they won't let you leave without a fight. You're the husband our Nevada actually wants, and as far as we're concerned, whatever Nevada wants, Nevada gets."

"So, what, I have no say in the matter?" Migel demanded, hands going to his fabric-clad hips.

"Not if you know what's good for you. Moreover, we took a vote just now, and it's decided. Rogen and Dar-shem will be staying here, because they're needed for the work on the desalinator. The rest of us, Baubin, Kristh, Talladen, and myself, will be accompanying you back to Althinac. That way you'll know Nevada has four bodyguards who are unswervingly loyal to her . . . and by extension to you. But only so long as you keep her happy," Cotter warned Migel, his expression sober. "Stabilizing the politics of Althinac is an important task, and having a Naccaran back in power—or rather, in co-power with you— will help with that. So no more talk of leaving her behind. Or us. Not even if she does divorce us. Not until the situation in Althinac is firmly stable. *Then* we'll consider moving back."

"Why?" The question came from Nevada, and even she was a little surprised to hear herself ask it. But she was curious and wanted to hear Cotter's answer.

"Because without you, *we* wouldn't have found our own happiness in one another. Even if it took us some relationship juggling at first. Migel makes *you* happy, and you make him happy. It's a good match. Now eat your mush." Cotter looked at the other man in the room. "One more question, Guardian. Do you love her?"

"Of course I do! Why else would I want to avoid endangering her, even at the expense of Althinac's future tranquillity?" Migel asked.

"And do you love him?" Cotter prodded, tucking another spoonful between his wife's lips.

Not wanting to choke on a purée of pungent, raw vegetables, Nevada merely nodded.

"Good. All else is just a matter of logistics. Here, *you* feed her," Cotter ordered, holding out the bowl. "I'm putting you in charge of overseeing her recovery. Rogen and I need to go start getting our co-husbands organized for the move to Althinac."

With a polite nod to both of them and an air of smug satisfaction at having settled everything for them, Cotter left the bedroom.

Bowl in hand, Migel sat down on the edge of the bed. He stared at the smeared contents and sighed. "Do I *have* to be husband number seven even after we've returned to Althinac?"

She managed a small chuckle. As unappetizing as the uncooked mush was, it had given her a smidgen of her strength back. "No. You and I will marry, and they and I will divorce . . . and they'll still come along. As *friends*."

"They do make good friends," he allowed. Scooping up a bit of vegetable paste, he offered it to her lips. She made a face. Migel wrinkled his nose as well, but didn't remove the spoon. "I know this stuff is awful, but you still have to eat it anyway. That Nightfallite mage was very strict about your diet and recovery schedule."

"Migel . . . what will happen to her?" Nevada asked after she swallowed the next mouthful.

"Socorro?" He shook his head. "Sheren and I worked it out. She'll be tried here in Menomon for attempted murder and tried again in Althinac for murder and for breaking the truce, and then she'll be jointly punished. Even if her surface personality didn't know there were poisons and spells in the things she gave to you, her true personality planned and executed everything with the intent to kill. We'll find out who her accomplices were, who trained her, what she has done in the past, and all of them *will* be dealt with," he promised. "Even if they're my own kin. I'm not proud of what my family has done, particularly since I'm the one left cleaning up *their* messes."

"You have new kin," Nevada reminded him, pausing to breathe between sentences. She felt as limp and mushy as the vegetables being spooned into her mouth, but she would regain her strength. "You can be proud of them instead."

"Ah, yes, six co-husbands," Migel muttered.

"*And* a wife—give me a kiss," she demanded as he lifted the spoon to serve her another mouthful. "I need something sweet to clear the taste from my tongue."

"You mean you just want to torture me by sharing it," he murmured. He leaned down anyway, brushing his lips against hers. "Don't ever leave me again, Nevada. You broke my heart when I thought you were dead."

"Not of my own free will, Migel," she promised, and kissed him back as thoroughly as her weakened body would allow. "Never of my own free will."

Sleeping Beauty

Author's Note: My editor and I weren't sure if this series would be called *Sleeping Beauties* or *Bedtime Stories.* Since I needed an eighth story to put on the list—yes, I know it's placed as number five in the book; just go with it—I decided to toss this one in to be on the safe side. Once again, I'm going to flip this over to the science-fiction side of things, because it's fun to do this tale in sci-fi. And, being a rabid equalist at heart, I've decided to flip the story a second time, too. Enjoy!

THE computer controlling the derelict laboratory and its defenses was not actually mad. Leo Castanides patiently reminded herself of this fact yet again as the projections from her headset showed a surrealist's fusion of security codes and bramble vines. *It's not insane. It's merely under the mental control of one of the greatest electrokinetics to ever come out of a Gengin lab . . . or rather, to never leave that lab.*

Lifting her gloved hands, she tried prying two of the bramble vines apart. Once again, the vines writhed and sprouted wicked thorns, trying to scratch and pierce her electronic intrusion, cutting into her code. She reached again, but the protection protocols thickened under the instincts of the dreamer she had been hired to awaken. Beyond the three-dimensional projection overlaying her view of reality, she could see the defensive turrets of the lab's security lasers swiveling her way, and backed off physically as well as electronically.

. . . Which means I am completely outclassed. I'm only half the electro-kinetic this guy was rumored to be, at my very best. Hiding behind the corner of her last secured safe-point, Leo paused to take a drink from the flask at her hip. It contained water only; she never drank while she was on the job. Liquor dulled the wits and the reflexes, inevitably leading the drinker into greater peril. *Just because the Raider Clan hired me to free this man from his stasis prison doesn't mean I'm stupid enough to risk my life heedlessly. They're not paying me enough for that.*

Then again, she couldn't just drop this quest; not everyone had her particular combination of talents. Leo was just barely good enough in reflexes and combat training to have qualified as a Minutemaid by her homeworld's strict standards. If she took on the normal sort of body-guarding and one-man-army mercenary contracts most Minutemen and Minutemaids took, she probably wouldn't survive long enough to go back home at the age of thirty-five and breed the next generation. Assuming she wanted to go back, which she didn't.

What she was really good at were the old computer languages. Ancient tech fascinated her; it was a hobby she had turned into some-thing of a career, raiding archaic tech sites on war-torn worlds and in abandoned spaceyards, places laced with unstable, deteriorating security measures and decay-worn traps. This, the Borgite Project, was the epitome of what she loved. Except this wasn't some mold-ering, hundred-year-old piece of abandoned technology. This was a self-sufficient, still functioning piece of hundred-year-old, lethally guarded research lab.

Not all the Gengin research programs had ended when the origi-nal subjects of the Genetic Engineering Project had rebelled against their captor-creators centuries ago. Enough of the various projects had been segregated in isolated pockets on different worlds to ensure that some of these programs would continue for hundreds of years more.

But as each of those projects was discovered, the Gengins targeted the research labs, freeing the captives wherever possible and inciting those inside to rebel if they couldn't be freed directly.

It had caused a lot of tech to be crippled, abandoned, and lost, with the outer edges of the known galaxy locked in constant pockets of warfare. Only in the Core Worlds was there a long history of peace and stability . . . but in the Core Worlds, there weren't many Gengins living among the Normals. Differences often meant unfamiliarities, and that led to fear and distrust. As much as even the Normals deplored the Gengin Projects, the average Core citizen didn't go out of his or her way to help look for hidden, illegal genetic manipulations.

Sometimes, the Gengins had spontaneously rebelled, and sometimes they had succeeded. The Borgite Project was one such internal rebellion. The researchers' mistake had been to put one of their own creations in control of the security measures. Leo had already seen the evidence in the outer edges of the complex that it had been a fatal mistake for many.

Shen Codah was the name of the man she was looking for, the man with the mind controlling this entire facility. According to the historical records from the escapees, he had wired himself fully into the facility's systems to ensure that his fellow Gengins could escape, but only at the cost of being trapped in the machinery. Some of the researchers and their security personnel had tried to converge on his integration chamber while the others escaped, only to be locked out of his particular lab. Others had tried to pursue the escaping victims of the Borgite Project, or had tried to flee for their lives, only to be locked in.

Only the Gengins had gotten out. Almost all of them save for Shen, and whoever might have died during the escape.

A brave and honorable act on his part, but a damn foolish one, too. He shouldn't have acted until he had constructed a means of his own escape, too. Now he's stuck in this bizarre, programmed dreamscape, metaphors merged with machinery. Until I came along, no one had the right com-bination of talents to get even this far . . . and I'm not even halfway to rescuing him.

She had some electrokinetic abilities as well as an affinity for old programming languages. Just not the strength of this man's mental might. Still, an analysis by the Raider Clan had proven it would take a combination of physical and mental dexterity to breach Shen's de-fenses, and she was their best shot. Possibly the only one who could do it. Considering the pool of talents the Raider Clan had at their command, it was something of a compliment. Maybe.

She had the strength and the speed to dodge some of the physical traps, and the skills to avoid being destroyed by the independently patrolling robots, but even the best of Minutemaids couldn't dodge a dozen simultaneously firing lasers. If she tried to press forward, that was what she would have to face. Lasers which were far more than the original, rough tally cited by the escapees in their accounts of what the place had been like. Which left her with trying to get through the coded defenses, since the physical ones were able to thwart her.

Psychic abilities were rare, though the Psians had been the first of the Gengins to successfully break free of their genetic breeding pro-grams. Like many victims of the various projects, they had retreated to a fringe colonyworld of their choosing, and had kept to themselves. But some had been interbred with other project strains in the early days, in the hopes of broadening the gene pool of psychic abilities. Some of that interbreeding had included the Minuteman Project. For that reason alone, Leo's services came with a very high fee, despite her comparatively mediocre physical skills as a Minutemaid.

Half up front for trying, and half at the end for succeeding. Enough creds to buy myself a small planetoid if I want . . . plus the ultimate prize, political asylum. If I didn't trust the Raider Clan's intentions toward all free-roaming Psians, I'd question why they'd be so willing to pay so much for this particular one.

Checking her chrono, Leo synched up with the less sensitive lab systems, the ones that weren't as likely to kill her. Ears straining for any noise that might come from a patrolling sentry bot, she reviewed the list of places she could get into. *Supplies lists, entertainment library, researcher personnel files . . . though not the files detailing the genetic experiments that were done. Not that I blame him for locking out any information on how he and the others were made.*

A glance around the corner showed the turrets still actively sweeping and the illusionary bramble vines still firmly in place. She eased back before they could flag her as an intruder, and wished she could just wave a truce flag at the security sensors built into the walls. *Turrets and brambles and flags, oh my . . .*

Wait . . . turrets, pennons, brambles, entertainment files . . . She scrolled quickly through the file lists, checking the status of the lattermost. *Yes! He's dreaming right now, and he's still connected to the security systems as well as the entertainment files. I'm seeing actual activity patterns, and recent ones at that. Now the only question is, can I hack into his dreams via those files? Oh, please, let it be so . . .*

It wasn't an overly complex system compared to modern entertainment programs, but it did include full stimuli programs. It also made sense that he would be using the files to keep his mind stimulated and occupied. *He's probably living the ultimate fantasy life, plugged into these entertainment files like a holovid addict. He's not going to welcome me into his sanctum . . . unless . . . Yessss, there it is! There's the holoprogram I want.*

He's trapped and he knows he's trapped, or he did know it at one point. The only way he's going to let me in is if I join in one of his virtual dreams and ride to his rescue like a legendary hero. All I have to do . . . is program . . . some suitable weaponry and armor out of this old code . . . borrowing from this story, and this one . . . integrate it into this file over here . . . and lure him into playing it. And *survive the occasional automated patrol,* she added silently, hearing a faint hum approaching her position. *Supply files, come to my rescue . . . yes! There.*

One of the doors in the hall slid quietly open. Moving near-silently on soft-padded slippers, Leo ducked into what had once been an office and tucked herself into the closet at the back. Shutting the door behind her, she settled cross-legged on the floor of the tiny space and continued her reprogramming.

I'll need some helper programs, in case I get into trouble. I can't tie those directly into the security system, but I can program them to prompt Sleeping Beauty in there to give them access anyway, as a subplot of the story line. Ah, good, as I suspected, he does have a random selector program set up to offer him story suggestions from time to time. If this works, he'll be helping me to rescue him, without being the wiser. And I know he likes this file; he's accessed it several times over the decades, though I don't think he'll be expecting the role-reversal I'm about to pull, let alone like it.

Of course, if this doesn't work, I won't stay alive long enough to uncover his opinion on the matter . . . I'd better hurry; it looks like he's three-quarters of the way through the current accessed file. I'd hop into that one and try to contact him that way if I didn't think his personal security programs would fry me on the spot. Far safer to integrate myself into a dormant program before he accesses it, and just go along for the ride . . .

Shen Codah stared at his face in the mirror with just one thought running through his mind. *I'm running out of time.*

The list of supplies needed to keep his sealed existence going was running dangerously low. He had three years' worth of nutrients in the dwindling storage bays. The power source that supplied energy to the research lab had maybe five years left. The suspension gel hosting his body, that was down to just two years, maybe three if the recycling system didn't break down again. He didn't trust the backups. It didn't matter that he had another seven hundred years' worth of regenerative medicines to keep his body young and fit; the aging of an adult human body could only be slowed by so much.

Here in the Administration Hall—which was nothing more than a simulated projection—he had long ago programmed the system to display his body as it actually was. His short-cropped hair was salted with gray among the stark black, and there were more fine lines beginning to form around his eyes and mouth than he could recall from his last self-examination. As always, his legs, arms, and chest were banded with metal from the sensor probes. Visible reminder of his self-incarceration.

His muscles were still in good condition, since his body did move at least somewhat in response to the scenarios playing through his mind, and the gel provided a decent amount of resistance, keeping his muscles reasonably strong. But while he still felt young enough, he looked middle-aged. Shen wasn't quite sure how many years had passed. He remembered giving up counting somewhere around fifty-six or fifty-seven.

And how many bodies lie dead all around? You couldn't count them, either . . .

Turning away from the mirror, Shen snapped his fingers, summoning up the Realm List. It hung in the air, a familiar holographic projection. He wanted something fantasy this time. Scrolling down through the hovering list, one of the filenames caught his eye; it seemed different, maybe a little bolder in its colors. Not sure if he wanted to enact a fantasy romance right after living through a western scenario, Shen continued down the list . . . and found the same filename coming up again.

That's odd . . . Maybe I just scrolled the wrong way. Again, the colors for the scenario's advertisement looked a little brighter and more lively than the rest. He stared at it, then shrugged. *Why not? I've usually enjoyed this one, with its bit of swordplay and some decent lovemaking.*

But I'll opt for some extra random variability this time. I know all of these programs too well by now on their normal settings.

Opening up the file, he flicked his hands, tapping hovering check boxes and shifting holographic sliders almost randomly. Slapping the start lever, Shen watched as the marble and glass hallways of the Administration Hall swirled and dissolved. But instead of the green meadow he usually appeared in, he found himself standing in a castle bedchamber—*the* castle bedchamber, in the highest room of the tallest tower, where the sleeping princess usually lay.

Frowning, Shen turned around, examining his surroundings. The fanciful canopied bed was over there, neatly made with crisp white sheets and a blue velvet coverlet. The chests of gowns and jewels sat neatly against the walls, which bore brightly woven tapestries, and in one of the window alcoves sat a spinning wheel, waiting for the princess to prick her finger upon it. Only he couldn't see the princess.

A glance down at his body showed it neatly clothed in the ancient garments that went with this setting, a red and gold doublet and matching striped hose. Red leather slippers protected his feet, and his waist was girded with a gold belt. But he wasn't wearing armor, and he wasn't carrying a sword.

"Computer! How am I supposed to rescue the princess like this? What role am I playing?"

Even the voice of the computer was different, feminine instead of masculine. *"You are playing the role of the Sleeping Beauty. Your rescuer will enter gameplay once you prick your finger and lie upon the bed."*

"And wait a hundred years? *No*, thank you," Shen muttered. "But at least this version is different . . . Computer, override any protocols which would automatically put me to sleep as the main character, Sleeping Beauty. Plus any protocols which would try to make me play out the hundred years of enchanted sleep in real-time. I'm doing enough of that on my own."

"Acknowledged."

Glancing at his fingers, he shrugged and crossed to the windowed alcove. Touching the distaff needle with the smallest of his fingers, he felt the mild sting. Virtually, he could see and feel the little bead of blood welling up, but he knew that nothing much had happened to his real body, other than that it had probably moved a bit in the pale blue goo supporting him physically.

One day, it might be interesting to feel real pain again . . . and I probably will when my supplies run out. Peering out the window, he saw nothing but the courtyard of the castle, some landscaped gardens, and trees in the distance. *Time to lie upon the bed, I guess.*

It was a comfortable bed, at least. In previous versions when he had been the prince, he had spent several enjoyable hours seducing and deflowering the real Sleeping Beauty. Stretching out on the velvet bedspread, Shen tucked his arms behind his head. "Computer. Tell me when my rescuer has entered gameplay."

"Understood. Princess Leo has now entered the game."

"Do I have to stay on the bed while she fights her way to the castle?" If he did, he would be utterly bored. *I never really thought of how passive the female's role is, in this particular scenario . . . and what kind of a name for a Princess Charming is Princess Leo, anyway? How far did I throw the normal scenario parameters out of whack, randomizing everything?*

"Consulting . . ."

That was an odd thing for the computer to say. Shen frowned, but it didn't take long for the systems monitoring the entertainment matrix to speak again.

"You are permitted to move around within the royal suite. You may watch the action from the windows. When your rescuer is within one minute of arrival, you will be given a warning to return to the bed and assume the correct position for your role. You will not be released from your prison until you cooperate."

That was a *very* odd thing for the computer to say. Rising from the bed, Shen crossed to the window. In the minute or so since pricking his finger and lying down, a massive wall of brambles had grown up between the castle walls and the forest beyond. He remembered previous versions of this game, the strain of his muscles as he hacked and hewed his way through the enchanted hedge, struggling with the cruel, barbed vines which "magically" slithered and regrew, attempting to thwart any entry. How good it felt to bash and slash, venting his frustrations with this self-chosen solitary existence.

How odd it is that I'm now the Sleeping Beauty. How very realistic, too.

BZZZZAPP!

The windows rattled with the force of the explosion.

What the—?

A huge chunk of thorn-sprouting greenery was now missing, and the edges of the gaping hole were on fire. *BZZZZABOOM!* Another chunk vanished, this time along with a section of outer wall. The windows rattled again and Shen swayed with the force of the explosion.

Staring, he watched the debris fall and the dust settle, revealing a strangely dressed woman. Instead of the armor and tabard of a medieval warrior, she was clad in black leather pants, matching vest, and a ruffled white shirt. Her hair had been pulled into a long blonde braid fastened with a black bow at her nape, and the top of her head bore an odd, triangular hat. In her left hand, she hefted a large canister of some kind, probably a power pack, and in her right, a cone-tipped cross between a small rifle and a handgun.

With the stock of the mini rifle braced between elbow and ribs, she spun to the side and shot the nearest patch of regrowing, enchanted vines, disintegrating them before they could grab and tear into her flesh.

Science-fiction meets fantasy? What random parameters did *I flip?*

As he watched, dumbfounded, she leaped with athletic grace over the rubbled remains of the courtyard wall. Once she was inside the castle boundaries, the brambles subsided as they were programmed to do. Dumbfounded, Shen watched her tuck the gun into a clip on the side of the canister and set it down. Stepping back, she snapped her fingers. Gun and energy canister dissolved, vanishing like a discarded game parameter.

She then tilted her tricorn hat back, shading her eyes peering up the length of the castle. Though he couldn't see her eyes over the distance between them, Shen knew the moment she spotted him at the window. He knew it because she grinned and lifted her black-clad fist, thumb poking up in ancient greeting. Stunned, he stayed at the window as she walked up the steps and entered the castle.

An interactive rescuer?

"This is your one-minute warning. Please lie on the bed and close your eyes so that the next scene may progress."

Bemused, Shen turned to do so. He caught sight of himself in the cheval mirror standing across the room and detoured abruptly. Up close, he could see the gray hairs stippled along his temples in his reflected image. Gray hairs he had seen just minutes before in the mirror in the Administration Halls simulation. *This isn't right . . . I shouldn't look like my real self. I always look young and handsome in these stories, not middle-aged and, well, like me . . .*

The computer spoke up. *"This is your thirty-second warning. Please lie on the bed and close your eyes so that the next scene may progress."*

"Computer, adjust my apparent physical age to about twenty-seven years old."

"Consulting . . . Negative. Your appearance is to remain true to reality. Please lie on the bed and close your eyes so that the next scene may progress."

What? Shen stared at his image, his brown eyes opened wide enough in shock that he could see their whites all the way around. *Something is seriously wrong—*

A knock startled him further. As did the voice, feminine and unfamiliar, calling through the stout oak door. "Hello in there! Could you please lie down on the bed and close your eyes, so I can come in? This door is not going to open until you do, you know . . ."

"You think so? Computer, end program!" Shen ordered. He didn't like the way this entertainment simulation was going.

"Consulting . . ."

"What the—? Computer, end program!"

"Player Two does not concur. Please lie on the bed and close your eyes so that the next scene may progress."

Something was *very* wrong. "Computer! Emergency override, code—"

"F.G. number three, *execute!*"

Shen tumbled backwards under the force of that feminine command before he could complete his own. He thumped onto the bed, arms and legs pulled out by the bonds that abruptly appeared. Before he could regain his breath, a leather strap wrapped around his mouth and a velvet sash covered his eyes, leaving him blindfolded and gagged.

He knew *this* scenario, but not from this side of things. He didn't arrange for it often, and Shen *knew* he hadn't tapped anything remotely like this on the options panels, because he hadn't accessed the subfolders for kinky sex scenarios. Even as he tugged futilely at the bonds holding his now shirtless body to the bed, he heard the door open.

"Thank you for your cooperation. I apologize for the forcefulness of my entry, but the circumstances have rendered it absolutely necessary."

"Comffufer! Wha fe heff if goih om?" Frustrated, Shen yanked at his bonds, but was unable to budge his arms more than a few centimeters. He tried spitting out the leather strap, but that didn't work, either.

The mattress on his left dipped. Fingers touched his face, making him flinch. They didn't harm him, just gently eased the blindfold up over his head. Greenish eyes and a warm smile met his furious glare. She wasn't the prettiest woman the entertainment simulations had ever generated for him, but she was reasonably good-looking for a blonde.

"I'll remove the gag and the other bonds once you've calmed down. In the meantime, you have my word of honor that I don't intend to harm you. Not that I could; this is only a simulation, after all," his rescuer-turned-captor offered wryly. "Allow me to introduce myself. Leo Castanides, Minutemaid and rescuer-for-hire."

"Wha?" None of this was making sense. Not unless his program had been hacked. The last attempt of *that*, however, had been over . . . Shen didn't know, exactly, just that too many years had passed. "Who ah hyu? Ah hyu *reah*?"

She frowned a little in concentration, then smoothed her expression and nodded, comprehending his question. "Yes, I'm very real. If you were to ask the computer how many people are playing in this simulation, it would tell you that there are two of us in here. Well, technically you're in the master control room and I'm hidden in a safe spot roughly halfway into the complex, because that's as close to you as I can physically get without getting killed by the defense mechanisms," the woman Leo added dryly. "But I'm very real, and very much interested in rescuing you. A real rescue, not a simulated one.

"I am here to unhook you from this forgotten machinery you've been protecting, pull you out of the suspension fluid you're floating in, and ensure you get physically back in touch with reality."

Shen stared at her, trying to comprehend her words. *Either I've gone mad . . . or the system is finally breaking down . . . or . . . she really is real, and here to rescue me . . . or she's here as a trick of the geneticists.*

That last one didn't ring very true. No one had tried to get at him for far too many years. Shen stared up at her, this youngish woman, confused.

She leaned over him, and he felt her lips pressing gently against his forehead. That felt . . . real. *Very* real. Only an actual kiss could have felt that good . . . or the simulated touch of another electrokinetic. A long, long time ago, he had interacted with others with similar gifts, geniuses at programming computers to do what they wanted because their minds could literally manipulate the electrons of the various programs. It had been so long, he had forgotten what it felt like.

Leo blushed as she spoke, sitting upright again. "See? I'm not going to harm you."

She has to be real, Shen thought, staring up at her. *She has too many contradictions to be a stable program. The no-nonsense approach, the sudden kiss . . . unless she's a symptom of the system crashing . . . and if it is, I have to fix it, fast. If this program crashes while I'm in it . . . !*

"Let me give you a brief synopsis of the last one hundred and two years. After you sealed yourself into—"

Closing his eyes, Shen concentrated and snapped his fingers, activating the inbuilt, wordless escape program. Three short, three long, three . . .

"*F.G. number thirteen, execute!*"

Shen *oofed* as she dropped on top of him, wrapping her arms tightly around his ribs while the bed and its bonds dissolved.

I can't believe I kissed him! Why in the stars' names did I kiss him? Most of her brain was devoted to wrapping her mental presence into a skin-tight package around the retreating electrokinetic in her metaphysical arms, but a corner of Leo's mind kept repeating that question as virtual existence stabilized around them. *There was no need for me to kiss him, so why did I do it?*

Unscrunching her eyes, aware of a long, lobby-like corridor lined with doors now surrounding them, Leo peered up at Shen Codah's face. He looked stunned that she was still with him—thanks to the coding of her Fairy Godmother program and the way she still had a bit of a death grip on his virtual body—but he was . . . well . . . in a word, handsome. Quite handsome. Quite fit, too; she could tell from his programming that this was a projection of his real body in her virtual arms.

"How did you . . . ?"

"I can explain!" Leo quickly asserted. Her virtual skin was beginning to buzz, a warning that his security programs were trying to lock onto her unauthorized presence. "Just don't shoot me! Pause your virtual security protocols, and I'll tell you everything."

He narrowed his eyes, thinking it over. Leo felt the security programs charging up and whirled them around. He stumbled in her arms, but their sudden change in position confused the intruder *targeting* systems.

"Call them *off*, Shen! The last thing *either* of us need is me dying in here," she ordered.

"If you're an intruder—" he warned.

"—I am your *rescuer*," she countered, jerking them around again as a metaphorical bolt of laser light shot past her waist. "Call them off, and I'll explain! I won't go anywhere or touch anything, I promise!"

Not that she *could*; her ability to be in this corridor, this deep into his systems, depended entirely upon her retaining tight virtual contact with his electrokinetic self-projection. The moment she let go, the moment she tried to look at anything else in this corridor, it would be a race to see which would happen first: her virtual presence being kicked out automatically by the system, or the defense grid vaporizing her mind.

Lifting his hand, Shen stayed the defenses. "Who are you? Who sent you? How did you get in here?"

She relaxed some of her wariness as the buzzing of her skin eased, but she didn't relax her grip. "Like I said, my name is Leo Castanides, and I'm here on behalf of the Raider Clan—they're a group of free

Gengins of broad diversity. They've formed a coalition where our kind can live in peace. No Projects, no breeding programs, and no internal wars for superiority. Just fellow human beings cooperating and getting along. *Some* of them are the descendants of Gengins you yourself freed. As soon as the Raider Clan realized this facility was still active, they hired *me* to break in, find, and rescue you."

"You?" he challenged, shifting in her arms.

Leo didn't let him pull back very far; she had to maintain close contact to maintain this direct link. She tried not to let the projected, firm warmth of his muscles distract her. "I'm an electrokinetic, like you. I've made a hobby of studying archaic tech, and combined with my electrokinesis and my Minutemaid skills, it's allowed me to get into old labs like this one to rescue many of the things we've forgotten or lost over the decades."

Shen frowned. His next question wasn't expected. "How long has it been?"

"Since you locked yourself in here?" Leo asked. "One hundred two years, six months, three days . . . or maybe four by now. I'm getting rather hungry and thirsty, and I haven't had a chance to use a bathroom for several hours. I'd appreciate it if you'd make up your mind to trust me, at least long enough so I *can*."

"You're *definitely* not a malfunctioning program." He stared at her a moment, then glanced down at the tight way she was holding him, still clad in her black-and-white clothes, her breasts pressed to his sternum.

His naked sternum, she realized belatedly. They were too closely pressed together, with her arms wrapped around his bare, steel-banded back, to tell if he was wearing pants or not, but his upper half was definitely shirtless.

"Do you have to hold me so tightly?" Shen asked her.

"It's the nature of my piggyback program. The moment I let go of you, I snap back out of the system . . . and given the sheer strength of the security protocols I've just slipped past, I might be knocked unconscious if I have to do it in a hurry. You have a few too many defense robots patrolling the physical corridors of this place for me to risk losing consciousness.

"I know you don't have reason to trust me," Leo added candidly, "and I wouldn't if I were you, having endured all that you have . . . but part of that lack of trust is your own fault. *You* destroyed all of the external relays that could have connected you with the outside universe. To use the metaphor of that entertainment program we were just in, you were your own evil fairy godmother, and grew your own barricade of briar thorns to keep everyone out."

"I *did* it so no one could override my mind and reopen this facility. I didn't . . ." He broke off and looked past her shoulder. She could tell he wasn't looking at their virtual surroundings.

"You didn't want the sadistic bastards in charge of the Borgite Project getting out and recapturing your fellow Gengins," she stated. He stared at her again. Leo nodded. "Well, you're not the only one who had to kill his creators in order to escape. Or to let others escape."

"So you're really here to rescue a murderer?"

"The first obligation of *all* prisoners is to seek a means to escape, and that includes by any means necessary. You weren't imprisoned because you broke the law. You were imprisoned because you were *enslaved*. You are a human being, Shen Codah, just like everyone else in this galaxy. You have the same right as anyone else to defend yourself, and to defend those around you. You have the right to life, liberty, and the pursuit of happiness—I should know; I'm a Minutemaid," she reminded him dryly. "My progenitors' Project was based on the ancient Earth belief of being ready to fight for one's freedoms and rights on a moment's notice. You fought to give others their freedom, as you had every right to do. Now I'm here to fight for yours.

"But I can't do it without *your* help," she stressed. "Yes, I broke into the entertainment files. And I just about gave myself a headache doing so. I'm surprised I don't have a nosebleed. But this is as far as I can get. From here on in, the physical and virtual security systems are under *your* active control. From what I uncovered in the reports of the fleeing Borgite Project survivors, whatever you did to hook yourself up fully to this complex, it has to be physically unhooked by a second person. But you also sealed yourself in your inner sanctum so that only *you* can unseal the place."

"How do I know I can trust you?" he challenged her, lifting his chin.

"Because I came alone. There were three attempts to get to you, roughly a hundred years ago. The records hold the speculation that the first two failed because you thought both groups were infiltration forces sent from the people backing the Borgite Project. The first two were sent by the Gengins you rescued. The third one . . . *that* group was backed by the Project managers, but civil war broke out on this colonyworld, and this corner of the continent was torched and abandoned. All three times, large groups were sent in to get you, and you treated them like hostile invasion forces.

"In the intervening decades, there were five more known attempts at getting into this facility. Most of them were tech treasure hunters. The only ones who got in past the first layers of security were solitary hunters. They didn't get very far, but it was far enough to know you're still expecting a large force to try to retake control of this place. I took a chance that a single visitor wouldn't trigger a massive counterattack . . . and it's finally paid off. Provided you don't trigger the system to actively hunt me down and kill me."

"I still might. How do I know you're telling the truth?" Shen demanded. He tried pushing her away again, but she clung stubbornly.

Leo kept her eyes locked with his. "Send a robot to sector B, level five, in the southwest room off the junction of corridors five and G. You will find a hardstate scholastic comm unit, one of the old Jayvisi 47s, sitting on one of the desks. I picked the Jayvisi 47 scholastic model because *all* it can do is transmit and receive signals from the hypercomm info channels.

"Pick it up, and do a remote search on all information pertaining to either 'Raider Clan' or 'Enalia System,' which is where the Raider Clan is based . . . or you can even do a search on 'Borgite Project' or the history of this colonyworld. There's no government left on this colonyworld strong enough and rich enough to spend its resources on reclaiming this place. It's a safe method of checking up on all of these things because there's no way the Jayvisi could threaten your control of this facility either; all it does is send and retrieve static information. But . . . do me a favor, and don't break it. Please," she added as he frowned at her. "I only have two of the 47s left in my functioning tech collection."

He gazed off over her head for a long moment, lifting his hand and gesturing with his fingers, then nodded. "I've sent a robot to pick it up. But I can't examine the truthfulness of your claim while you're clinging to me. If you're an electrokinetic like me, you *could* be trying to distort my perceptions of reality versus virtuality."

"That's easily fixed," Leo promised. "Take us back to the Sleeping Beauty program. It's a far less sensitive subsection of the system. I can safely let go of you once we're there, and from there, I can make my way back to my body with no problem—and you *do* want me to get back to my body with no problem for one very important reason: if I'm telling the truth, then I *am* here to rescue you . . . and somehow I don't think that's a chance you'll want to throw away. Not when you're the man who saved three hundred and fourteen fellow Gengins so *they* could have a chance at freedom. Now it's your turn, and you *do* deserve your freedom."

Shen didn't say anything. Lifting his hand, he flicked his fingers. The long corridor they were in dissolved again, and again Leo clung tightly to him . . . until her arms were dragged free by the force of his programming. They *were* back in the Sleeping Beauty entertainment program, but *she* was the one now tied to the bed. Fully clothed, but bound hand and foot to the four posts of the canopied bed and gagged with a leather strap.

He was definitely the better electrokinetic; she hadn't even sensed him reversing their positions in the programming. *Then again, after more than a hundred years, he probably knows everything there is to know about how to program this place on the fly.*

"*You* will stay here until I have examined the veracity of your claims," he ordered.

His hand swept through the air over her body, making her skin tingle from the invisible layers of security he was adding. Her heart skipped a beat, speeding up with adrenaline-tinged fear. Not a lot of fear; she was fairly sure Shen Codah was taking her invasion and her claims seriously enough to investigate in full rather than just mindlessly terminate. But he was definitely the better electrokinetic.

The sight of him stepping back from the side of the bed prompted her to speak. "Heh! Ar' hyu gomma fiff me?"

Shen frowned, confused. "What?"

Leo winced. *Oh, dear stars in heaven, why did I try to say* that? She wanted to berate her subconscious, but he was patently waiting for a reply. As she tried to think of a way to tell him "never mind" without the leather gag muffling it beyond all recognition, he leaned over and tugged the strap out of her mouth.

"*What* did you say?" he repeated.

The tingle of the security measures was still there. Licking her lips, Leo gave in and repeated herself. "I said, 'Hey! Aren't you going to kiss me?'"

The befuddled look he gave her was rather cute. "Aren't I going to . . . ? *Why* would you ask *that*?"

"Well . . . here I am, in a romantic entertainment program, tied spread-eagle to your bed. I'm lying here at the mercy of a handsome man, prepped and ready for you to do all manner of kinky things to me . . . and all *you're* planning on doing is leaving me here alone," she stated as boldly as she could. *In for a processor, in for a program, and all* . . . "It's probably just the setting stirring up the mood, but . . . well, I'm feeling a bit disappointed."

"Disappointed?" Shen repeated skeptically.

"Yes. Disappointed. When I had *you* tied to this bed, bound and at my mercy, *I* kissed *you*. I was just . . . you know . . . Just because I was hired to rescue you doesn't mean I don't find *you*, the person, attractive," she pointed out. Then she shrugged as best she could, given her tied-down status. "Because I do. I *am* human, as well as a Gengin."

He surprised her by kneeling on the bed and bracing his arms on either side of her head. "Tell me, Leo Castanides . . . how much are you being paid to 'rescue' me?"

The question made her smile. It was a lopsided smile, but mostly because she didn't know if he'd believe her or not. "Aside from enough to cover my operating costs? The same thing they pay a lot of the other Gengins who work for them. A priceless treasure beyond compare. There's the sundry fees for itemized expenses, of course, plus hazardous duty and potential medical coverage . . . but the bulk of what I'm being paid, no one else can afford to give me."

"And that is?" he prompted, lowering his head close enough to block out some of the virtual sunlight slanting in through the castle windows.

"A *home*."

He blinked, visibly confused. Leo took pity on him and clarified her meaning.

"The Raider Clan has offered me amnesty and political asylum. Like a distressing number of Gengin settled worlds, my homeworld has turned a bit insular . . . and rather Project-like in its regards as to who can breed and even when. I'm just genetically 'superior' enough to qualify for Minutemaid status, *and* I'm expected to go out and be a Minutemaid, a mercenary-for-hire . . . but *as* a Minutemaid, I'm not allowed to breed until I've proven I can survive to my thirty-fifth year. Plus, once I do, *if* I do . . . I'm supposed to breed only with a Minuteman. While I'm sure any number of my fellow Minutemen are worthy enough individuals, I don't like being *told* I can or cannot do something as intimate as . . . well, intimacy itself.

"There's not a single government outside of the Core Worlds which could offer me a better deal than my freedom to choose my own life . . . and the Core Worlds don't like dealing with Gengins. Particularly not ones who were bred for violent purposes . . . though at least if you *look* like a Normal, they're a little more tolerant."

"It sounds like the universe hasn't changed much in the last hundred years," he muttered.

"Some places are worse. Some places are better." Leo shrugged. "But it's reality . . . and reality will always be more interesting than virtuality. Living in a virtual world is *safer* than reality but it's not actually *living*, is it?"

He stared at her, his short-cropped hair stained gray with middle age at his temples, his expression shuttered, inscrutable . . . and leaned down, touching his mouth to hers. Slanted it over hers, claiming the kiss she had offered. Leo lifted her chin, parting her lips and returning every nip and taste. Holographic or not, he was a talented electrokinetic, putting every sense into full play in his kiss. Touch, taste, scent, sound, and sight—for all that Leo knew she was only seeing and feeling these things inside her mind.

Breaking off the kiss, he backed off the bed, stood, and vanished. Left on the bed, tied and bound, Leo gauged her programming ability versus the tingling pressure of the security programs keeping a close eye on her virtual location. In the end, she stayed where she was. It *was* likely that once she left, she would have a very hard time getting back in again. But that wasn't the reason she stayed.

She stayed because she didn't want to break his trust. Breaking into the entertainment subsystems had been a risky move. Hacking his defenses so that he had taken her with him into the main access command zone had been very risky. But he *was* searching for her Jayvisi comm set . . . and he *had* left the gag out of her mouth.

And he is *one heck of a kisser. At least in virtuality,* she acknowledged. *I hope he believes me, because I'd love to know if the real Shen Codah can kiss like that, too.*

It wasn't as if she had anything else to think of, bound as she was to a bed in virtuality and crouched in a closet in reality.

SHE was telling the truth.

Shen remembered being educated on a Jayvisi 49 model; they were popular with educators because all they did was access information, ensuring that their users studied, and only studied. They were boring for students, because they couldn't be used to communicate. But the scholastic units did connect to the archived files of hundreds of worlds in a vast, redundant library of information. The Jayvisi 47 was old and slow, but it did what it was supposed to do: collect and collate data.

The history of his colonyworld was turbulent. There were now five separate governments, none of them claiming territory within a thousand kilometers of his location, and only three of them strong enough to have reestablished interstellar trade with the other worlds out there. More worlds than he remembered . . . and many of them shattered by civil wars, including his own. The Borgite Gengins had abandoned this world shortly after his self-imposed isolation, but because he had destroyed all means of anyone gaining remote access to his systems, he hadn't known that the old government and its Gengin Project funding had completely collapsed within the first five years.

It was a sobering thought. *All this time . . . all this time I've been barricaded behind my briar thorn walls, sleeping my way through virtual worlds . . . and I could have been free . . .*

Given the layers of security he had cocooned himself in, it would have taken a fellow electrokinetic to reach him. With the other Borgite Gengins offworld and the rest of the planet rocked by strife, no one had made a concerted effort to come back for him, beyond the three group attempts she had listed. That was in the history files, dispassionately collated by the archival programs of the Core Worlds, which even a model as archaic as the Jayvisi 47 could still access. He could even tell who had accessed and collated all that information, and from where, since that was part of the scholastic archive's information gathering parameters.

Who was Leonida Castanides? *Where* was Prism Station in the Enalia System? *Why* . . . was not listed. But he did find a number of footnotes when searching for the "Raider Clan" she mentioned. Some rather interesting history files of their own.

She *was* telling the truth . . . as far as he could tell.

The question now is, what am I going to do about this information? Do I stay where I am . . . safe but running out of supplies and thus out of time? Or do I take the chance that what I've read is real, and risk returning to reality?

Returning to the real world meant disconnecting himself from the facility. After literally more than a century, Shen feared it would be like trying to amputate his own legs. More than that, disconnecting himself didn't mean just freedom; it meant abandoning his sense of safety and familiarity for the unknown.

It wasn't an easy choice to make. *I can't make it blindly. I need to know what awaits me, if I do choose to disconnect. I need something more—a lot more—than an abstract like "freedom." I need . . .*

Snapping his fingers, he rematerialized in the entertainment program. Leonida Castanides still lay on the bed where he had bound her, though she stared up at the canopy with a glazed, unseeing expression.

"Leo?"

She blinked, focus returning to her gaze. Twisting her head, she peered at him. "Ah . . . you've returned—you believe me, too."

"What makes you think that?" he asked warily.

"You're too integrated into these programs not to project your feelings; it's the blessing and the curse of a really good electrokinetic holo-programmer. Now that you *do* believe me, could you *please* deactivate all the security systems and robots in sector C? *Just* sector C," she added quickly.

"Why?" he asked. There wasn't much in sector C beyond some offices, though he did realize there were a lot of remote access sensors in those offices. *That's how she's accessing my virtual zones, isn't it?*

Her answer was fervent. "Because I *really* have to pee, I *don't* want to do it in a corner, and I'm *not* suspended in a self-cleaning biomaintenance tank like you are. And I'd *really* rather not be shot while running for the nearest facilities."

Shen chuckled. He couldn't help it; *none* of his former captors had plea-bargained for bathroom access. Bargained and threatened for other things, but not for that. Lifting his hands, he summoned the security task panels into the entertainment subprogram. "As you wish. Sector C . . . is now in safe mode. You're free to move about the corridors. But *only* sector C."

"*Thank* you!"

Her reply was so forceful, he almost expected her to leap off the bed in spite of her bonds, but she didn't move beyond a few twitches of her muscles. Curious, Shen tipped his head, accessing the cameras in that sector. It took him a few moments to find her in reality, but there she was. A black-and-white-clad woman with an actual ancient three-pointed hat on her head, her blonde hair caught back in a braid, all but sprinting down the hall toward a door marked *Women*.

She did so, he noticed with a twinge of shame, by leaping over a trio of mummified corpses left long ago on the hallway floor, fallen where the security robots had slaughtered them under his control.

I killed all of those people. It was long ago, and it was for a good cause, or so I believed. But . . . I still killed them. Do I deserve my freedom? Do I deserve to live in reality?

Did the real Prince Charming—if there ever was one—ever ask himself if the sleeping princess deserved to be awakened? On the surface, of course she deserved to be awakened; the princess hadn't murdered anyone. His had been a deliberate slaying of hundreds of research workers and guards. *Not to mention, the whole royal court had been put to sleep alongside her, not slaughtered, so that she would awaken surrounded by familiar faces. I don't have that option. Everyone I know is most likely long dead.*

Leo drew in a deep breath, recapturing his attention. She let it out in a long, happy sigh and blinked, refocusing her gaze on him. "*Thank* you. Your civility and courtesy are deeply appreciated. Now. How do we go about freeing you? I know you have to have someone else physically disconnect you, and that only you can let that person into your inner sanctum to do so, but beyond that, the details I researched were rather sketchy."

Shen was somewhat surprised; he had expected her to ask to be released from her bonds first. Folding his arms across his chest, he didn't answer her question. He still had a few of his own.

"*First*, you tell me what is supposed to happen to me after I've been disconnected from this facility. You say you're here to free me, but what then?"

"That's easy. I'm authorized to offer you amnesty and political asylum in the Enalia System, under the governance of the Raider Clan. You'll have a six-month trial citizenship, to include housing, feeding, and rehabilitation services—strictly in the educational sense," Leo clarified quickly. "While the various civil wars have made certain advances in technology sporadic at best as governments collapsed and formed and collapsed all over again, you *have* been out of the loop for slightly more than one hundred years."

"And how do I pay for this housing and feeding and reeducation program?"

"Well . . . the Raider Clan *would* like access to the tech of this place," Leo admitted. "Anything deemed commercially revivable, they'd like to market on your behalf at an even fifty-fifty ratio of the profits above production costs. Plus you'd get free housing beyond the initial six months of your adjustment period, which is how long they calculated it would take you to adapt to the future. If you *don't* want to accept their offer, either of amnesty or of tech rights and split residuals . . . I'm offered to set you up with an official identity as a worldless free-spacer under whatever name you like, arrange for an account in that name filled with ten thousand Core creds—which is the maximum allowable untaxable gift by Core World law, or half a year's minimum wage salary—and give you a lift wherever you want to go, whether on this world or to any other."

"That's it?" Shen asked, taken aback by the offer. "If I don't want to work with this Raider Clan . . . I go free? With money and an identity?"

Leo shrugged. "You don't know how the modern world works, so turning you lose isn't exactly doing you a favor, but you're not being kicked out the door, either. I *wouldn't* advise trying to stick around here. Once you get outside the complex, the local region is a war-torn wasteland. There aren't any farms within six or seven hundred kilometers of here, let alone towns and cities. At least with ten thousand Core creds in your pocket and a free ride elsewhere, you'd have enough money to get yourself established somewhere, with enough time to start figuring out what you want to do to make a living. The Raider Clan isn't heartless, and they aren't thoughtless. They give these options to all the Gengins they help set free.

"Oh—I almost forgot, I'm *also* authorized to offer the services of the Raider fleet in destroying this facility, if you decide you'd rather see it obliterated than allow any of its tech or information to fall into other hands. But only at *your* command," she emphasized. "It's not meant to be a threat in any way, shape, or form, just an offer of assistance if you'd like to see this place blown off the map once you're free of it."

If her previous words hadn't rocked him to the core, Shen might have indeed taken the thought of blowing up this place a lot more like a threat. But her words did disturb him all the same. *To start figuring out what you want to do . . . to make a living. But . . . I* haven't *been living . . .*

Needing to think, he sank onto the edge of the bed, staring at the tapestry-covered wall across from him.

"Shen?" the woman lying next to him prompted after several moments had passed. "Hey, if you're going to sit and think for a while, can you at least untie me? I know I'm only bound in virtuality and all, but if you're not going to do kinky things to me anytime soon, I really don't think there's a point in keeping me tied up like this. I'd rather not break your programming or myself in trying to get free, so there's no reason. You've only turned off the security measures in one sector out there in reality. You haven't done anything to the security measures here in virtuality."

Shen turned to look at her. An idea formed in his mind. "You say all these things are being offered by this Raider Clan . . . but the only person I know from the current era is *you*. What are *you* going to promise me, to hold as a bond that all these things you're offering are true?"

She blinked, considering his words. "Well . . . lessons in modern tech, I suppose. As a fellow electrokinetic, I can teach you what you need to know in ways that a non-Psian couldn't."

Bracing his hand on the other side of the mattress, he leaned over her. "What about *tangible* benefits? You offered me an opportunity for 'kinky things' in virtuality. Would you be willing to try them out there in reality, once I'm free?"

Her brows rose at his suggestion, but it didn't take more than a moment for her to smile. "Well, if I get to do kinky things to you in return, out in reality, then I think that could be arranged."

Another thought crossed his mind. "What about that offer to explore all the 'archaic tech' of this place? Would you be one of the people working on it?"

"I suppose, if the Raider Clan extends my contract."

He wanted to kiss her again . . . but a virtual kiss was nothing compared to a kiss in reality. A kiss and much, much more.

"Tell them to extend your contract. I'll accept the offer of amnesty and six months of rehabilitation. They can have access to the physical tech of this place, but *not* the research files. Not that it would do them any good. I destroyed most of it long ago, physical and virtual," Shen stated, lifting his chin a little.

"I would've been surprised if you hadn't. Most Project escapees tended to destroy or steal away their creators' research notes. Now, are you going to unbind me and help me get safely to your inner sanctum out there in the real world?" Leo asked him, smiling slightly. "Or are you going to take advantage of my virtual vulnerability and do some preliminary kinky things with me?"

Tempting as her offer was, the thought of doing kinky things to her in reality was too compelling. A simple sweep of his hand dissolved her bonds. Shen shifted back to the edge of the bed so she could have the room to sit up now that she was free. "It'll take me over half a day to disable the security measures between sector C and my location. If you're still in that bathroom, go out the door, turn right, and enter the second room on the right; there's a couch large enough to sleep on and a sink with still potable water. You're out of luck for edible food, but otherwise you should be comfortable."

"I brought nutribars. They probably taste as old as the age-powdered packets of food that used to be in the staff vending machines I've seen, but they'll keep me going. And I can always head outside and go back to my ship if necessary. Sector C has an emergency exit tunnel that emerges not far from where my shuttle is parked."

Curling her legs to the side, Leo leaned forward, braced her palm against his thigh, and swayed almost close enough to kiss him. But she didn't. Shen frowned in disappointment.

Pulling back, she grinned at him. "Oh, no. I still need to motivate you. You'll have to wait for a *real* kiss, with *real* lips. Go on. You've got a lot of work to do. I can't rescue you without your help on the inside; I'm good, but I'm nowhere near as good an electrokinetic programmer as you."

Her smile was too tempting. *To hell with it. I want something to tide me over while I wait for that rescue. My Princess Charming will just have to deal with it.*

Cupping the back of her head, almost dislodging her tricorn hat, Shen pulled her close enough for a very thorough kiss. It wasn't completely satisfying, but it was enough for now. Releasing her, he stood up and vanished, taking himself back to the main corridor of the research facility's virtual systems.

Now, where the hell did I put those release codes?

He was, more or less, the same physical age he had projected in virtuality. There were quite a few more wrinkles on his hide than his virtual self bore, but that could easily be attributed to fluid retention, also known as the bathtub effect. And his face was seamed around the edges by what by now was probably a permanent imprint of the breather mask and headset goggles he had worn. But he had the muscles, and the eyes, and the gray-tinged black hair.

The only thing she still couldn't tell if it was the same or not was his smile. He was too busy coughing from having to breathe dusty, unfiltered air and grimacing at the pale blue goo clinging to his fluid-wrinkled skin to bother. Smiles weren't on his immediate agenda.

Switching to a clean towel and rubbing at another section of his body, scrubbing off the blue goo, she waited for his coughing to ease. There wasn't much she could do to stop it, not when real air was just something his lungs would have to get used to breathing.

Besides, she thought, rubbing the age-worn fabric over his legs, *he's damnably sexy in person. What red-blooded woman* wouldn't *want to get her hands all over a man like him? Well, presuming she doesn't mind older men. Which I don't.*

That thought made her smile. He might look like he was forty-seven to her twenty-seven, but according to his file, he was closer to one hundred thirty-three. *That stuff he was being injected with, the anti-aging agents . . . that's an old tech we've lost. It'll be worth a fortune if it can be redeveloped. If we want it redeveloped. The problem is, it'd be worth a fortune* and *a massive interstellar war.*

I'll have to warn the Raider Clan how effective the stuff is. They weren't sure if I'd be rescuing a wizened old gnome of a man or maybe just a virtual ghost running all these machines. But if it really works to slow down aging—as it seems to—and word gets out that the tech is still viable . . . well, it won't be the first time I've destroyed a bit of technology I didn't think was safe to let loose in someone else's hands. Even the Raider Clan's . . .

"Hey." His voice was rough, gravelly. Rusty with disuse, though he had undoubtedly used it in the same intermittent way his muscles had used the resistance of the fluid for a source of exercise as well as support, keeping himself more or less in shape.

"Yes?" Leo asked, curious.

"I'm waiting . . ." He gave her an expectant look. When she only returned it with a blank, noncomprehending one, Shen sighed and sagged back on the floor of the platform next to the rim of his control tank. A moment later, a strangled snort escaped him. It was followed by a second one.

Oh! She bit her lip to keep from giggling, but couldn't stop her smile as he *snorked* a third time. "Don't even bother, Shen. You may have been 'asleep' for a hundred years, but you fail miserably at snoring."

Leaning down over him, she kissed him on his lips. It was soft, sweet, and he tasted vaguely of plexi, suspension goo, and recycled air. Nor did his lips move as smoothly in reality as they had in his virtual world; he still had most of the muscles of his virtual self-projection, but he wasn't used to consciously using them in reality yet, which made his responses a bit awkward.

She wasn't going to hold any of it against him. *Practice does make perfect, after all.*

Shen smiled, letting his head drop gently back to the floor. "I'm free. I'm really, truly free . . . Ow."

"Ow?" she repeated, confused.

He frowned, but not at her. "I think I bruised my arm on the edge of the tank when you hauled me out. And my thigh . . . and this platform is disturbingly hard. And, as much as it pains me to admit it," Shen added, his voice still somewhat rough, "I don't think I'll be able to walk all the way out of here. I have muscles, but . . . not the memory of how to move them."

"I guessed as much. The reality-is-stranger-than-virtuality syndrome. I get that way if I spend more than eight or so hours at a time inside a virtual program, and holoprogram addicts suffer for it when they spend weeks and months in virtuality. Luckily, it's nothing that a few weeks of physical therapy won't cure. Come on, on your feet," Leo coaxed. "I found a hoverchair in the medical wing to give you a ride out to the ship, and some sheets and blankets to preserve your dignity, but that's all down on the main floor. We have a set of steps to navigate, first."

Nodding, Shen looped one arm around her shoulders, letting

her reposition herself at his side. He kissed her cheek while she was shuffling into a sturdy squat. "For good luck," he told her when she glanced at him. "And as the first down payment on a thank-you. I . . . would have run out of supplies in just a few more years, if you hadn't come along." He grimaced wryly. "I also don't think I'll be ready for anything more vigorous until I've been looked at by modern medical techs. I know I'm fine in virtuality, but . . . I have no idea if, you know, everything still works in reality."

She smiled, and carefully did not look at his groin. "Then I'll just wait and take the rest of those installments after you've had some physical therapy and regained your equilibrium. Of course, the sooner we get you out to my shuttle, the sooner the Raider pilot who brought me here can fly both of us back to the Enalia System."

"These Raider Clan people had better be all that you've promised," Shen muttered.

"They will be. If not, you can take me captive and do kinky things to me in reality—feel free to do so anyway, once you're feeling better," she joked. "It was quite arousing. Now, I'll pull you to your feet on three. I can support most of your weight since I'm bred to be stronger than I look, but all that tech welded to your flesh makes you heavier than *you* look. So you'll have to do some of the walking, too. We'll just take it slow and easy, since we have all the time in the world, now that you're free.

"Ready? On one . . . two . . ."

THE first thing Leo Castanides saw when she opened the door of her home was a plexi sword. A cheap, child-sized plexi sword, as light as a datapad and no sharper along its edge than the side of a pencil. It dangled from a string hung from the ceiling of her entryway. Next to it was an equally child-sized shield, both of them painted in fake silver and gold.

After a long day of cataloguing yet another fraction of the tech they had literally stripped out of the Borgite Project stronghold, leaving nothing behind but bare concrete walls, unlocked doors, and a note painted on a couple walls to contact the Raider Clan in the Enalia System if anyone had any further inquiries . . . a cheap toy sword and shield were not what she'd expected to see.

Pushing her tricorn hat back on her head—she loved her Minutemaid hat, even though she was firmly an Enalian citizen these days—Leo reached up and plucked the sword and shield free. The strings were easily snapped, being little more than threads. Beyond them, she saw more threads holding up more objects. Long strips of crepe and tissue paper, crudely colored in shades of brown and green and scribbled with crude approximations of leaves and thorns.

Comprehension dawned.

Grinning, Leo adjusted her hat firmly on her head, gripped the shield in her left hand and the sword in her right, and "hacked" her way through the makeshift walls of mock briar thorns. As suspected, the display of suspended barriers led through the living room, past the door to the kitchen, and down the back hall to the bedroom. *Her* bedroom, not his. Another telling point in this mock dramatization.

Batting aside a last bit of paper vine, she pushed the button for her bedroom door. It slid back quietly, revealing a brand-new, archaic-styled canopy bed in place of her older, simpler one. A bigger bed, she noted. A bed occupied by the recumbent form of a middle-aged man.

Three things caught her attention in the glow of the setting sun visible beyond the gauzy bedroom curtains; two of them had grown familiar over the last six weeks since his rescue. His gray-streaked black hair was somewhat longer than it had been, though still quite short by local fashion standards. His calves, thighs, forearms, and biceps were banded with fading scars where the old metal bands used to reside; more body-friendly organic transceiver nodes had been transplanted in their place, similar to the ones in her own limbs, which boosted her electrokinetic abilities.

And he was quite, quite naked, with not a trace of pale blue goo, bathtub wrinkles, or metal implants to be found. That was a new twist on the man she had come to know and love.

The warmth of the Enalian summer night at the latitude where they lived was enough to keep him comfortable as he rested on what should have been her original bed. The fact that it wasn't her bed anymore didn't upset her. Rather the opposite. In fact, the mere thought of all this effort on his part was doing a very good job of arousing her.

If he's in here, re-creating how we first met, that means he's finally been given the all-clear by his therapists for lovemaking. Good! Excellent, in fact.

Stepping quietly into the bedroom, Leo poked the toy sword at the controls, shutting the door. She set her weapon and shield on top of her dresser, then removed her hat and hung it on its wall hook by the door frame. Another glance at the bed showed what could have been a flickering eyelid, but she couldn't be sure.

Leo toed off her cuffed, ankle-length boots and untied the laces of her vest as she stepped out of them. It looked like his eyelids flickered again at the soft *flump* of the leather hitting the floor, but otherwise he didn't respond. He also didn't try to fake a snore while she finished approaching the new bed, for which she was grateful. As much as she was pleased he was ready and willing to take this next step with her, she didn't think giggling would be appropriate. *Not after all the trouble he'd gone to, creating that fake paper briar patch and finding those silly toys . . .*

It was really quite sweet of him. Loosening the ties at her wrists and throat, she sank onto the side of the bed. This close, she could see a faint shiver cross his skin at her proximity, and the tightening of his dusky nipples. Not to mention the slight twitch of his not quite flaccid shaft. A lift of her hand and a bit of concentration was all it took to tap into his organic transceivers. Shivers rippled across his muscles as she dusted his limbs with phantom caresses. With her hand ghosting several centimeters above his skin, she touched him with just her mind, preparing him for the reality ahead.

A glance at his face showed his eyes still shut, but his lower lip was caught in his teeth. A second glance at his loins showed his flesh thickening in tiny but visible jerks, tied to the blood pumping in time with the beating of his heart. Not wanting to torment him too much, she lowered her hand to the bed on his far side, leaned down over that handsome pair of lips, and kissed him.

This time, he tasted of mouthwash and man. This time, his lips parted and pressed with a lot more skill. This time, he wrapped an arm around her shoulders to pull her down closer, rather than lift himself higher. Satisfied that he was very much awake and willing, Leo kissed him hungrily.

Shen returned it greedily, until kissing wasn't enough. Impatient fingers tugged at her shirt, pulling it up over her head. That broke their kiss, since she was forced to detangle herself from the fabric. As soon as he flung her top to the floor, he cupped her breasts in his palms. The skill he used to rub and stimulate her nipples with his thumbs surprised her a little, until she remembered just how many of those entertainment files had included romantic interludes in their programming. Grinning, Leo pushed her breasts into his hands, encouraging him.

The sight of his eyelids still shut made her frown a moment later. She could have sworn she'd kissed him thoroughly enough to wake him. A glance at his loins showed his shaft arcing up over his lower abdomen in an inviting curve the length of her hand. *Well, if kissing him on the* lips *doesn't open his eyes . . .*

Shifting free of his grasp, she bent over his hips and bestowed a tender kiss on the turgid tip of his shaft. His sharp inhale made her slant her gaze at his face. Grinning at the sight of his blinking brown eyes, she licked around the little head and sucked him deep into her mouth.

That snapped his eyes wide. Body tense, hands clutching at her head, Shen arched into her bobbing, inhaling, enthusiastic nether-kiss. He groaned when she swirled her tongue, and choked out her name when she rapidly flicked his tip. "Leo!"

Leo released him with a chuckle. He groaned again, this time in disappointment, but she avoided his hands. Rather than letting him drag her back down, she moved off the bed completely and unfastened her pants.

Pushing up onto one elbow, Shen watched her strip off the last of her clothes. Moving his other hand to his groin, he caressed himself lightly as she peeled off her socks and underwear. To Leo, the sight of him touching himself was erotic. So was the way he reached up and circled one finger around her breasts, then slid it down between her thighs, boldly proclaiming his right to touch her flesh. Head tipping back, eyes drifting shut, Leo rocked into his gentle, stimulating strokes.

A moment later her own eyes snapped open from the sudden spark of energy crawling like tiny nibbling mouths across her skin. His wicked grin told her she wasn't the only one capable of invading a fellow electrokinetic's transceiver nodes for pleasurable stimulation. Probing deep with two fingers, he hooked them in her body and gently tugged her close, sitting up so that he could meet her approaching breasts with hungry, lustful nips from his real mouth, letting the phantom ones he was projecting electrokinetically caress other, more peripheral parts.

Clutching his shoulders, Leo caressed his skin, then pushed him down. He murmured a protest, clinging to her with his free arm and lips, his right hand still occupied with a very skillful exploration of her flesh. Still, she persisted until he was lying on his back again, though it meant she half-straddled him in his wordless, insistent demand to keep her close.

A few moments later found him pressing *her* onto her back, when all she did was shift so they could continue their kiss. Complying, Leo groaned; his suckling kisses wandered from her mouth to her throat, turning into teasing nips. The controlled scrape of his teeth was undeniably erotic, but also a little alarming. She gasped, startled, when he bit and suckled at the same time, accompanying the act with a deep growl.

"Easy!" she hissed, alarmed by his increasingly feral touch. He released her flesh with a wet *pop*, peering up at her. She smiled wryly at him. "Hey. I thought this was supposed to be the tale of Sleeping Beauty, not Beauty and the Beast."

He grinned and licked her breast. "We can always explore that one later . . . but you're right. Ours is definitely a Sleeping Beauty story."

"Good. Now . . . having rescued the handsome, slumbering prince," Leo purred, coaxing him higher on her body with a gentle caress of her finger under his jaw, "I would like to claim my reward."

Shifting a little higher, settling between her thighs as she parted them, Shen braced his elbows on the bed to either side. "Anything I have is now yours."

"Good." She smiled. "I want it all." To make sure he got at least some of her point, she shifted her hips, lifting her knees so she could tip her pelvis into his.

His brown eyes darkened and he flexed his own hips, sliding his shaft against her damp flesh. "All of me?"

She shuddered, enjoying his firm, gliding touch. "*All* of you."

Shen stilled. Despite the now dim glow from the tail end of sunset outside, she could see the teasing look in his eyes fade, replaced by something much more serious.

"Is that . . . a proposal?" he asked.

Leo stilled as well, holding her breath as she thought about it. Thought about him. Shen. A man who looked twice her age and had lived five times it, though not as freely as she had. A man who was bright, caring, and completely one of a kind. Her kind.

She didn't stop the smile that spread her lips. "Shen Codah, will you marry me?"

Emotion gleamed in his eyes. Cupping her head, Shen captured her mouth; he devoured her with a deep kiss, his hips moving in time with his tongue, rubbing himself sensually against her.

Enjoying the gliding tease of his erection, it didn't take long for her to grow impatient for more. Squirming a little, she reached between them, capturing his shaft with her hand. He groaned into her mouth, then shifted, helping her find the right angle to prod him into her depths. That made both of them groan, and he bucked a little, sinking deeper.

Leo sucked in another breath at the sting of being stretched; it had been a while since her last lover. But it was the pain on her new lover's face that concerned her. The lines deepened on Shen's brow as he grimaced, making her wonder if this attempt at intimacy was too soon in his recovery. Teeth bared, he pushed a little deeper, muscles straining in what looked like an internal war between forging forward and holding back.

"I . . . I can't . . ." His abdomen spasmed, followed by the rest of his body. Driving deep, he nipped and licked at her mouth, her throat, her shoulder, sucking strongly on the skin at the base of her neck. He took her roughly, fiercely, claiming everything she had just given him, rocking the bed until the canopy fringe swayed.

For a moment, it seemed inevitable that he would leave her behind, his passion had boiled over so fast, so furiously. Leo didn't care; even without those half-lost rejuvenation medicines, the physicians who had examined him after his rescue had promised both of them that he still had a good sixty or more years left to live. He could make it up to her another time; right now, she just wanted to give him as much pleasure as he could stand, because he deserved it. Reopening her transceivers, Leo caressed him electrokinetically.

Tearing his mouth from her throat, Shen gasped. "Stars! Oh, yes—let me in!"

Guessing what he meant, she pulled down her inner walls, the part of her that guarded her against intrusion, whether from a random electromagnetic fluctuation or from another soul with Psian genetic engineering in his veins. To Shen, she opened herself up—and bucked herself as raw sensation flooded her nerves.

For a moment, he and she were one; his lust, his passion, his love were now hers. She was him, hard and aching, driving into soft, clinging heat over and over again. He was her, wet with acceptance, clenching around him with need. Passion crested, climaxed, crescendoed in an actual, physical spark between their bodies, flaring blue white in the indigo darkness of the bedroom. If that spark sizzled, neither of them heard; her cries mixed too strongly with his groans, accompanied by the wooden creaking of the old-fashioned, canopy-draped bed.

He didn't collapse on her, so much as slump slowly by degrees. Clinging to him, her own mouth nibbling on his throat, Leo accepted his weight. Without all the cumbersome metallic implants, he wasn't as heavy as when she had rescued him. He was solid, pinning her to their new bed as surely as if she were still bound by his virtual programming, but not a burden. Of any kind.

For a moment, she let memory color her perceptions in electro-kinetic detail, conjuring up a virtual replica of that room in Sleeping Beauty's castle. Shen grunted and shook his head, dispelling the shared vision.

"No," he ordered gruffly, lifting some of his weight back onto one elbow. "No more dreams. No more programs. I want nothing but reality with you."

Sighing, Leo nodded. "All right . . . but that does mean actually getting up and trying to find something suitable with which to tie me to the bed."

Shen groaned, dropping his forehead to hers. Physically, he was still soft with satisfaction, but she could feel the mental undercurrents of his reaction to her suggestion. They were still linked electrokinetically, still sharing their arousal, and more. Reaching up and out with her mind, since her arms were occupied in the important task of holding him, she sparked the bedside lamp to life.

The sideways glow highlighted the silver strands at his temple and the wrinkles at the corner of his eye. Leo shifted her left hand from the sweat-damp skin of his back. Cupping his cheek, she guided his mouth down to hers for a gentle, loving kiss. She didn't quite invoke true virtuality between them, but she did link and share her pleasure. Shen accepted it, as he accepted her into the inner sanctum of his mind . . .

A long while later, Leo woke from a vivid, disjointed dream of roving hands and roaming lips to find it wasn't a dream. Her lover *was* caressing her, kissing her in the dim gray light of dawn. Smiling sleepily, she wrapped her arms around him and returned the favor, tangling her tongue happily with his.

It didn't actually matter which one of them was the other's Prince or Princess Charming. It only mattered that they were both awake.

Beauty and the Beast

Author's Note: When we were discussing a list of stories for this anthology, my editor requested that I write a version of this particular one, as it happens to be her favorite fairy tale. Since a lot of these stories have been popularized by various movie and television production companies—along with a particularly fine novelization by fellow author Robin McKinley—I worked hard to find a new twist of my own. In the end, I decided to take it completely out of the fantasy genre and tuck it into science fiction. Cindy, this tale is dedicated to you.

H AND snapping up and out with the same speed he would have used to break a neck or crush a skull, Viktor snagged the rose being thrown his way. The only damage he did to its stem, however, was a slight nick from one of his claws. There were other flowers he could have plucked, for there were literally hundreds being tossed his way—enough to make more than one of his fellow Haguaro sneeze from their thick floral scents—but roses were special to him.

Roses were his link to his humanity.

Lifting the bloom to his muzzle, he inhaled deeply, savoring its sweet, rich perfume. Except, there was more to the smell of this rose than mere perfume. *Something* wafted up from the flower in his hand.

Something that pricked at all of his senses, fluffing the fur along his neck and arms. Something that made his tail want to lash, something that made his ears flick up and strain, despite the tumult of noise from the cheering crowd tossing yet more flowers around him.

Burying his muzzle against the deep pink flower, he sniffed his way first along the petals, then down to the stem. There lay the strongest traces of that mysterious scent, down where its former owner's fingers had cut the bloom from its bush, snapped off its thorns, and handled it for untold minutes while waiting for this parade before tossing it into his hand.

A feminine hand had wielded this bloom, but not just a feminine one. Something more basic than that. So basic, it struck his senses like a blunt weapon.

Female.

One moment, he was seated sedately among his fellow Haguaro Gengin on the parade float, accepting their accolades once again as the saviors of the small, enemy-beset nation of Sullipin. The next, he launched instinctively into the crowd. The Normals scattered, startled by his sudden movement; men, women, and children, they shrank back with wide, wary eyes. Not fearful, thankfully, just startled, but Viktor couldn't think about that. He couldn't think about anything, but stretched up on his hind legs, sniffing the upper currents of air and trying to calculate the point in the capital city's parade route from which the flower in his grip had been tossed.

There! Dodging around a knot of staring men, he approached the spot he had matched up in his memory with the trajectory of his rose. It had to be one of the five or six women edging back from him, all but leaning against the plexi windows of a bakery. The warm, yeasty scent of freshly baked bread and spicy-sweet sticky buns couldn't mask the scent of *her*, however.

Her. That heady scent of pure, intoxicating *female* came from *her*. Viktor stalked toward her, sniffing the air to be absolutely sure. The smell of her was too important to pick the wrong woman; he had to be sure the redhead with the wide blue green eyes was his rightful—

A body interposed itself between him and his . . . well, she wasn't his *prey*, per se, but she *was* his, somehow. The blocking figure was an older man, his dark hair salted heavily with iron gray. He smelled somewhat like her, some sort of relative, but he also smelled of a mix of courage and fear. The scent of a confrontation.

"What . . . what do you want?" the man demanded, lifting his chin a little.

Lifting up again on his hind legs, towering over the older man, Viktor sniffed at the air around the redheaded woman. It was definitely the redhead, no mistake. He pointed at her, his hand still holding her flower. "Her."

The gray-haired man spluttered. "My . . . my daughter? Well . . . you can't have her! We're free citizens! We haven't done anything wrong!"

A hand touched his arm. Viktor glanced at its owner. Keisia Bloodthunder blinked her cat green eyes at him and murmured, "Viktor, what are you doing?" Her ears flicked down and back, and she snuck a look at the other Normals around them. "Why have you stopped the parade? What have they done?"

The slight breeze wafting through the city shifted, bringing his fellow Haguaro's scent to his nose. It didn't completely diminish *her* smell, but it did reduce some of its impact on his instincts. Enough that Viktor felt embarrassed by his wildly impulsive actions. "Nothing . . . they've done nothing."

"Come back to the float," Keisia murmured, patting his arm. "Let the Normals see how nice we are."

He knew she was right, but he couldn't quite leave things at that. Turning his attention back to *her*, he lifted his chin a little. "What is your name?"

The man between them lifted his own chin. "I am Godo Chavell, and this is my daughter, Raisa. What do you want with her?"

Raisa . . . how appropriate. Briefly satisfied with that much information about her—which would hopefully be enough—Viktor lifted the flower again. "Thank you for the rose, Raisa. It is . . . *very* beautiful."

She smiled tentatively at him, making his chest swell at the sight. She had a beautiful smile, with a hint of a dimple on one side. Remembering his manners, Viktor bowed to both of them and turned away, following Keisia back to the float. Leaping back up onto the flower-piled transport, he ignored the curious looks from the other Gengins, focusing instead upon the flower still caught in his hand.

Raisa Chavell. Raisa. Ancient Russian for "rose" . . .

My Rose.

"WHAT do you mean, you want this Raisa Chavell?" Cameron, the defense liaison, demanded. The Normal man gave Viktor a look that, if he had been an Haguaro himself, would have included downturned whiskers and flattened ears. "We don't do slavery in Sullipin!"

"Not like *that*," Viktor growled, though he wasn't particularly mad. Disgusted, more like it. He could not get her scent out of his head, but he *was* a civilized man, despite his genetically engineered shape. "I want to know who she is, where she's from, what she does for a living, who her friends and family are. I want to meet with her, and I want to talk with her."

"This is highly irregular!" the defense liaison protested.

"Our contract with your government is that for each time we risk *our lives* in defending this nation, we get to make a request for a special item or privilege commensurate to our efforts on your behalf," Viktor reminded him. "We are on call every hour of every day, in exchange for food, living quarters, medical treatment, and a modest stipend. But when we actually risk our lives—as I clearly did this last week— we can ask for something more. I am asking for information about the redheaded woman, Raisa Chavell, and for the chance to talk with her. To start with . . . since this is such a *little* thing, compared to risking my life on behalf of all of yours."

"She is a free citizen of Sullipin!" Cameron protested.

"And *I* am a civilized man, not a monster, as you *seem* to be implying," Viktor pointed out, doing his best not to growl this time. He couldn't keep the tip of his tail from twitching, though he did restrain it from fully thrashing. "I want her background investigated and a report sent to my quarters by this time tomorrow. To start with. More meetings might follow, but they'll be with her cooperation and consent. *End* of discussion."

The other Haguaro in the debriefing room eyed him askance. Viktor didn't care. He wanted to know more about her, and to smell more of that intoxicating, bone-deep scent.

The Haguaro were the Sullipins' primary weapon against their enemies. Civil war had devastated the backwater colonyworld of Pinnia three hundred years ago, fragmenting their original government into five factions. Sullipin didn't have the one remaining, functional spaceport; that belonged to the nation of Arapin, up at the northern end of the small continent. Between them lay the jungles of Kessepin, where exotic and transplanted foods and medicines were grown. Danispin had the fruitful plains to the west, with grains and herds and farms, while Hallapin had various petroleum deposits to the south.

Sullipin had all the mineral resources of the Pinnit Mountains, which the other four factions were in dire need of, and the shelter of the Sullivan Rift, a broad valley near the heart of those mountains, suitable for farming and living. With technology heavily reduced by centuries of war, and lacking the resources to build forms of airpower strong enough to assault the mountain kingdom the easy way, the militaries of Danispin, Hallapin, and Kessepin did their land-bound best to raid the outer mines of Sullipin whenever they thought they had a chance, rather than constantly pay the Sullipins in a more civilized way for the value of the ores and jewels.

Up until the arrival of the Haguaro, they often succeeded. The crash landing of the original Gengins' ship, stolen in their escape from the genetics lab that had created them, had occurred in the southern Pinnit Mountains. A trio of brave miners had treated the survivors of that crash like human beings rather than like monsters, and the survivors had allied themselves with the local government in gratitude.

Bred and trained for speed, strength, tracking, and hand-to-hand combat, the Haguaro Gengins were warriors above and beyond anything this planet knew. For five generations, the Haguaro had defended Sullipin, and the Sullipins had honored them as its heroes.

Is it really so damned much for me to ask for information about a damned Normal female? Viktor thought, tail flicking restlessly. *I am a man! I am human, just like they are. With the same needs and wants and interest in my fellow human beings.*

He could feel Keisia eyeing him and knew she was concerned about his interest in a Normal woman. They had grown up in the same crèche group, had trained in many of the same combat forms, and had similar tastes in entertainment, humor, and favorite foods. The elders who oversaw the breeding lines had even made gentle suggestions that the two of them should consider forming a breeding pair, since they weren't too closely related and did seem to get along so well. Before the parade, Viktor had considered those suggestions as a future possibility. A distant future possibility, but one nonetheless.

Now all he could think about was *her*. Those blue green eyes with their round pupils instead of cat-slit ones. That faint dusting of freckles on her creamy cheeks instead of a stippling of dark whisker-spots. The sun-streaked copper and cream curls she bore, rather than a fluffy mane of golden and dark brown fur.

Her scent spoke strongly, compellingly, undeniably of *home* to him.

Of home, of woman, of something more. Something which he hadn't had time to puzzle out just yet, other than that it was important. Something which he couldn't dismiss from his thoughts. Why a Normal would make him react this way, he didn't know, but she did.

The mystery of his strong reaction to her only added to his desire to see her again. It didn't matter what the others thought. He *would* see her again.

He had to, even if he didn't know why.

"VIKTOR, I present to you Miss Raisa Chavell." Giving him a look filled with the protests and misgivings, voiced and unvoiced, which he had argued over the last three days, the defense liaison reluctantly stepped aside. He left just enough room for the young woman behind him to enter the conference room. "Miss Chavell, this is Viktor Ragerip, defender of Sullipin."

Miss Raisa Chavell looked just as beautiful as she had during the parade three days ago. Viktor had been vaguely aware of a bluish blouse and tan slacks the previous time, and she seemed to be wearing something similar, this time greenish on top and brown beneath. The last blouse had been flowery; this one seemed to be an abstract sprinkle of greens. It made her skin look creamy and her hair a little redder than before. He liked it.

He also still liked her scent. The flow of air currents in the air-conditioned conference room held back most of her scent, but it was there. Threatening to distract him.

He had done his own best to look civilized, with a fitted black jacket and a black and gold kilt. There wasn't a comfortable way for a Haguaro to wear pants, thanks to their tails, though they did wear loincloths under their kilts. Nor could they wear a traditional plaid, since the crisscross of stripes clashed horribly with their spotted fur, but this kilt had been made with an attractive spotted print somewhat reminiscent of Viktor's jaguar-patterned hide.

Aware of how important a good first impression was, Viktor had taken extra care with the selection of his clothes, the combing of his tail and the fluffing of his mane, even going so far as to decorate his ears with thin gold hoops, following current fashion for Sullipin males, Normal or otherwise. He thought he looked rather attractive. Gentlemanly. He deeply hoped she thought so, too, and he let his chest puff up a little as she swept her gaze slowly from the top of his head downward, perusing every centimeter of him.

She giggled. Her hand flew up to her mouth and her face flamed with embarrassment, and she did her best to choke it back . . . but she undeniably laughed. Ears flicking back, Viktor wondered what had set her off.

Cameron scowled and grabbed her elbow. "Behave yourself! He is a defender of Sullipin, and you will give him every respect!"

The defense liaison's harsh act startled her out of her laughter. It affected Viktor, too. For a moment, he trembled with the urge to leap across the conference room and fling the other man away, just for daring to touch her. Struggling against the uncomfortably violent impulse, he pinned the other man with a glare, ears flat and whiskers pulled back. "Thank you, Cameron. That will be all."

Cameron glanced sharply at him but did not release her elbow.

"*Thank* you, Cameron . . . that will be *all*," Viktor repeated firmly, his voice deepening almost to a growl. He let his tail lash sharply when the other man didn't release her fast enough. He didn't have to move anything else; the defense liaison was well trained in reading Haguaro tail, whisker, and ear moods.

Withdrawing his touch, Cameron gave Viktor a hard, chiding look. He followed it with a stiff half bow before striding back out through the conference room door. Deliberately leaving the door open behind him and deliberately not going very far. Annoyed, Viktor did his best to ignore the older man. He wanted to ask Raisa what had amused her, but first he had to get them past this moment of awkwardness.

Soothing his tail, pricking forward his whiskers and ears, he offered her a smile. "Would you like to see the gardens? They're at their best right now."

She gave him a dubious look. "Is that why I'm here? To see your gardens?"

"For a start. Come. We can talk while we walk outside." Holding out his hand, he waited to see if she would take it.

She stared at his fingers, callused skin on the palm side, plush, velvet-short fur on the back, his nails pointed like claws, though they were not actually retractable. The ones on his toes were, but not his fingers. The fact that she hesitated hurt him a little, reminding him that for all he *felt* like a man inside, he still looked more like a beast. Stubbornly, he kept his hand out and his ears up, and hoped.

Slowly, she lifted her hand. Slid her fingers against his. Curled them around his flesh. Touched him of her own free will.

Something sparked from her flesh to his, something deeply primal. Viktor heard the fabric of his jacket shift and strain with the swelling of his muscles, and suppressed the urge to roar in triumph. Instead, he did his best to keep his expression polite and pleasant rather than ferally possessive, and guided her back through the doorway, past the frowning Cameron, and out through the glazed doors leading to the gardens of the Haguaro Headquarters.

His ancestors had requested a large tract of land be set aside and developed for their use, more or less centrally located in the Rift Valley. Some of the buildings were training salles with all manner of equipment to train and test their combat abilities, some were medical facilities with staff dedicated to the study and maintenance of Haguaro biology, and some held meeting rooms and offices such as the conference room they had just left. The rest were personal residences, interspersed with stretches of lawn, trees, streams, fountains, and gardens.

Viktor's home wasn't visible, having been built beyond some of the trees off to the left; if it had been, he would have pointed out with justifiable pride the heavily blossoming rose vines he had trained to grow up over the many trellises he had erected with his own hands. Maybe he would show her his home later, if things went well. As it was, there were plenty of other flowers for her to see, and the need to reassure her that his intentions were civilized.

Given how the weather was on the cusp between late spring and early summer, everything that could be in bloom was in bloom, and vigorously so. From carpets of violets to bunches of bluebells, the view was a riot of colors and smells. Nothing quite as intoxicating as *her* scent, but some of the pollen was strong enough to make him want to sneeze after only a minute of strolling along the path. A subtle attempt to rub at his nose with his free hand made her glance at him. Viktor barely had time to turn his head into his far shoulder to muffle the explosion he had failed to subdue.

She *snerked*. She quickly averted her head, but his ears had picked up the muffled, suppressed laugh. He felt it in the subtle tremble and squeeze of the fingers still cupping his. Strolling with her along the winding brick path felt right, even if he had given her a laugh at his expense.

"I am glad I can amuse you," he murmured, catching her startled glance.

"I . . . I didn't mean . . ." she stammered in apology.

"Your laughter is a gift, and quite understandable. There is nothing more amusing than watching a creature as dignified as me letting out a hearty sneeze," Viktor reassured her. "Of course, I am also curious to know why you laughed the first time. Would you care to let me in on the joke?"

She blushed and shrugged. "It's stupid. I shouldn't have thought it. You're a hero, not a . . ."

That intrigued him. "Tell me anyway. I'm a hero, not a . . . what?"

Raisa blushed deeper. "You're a hero, not a fairy tale creature." A glance up caught the perking of his ears. She offered him a tentative smile. "I looked down, saw your feet, and, um . . . well . . . I immediately thought *Puss-in-Boots* . . ."

Viktor glanced down at himself. While his hind legs weren't entirely human in shape, neither were they quite the exaggerated ones of a true cat, and the fit of his footwear reflected that. Still, he could see her point. Permitting himself a chuckle, he gently squeezed her fingers. "We Haguaro are well aware of how we look. We often take pains to look more human, even if we can't look Normal."

"Well, you are very, um . . . exotic looking," she offered politely.

This close, with the wind shifting direction, her scent filled his senses, permeating him with a feeling of rightfulness. "On the outside, perhaps. On the inside, I am still a man."

She flushed again. "Erm . . . why do I get the feeling the reason you wanted to see me is because . . . you're a man?"

He couldn't hide it. "Because you have excellent instincts."

"Why?" Stopping, she turned to face him. "Why me? I don't look anything like, well, an Haguaro woman. Aren't you . . . um . . . Wouldn't you prefer one of your own kind?"

Viktor shrugged. "I'll admit it's more common. But there is something about you which I find . . . compelling."

"Compelling? Me?" Raisa shook her head, her sun-streaked locks sliding over her shoulders. "I'm surprised they even let me come here. That is, presuming you know . . ."

He didn't pretend ignorance. "You and your father and brother were former Danispin citizens. Your father was—and is—a baker, yourself a massage therapist, and your brother a clerk in the Danispin military. A dissident clerk. You have my condolences for his loss," he offered.

She shrugged, but he could see the tension in her shoulders, smell the subtle tinge of sadness in her natural perfume. "He was trying to do the right thing. Father raised us to think about the differences between wrong and right, and my brother believed in it. He died getting us across the border, along with the information he had smuggled out of his work." Raisa breathed deeply, gazing at the trees in the distance. "I still wish my mother and sisters had seen reason, too. Bombing these people just to get their hands on rare minerals . . . it's an insane idea. We should be working *together*, all of us, to rebuild the technology we've lost.

"Arapin has a spaceport, yes, but we're on the back end of colonized space; hardly anyone ever visits, and we don't have enough resources individually, nor enough cooperation as a group to rebuild our half-lost spaceship technology. The only way we're going to regain solid contact with everyone else, and regain all the advantages that will entail, is if we stop fighting each other—I'm sorry if that kind of goes against your entire purpose for existence," she added quickly, looking up at him. "But it's how my father and I feel."

Viktor wrinkled his nose. "I wouldn't call it our purpose for existence. It's more our purpose for employment. Saying that we exist for no other reason than to fight and kill is to render us less than the beasts we resemble. I don't deny we were made to be tools of war, and that we look more like beasts than like men and women, but we are still human beings inside."

"I'm sorry if I offended you," she murmured, tugging on her fingers to free them.

He kept them tucked in his. "You didn't. I know what I am. I was just hoping that you did, too. Or that you'd be willing to learn."

"Which brings me back to why I am here." Lifting her chin, Raisa looked up at him.

She was about average in height, which made her around forty centimeters shorter than him—and that was without him rising up on his toes. Her height and slender build made Viktor all the more aware of how fragile and delicate she was, and how that comparative delicateness dug its claws into his protective instincts.

"Why am I here, Viktor Ragerip?"

"Rose," he corrected. She blinked and frowned softly, confused. Viktor sighed. "A few years ago, I dug through the records our ancestors brought when they escaped the Gengin facility which had created them. My paternal bloodline is descended from a man named George Rose . . . so by rights, Rose is my true family name. Not the battle name I was given in an effort to make me sound all the more ferocious to our foes—which is a stupid practice, if you ask me."

"Oh?" she asked. "How so?"

"Well, it's not like we stop to exchange names and hobbies and interests first before entering a battle with our attackers," he pointed out. "Our names might occasionally get across the borders through rumor and so forth, but the people who hear them every day are our fellow Sullipins. With names like Ragerip, Throatgouger, and the like, all we're doing is intimidating the people we're sworn to protect."

Raisa tipped her head, acknowledging his words. "You're right. It does seem excessively intimidating. But to quote Shakespeare, would a Ragerip by any other name sound as fierce? To call you a Rose would make you sound sweet, and you *are* supposed to be a symbol of ferocious defense for this land."

"That may be reasonable for when I'm working, but what about my leisure time?" Viktor argued. "Shouldn't I be allowed to seem sweet and kind? Do I *have* to remain a beast every hour of the day? Or can I also be a man at least some of my time?"

She gave him a dubious look. "Viktor . . . you don't *look* like a man. As sad as it is to say this . . . people tend to judge first on how people look. They see you, they think, *fierce jungle beast.*"

"Then that's all the more reason for me to be looked at as a man. To have the opportunity to be *seen* as a man. Which is why *you* are here," he murmured pointedly.

"Yes, but why *me*?" she asked again.

Viktor shrugged. "Because you smell right."

"Because I *what*?" Raisa demanded, her brows rising with her incredulity. "I *smell* right? I thought you wanted to be seen as a *man*, not a beast, but if *this* is your selection criteria . . ."

She tried tugging her hand free again, but Viktor kept it. He pulled it to his chest, turning it gently but firmly in both of his hands so that her palm pressed flat against his golden fur. He didn't smell any fear about her, which was good, but the combination of her scent and her touch made it a struggle for him to focus on mere words. "I have a heart. I have a brain. I have a soul. I also have a body, which by these measurements is merely one-quarter of me. I'm not going to ignore my appearance or my abilities, but neither am I going to deny the other three-quarters."

Her blue green gaze dropped from his face to his chest. He felt her fingers move slightly, a subtle caress of her thumb. "Your, ah, fur. It's very soft."

"Lots of vitamin E. Both in my diet and in my shampoo." He smiled when she glanced up, inviting her to enjoy the mild joke. "It takes forever to wash and dry, and I have to use a conditioner if I don't want problems with static electricity, but at least I don't have to lick myself."

She blushed at his choice of words. Dropping her gaze to his chest, Raisa splayed her fingers over his fur. Viktor released her wrist slowly, giving her silent permission to explore him. Released, her fingers rubbed against the grain of his fur, then with it, stimulating and soothing the underlying skin. She frowned slightly, thoughtfully, and raked the pads of her fingers through the longer, golden strands cresting his sternum.

"Does it interfere with massage therapy? Or have you ever had a massage?"

Her clinical interest gave him hope that he could capture other facets of her interest as well. Viktor shrugged. "It does take a certain talent to massage a Haguaro, and the right tools of the trade. I'm not quite sure what oils are used, since our therapists don't use them very often. I think some of it is aloe vera gel, maybe with some vitamin E. They often follow it with an oatmeal powder scrub, which is very invigorating.

"But most of the time, they just use their bare hands and our natural body oils." Stooping a little, he picked up both of her hands and guided them into the thick, long, hairlike mane covering him from scalp to shoulders. "There are glands on both males and females at the back of the head, below and behind each ear . . . Feel that, the bit that's a little more oily? Plus more glands down by our tails and around the bases of our whiskers." Pulling one of her hands free after it had wriggled experimentally for a little bit, he guided it to her nose. "For the men, the oil glands are a bit muskier in their scent than for the women. Here, smell it for yourself."

Hesitantly, she sniffed. Blinking, Raisa looked up at him. "It's not bad . . . Kind of like a perfume, actually. Or a cologne."

Stooping again, Viktor twisted his head and shoulders, offering her his mane. "Stick your face in it and breathe deeply."

She laughed and swayed back. "I can't do that!"

"Sure you can! You just might like it . . . but you won't *know* until you actually try," he teased. "Go on, do it."

"Well . . . okay." Steadying herself with a hand on his shoulder, she buried her face in his fluffy gold and brown mane. Most of the Haguaro feline genome had come from jaguars, but some had been borrowed from other cat species, including Viktor's lionlike mane. He heard Raisa inhale deeply, then exhale on a humming sigh. "Mmm, yes . . . like a very nice cologne. Unless you applied some actual cologne to your fur?"

"I'm not wearing any. What you're smelling is the real me." Turning to face her, still stooped over, Viktor found their faces close enough to mesmerize him. Partly because of her own perfume, natural and heady, but partly from the fearless curiosity in her blue green eyes.

This close, he could see they were definitely too dark to be called aquamarine, and she had two tiny flecks of amber in the iris of her left eye, while there was only one fleck in the right.

She was also close enough that he couldn't resist. Angling his head, he pressed his mouth to hers. Kissed her. Raisa sucked in a startled breath, both of her hands coming up to his shoulders. Balling his own hands into fists to keep from touching her, from pulling her closer, from obeying the instinct to snatch her up and carry her off to his lair, Viktor instead gave her parted lips a teasing lick. He pressed further when she gasped again, claiming her mouth as gently as his instincts would allow.

Apparently not gently enough; she pushed at his shoulders, stepping back. Cheeks flushed, she didn't meet his gaze. "You really shouldn't do that. You're a . . ."

"I'm a . . . what?" Viktor asked, angry that she was daring to call him *that* in spite of his explanations.

She lifted her chin and her gaze, meeting his stare firmly. "You're a stranger, and we've only just met. I may be a Sullipin now, but I was raised a Danispin, and in Danispin, we don't do that on a . . . on a . . . I can't even call this a first date!"

He would have backed off, if it weren't for two things. The first he noticed at the lower edge of his vision. Spotted in shades of green though it was, her blouse couldn't camouflage the evidence of her reaction poking against the soft, supple fabric. The second was her smell. His wasn't the only musk now tangible in the air, though hers was yet so faint no Normal nose could have detected it.

Acting on instinct, Viktor cupped her chin in his hand. Holding her still, he kissed her again. A claiming kiss, for all it was gentle. It pleased him that within just a few licks, she parted her lips enough to return his kiss. It pleased him even more that the hands which touched his shoulders a few moments later cupped the material of his jacket, pulling him closer, rather than pressed to push him away. It was a good thing; Viktor didn't think he could stop kissing her, now that he'd had this second taste.

Indeed, he didn't care about the chatter of young, approaching voices, until one of the youths let out a disgust-laced "Ewww! He's kissing a *Normal*!"

Rage seared through him. Gently—very gently—Viktor pulled back from his startled, embarrassed mate. Using the thumb of the hand still cupping her chin, he gently covered her mouth, preventing her from saying anything. "Please excuse me a moment . . . and you may want to cover your ears."

Visibly flushed with embarrassment, Raisa watched him as he used his free hand to unbutton his black jacket. With his chest and abdomen given room to expand, Viktor turned to glare at the three young Haguaro who had approached along the path. It wasn't easy to tell which one had spoken, since all three sported flattened ears and wrinkled muzzles, but it didn't matter. They were mere teenagers and he was a full adult; disciplining them was well within his rights as a blooded warrior.

Inhaling deeply, Viktor roared. All three youths jumped back at his full-throated thunder, eyes wide with shock. Birds squawked and flapped into the air, abandoning their perches in the nearest bushes and trees. More than that, Raisa jerked back out of his grip, gentle as it was. He spared her a glance, making sure she hadn't actually fled, then glared at the trio again.

"You have *insulted* my guest. You will apologize. Now!" Lashing his demand like it was his tail, he waited. Thankfully, they did not try his patience.

"Sorry, sir, miss . . ." "I apologize." "We didn't mean to offend!" Bobbing in short Sullipin bows, the three boys edged off the path and around Viktor in a wide, wary circuit.

Sighing, Viktor let his rage go. More worried for his guest than still mad at the boys, he turned back to Raisa. She smelled more of startlement than of fear, but there were some traces of fear. "I apologize as well. They are young, and the young are often idiotic. I hope I didn't hurt your ears."

She stared at him for a long moment, then managed a tentative smile. The redhead even lifted her hand, cupping it around her ear. "Eh?"

Viktor chuckled, nervous that he had scared her but relieved she didn't seem too offended. Cupping her chin again, he leaned down and gently kissed first one ear, then the other, indulging himself one last time in the chance to inhale her sweet, beckoning scent. He felt her shiver when he did so, and saw the desire returning as a faint, rich gleam in her blue green, amber-flecked eyes.

"Would you join me for dinner?" he asked, pulling back. "I know you have massage sessions scheduled for later this evening, and you're on duty tomorrow as well at your clinic—I hope you don't mind that I made inquiries about such things—but would you be willing to share a meal with me two nights from now?"

She ducked her head a little. "I don't know . . ."

"Please," he murmured, hunkering down a little in the hope that it would make him look more harmless. The full-throated roar of an enraged Haguaro was very intimidating to most, even if it had been aimed on her behalf rather than at her. "I would like you to get to know me better, and I would love to know you better, too. Please, have dinner with me."

She nibbled her lower lip and snuck a glance up at him. "You, um, don't eat your meat raw, do you?"

Viktor wrinkled his nose in disgust. "Hardly. I prefer my red meats cooked at least to medium-rare, and my fish and poultry fully cooked. And I *do* eat vegetables."

"Ah." She hesitated, considering his offer.

"Plus, I'm an absolute slave to cheese," he said, half teasing, half coaxing. She looked up at that, arching one reddish gold brow. "Oh, yes," he agreed, nodding to emphasize it. "Feed me cheese from your dainty fingertips, and I'll purr and sprawl and do almost anything you ask of me. I might even play 'fetch' if you asked nicely . . . say with a hunk of smoked gouda in your other hand?"

She wrinkled her nose at that, but thankfully only in laughter, not disgust. Pleased he had tickled her sense of humor, Viktor lifted her hand to his lips, giving her fingertips a kiss and a featherlight lick.

"Come, I'll walk you back to the visitor's center—you will go out with me in two nights, yes?" he asked, needing to know. "Please?"

Again, she hesitated. Finally, Raisa nodded, her body posture shy, her scent both curious and trepidatious. "All right. Here, or . . . ?"

Viktor considered the strength of his reaction to her, versus the likely reaction of others. *Bringing her to my home for a private meal could tempt me into things she's clearly not ready for yet . . . but taking her out into public might make others voice a few "ewws" of their own . . .* There was really only one choice in the matter. He could take whatever insults might be flung his way, but he didn't know about her. "I will leave that choice up to you. We can dine in my home, in your home, or in a restaurant of your choosing."

She tilted her head again, looking up at him. "Since I don't know if you can cook . . . and the way those boys reacted . . . it should probably be my house. If you're willing. You may be brave in the face of combat," Raisa added, her dimple making its lopsided appearance, "but I'll bet you haven't faced a disapproving, highly protective father over the dinner table."

He laughed. "I look forward to the challenge."

Six dates. Six long, wonderful, impatient, agonizing dates. Long, because they inevitably ended up talking all the way to midnight. Wonderful, because it didn't seem possible they could run out of things to say to each other; even their moments of silence together were companionable rather than awkward. Impatient, because her work schedule only allowed them to meet two nights a week; having served in a combat zone recently, Viktor had arranged to take a few weeks to teach the latest tricks and tactics of the enemy to the next generation of Haguaro warriors, which allowed him to stay near the capital. His work took place in the mornings, and that left him at the mercy of her much more varied schedule. Agonizing, because he was doing his best to proceed at *her* pace regarding intimacy.

Even with only a few kisses here and there for his meager satisfaction, Viktor had never enjoyed anyone's company so much before. They might have two disparate backgrounds and careers, but they also had many things in common: a good sense of wrong versus right; a love of archaic literature; and strong ties to their family history—or at least, in Viktor's case, as much history as he had been able to find out. Raisa could trace hers all the way back to ancient Earth. And with every wide-ranging conversation, they kept finding more things in common, more subjects to discuss, debate, and enjoy.

Their first three dates had been in the privacy of her home; she was a good cook, as was her father, though her father still wasn't too sure about Viktor's intentions. The next two dates had taken place in public restaurants. Those had been awkward, but necessary. Word had already gotten out that an Haguaro was seeing a *Normal*. As in *dating* her.

Viktor wanted to show everyone that he *was* a man, a civilized, normal man, for all he wasn't a Normal. Thus, this was their third time venturing into public together.

What he longed to do was bring her back to his home, where there was no lurking, wary father—though at least Godo Chavell seemed to be coming to terms with Viktor's presence—and no other distractions but the two of them. Nothing for them to do but interact, in whatever way she might desire. Instead, tonight they had attended a play.

As much as Viktor normally enjoyed the archaic comedy *Much Ado*

About Nothing, the padded theater seats had been designed with Normal backsides in mind. His tail hurt from his being forced to sit on it through every act of the play. An awareness of his broad shoulders and height even when seated had forced him out of politeness to request seats in the back of the house, distancing them from the action. But in compensation for all the discomfort, she had held his hand. All the way through the performance and all the way outside.

The popularity of the acting company performing the play had forced Viktor to park his hoverbike a couple blocks away, but that was all right; it really wasn't a bad night for a stroll. The air was warm, the stars were out, and the gold and green glow of Thesten's Nebula could be seen rising off to the east, through the buildings of the Sullipin capital. Dressed in a buff gold vest and matching kilt, with sandals on his feet so that she wouldn't have to suppress the urge to giggle whenever she looked down at them, with her in a golden summer dress that almost matched his clothes, Viktor strolled contentedly at her side.

His contentment vanished when five men, ages ranging from early twenties to perhaps a little older than his own twenty-seven, stepped out of the shadows and crowded the sidewalk in front of them. Blocking their progress. The antagonism in their eyes, the mixture of alcohol, belligerence, and fear in their scent told him it wasn't an accident. No, seven men, for two more moved up behind them.

The liquor oozing from their pores told him that what they were planning wasn't based on wisdom or common sense. The fact that two of them had lengths of pipe held at their sides added to the impression. The scent of the woman at his side, startled and a little fearful, reinforced his bone-deep belief that Raisa had to be kept safe at all costs in this witless confrontation. That meant using calm, rational logic and civilized courtesy.

"Gentlemen, I will remind you that I am a government agent," Viktor stated calmly. "Attacking me is a crime. Committing any crime in my presence, such as attacking myself *or* someone else, gives me the legal right to stop you. As it is a lovely night and there are a *lot* of witnesses around, witnesses who can see the weapons in your hands, I suggest you reconsider whatever it is you have in mind, and step aside."

The ones in front glanced around. There were, indeed, several witnesses to this confrontation. Not only several of the other theater patrons on their way to their own vehicles, but the drivers of the hovercars gliding just half a meter off the pavement next to them. Wisely, the group parted to either side. Viktor shifted from holding Raisa's hand to cupping her shoulders, visibly protecting her at his side as well as guiding her between the inebriated men.

A sting of sweaty adrenaline and a whisper of sound were his only warning. Sidestepping quickly, Viktor grunted under the blow, absorbing the burning impact.

"Freak!" his attacker shouted from behind, yanking the knife free. "You don't take our women! Stick to your own kind, you freaking beast!"

Viktor grunted again as the knife stabbed deep a second time. Through the pain reddening the edges of his vision, he heard the youth panting, felt him release the hilt, and turned slowly to face the drunken Normal. The younger man paled, eyes widening as Viktor faced him. He bared his teeth a little, displaying his slightly longer than human canines. That made the idiot blink, then flush.

When the idiot drew in a deep breath and balled up his fists, leaning in to attack, Viktor sighed and planted his right palm on the younger man's face, holding him at arm's length. The movement pulled at the wounds in Viktor's back, and it hurt, but being a lot taller meant the drunkard couldn't quite reach him. He endured the first two whiffing, would-be blows patiently, then shoved the idiot back. The dark-haired youth stumbled and sprawled onto the pavement with nothing hurt worse than his badly bruised dignity.

Pleased he had controlled his battle rage in spite of his pain, Viktor turned back toward the others . . . just as one of the older fools grabbed Raisa by the arm, pulling her away from him. Touching her.

Her.

Possessive fury exploded through him in a thundering roar of blood-rage red, destroying his careful self-control.

"Viktor!" Raisa's shout called him back to his senses, her voice hoarse with both fear and anger. A glance showed her released and unharmed, untouched by anyone else. Of course, he had just attacked the only one foolish enough to try. Trembling, hands clenched in fists, Raisa lifted her chin. "Put him down. Now!"

Blinking to clear the fury half-blinding him, Viktor lowered the man half-throttled in his grip, returning his feet to the ground. He did not immediately let go of the second idiot's throat, however. Leaning in close enough to smell the urine as well as the sweat soiling the other man's clothes, he growled, *"You do not touch my woman."*

Unpeeling his fingers, he released his prey. Unsure if she would let him touch her, now that she'd had a glimpse of how violent he could be, Viktor bowed and politely gestured with both hands for her to precede him. For a moment, she didn't move, just stared at him and his hand. Then, giving the others a defiant glare, Raisa placed her fingers in his. Deliberately touching him.

Relief washed through him in a shiver of anticlimax. Aware of the extent of his injuries, one deep wound bleeding freely and the other still stoppered with the knife causing it, he held himself stiff yet proud as they walked away together.

She chose *me*, he thought as they crossed the intervening street and entered the hovercraft garage. *She chose to take my hand in the face of their asinine prejudice . . . My woman* chose *me . . .* It wasn't much, but it was a balm soothing some of his pain.

Reaching his hoverbike, Raisa climbed onto the seat first, shifting forward as she straddled it so that he could climb on behind. She glanced over her arm . . . and froze, staring at the ground. Her eyes widened, taking in the red smears. "Viktor, you're bleeding!"

"I know," he grunted. He quickly stopped her with a hand on her arm when she tried to dismount. "We have to go back to Headquarters to file an incident report."

"Incident, hell! We have to get you to a hospital!" she swore.

He managed a smile as he pressed her back into place. Swinging his leg over the rear end of the bike certainly hurt, but it wouldn't kill him. "That's the other reason we have to go back. A regular hospital won't do me much good. They don't know enough about Haguaro physiology to help quite as well.

"Besides, I heal a lot faster than a Normal. By the time we get back, most of the bleeding will have stopped." That was an exaggeration, but he didn't want her to worry. "I am concerned about the knife still stuck in my lower ribs, but so long as I don't move too much, I'll survive. I've had a lot worse, too, fighting on the border. And they'll need the evidence on the blade to track down the man responsible."

"Is there anything I can do?" she asked, concern keeping her eyes wide and her face pale. "Do you want me to fly the bike?"

"It has an auto-return program. Just stay with me," he murmured, activating the controls and setting the autopilot. "That'll be enough."

"All right." Gripping the support struts for the handlebars, she nodded, then shrugged. "I've never . . . never seen anyone move so fast. You just . . . Wow. It was rather . . . scary."

"They threatened you. I couldn't let them hurt you." Punching the button that engaged the thrusters, Viktor set the bike moving under auto-return. As a government vehicle, his bike didn't have to stick to the meter-high rule, particularly under auto-return; within moments, they glided up out of the multi-story garage, soaring into the night air. Using the comm, he gave a terse report of the incident, the fact that he was injured, and was returning to the Haguaro compound for medical aid.

The safety field snapped up as they angled to the southeast over the city, cutting out the increasing force of the wind stirred by their flight. That trapped her scent in the cocoon of static energy sheltering them. Lowering his face to her upswept hair, Viktor soothed some of his pain by resting his chin on her shoulder and breathing it in, until nothing mattered but the fact that she was safely unharmed.

"I need to thank you," he admitted a few moments later, distracting himself from the pain in his ribs. "I was so upset at the thought of them hurting you, I don't think I would have stopped without you telling me to. I don't normally get that upset. They didn't deserve to be hurt just because they were a bunch of drunken idiots."

"You *really* scared me," she confessed quietly over her shoulder. "I thought you were going to tear those men to pieces right in front of me."

"I'm sorry," he murmured. "But this is part of what I am, and what I do. All I can promise is that I will never hurt you."

"How do I know that?"

Her doubt hurt as much as his wounds. He could ignore the ache in his back, but not this. Leaning forward just a little more to purr in her ear, Viktor gave her the truth. "You're my mate."

Raisa shivered, but she didn't move away. Not even when he leaned in close enough to rest against her back. Breathing in her scent, soaking in her warmth, Viktor let the bike carry them back.

SHE wasn't there when he woke up from the anesthetics. His spleen was still there, despite the severity of its lacerations, but that was more due to the recuperative abilities of regen paste than due to Haguaro healing abilities. Lying on his side in the recovery bed, Viktor listened to Cameron explain how he had taken Raisa's statements and that Keisia had offered her a ride back home. Hearing that Raisa was gone was a painful disappointment to him.

And then the liaison officer had the gall to lecture him on how disruptive it was to try and date outside the Haguaro. How his abilities as a warrior needed to be preserved and passed on to the next generation, and shouldn't be diluted by the Normal genome. How he had a responsibility to ensure that the future citizens of Sullipin would still enjoy the protections of his own kind decades from now.

If Viktor hadn't been muzzy from the surgery drugs, he would have growled at the other man. Allowing himself to fall back asleep instead, he saved pondering the implications hidden in the defense liaison's statements for later. He hurt too much right now, inside and out, to do anything but sleep.

It wasn't until he returned to his own quarters the next day and had the chance to catch up on the news feeds that he saw part of the reason why Cameron had been so upset. Journalists were still talking about the near-fight that had happened outside the theater . . . and soliciting opinions on the thought of an Haguaro trying to date a Normal. Some of the average citizens' reactions were positive, but many more started with something along the lines of "Well, he *is* a hero and all, and we're very grateful, of course . . . ," only to end with a variant of "he really should stick to his own kind, for her sake" or "just to be safe."

It didn't take long for him to hear what his fellow Haguaro thought of the matter, either. While he was debating watching a boring football match or yet more gossiping vid journalists trashing his attempt at a love life, Keisia knocked on his door. He knew it was her because she entered a moment later, bearing two bags of food. From the smell of it, one bag contained a roasted chicken, the other stir-fried vegetables.

"I figured you'd be ready for lunch by the time they let you out," she stated, carrying everything over to the lounger where he had settled to watch the news. "Hospital food always tastes wrong to me, like they're trying too hard."

Her left ear twitched back and forth as she set the bags on the table and started extracting the contents. There were even two slices of cheesecake in little plexi boxes, he noted. *Finally, something much more interesting than the news.*

Keisia smiled slightly, seeing his ears prick up at the sight of his dessert. "I'll go fetch the plates. And a glass of milk?"

She paused, and her ear twitched again. Viktor sighed. "Spit it out, Keisia. I know you have something to say; your ears never lie."

Sighing roughly, she dropped to a crouch on the other side of his coffee table. Elbows on knees, with the pleats of her red kilt draped between them, she met his gaze steadily. "You shouldn't be pursuing a Normal, Viktor. You are an Haguaro. Nothing you do, nothing you try, will ever change that. We are what we are, and we will always be it."

He returned her steady stare. "What I *am* is a human being. First and foremost."

"You *aren't* a human! You're an Haguaro!" she shot back.

"I am a genetically engineered *human*!" Viktor argued firmly, ears flattening against his skull. "Genetically engineered, but *still* a *human*. We know for a *fact* that Haguaros and Normals can interbreed, because they were still doing it to us when our ancestors escaped!"

"Yes, and *most* of the time, the Haguaro side breeds true!" Keisia snapped, tail thumping on the carpet as she lashed it. "Do you think the Normals want to hear that? Do you think *she* will want to hear it? Do you think she would want to bear your children, knowing that? Do you think she'd *do* it willingly, if she knew three out of four of her kids would end up furry, with teeth?"

"I don't know. I haven't asked. *Yet*," he added daringly.

She narrowed her eyes, blinked slowly, and let out a sigh of disgust. "She's only going to disappoint you. And you're going to piss off your superiors. They won't stand for you dallying with a Normal."

"That!" Viktor exclaimed, pouncing verbally on her statement. Keisia jumped, started. "*That* is what bothered me yesterday!"

"*What* bothered you?" she asked, frowning. "The truth?"

"The attitude that we're supposed to keep to ourselves, breed with ourselves, and continue to propagate a perfect warrior species! Don't you see it?" he demanded, hoping that she did see it. Keisia was his friend. He hoped the intelligence he knew she possessed would connect the dots. "This is *exactly* what we were bred for."

"I know! That's what I'm trying to tell you! Haguaro stick to our own kind!" she repeated, flipping up her hands.

Groaning, Viktor sagged back onto the cushions of the lounger. "Stars give me strength . . . Keisia, our ancestors were *bred* to be warriors, and *kept* as warriors . . . but our ancestors *knew* that we were still human beings! We have the same rights to life, liberty, and the pursuit of happiness as the ancients did back on Earth! It is *wrong* to demand that we stick to our own kind. It is *wrong* to demand that we take mates only among each other! If *we* restrict ourselves, we are no better than the Gengin-crafting bastards who made us, because they wanted to *enslave* us!

"*They* created us because they wanted an army of genetically modified beasts they could command! *They* forced us to breed *more* of our kind, to concentrate our genome and strengthen it by *breeding* with each other. They only used Normals because it still takes an Haguaro woman nine months to carry her child to term, and they wanted to increase their breeding stock exponentially—but they still wanted us to *be* Haguaro.

"They *culled* the non-fuzzy, non-toothy babies, Keisia! How is *that* any different from the idea that the Haguaro of here and now are '*supposed*' to stick solely to our own kind, and not risk breeding *Normal* children with *Normal* mates? Is that what you want? To be *forced* to stick to our own kind? In *another* damned breeding program?"

Expecting a counterargument, he waited, ears flat and eyes squeezed shut. She didn't say anything. Prying open one eye, Viktor peered at her. Keisia still crouched on the other side of the low table, and her ears were flat, but her whiskers were pulled down in unhappiness.

Only the tip of her tail twitched, echoing the subdued restlessness of her thoughts.

Sighing, he relaxed a little.

"You *know* I'm right. And you can't argue that it's just about me gone over my head for some Normal woman. Cameron and the others may have the best of intentions toward ensuring there are always Haguaro to defend this land, but those attitudes are paving a road right back to the genetic captivity our progenitors fought so hard to escape. They and we *are* still human beneath all this fur. When our great-plus-grandparents crashed here, they signed a charter that *guaranteed* that they and their descendants would be free to choose their path in life. Which *includes* who they would mate with, and when, and how often.

"That each generation has agreed to use our strengths and skills to protect Sullipin is a testament to our continued honoring of that pact for freedom of choice. *Not* an indictment of our willingness to return to being warrior-slaves." He fell quiet for a few moments, letting her think, then flicked his hand in the direction of his kitchen. "And yes, I *would* like a glass of milk."

Her ears flicked back at his peremptory order, but she wrinkled her muzzle more in a grin than in a grimace. "I should make you get it yourself, you lazy tail . . ."

Pursing his lips in an attempt to avoid a grin of his own, Viktor draped his wrist over his forehead. "My injuries have left me so weakened, I don't think I'll be able to walk—have pity on me, Keisia; I'm dying, here! Dying of *thirst* . . ."

"Dying of overacting, maybe," she muttered, but pushed herself upright. Padding toward the kitchen, she stopped as his comm unit chimed. "You want me to get that?"

"Yes, please." It was probably a call from someone at Headquarters, though it could be one of his parents; his mother and father were stationed on the Kessepin border, now that all their cubs . . . all their *children* were fully grown. He'd get up for the latter, but not the former. Viktor was officially on medical leave for the next week, to make sure the newly regenerated tissues weren't strained by the rigors of combat . . . and right now, if it was the defense liaison, he would probably say several things that should wait for a much more formal and politely worded draft.

Besides, leaving Keisia to catch the call meant he could investigate the delicious smells wafting out of the carry-out containers she had so generously brought. He might not love her as a mate, but there were several reasons he loved her as a friend.

"Hello, you've reached Viktor Ragerip's . . . Oh. It's you."

Viktor looked up. Keisia quickly swiveled the comm unit, which sat on the end of the counter dividing his living room from the kitchen and dining areas, so that it faced into the kitchen. She looked over at him as she did so, but rather than chiding him for getting into the plexi container holding the roasted chicken without waiting for her, she dipped her ears and returned her gaze to the screen.

"Look . . . forget everything I said to you last night when I took you home," she told the caller on the other end of the screen. "Drop everything and get over here . . . because even I'm not going to go against the wishes of a dying man."

"A *what*?" he heard Raisa's voice exclaim through the comm unit's speakers.

Viktor, caught in the act of nibbling on one juicy drumstick, froze. *A* what? he echoed silently. *A dying man? Who is she . . . ? Ohhh . . .*

Hope made his heart pound in his chest. He knew this could turn out to be a very dangerous ploy if it backfired, but he also knew he had his best friend firmly on his side. If nothing else, he knew he could let her take all the blame and she'd do it. He'd *owe* her majorly—what else were best friends for but blackmail opportunities and owing giant favors, anyway—but she'd do it.

I'll have to help her when it comes time to bag her own mate, of course . . .

"Please, drive carefully," he heard Keisia cautioning his caller. "It would be far too tragic if anything happened to you before . . ." She paused, glanced his way, and lowered her whiskers. "Anyway, I'll let Security know you're on your way. Here, let me pass you a map to his home address, in case you haven't been here yet. If you haven't, I'm sure you'll recognize it anyway, since it's the only house covered in roses . . ."

A few murmured words later, she ended the call. Fetching two glasses of milk and two sets of tableware, she set them on the coffee table and snagged a cushion from a nearby chair. Settling onto it, she smirked. "You *totally* owe me for that."

"You're right, I do. If she gets upset at the trick you've just played, I'll point out that *you* played it. Here I was, minding my own business as I recuperated from a *minor* combat injury, totally innocent of your machinations," he said mockingly.

"Minor, like hell; I saw the scans they took of your spleen," Keisia snorted. "And don't eat all the chicken. Have some vegetables, too—not the stuff with garlic! If she smells garlic on your breath, it'll give the game away."

"I *like* garlic. I'll gargle with mouthwash." He reached for the container of garlic beef again, only to have his hand slapped.

"Seriously, stay away from the garlic! You can't kiss someone unless they've eaten it, too, and mouthwash only goes so far in masking it," Keisia argued. "Garlic burps are *not* romantic."

"Fine. But I get to keep *both* slices of cheesecake." Viktor ignored her mock growl and her mock flattened ears. Her tail wasn't lashing. "I'll need *something* to sweeten her mood after she's discovered your little trick, and I know she likes cheesecake. If I lay off the garlic . . . well, with any luck, we'll be eating our dessert in bed."

Keisia rolled her eyes. "Please, I don't need to hear about your sexual exploits."

"We haven't had any, yet. I was thinking more along the lines that I should be lying in my bed like a good little invalid, to further your little illusion," Viktor told her. "I'd also better make sure my sheets are clean and that I don't have any dirty kilts lying around . . ."

"That reminds me, they threw your vest into the recycler since it was too cut up to salvage, but your kilt and loincloth were cleaned. I left the package in my car," she told him, licking a bit of garlic beef sauce from her lips. "You owe me for picking up your laundry, too."

"You're a very good friend, Keisia," Viktor murmured.

She wrinkled her nose. "You know, I used to wonder if we'd ever make a go of it together. But now I realize I think of you more like a brother. A *little* brother."

"Careful, or I'll dip your tail into the nearest inkwell," he teased. He had a couple of brothers and sisters already, and was happy to number her as an honorary member of his family, but it was a distinct relief to know she felt the same way about him.

Keisia snorted and poked at the carton in his hands. "Eat your vegetable delight."

THE muffled sound of Raisa arriving, audible over the low, ongoing drone of whatever entertainment show Keisia had been watching while she waited, threatened to make his heart pound all over again. It had been a race to finish tidying his bedroom on top of making sure the scent of his lunch had been scrubbed and gargled away, and a struggle to make himself calm down so that he could appear to be fast asleep. Focusing on breathing slowly and calmly, he relaxed into the bedding.

The door opened. Viktor stilled the urge to twitch his uppermost ear; thankfully his tail was already weighed down by the bedcovers.

"There he is," he heard Keisia whisper.

"Oh, Viktor . . ." Raisa breathed, her voice trembling with grief. Viktor felt an ambivalent mix of guilt for deceiving her and joy that she cared so much.

"I'll leave you two alone," his friend murmured, and he heard the door close again. Raisa's scent filled the air-conditioned room, wafted his way by the ventilation currents. Manfully, he resisted the urge to breathe deeply. As much as he loved her scent, he was supposed to be playing the part of an invalid.

"Oh, Viktor . . . I'm so sorry. I didn't mean . . . I thought we had time, that I could find the . . . the right moment to tell you how I *felt* about you," Raisa murmured.

And how do you feel about me? he wondered, listening to her slowly cross the room. The bed dipped as she eased onto it, prickling his nerves with anticipation. His whiskers thrummed, sensing the proximity and heat of her hand moments before she gingerly touched his forehead.

"Now you're dying," she whispered, stroking his mane back from his face. "And I never had the chance to admit how much I've fallen in love with you."

YES!! His tail twitched under the covers, and his whiskers trembled, but he managed to keep his ears relaxed. She stroked his mane again, dipping low enough that he could feel her breath on his face. He could smell a hint of tea in it, but nothing of lunch. He could also smell hints of saline in her scent, and knew she was crying, or at least struggling with her tears.

"And now . . . now you're so far gone . . . I don't even think you can hear me." Her voice broke.

He couldn't bear it anymore, but before he could open his eyes, before he could confess he would live, she kissed him. His Raisa kissed him of her own volition, entirely of her own free will. All it took was a slight tilt of his head and he kissed her back. Sliding his left hand free of the pillows, he cupped the back of her neck, burying his fingers in the soft waves of her strawberry, sun-streaked hair.

One moment, their tongues were tangling; the next, she shoved back, breaking the kiss. "Viktor! You're alive! You're awake!"

Opening his eyes, he smiled. Not too much; he didn't want to seem smug. "After a kiss like that," he murmured, "how could I be anything less?"

Apparently, he hadn't tried hard enough.

"You . . . Oh! *You!*" She shoved at his shoulder, twisting him onto his back. Viktor grunted, but she didn't give him any sympathy. "I honestly thought you were *dying!*"

"*That* was Keisia's idea. While my spleen wasn't too happy for a while, it's all been safely regrown—it's just *tender* right now," he warned her, catching her wrist as she tried to shove him again. She shoved him with her other hand, so he caught that wrist, too. Grinning, he pulled her down so that she had to lie on top of him. She dug her elbows into his chest, lifting up her head so that she could glare at him, but he wasn't fazed by it. "I missed you, yesterday. I asked you to stay with me, but when I woke up, you weren't there."

"I was told to go home, that there was nothing more I could do. And then Keisia told me . . ." Raisa broke off and shook her head. "No. No, I *won't* listen to those words. Nor to any of the nonsense they've been blaring on the news nets." Lifting her chin, she stared him in the eye almost defiantly. "I love you, and . . . I hope you love me, too."

"I do. Very much so," he agreed, all but purring at her declaration.

Releasing her wrists, he let her settle more comfortably on his chest. Then, because she was simply too beautiful, and he loved her too much not to seize this moment, Viktor threaded his fingers through her wavy, red locks and pulled her mouth firmly down to his. They had kissed a few times over the course of their dates, but never for long, and never in such an intimate setting as this. Always before, he had let her set the pace in such things. This time, he hoped she would let him not only set the pace, but go a lot further.

It was a shock when he felt her not only pull back from his kiss, but tug and shove at the blanket and sheet between them. Her voice low and a little breathless, Raisa growled, "I *need* to make sure you're not hurt."

Viktor grinned. Completely willing to be examined by her, he helped her shove the bedding down past his feet. Only when it was too late did he remember that he had decided to leave off even a loincloth under the sheets. There was no way to hide his growing excitement, no undergarment to restrain his eagerness and no loose kilt pleats to conceal anything.

Raisa stared. "Oh . . . wow."

A corner of Viktor's mind marveled how he could feel both embarrassed and smug at the same time.

"You're very, um, large," she observed, her hand reaching out and hovering near his half-aroused shaft, though she didn't quite touch him. Not that it stopped his flesh from twitching upward in excitement at the thought she might.

"I *am* over two meters tall," he reminded her. "Everything is perfectly proportionate. *And* within Normal parameters. It won't kill you. *I* won't kill you. I promise."

She shook her head, but not in a denial. "I still need to see your wounds, to make sure you're all right. Turn onto your stomach, please."

Viktor complied, smiling slightly. "That must be what you sound like when giving a massage. Does this mean you'll take me on as a client?"

"I don't sleep with my clients . . . and I don't know Haguaro physiology well enough to know what changes I'd have to make in my normal techniques," she confessed as he settled carefully on his stomach. She sucked in a sharp breath, and he felt her fingers touching his ribs. His ribs had been surgery-shaved in a palm-sized swath around each wound. "Oh, your poor fur! Did they *have* to shave you so much?"

"To keep it from regrowing down into the wound when they apply the regeneration salve, yes, they do have to shave it so much. I always look piebald after a battle if I get injured. We all do." Reaching underneath himself, he adjusted his erection, then snagged a pillow and pulled it under his chest and cheek. A stray thought came to him as she spread her hands gently over his back, one which had to be voiced. "I, um, have something to ask of you . . ."

"And that is . . . ?" Raisa inquired, finding and outlining the major muscles in his back.

"I know your job is important to you, but . . . could you maybe restrict your efforts to female clients? It's the *smell*," he explained quickly, before she could object. "I know you're very professional, and I do trust you, but . . . it bothers me whenever I visit and you have the scent of another man still clinging to your hands."

"I *do* wash my hands after each client," she muttered, stroking the pads of her fingers through his fur.

"Yes, but I have a very sensitive nose . . . and horribly jealous instincts," he confessed.

Her hands paused on his back, then resumed their stroking. "Really? Aside from that incident outside the theater, I haven't *seen* any signs of jealousy."

"Well, it wouldn't be civilized to growl and snarl at . . . Ohhhh, right *there*." He purred as her explorations reached the base of his tail. His hips lifted up into her touch, it felt so good. "Ohh, yessss . . . !"

Raisa giggled and rubbed harder, adding a bit of scratching from her short-trimmed nails. "This is classic. You're actually doing the 'elevator-butt' thing!"

Viktor couldn't take her teasing, vocal or physical. Whipping around, he scooped her up and flung her onto the bed next to him, aiming so that she landed with a gentle bounce on her back. Eyes wide, she gaped up at him. He would never willingly hurt her, but he wouldn't put up with being teased, either. Not like that. Unbuttoning her blouse, he tugged it out of her slacks and flicked the edges open, baring her bra-covered breasts and tender, pale abdomen.

"The base of the tail is a *major* erogenous zone on an Haguaro," he warned her in a growl, unfastening her trousers next. "Messing with it calls for *retaliation*."

Pulling the waistband open, he dipped his head and licked her navel, making her squirm and choke out his name. "Viktor!"

Mock growling, he licked and nipped at her stomach, then kissed his way up toward her breasts. Her hands beat him there, but not to stop him. With a brief fumble, she unfastened the front clasp of her bra, baring her flesh to him. Purring in pleasure at her open acceptance of his intentions, he plumped her breasts in his palms, nuzzling them.

Casual, recreational sex wasn't unknown to him—nor was it frowned upon by Sullipin culture—but it had always been with willing Haguaro women before now. The feel of all that smooth, satiny, furless skin was undeniably erotic to him. Nipples, he had seen before, but never ones surrounded by so much hairless, creamy-pink skin. He groaned, wanting to touch and taste and smell every part of her.

Tonguing her flesh in wide, hungry circles, Viktor reveled in her squirms and breathy moans, the encouraging way she dug her hands into his mane, tugging erotically on the fluffy gold and brown strands. Her scent, enough to make him light-headed on its own, blended with the musk of her rising, undeniably feminine desire.

With his nostrils filled with the sheer scent of *her*, knowing—believing—that she wouldn't ask either of them to stop this time, he abandoned himself to his instincts. The only self-controls he retained were just enough care with the remainder of her clothes to refrain from damaging them, and the vital care he took with her person. Mindful of his claws, he stroked her with the pads of his fingers and the warmth of his palms. Laved her with his tongue and nipped far more with his lips than his teeth. Loved her with every millimeter of his being.

Not caring that she still had one sock partially clinging to her foot, Viktor nuzzled his way up her thighs until he could bury himself nose-first in her mound. Nothing else mattered once he was there. Not the groaning of her voice, not the squirming of her hips, and not even the hands that gripped and tugged at his mane, threatening to pull out tufts of his hair.

Even when she grabbed at his sensitive ears, he only shook his head long enough to free them before diving back into her divine, desire-reddened folds. Rose-colored folds. His to devour and enjoy. Possessive instincts drove him, and he had no desire to resist.

Overwhelmed with sensation, Viktor pursued every single action that caused her to react. He pursued them, licking, rubbing, even growling, listening as her moans turned into gasps, which in turn became panting cries. Even when she shouted hoarsely, undone by her climax, he continued to lick and kiss, though he gentled his touch. But he didn't stop. Not even when she grabbed at his ears a second time, though it forced him to catch her hands and press them to the bed, leaving her thighs to flex and flutter like demented, overgrown butterfly wings while he gradually increased his efforts once again.

There was nothing he wanted more in this world than the taste and the feel of his rightful mate, to hear her joyful cries, to see her writhing in bliss, to smell the scent of *her*, all of it weaving its way through his blood and his bones and his brain.

Her third climax rendered her limp and nearly senseless. He could tell by the lax slumping of her legs, the way her flesh shivered but didn't fully tense under his touch. Instinct said that now was the time to hold her, to bond with her emotionally in the aftermath of such intense pleasure. Crawling up the length of her, Viktor rubbed his furred chest against hers. Raisa hummed and lifted one limp arm, pulling him closer, so he did it again. A shift of his weight allowed him to settle onto his side; a lift of her torso allowed her to roll up against him.

A subtle adjustment of his hips allowed his engorged shaft to slip between her thighs. Unlike the velvetlike fur on his face and the back of his hands, his erection was nothing but bare, naked, masculine skin, a point of familiarity he hoped she would enjoy. Unlike the soft tufts of fur decorating the mound of an Haguaro woman, her feminine curls were crisp and crinkly, a point of exoticness which fascinated and aroused him. Flexing his hips, he enjoyed the soft scrape of them against his flesh as he rubbed himself along her pleasure-damp folds.

He couldn't stop making love to her now that she had confessed she was his, but he could slow things down long enough to wait for her recovery. It came with a humming sound that was almost an Haguaro purr. She accompanied it with a press of her hand on his chest, tipping him onto his back. That allowed Raisa to slither up over him, rubbing her body from breasts to shins against his fur and nuzzling her face into his shoulder, neck, and mane.

"Mmm . . . that was *magnificent*. Unbelievable . . ." Drawing in a deep, luxurious breath, Raisa grinned smugly at him. "So . . . How soon can you do it again?"

Another time, he might have chuckled. Instead Viktor captured her mouth in a heated, tonguing kiss. Sighing, she cupped his face and kissed him back. The stimulation roused by her thumb gently rubbing the base of his whiskers was almost unbearable. He gently nipped the edge of her thumb, then sucked on it with instinctive hunger.

It wasn't enough; he needed more. He needed *her*, wrapped around him, holding him, loving him. *His*. Rolling them over, Viktor parted her thighs with his own. Feeling her tilting her hips up to his, welcoming him intimately, he growled his pleasure. The instinct to drive straight in, to claim what was now his warred with the need to be gentle with his chosen woman. Either way, his need to move, to mate with her, was undeniable.

Nudging himself into the right spot, Viktor rocked into her, pressing in centimeter by centimeter. Elbows bracing his weight, he dipped his head. Not to kiss her, but to press his cheek against hers. He nuzzled her, purring into her throat in time with each advance and retreat. That purr increased to another near-feral growl when she raked her fingers through the short fur on his back. Clawing him in her clawless way.

Encouraged, he thrust a little harder, a little deeper. That made Raisa moan and tilt back her head in subconscious submission, which made him glad. Sparing enough attention to lick the proffered skin, he increased his pace, until all he could feel was her warmth and her wetness enveloping him from tip to root with each long, smooth stroke.

The bed creaked with each circling thrust of his hips, joining her soft, rhythmic groans and his panting breath. Vaguely aware that he was starting to push her physically with each stroke, Viktor wrapped his hands under her shoulders, holding his mate carefully in place for each controlled, considerate thr— She raked her fingers all the way down to the base of his spine and rubbed there. Right *there*.

He broke. It was too much, too stimulating. Too sexy. Crying out—not quite roaring—Viktor snapped his hips in full passion. Raisa cried out, too, cried out and dug her short fingernails into his furred buttocks with each stroke.

She wanted him? She *got* him. It was his last semi-coherent thought. Growling wildly, Viktor pounded into her, poured himself into her, fused every sense with her and absorbed everything that made her his mate. Mouthing her tender neck, he sealed his lips against her skin, passionately tonguing the rapid pulse of her heartbeat. Sucking on the vibrating thrum of her cries.

The scent of her passion, the feel of her overwrought spasms—this time with her flesh rippling intimately around his own—drowned his last rational thought. Releasing her throat, he threw back his head and roared with triumph. Shaking with the bliss of his own release, he sagged slowly down over her, until some last vestige of consciousness prodded him into shifting to the side. Bringing her limp, sated figure with him, he rolled gently over until she lay sprawled against him. Only then did he relax fully, letting sense seep back in among his sensibilities.

His fur clung to her sweaty skin. He could see the stray hairs clinging to the arm draped in a loose cuddle over his chest, most of them golden, some of them brown. As his strength slowly seeped back into his brain, Viktor chuckled. Raisa drew in a deep breath, but instead of actually asking anything, she merely hummed at him in an inquiring way.

"I seem to have shed on you," he pointed out, amused.

"Mm. Marking your territory, I guess," she murmured, nuzzling his chest with her cheek.

Yesss . . . Pure happiness purred out of every last one of his pores. Not only was Raisa his mate, she willfully recognized it out loud. It didn't matter that his back now felt sore from all that activity. The pain didn't matter; he was unabashedly happy.

The comm unit by his bed beeped, startling both of them. Ears flicking back, whiskers pulling down, Viktor gave it a disgusted look.

Raisa chuckled. "At least whoever it is has good timing and didn't call about two or three minutes earlier."

He grunted. Stretching out his left arm, he found the switch for audio-only, made sure it was pushed firmly to the left, and activated the call. "You've reached Viktor; who is this?"

"Viktor Ragerip? This is Dr. Morrigan Galoise, psychobiologist. Having reviewed your actions during the incident on Thrasker's Street the other night—as per standard debriefing procedure following any incident involving civilians—I went ahead and ordered a full workup of your genome."

His ears flattened further. If he hadn't been lying on his tail, with the tip of it caught under the back of his knee, it would have flicked and thumped in annoyance. "What for? Just because I was involved in an almost-fight is no reason to examine my DNA for abberances. No one was severely hurt. Other than *me*, I'll point out."

"The details we have of the Gengin Project records are sketchy at best, but after having studied your genome, and comparing it with the ferocity of your response to a threat toward the, ah, woman you are dating," the doctor on the other end of the connection stated, "I have reason to believe you are harboring Phrodesian encoding in your genes. As I said, the records of what the full implications of this possibility could mean aren't completely known . . . but I'd place the probability at or near seventy percent.

"I therefore suggest, Mr. Ragerip, that you proceed with great caution when contemplating intimacies with this Miss Chavell. It wouldn't do to imprint yourself on her without her knowing what this possibility entails."

Viktor wrinkled his nose. "I'll take that under advisement. Thanks for calling."

Shutting off the unit, he looked at the woman in his arms, unsure how to explain what all of that meant without possibly scaring her off.

Raisa lifted her head from his chest, curiosity in her blue green gaze. "Phrodesian? Is that another Gengin race? Or sub-race, rather?"

"A sub-race." He closed his eyes, reciting what little he knew. "The Phrodesian genome project was designed to biologically influence its inheritors, forcing them to comply with demands for breeding more of their own kind. It's been presented as a classic case of nature over-coming nurture, since the biological imperative to mate drives the Phrodesian wild with lust, while other imperatives encoded in the genome encourage the sufferer to 'imprint' upon a specific person, ostensibly to keep a particular genetically engineered bloodline pure.

"Unfortunately, the engineers never managed to key it to a specific Gengin race. Nor could they get the genes to activate on demand. They can lie dormant in the blood for years, even lie dormant for a few generations, and then they just . . . activate," he finished, gesturing vaguely with his free hand. "Sometimes with very unexpected results, and usually about five to ten years past puberty. But utterly unpredictably."

"That sounds like it would be more trouble to the genetic engineers than it was worth," Raisa observed idly.

His ears pulled down, as did his whiskers. "No. It was considered worth it. You see, they enslaved many of the Psians that way . . . and it did ensure that at least *some* of their creations would *have* to breed, whether they wanted to or not. Most of the Gengin Project managers paid enormous sums for access to the Phrodesian genome, preserving and passing along each snippet of the code. It wasn't ever predictable in the Haguaro line . . . something about our feline sides provoking a greater level of independence," he half joked, opening his eyes to slits to gauge her sense of humor. It pleased him to see her smiling a little. Shrugging, he continued. "But there *have* been a few rumors of Phrodesian Haguaro in the past."

Resting her cheek on his chest, Raisa considered that for a little while, then sighed. "All right . . . I'll bite. How do we know if you're a Phrodesian or not?"

Viktor grinned. "It's hard to tell. A Phrodesian is possessive of his or her mate . . . but so is an Haguaro, *when* we finally pick someone we want to marry and settle down with. Phrodesians also want to make love frequently . . . but so do the Haguaro. Of course, the third way to tell a Phrodesian is a lot more accurate than that, and is usually the best way to determine if that person's genome has been activated, regardless of which Gengin race is being tested."

"So what is this fail-proof third way?" she asked, curious.

"Once fixated on a specific person, a Phrodesian literally can't get aroused by anyone else. Not even if he or she actively tried."

"If you try with anyone *else*," Raisa growled, "I'll rip out your fur!"

That made him laugh. Cuddling her close, Viktor kissed her disheveled hair. "As if I'd be interested in anyone else, ever again. But, um . . . Keisia did have a good point to raise, when we talked earlier."

"Oh?" Raisa asked. Then frowned warily. "You and she aren't . . . ?"

He shook his head. "No, just best friends. Or more like honorary siblings. No, she pointed out that the odds of, well, any children of ours being born Haguaro are rather high. That wouldn't bother you . . . would it?"

"Nope. Haguaro kids are cute . . . and so are *you*." Squirming a little in his grip, she managed to get her lips up to his for a real kiss. Then pulled back and peered down at her fur-streaked chest, wrinkling her nose. "You're furry, and I'm sweaty. Not only am I going to have to deal with your sheddings everywhere, as well as any from whatever kids we might have, you're going to be a fuzzy furnace to sleep with when late summer rolls around!"

"If you haven't noticed, Raisa my love, my house *is* air-conditioned," he quipped. Viktor paused, flicked one ear, and gave her a wry smile. "I trust, since you're talking about liking kids and still being with me in a few months' time, it means you'll say yes when I ask you to marry me?"

Her dimple appeared, accompanying her smirk. "*Are* you going to ask me, Viktor Rose?"

"Raisa Chavell, will you marry me and be my mate?" Viktor asked her politely, dutifully, knowing the answer was a foregone conclusion. She *was* his mate, after all. Phrodesian or otherwise, she was now firmly his, and both of them knew it.

She gave him a smug look. "No."

What? His mouth fell open and his whiskers pulled back. He couldn't even find enough breath to ask her why not, he was so shocked.

"No, no, no, no, no," she repeated, flicking her fingers as if counting on them, "no, no, no, no, no, no . . . *yes.*"

And then she giggled. The same muffled giggle she normally used when comparing him to certain fairy tale creatures. Breathing once again, he gave her a mock-dirty look.

"You may be an undeniable beauty, my dear Raisa, but *you* are also a *beast*. Come here," he growled as his mate's giggles turned into outright laughter. Cupping the back of her head, he coaxed her parted lips back into range. "Kiss your poor beast back to life . . ."

Puss-in-Boots

Author's Note: Question—How can you possibly compete with a suave, seductive, ginger-furred Antonio Banderas? Answer: You can't. Or at least I knew I myself couldn't. So—since I wasn't in the mood for another science-fiction piece—I just swapped genders. Let's see if this one works . . . and yes, we're actually returning to the Sons of Destiny universe for another brief visit . . .

SIONA cursed, as only a cat could curse—by yowling, hissing, growling, and clawing up the earth behind the stables. If there had been a rat within her reach at that moment, it would have died in a rather bloody fashion . . . but even that level of violence wouldn't have satisfied her. Only the death of the figurative rat responsible for her predicament would solve her problems. The filthy, overgrown rodent had expanded his catch wards; she couldn't take her natural form any closer than this inn, which was *outside* the range of her estate, and at that, she could only do so under the heaviest of wards.

Someone *else's* wards.

Unfortunately, her fit of rage caught the attention of the stable hand. He peered around the side of the building, scowled at her, and shouted, snapping his fingers, "Hey! Hey—scat! Get out of here!"

"That sounds like a real scrapper," another male voice stated, amusement lacing his words.

Startled out of her rage, Siona flicked her ears. That voice . . . she *knew* that voice. Instead of leaving, she trotted after the stable hand. Her viewing angle was wrong, coming from down low instead of close to level with his head, and he had a beard now, a neatly trimmed growth of rich brown hair covering him from nose to chin, but she thought she knew who he was. It was confirmed by the way he lifted his hand and rubbed his chin, then slid his finger up to rub behind his ear, giving the expected little tug on his earlobe as he finished. There was only one man she knew of with *that* little habit, though she hadn't seen it in at least four, maybe five years.

Marc Tresket of Thessalina . . . finally, a fellow mage! Of course, he spent all his time studying Arithmancy and not nearly as much on the offensive and defensive spells most of the rest of us studied. I don't know how much help he'll be in my current quest, but any—

"Hey!" the stable hand shouted, kicking at her. "Scat!"

Siona jumped out of the way. Dodging a second kick, she darted between Marc's boots, twined quickly around his ankles in a deliberate show of affection, and hissed at the stable hand.

"Damn feral cats," the inn worker muttered, reaching for the pitchfork hung on the stable wall. "The barn cats are good mousers, but they attract all manner of strays, which end up fighting at all hours, clawing at the patrons, and plague us with too many useless litters that have to be drowned. Mind stepping away? I don't want to get you."

"You're actually planning on killing this cat?" Marc asked as Siona narrowed her eyes and growled.

The stable hand gave him a sardonic look. "No, I'm planning on crowning it our next sovereign king." He stepped forward, but Marc shifted, blocking him. "Out of my way, milord. The innkeeper doesn't want feral strays hanging around."

Come near me with that pitchfork, you idiot, and you'll need a healer, she growled, though she was unable to say the actual words in her current form.

"Excuse me, but this is *my* cat." Hands came down and scooped her up, one under her ribs, the other under her hind legs. Wisely, Siona didn't protest being manhandled. Switching from growling to purring wasn't possible, but she did manage to nuzzle her former academy mate in a show of affection.

"Hmphf." Backing off, the stable hand hung the pitchfork back up on its pegs. "Make sure you keep it in your room while you're here. One of the other servants might not wait to find out if it's yours or not. We're *dog* people hereabouts."

Balancing Siona in the crook of one arm, the mage holding her slung his saddlebags over his other shoulder and headed for the inn. The scents of horses and hay were exchanged for the scent of cooking and canines. Siona sneezed, catching the attention of the innkeeper. He scowled, but allowed Marc to rent a room for the night. Their path through the common room took them past a table where three men sat, clad in the yellow and blue tabards of her enemy.

Restraining the urge to hiss and fly at them took most of her attention. It wasn't until Marc hissed at *her* that she realized she had dug her claws through the wool of his sleeve. Relaxing her paws, she let him carry her up to the assigned room. Once the door was closed and he had draped his saddlebags over the footboard of the bed, Marc lifted her in both hands so that they were nose to nose.

"*No* claws, got that?" he ordered, giving her a slight but gentle shake. Lowering her to the bed, he stroked her from head to tail. "I have just rescued you from being pierced by a pitchfork. It would be a sign of gratitude on your part to refrain from playing the part of a pitchfork around *me*. Not that I expect you to understand, of course."

I understand more than you know . . . and I owe you a debt for sav-

ing me from having to dodge that stable hand, she thought. *More than that . . . I think I can trust you. It's not like I have many options to find a better mage to assist me, this far from the more heavily populated lands.*

From her position on the bed, Siona could just see onto the nearby table. As she watched, he pulled out some of his belongings and set them on the age-worn surface, including some of the tools of his mathemagic trade. Jumping down from the bed, she trotted over to the chair, leaped up, worked her way as close to the back as she could, and leaped again.

The gap between the back of the chair and the edge of the table was narrow; she barely made it. Marc frowned softly at her. "What are you looking at, puss? Are you a curious cat?"

Sure enough, he had set some shrunken chalkboards on the table, as well as a slender book with an interesting title, *The King Who Heard a Joke, and Other Salacious Tales*. Unfortunately, she didn't have time to investigate it; stopping her family's killer was more important. Pawing at the dusty surface of the topmost slate only got her scooped up, however.

"Bad cat! Don't go messing with my equations, you got that? Do I have to spank you?"

Meeting his gaze, Siona deliberately shook her head *no*. Firmly, from left to right. Marc frowned softly.

"Did you just . . .?"

She nodded just as emphatically.

He blinked. "You're not a regular sort of cat, are you?"

Again, she shook her black-furred head. *No.*

"Are you . . . trapped by a spell? Do you want me to free you?"

She hesitated, then shook her head.

That made him frown. "Then why don't you just pop out of your fur and talk to me?"

Looking around the table, Siona spotted a snapped-off stub of chalk. Though her paws weren't exactly designed for holding things, she padded over and did her best to pick it up. Carrying it back over to the topmost slate—patiently, since she dropped it twice—she placed it on the surface and gingerly pushed it and patted it, marking what she wanted to say in crudely drawn squiggles.

sIOnA

Moving aside, she let him read the letters. His jaw dropped and he peered at her. "You're *Sio*—"

She hissed loud and clawed at him, ears flatted to her skull. She didn't get near enough to actually touch him, but at least it shut him up.

Marc gave her a wary look. "Do you mean that you're trapped in this form because of a spell that Sio—"

She hissed and clawed again, then shook her head hard. *Come on, figure it out!*

"So you're *not* trapped in a spell?" he asked cautiously. She nodded firmly. Marc frowned again. "You're in a cat shape because of your own free will?" Again, she nodded. Pulling out the chair, he sat down and braced his elbows on the edge of the table. "So what does that have to do with Sio—"

Hiss! She thumped her tail for emphasis. His brown brows lifted.

"So it's the *name* you don't want me to mention?" he asked. Siona nodded sharply. Marc eyed her speculatively. "Are *you* . . . her?"

She nodded, glad he had finally caught on and *wasn't* going to state her name out loud. That would cause the mage-wards seeking her to trigger.

Marc slumped back in the chair, staring at her. "But . . . you're *dead*!"

Shaking her head, she turned back to the chalkboard. Scraping with the little piece of chalk, she managed another word.

OgeR

He leaned forward and read it. "Baron Oger? *That* doesn't make sense. From what I've heard, His Majesty sent Baron Oger to manage the Marque of Calabas while the deaths of your family are being investigated. It's even been rumored he'll get the estate permanently if a living inheritor can't be found."

She patted the chalk on the board, squeezing in a few more letters. The piece was melting down as it scraped across the slate, dragging her toe-tips through some of the marks she made. It took him a bit of squinting and muttering to make out what she wrote, for all it was a single word.

muRdEr

"Your parents . . . were murdered?" At her nod, Marc tapped the previous word. "So what about the baron?"

Deliberately facing the chalkboard, Siona hissed and swiped her paw at the name, raking her claws across the four letters. Both of them shuddered at the nerve-wracking *scree*, but that was all right; it made her point all the more effective.

Marc sat back again. "But then why . . . ? Of *course*. He's a fellow mage, and a powerful one. I remember you from the Academy; you weren't bad at spellcasting, but Baron Oger . . . he has a reputation as one of the best. And the ear of the king. As His Majesty's officially sent investigator . . . he could easily cover up any evidence that pointed to *him*."

Siona nodded.

"The question is, *what* evidence?" Marc muttered. "I wish you could talk; I have a lot of questions I'd love to ask you."

Pawing the surface of the chalkboard, Siona wiped away the three previous words and started scraping new ones on the cleared surface. She ran out of chalk when she had only written "*BiG wA*," and had to mark the "*Rds*" in the dust of the slate with her furry little foot.

"Big wa . . . big . . . Big wards?" Marc asked, and received an equally

big nod. He mulled that over for a few moments. "I think I understand. I saw some artifacts set up at the crossroads outside. The curves
of the wires caging the crystals looked like tracking symbols. No doubt
he's told everyone they're up there in the hopes of tracking the murderer . . . but given how even your family's few cousins to the third and
fourth generation on your father's side have wound up dead in their
beds over the last week, they're probably designed to track down the
Calabas bloodline instead."

Siona nodded.

"Well. If there's one thing I'm good at as a mathemagician, it's pre-
cision, getting the most magic out of the least amount of spellpower.
It'll take me several hours to craft something appropriate, but I should
be able to come up with the right runes for a ward circle tight enough
to disguise a major Netherdemon, never mind a mere former Academy mate—if you don't mind my putting it that way," he allowed.

She couldn't shrug very well in cat shape, so she settled for blinking
at him, tail curled patiently around her haunches. Marc rubbed at his
bearded chin for a few moments, then slid his finger up to his ear for
a little rub and tug, ruffling his brown curls.

"Right. How about I go tell the innkeeper I'll be staying here for a
few more days, get us something to eat for later, and then the two of
us hole up in this room while I craft a means to safely talk with you?"
he asked. Siona nodded. Marc lifted his hand to the nape of her neck,
smiling as he scritch-rubbed gently. "You know, you are just as pretty
in this form as you ever were as a student. I'm regretting not spending
more time getting to know you back then."

Siona decided it was a good thing cats couldn't blush.

SHE had forgotten what she was, or rather wasn't, wearing. The moment her senses finished testing Marc's carefully drawn wardings, tell-

ing her it was safe to expand back into her normal form, Siona had done so . . . only to find herself wearing a very short sleeping gown and a pair of low boots.

Marc, seated inside the chalk-drawn circle with her, whistled slowly as he looked up, and up, and up. Blushing, Siona squeezed her bare thighs together and folded her arms across her chest. "Hush. I didn't exactly have time to dress the moment I realized a foreign mage was casting magic inside the manor."

"You had enough time to throw on some boots," her former Academy mate pointed out, still studying her curves.

"I thought the attack was coming from outside, and they were right there by the bed." Sinking down, trying her best not to flash him, Siona settled on the floor with a sigh. "I was just starting to grab my dressing robe when I felt a spell being targeted at *me*. Specifically, at my name."

"Name magic?" Marc asked. He focused on her face, now that she was seated at his level. "Isn't that Mendhite magic?"

"Yes, it was among some of the spells Don Carlo taught in his Runic Theory classes. And Don Carlo is old enough, he could have taught the baron," she added grimly. "That was when I shifted my shape."

"I didn't know you studied Animism. Don Marie only took on those students who showed an aptitude for spellshifting," Marc admitted. "I'll confess I never passed the entrance test for her classes."

"It's . . . not spellshifting." She blushed as she admitted it, but forged on. "The Marque of Calabas is a bit unique in the Kingdom of Guchere. The estate is entailed. *Magically* entailed. Some of that entailment is tied to the title of 'marquis' or 'marquess,' but some of it is tied to my family's blood. So long as one of the line of Calabas lives—a legitimate descendant—certain spells and spell-like effects will remain in existence. The king knows this, and I suspect the baron does as well, considering how careful he's being in exterminating anyone with a legitimate claim to the place."

"What's so important about these entailed spells?" he asked her. "If the Calabas line is wiped out, doesn't the magic go away? Is that what Baron Oger wants, to get rid of whatever magical benefits you're enjoying and thus make Calabas a normal sort of marque?"

Siona shook her head. "No, he wants the spells attached to the title. A long time ago, an ancestor rescued the people from enslavement to a vile sorcerer. The bloodlines of most of the villagers and farmers within the marque were enslaved to the marque. Permanently enslaved. They *had to* obey the person who held the title marquis or marquess of the estate. My father's ancestor came in, defeated the sorcerer, and when that didn't stop the enslavement, he oath-bound his life and the lives of his descendants to protect these people, rather than exploit them."

"What sort of exploitation?" her former classmate asked.

"Imagine, if you will, being able to order a family to give you every last bushel of beans, haunch of meat, and copper coin they had saved . . . and them actually doing so, even if it meant their starvation and death." She held his gaze as he paled. "That's the level of abuse Baron Oger wants to inflict. He's not bound to protect this land like my bloodline is. And there's worse—the sorcerer who originally enslaved the local peasants . . . sometimes he'd order them to fight against and kill each other, just for his amusement. They had no choice but to obey. It wasn't pretty."

Marc rubbed at his chin, then tugged on his ear. "So what does the cat thing have to do with all of this?"

She blushed. "That's something from my mother's side. Her great-plus-grandmother saved the High Priest of Cheren from being eaten by rats—it's a very long story—and the God Himself blessed her family line with the ability to become cats. The reason it helped me escape the name magic is because I've never been *called* by my name when

I'm a cat, and I've never answered to it as a cat. That name has no power over me as a cat, and thus the name magic has no power over me . . . but only while I'm a cat—you know, I'm giving you a lot of my trust by telling you these things."

"I won't betray that trust," Marc reassured her. "Besides, I agree: if you don't ever answer to it, then it's not your name. I remember Don Carlo's lectures on the subject. 'If you don't like what someone is calling you—'"

"'Then don't respond to it, Stupid,'" Siona agreed, smiling. "I remember them, too. Anyway, the spell missed. Barely, but it missed. It's still out there, too. I can feel it." She grimaced. "Unless Baron Oger recalls the spell . . . or if he dies . . . I'm stuck either living out my life as a cat, or living it inside very tight wards. Just saying my name outside these wards will cause his finding spells to focus on the speaker. The last think I needed was for him to magically overhear you speaking my name while you were figuring out my identity.

"I can also sense the spell hovering near those catch-ward crystals he's been putting up . . . and I'm now *outside* Calabas lands. Just barely outside, since the other side of the crossroads is Calabas land, but those wards now extend beyond my family's property. With the king backing him, he could have every major and minor city covered in just a few more weeks, plus all the crossroads watched . . . I'd have to flee the kingdom practically.

"I need your help, Marc," she murmured, holding his green gaze. Hoping he could help, somehow. "I need to figure out some way of taking him down before every last relative within seven generations ends up dead. Time is running out."

"If you don't have solid evidence he's doing it . . . he's too politically powerful to demand that he be Truth Stoned. Not without evidence to cast enough doubt on his innocence. Not to mention there are a few spells in existence for getting around that sort of thing, or at least the standard truth-sensing spells—I actually started out studying Veritamancy, thinking I might become a royal inquisitor," he explained. "But I have a better head for math and logic, so I ended up studying for my degree in Arithmancy. In some ways, I should have stuck with Veritamancy; there's always a demand for truth-discerning in the court systems, both here and abroad.

"My last job . . . I quit because my employer wanted me not only to do an audit of his business to find where he could tighten up production costs and lessen the amount of magical energy expended on his creations, he wanted me to *fix* the numbers magically so that the records would never show how much money he was really earning in his glassmaking shop. Particularly whenever tax time rolled around."

Siona smiled. "You're an honest man, Marc Tresket. We didn't have more than a handful of classes together, and we weren't ever paired for assignments . . . but I did see that much in you. It's why I decided to trust you."

He gave her a lopsided smile. "Honest men don't always find honest employment. Which is ironic, because I left the last job due to an ethical conflict, yet here you're asking me to help you in exposing . . . or even eradicating . . . a government official."

"A murderer," she corrected.

"How do you *know* Baron Oger is the murderer you seek?" Marc challenged her.

Siona gave him a sardonic look. "Because I studied Auramancy under Don Divestia . . . and because I got close enough to him as a cat to sniff the baron magically. I have a hard time casting active magics when I'm in cat form, but the passive ones still work well enough. That name spell came from his own energies. I'm so sure of it, I'm staking my life on it, because if I had any *sense*, I'd flee to the far side of the world. That . . . and if I weren't oath-bound to protect the land-bound peasants of Calabas. So long as they're in danger, I *have* to stick around and figure out how to save them all."

"Ah." He mulled that over. "So how do we get him to confess?"

She shrugged. "I don't know. I don't know what his weaknesses are or where his skeletons lie."

He rubbed at his chin and his ear, then tugged on it. "I suppose I could offer my services to him as a freelance Arithmancer, offer to go over the estate books, see if there is any sort of monetary motive behind the killings. Then we'd have an 'inside man' on the scene."

Siona nodded. "That could work . . . particularly if you claimed to be working on behalf of Dowager Queen Jalta—she's related to the family by marriage. I also happen to know something which has been kept hushed up from general knowledge. Her Majesty's been forced to take to her bed because of a stroke and is under healer's orders to have strict peace and quiet while she struggles to recover full speech and mobility—her primary healer sent a note to my parents just days before . . . well. The note explained why she wouldn't be visiting us later this summer as planned."

"That just might work . . . With her out of touch and the reason why she can't be reached hushed up, I can drop her name to get my foot in the door. I can also bring you onto the estate as my pampered pet cat, though I'd have to give you a suitable name—hey, how about *Boots*?" he teased, giving her feet an unabashed grin.

With his beard framing his white teeth, he looked a little wicked and rather sexy. As a younger, beardless man, he had been kind of cute, if shy and self-effacing. With the beard and that grin, he looked rather handsome. Siona felt her face and other parts farther south warming. "I suppose that one will do, if you *must* give me a name."

He scratched his chin, then his ear. "We'll also need to ensure some way of communicating while you're in cat form. It's been a while since my Artificing classes, but I think I can cobble together an amulet you could wear on a collar, something which would translate your verbal intent, your yowls and such, into actual Gucheran speech. It would have to be recharged each night, though, since I don't have the right ingredients on hand to make it long-lasting. The rather *expensive* ingredients. Unless you'd prefer to wait?"

She wrinkled her nose in distaste. "I'd rather not wait for the expensive stuff. I—"

She was interrupted by the *boom-boom-boom* of someone thumping on a large set of drums. Royal messenger drums. Siona quickly resumed her cat shape, allowing Marc to break the chalked lines of the wardings. As soon as both of them were free, they hurried to the window. Marc scooped her up in his arms in time to hear the drumming stop and see the royal messenger unrolling his scroll.

"*By royal decree!*" the man mounted on the horse called out in deep tones. "*His Majesty has commanded that, due to the unexpected and tragic loss of all known inheritors, Oger Havant, Baron of Shellid, shall be named successor to the Marque of Calabas. This proclamation is to be made all throughout the bounds of the Marque of Calabas and its immediate environs. Let all hear His Majesty's decree and honor your new governor, the Marquis Oger of Calabas!*"

Siona hissed. She didn't realize she had dug in her claws, too, until Marc himself hissed. Squirming out of his arms, she stalked over to the center of the broken wards and paced, waiting impatiently for him to return and begin inscribing the circles and runes all over again.

As soon as she safely could—many minutes later—Siona shot back to her natural form and glared at her former classmate, hands clenching in fists. "They're *both* in collusion on this! It's the *only* explanation why His Majesty would act so fast, when it's barely been a week!"

"Calm down," Marc ordered her, catching her wrists. "What you're suggesting could be considered treason *if* someone else hears us mentioning it. I did put up sound-dampening wards, but they'll only go so far. If we can't catch him by taking your evidence to the king and demanding a truth-testing . . . then we'll have to find evidence some other way, and . . . I can't believe I'm even thinking this . . ." he muttered.

"And what, take justice into our own hands? I'm more than willing!" Siona asserted. He hushed her again, glancing at the door and the walls around them. Subsiding, she thought out loud in a lower, quieter tone of voice. "You're right. We need evidence. But not just to prove it's Oger. We need evidence to hold over His Majesty's head. I don't want anyone else trying to gain control of Calabas once Oger's out of the way, and I don't want the one man who is *supposed* to be protecting all Gucherans to just turn around and back *another* greedy murderer."

"I'd better get to work crafting that collar—if there's anything you can do to help, we'd better brainstorm what that is right now," he added, releasing her hands. "It takes too long to set up these ward circles. We'll want to be prepared and ready before we start, if you're going to help make that collar, and help me think of ways to get the evidence we need. Here—I have a couple of miniaturized slate boards and some chalk in my pouch. You take one, I'll take the other, and we'll list out our objectives, requirements, and goals."

Siona smiled wanly. She settled back on the floor, tucking the hem of her nightdress down for decency. "Were you always this organized?"

"Third best Arithmancer in my graduating year. The only thing keeping me from a higher ranking was my lesser magic. I wasn't even a quarter as powerful as that Serina girl, the one from outkingdom," he admitted with a shrug. "She took the top honors."

"Serina . . . Serina . . . tall, skinny, pale blonde?" Siona asked. "Skinny, but really pretty?"

Marc wrinkled his nose. "Too tall, too skinny, and her hair was too straight." He smoothed his expression into a smile and added a wink. "I like curly haired Gucheran girls."

Mindful of the uncombed state of her own curls, Siona ducked her head and concentrated on writing down whatever ideas might be of use in her—their—quest.

❧

FROM the ends of her whiskers to the tip of her tail, Siona trembled with rage. It was all she could do to keep from growling and flexing her claws, the latter of which might have caused Marc to drop her. As it was, her tail *thumped* repeatedly against his chest.

Baron Oger lowered the lash in his hand, giving the whimpering man at his feet a brief respite. Strolling around to the front, he grabbed the peasant's curls and lifted his tear-streaked head. As he was a very large man and the peasant somewhat short, the Baron managed to lift his victim almost off his knees. "*Now* will you call me by my new, rightful title?"

"I'm so sorry, milord! Bright Heaven, I'm *sorry*, but I can't call you that!" the man begged.

"And why not?" Baron Oger all but purred. "Why can't you call me 'milord Marquis,' hmm?"

"Be-because there *isn't* a Marquis of Calabas!"

"I should beat you until—"

Marc cleared his throat, interrupting the older mage. As soon as he had the baron's attention, he spoke in a dry, bored tone, "Is this going to go on much longer? My time is very valuable."

His languid, foppish drawl made Siona blink. *Where did he learn to sound like a pampered Draconan nobleman?*

Baron Oger, would-be Marquis of Calabas, frowned. He dropped the farmer he had been whipping, shifting his hand to his hip. The stance only emphasized the breadth of his shoulders, making him look like a muscular wall. "*Your* time is valuable? Who are you, and why are you here?"

"My name is Arithmancer Marc Tresket. I was sent here as a favor of a *certain* high-ranking *someone* to offer my services in investigating any possible reason as to why the Calabas line has been slaughtered. Certain *other* parties insist on having an Academy-trained Arithmancer rule out financial gain as a motive. After all, Calabas is a prosperous marque, and money is always a motive." Pausing to pet the black cat lounging in his arms, Marc shrugged and continued. "Of course, if you think *you* could do a better job at figuring out how money could be a motive, and the truth of the estate accounts covered or uncovered . . .

"Oh, wait, *you* don't have a degree in Arithmancy. Any attempt *you* might make at trying to uncover embezzlement and so forth would be about as successful as any attempt you'd make to cover it all up." Another pause, a shift of his weight, and Marc tossed his head, settling his curls back from his face. "Either way, the longer I'm delayed, the more likely my employer is to recall my services . . . and send a more formal inquest as to why they were delayed."

"And who, pray tell, is your employer?" Oger sneered. The peasant was all but forgotten; Siona could tell the farmer was struggling to keep silent in spite of the blood-speckled welts on his back.

Marc gave a languid, graceful gesture with his free hand. "The Dowager Queen Jalta . . . but I'm here on her behalf *discreetly*. One of her uncles was related by marriage to the Calabas line, you know, and she is eager—out of sentiment, I'm sure—to settle the question of who inherits what, now that the family line is dead. Not to mention the death taxes need to be assessed and independently verified, for which reason I am also here. I do realize my appearance at this juncture is *unannounced* . . . but then that *is* the way these things are done these days. I *am* supposed to be an independent assessor of the situation, after all.

"I will require access to the entire estate, its storerooms, barns, warehouses, flocks, herds, and other accountables, plus of course all fiscal records for the last fifty years, and the original copies of any wills or other entailment documents. Personal correspondences if they can be found, in case anyone wrote any uncivilized, inflammatory letters at some point. I also require a study with a writing desk, several expandable slate boards . . . if they *have* any in such a backwater marque as this . . . and of course my own private suite of rooms," Marc added, as if such an endeavor were unthinkable otherwise. "I refuse to share quarters with anyone of lesser rank and status. The staff must also be informed about the needs of my precious puss here. It wouldn't do for my pretty little Boots to go hungry while I'm working, now would it?"

Siona affected a purr as he kneaded the nape of her neck. It wasn't too difficult, since Baron Oger's mouth had sagged open under the impact of Marc's performance. Marc paused once more, sighed, and tossed his head again, bouncing his brown curls.

"Now, if you're done punishing this criminal, or whatever he is, I'd be *deeply* obliged if you'd instruct the staff to prepare my rooms— unless this is some member of the staff and they're being unruly?"

"They're *all* being unruly." Shoving the farmer away, Baron Oger gestured behind him at the steps leading up from the courtyard into the manor house. Like most Gucheran noble homes, it was arranged in a square two stories high, ringed with arched balconies and centered around a garden courtyard shaded by trees and cooled by fountains. There was enough room on the flagstones directly in front of the wrought-iron entry gate to receive guests. Or to punish someone. The baron gestured for Marc to follow. "This way."

It didn't take long for a servant to show Marc to a guest suite on the second floor. Once there, and once his baggage had arrived from the coach hired to bring him to the manor, Marc warded the front room against scrying. Siona, set free to sniff around while they waited, joined him on the overstuffed cushions lining the wicker couch.

"Your assessment?" he asked quietly.

She squeaked and *mrraurred*, and the collar they had crafted for her over the last two days translated her intentions in an approximation of her own voice. "This is *bad*. He'll beat them until they call him the

Marquis of Calabas, but the entailment means they literally can't. Not the spellbound ones. The others, the freeholders, they can call him whatever they want, but the enslaved ones cannot lie."

"What if *you* told them to lie?" Marc asked.

She shook her head. "They can't. Unless there is an actual Marquis of Calabas . . . they can't. They can only say that someone is the marquessa, which would be me. Or the marquess if I were married . . . *Ohhh*."

"Oh, what?" he asked. She blinked up at him and he reached over, scratching the top of her head. Siona enjoyed it for a moment, then pulled both her head and her mind back, concentrating on the business at hand.

"Well . . . if I got *married*, then they could say there was a Marquis of Calabas. But . . . I still can't order them to lie to a government official. That's part of my own family's spellbound covenant with them, part of the things which ensure we'll never abuse our powers. Particularly that we will never abuse those powers and then try to conceal it from the law."

He mulled that over. "What about . . . if you ordered them to obey *me*, and *I* told them to lie?"

"They wouldn't have cause to obey unless you were my husband. And even then . . . I don't know how much of the spellbinding on the Calabas line would affect a spouse's commands." Siona sighed and groomed her shoulder, thinking about it.

"What if I told them—or even if you told them—to *seem* as if they were addressing him as the Marquis of Calabas . . . so long as *I* was present and was your husband? You know, like the way how you can be looking directly at one person, but are actually talking to someone else?"

She paused in her grooming, tail tip twitching. "That . . . might work. Of course, it would require us to get married, but such things aren't irreversible. We could always get an annulment afterward."

Marc slowly shook his head. "No . . . I don't think so."

About to lick her paw and groom her face, Siona quirked her furry brows. "You don't think so? I know marriage is a bit extreme, but I'd really rather my people weren't beaten for something beyond their control."

"No, I meant an annulment would be out of the question, not the marriage itself." Reaching over, he scooped her up and cuddled her against his chest, putting their heads close together. His was large, brown, and curly; hers was small, black, and furry. Meeting her green gaze with his own, Marc quirked up the corner of his mouth. "You're a beautiful, intelligent woman, Boots. I'd have to have the willpower of a god to resist the thought of making love to you if I had the chance. As it is, I'm a young, healthy man, and you're a young, healthy woman. *If* we marry . . . I'm afraid we'd have to get a divorce. I insist on having a wedding night. And any other following nights."

She opened her mouth to *mrrau* in protest at him, only to have his fingertip lightly bop her on the nose.

"Besides, how do we know I'll even *count* as your husband, at least where the entailment spells are concerned, unless the marriage is first consummated? Hmm?"

He had her there. Subsiding in his arms, Siona mulled it over. *He isn't a bad catch, as far as husbands might go. He's not a messy roommate, and he did buy me a set of clothes to wear so I'm not stuck reshaping myself into nothing but my nightdress and boots. He's smart, and funny, and cute . . . and he smells nice,* she admitted. *Plus he's rather good at finding all the right spots to scritch while I'm in this form. Hopefully that should translate into reasonably good skill as a lover . . .*

Marc lifted his brows, waiting for a reply. Making up her mind, she nodded. "All right. We should probably do it in the manor chapel, too, as soon as possible. After supper. That is, presuming Priestess Selva hasn't been retired precipitously. She's one of the few surviving people within the marque who know I can take on a cat form. Just caution her not to say a certain spell-targeted name, to avoid catching the attention of Oger's wards, and we should be fine."

"Agreed. And if she can't do it, well, whoever *is* there will just have to put up with my wedding my cat," Marc muttered, though he wrinkled his nose.

Cats, Siona discovered, could actually smirk. "I look forward to seeing you pull off *that*."

THANKFULLY, the priestess was still there. She had almost turned them away, citing the need to continue preparing the bodies of other Calabas family members still in the process of being brought to the family crypt for interment, but she consented eventually. Namely after several surreptitious, thoughtful looks at Siona, and Siona's own solemn nod upon the third viewing. Their sole witness was the young acolyte who served as Selva's altar boy. The youth stared with wide green eyes at the amulet-translated cat while "Boots" meow-spoke her vows but otherwise didn't comment.

Baron Oger confronted them not more than a minute after they left the chapel with the blessing of their patron god Cheren still dampening their brows in an oily blue dot. Or rather, he confronted Marc. He met them on the winding garden path leading through the back gardens to the rear entrance of the manor.

"I tried getting ahold of Her Majesty via scrying mirror," Oger growled, glaring down at the shorter man, "but it seems the dowager queen is currently experiencing a bout of religious fervor and is 'contemplating her life.' Which means I cannot ask her directly to confirm your presence here."

Marc tossed his hair and stroked the cat in his arms. "It's not *my* fault her relatives have been dropping like day-flies. Her Majesty is probably busy confessing her sins and purging her guilts in the understandable effort to avoid spending part of her afterlife in a Netherhell. Besides, I'm supposed to be here as an *independent* investigator of the nature and status of the Calabas estate. It wouldn't do to connect me too strenuously with a potentially interested party."

Out of the corner of her eye, Siona watched this languid, foppish version of the normally sane Arithmancer give the larger man a wink . . . and then purse his lips. Oger paled and backed up. Marc smirked and strolled past him for a few steps, then turned and spoke again.

"I'll need access to all books, scrolls, logs, journals, letters, receipts, and other forms of record-keeping bright and early tomorrow morning. Now, if you'll excuse me, it's been a terribly long day of traveling already, and I'll need to spend what is left of this evening preparing my mathemagics for the morrow's accountings." He paused, glanced around the lantern-lit shadows of the garden, then stepped close enough that Siona had to suppress a sneeze at the musky-sour scent of the baron's body odor. "If you have any *specific* instructions on what I should or shouldn't find . . . slip them under the door. I'll set up a catch spell to hold them confidential until I can attend to whatever you have in mind."

Baron Oger stepped back. His lip curled up. "Are you *flirting* with me?"

"Hardly. I save all of my passion for my sweet puss. Isn't that right, Boots?" Marc asked, lifting Siona and turning her so that he could nuzzle her face with his own. She licked his cheek above his beard, doing her best to look like an affectionate, pampered cat. Cuddling her to his chest, he gave the baron a superior smile. "I am, however, smart enough to seize an opportunity, or even just see the possibility for it. Particularly if there is some profit in it for me. I *am* an Arithmancer . . . and manipulating money is just one more form of mathemagics, isn't it?

"Sleep well, Your Excellency," Marc added over his shoulder as he turned back toward the manor. "I certainly intend to . . ."

∽

AN hour later, as soon as the last chalk mark sealed most of their suite against any possible intrusion, physical or magical, Siona unfurled herself into her human form and smirked at her ersatz husband. "*You* are unbelievable. Whatever gave you the idea to act like *that* around him? Did you want to risk having him throw us out?"

"It's a trick I learned from a classmate from my primary schooling years. Well, not a classmate, per se," Marc amended, putting his chalks back into their pockets on his satchel. He had marked all of the walls, plus the edges of the ceiling and the floor in shades of blue, white, pink, green, and silvery gray. "Eremen Gestus was an extraordinary eleven-year-old con artist. He would affect a brash, over-the-top personality to distract anyone and everyone around him during the luncheon break . . . and while we were all distracted, he would swap out bits of lunch brought by the others.

"Pocket breads, fruits, even baked sweets would end up in *his* hands, if we weren't careful. And though many of us swore time and again we wouldn't let his antics distract us . . . sooner or later, his little theatrics and gestures would draw our attention away from guarding our sticky buns and our pasta bowls, and there would go a spoonful of this and a nibble of that into *his* mouth, and down into *his* gullet." Wiping his hands on a rag taken from his satchel, Marc smiled wistfully. "It took me more than three months to realize he *never* brought food of his own from home. I don't think his family had any to spare. Not and still afford to give him an education.

"When I realized why he did it . . . I didn't begrudge him the way he cadged his meals, since it spared him his dignity. He went on to be quite famous—I'm sure you've heard of him, Gestus nii Vestas?"

"Gestus nii Vestas?" Siona repeated, startled. "The Magicless Wonder? The entertainer who has successfully challenged hundreds of mages to explain how he makes things appear and disappear *without* any traces of magic? You grew up in the same school as him?"

"Primary school only, since I went on to the Academy to learn real magic, and obviously he didn't follow, but yes. *However*," he stated, moving close enough to cup her shoulders, clad as they were in the short-sleeved, short-cropped tunic he had bought for her to wear, along with the matching rose-pink skirt wrapped decorously around her hips, concealing her legs down to her ankles. "This is our wedding night, and I would rather you paid attention to *me*, tonight."

Twisting, Siona double-checked the wards he had scribed. "Did you remember to ward against the passage of excessive sounds, as well as intrusions and scryings?"

"That's what the pink runes are for." Sliding his hands from her shoulders to her back, he stroked along her spine, subtly tugging her closer.

When Siona looked back at him, he seized the opportunity to kiss her. His lips were sweet, warm, and slightly scratchy, thanks to his mustache and beard. They also grew on her rather quickly, coaxing her into responding with soft, savory nibbles. It had been a while since her last lover; she had forgotten how satisfying in and of itself a good kiss could be . . . and Marc was undeniably a good kisser.

By the time it ended, her lips stung a little from the scratching of his beard, but she didn't mind; his kisses were quite enjoyable. He had also loosened the ties of her blouse and had splayed his hands across her bared back. Siona smiled. "I take it you've done this before?"

"Just because I'm an Arithmancer doesn't mean I'm as passionless as my numbers and formulae," Marc admonished. He smiled as he said it, rippling his fingers in a subtle massage along either side of her spine, then sliding them down to the ties of her skirt. "Besides, I tutored Stasia Nicolmo in applied statistics and Geomancy in exchange for lessons on how to please a woman properly."

Siona wrinkled her nose, remembering the girl in question. "Stasia Nicolmo? But she looked like a . . ."

"As *she* put it, since she never had the looks to catch and hold a man's attention, she always had to rely upon pure skill," Marc told her. "She exchanged tutoring lessons with at least five other classmates and managed to graduate with decent grades. Last I heard, she had moved west to Nightfall to work for some guild in the brand-new kingdom.

"But enough about her," he added, drawing his hands around her waist. The action brought the ties of her skirt around as well, unwrapping the garment. "We need to focus on me and you."

Siona mock-frowned and tucked her hands around his waist, finding and tugging at the ties of his own trousers. "Not fair. If I have to get naked, so do you."

Marc grinned. "It'll be my pleasure."

I don't know why, Siona mused as she backed off, divesting herself of clothing and giving him the room to do the same, *but somehow, getting naked so I can make love to my* husband, *and not just a casual lover, is rather titillating. Illicit, even. Possibly because it's only temporary . . . but possibly because it* is *a commitment. A legal right to pleasure. In other words,* she thought, moving back to run her fingers over the whorls of hair dusting his now naked chest, *mine, all mine. Acres and acres, and it's all mine . . .*

She paused and pulled back, looking down. His trousers had fallen, thanks to her own efforts, but while he was still wearing a loin wrap, it was the impediment to the removal of his trousers that had caught her attention. Smirking, she looked up at him. "Perhaps I should start calling *you* 'Boots' as well?"

"Just for that, I'll make you remove them," he quipped. He shuffled over to the side of the bed, sat, and stuck out his feet, draped in a tangle of cloth and leather. Kneeling, Siona untangled his clothes and removed them, noting with approval the contraceptive amulet tied around his ankle. She crawled up onto his lap when she was done, meeting his lips even as she straddled his hips.

With each of them clad in a loin wrap and nothing else, she was free to touch almost anything she wanted. What she wanted to do most, she did: Siona ran her fingers through the hair on his chest. "Mmm . . . *very* manly. Last time I saw you, Marc, well, you still looked like a boy. Young and hairless. But *this* makes you look very much like a fully grown man. I like it."

Grinning, he lifted his palms to her breasts, gently cupping the soft curves. She shivered when he rubbed his thumbs in slow circles around their peaks, and shivered again when he spoke. "Alas, I can't say the same, since you already had *these* when I first saw you . . . but they're a *very* nice pair of these."

She laughed, tilting her head back. Marc shifted, taking advantage of her bared throat. With the edges of his thumbs rubbing her nipples, he nuzzled and gently bit the exposed skin, feathering his teeth over her skin. The combination was simple, yet stunning, connecting not only her breasts to her throat, but her throat to her loins. Breath hissing in, she raked her fingers gently through the coarse fuzz of his chest and tugged lightly on the strands.

Marc shivered under her. "Mmm . . . are you sure you didn't tutor Stasia in anything yourself?"

That made her laugh a second time. "Maybe I'm just naturally talented. Or maybe I just prefer practicing on hairy men."

He pulled her close, pressing them together from pelvis to chest. Nipping at her ear, Marc growled, "Well, you're married to *me*, now. For however long this marriage may last, I *don't* believe in sharing."

That was titillating, too. Digging her fingers into his dark brown curls, Siona tipped his head back, baring his own throat to her lips. "*I* don't believe in sharing when married, either."

"Mmm, good," he murmured. "Then we're agreed . . . we'll have lots and lots of lovemaking together—and if we don't get it right, we'll just keep practicing until we do."

Chuckling, she nibbled on his ear. He growled again and nipped back, somehow finding a ticklish spot she hadn't known existed. Squirming, Siona fought back to nibble while avoiding being nibbled on in turn. Somewhere in there, their mouths met, this time for a much more heated kiss than before. Fingers buried in her long black curls, tipping her head this way and that, Marc kissed nearly every inch of her skin from brows to collarbone.

The pleased, hungry noises he made as he did so thrilled her. It had been a while since she'd had a lover, particularly one so enthusiastic. As the sole heir to Calabas—in the immediate family sense, before the odious baron began his killing spree—she had been caught up in learning how to manage the marque in a responsible, oath-sensitive manner. That hadn't left a lot of time for pursuing anything other than a casual romp. This wasn't a casual romp, though; for however long or short it lasted, they *were* married.

Recapturing his mouth, Siona kissed him hungrily. She didn't know if or when Baron Oger might uncover their deception, or how long it might take to find evidence solid enough to prove his guilt, or how to deal with him once they did. It felt right to seize the moment with this man. With her husband.

Pushing him down onto the bed, Siona kissed her way down his chest, nuzzling her face into the crisp strands of his chest hair. Marc played with her curls, letting her be aggressive. She had to slip off the bed in order to kiss lower than mid-chest; by the time she did, the modest bulge in his loin wrap had formed a distinct ridge. Unbuckling the thong holding the wrap in place, she freed the spike of his flesh from the folds of cloth.

The reddened head was peeking out through its little cowl, encouraging her to gently grasp and stroke it. Marc sucked in a breath, lifting his hips into her touch. He reached for her hands, curling up a little so that he could tug on them. "Come up here on the bed. If you're going to play with me like that, I want to play with you, too."

She complied. He guided her into lying down diagonally on the bed, giving both of them enough room to stretch out past each other, heads to loins. Siona lifted her upper leg, bending her knee so she could brace it upright, but he didn't accept her silent invitation immediately. Instead, he leaned over her thighs and kissed their soft skin. Enjoying it, she returned the favor, exploring the differences between the smoother, nearly hairless expanse of his upper thighs versus the hairs scattered with increasing thickness over his lower legs.

His erection bumped against her shoulder and throat. Gradually, the accidental brushes became more deliberate touches, until with hungry little moans of her own, she kissed her way from his sack to his spike and back. He returned her efforts by nuzzling his way into her folds, proving within moments that he had been well paid for his tutoring efforts. Siona enjoyed it thoroughly, until he murmured something she couldn't quite catch.

Lifting her mouth from his spike, she pushed up higher on her elbow and craned her neck. "What did you say?"

Beard glistening, Marc removed his head from between her thighs. He flashed her a grin. "Just a little spell I read about, a few years back. *One* which I'm sure you'll enjoy."

The moment he said *one*, her loins throbbed. It was a subtle vibration, but a distinct one. Blinking, Siona eyed him. "Did you just . . ."

"I *am* an Arithmancer. Numbers are my specialty." Smirking, he paused, pursed his lips, and carefully enunciated, "*Four.*"

The subtle thrumming became a distinct buzzing in her flesh. Siona gasped, hips bucking. Rolling onto her back, she squirmed in the attempt to escape, but she couldn't. It stayed with her, enervating her senses. "What did you . . . ?"

"What, don't you like that number? How about *five*? *Six*?" he asked.

The tremors strengthened, spreading from the little peak at the top of her folds to the base of her spine, making her buck again in surprise. "Or would you prefer *three*?"

The intensity backed off, allowing her to unclench her hands from the bedcovers. It didn't fade completely, but it wasn't quite so strong. "How . . . how high does it go?"

"*Five* plus *five* . . . but I won't say the exact number just yet," he added. He waited until she stopped arching her back before continuing. "You're not quite ready for that."

"Gods, no!" she breathed, panting through the pleasure stirred by the vibrations. Then she reconsidered when he curled himself around so that he lay the same way, allowing him to massage her breasts. He rotated them in time with the restless circling of her hips, until Siona panted, "Well . . . maybe . . ."

"Did you know that most people consider mathematics—the plain, non-magical kind—to be quite boring?" he asked. His tone was idle, but his fingers were not. They toyed with the peaks of her breasts.

"No, really?" she managed to pant.

"Oh, yes. I consider it *one* of my missions in life to instruct people in all the joys of counting." As she relaxed under the lessened sensations, he smiled, abandoning her breasts for her thighs. Nudging them apart, he stroked through her now palpably slick folds for a few moments, then probed into her depths. "Ah, yes . . . I do believe you are now receptive enough to learn all about *three* of my favorite numbers."

Shifting over her, Marc settled between her thighs. Ready and willing, Siona lifted her knees, giving him more room to find the right spot. But he didn't do more than prod.

"My first favorite number is *zero*." He waited a moment, allowing her to absorb the lack of vibration. "Before it was 'invented,' math was sometimes awkward to calculate. And if I say it twice—since I'm the *one* who cast the spell—it'll end the magic. But I won't. Not just yet."

Siona sighed, glad the buzzing had come back. She tried to coax him closer with her hands and her heels, but he didn't move. Giving up, she raked her fingers lightly through the manly fur on his chest. "What's the next number?"

"My next favorite number is *pi*," he added, bracing his weight comfortably on his elbows and knees. "*Three . . .*"

He pushed in a little. Moaning, Siona arched her hips up into his. "Mmm, yess . . ."

"Point *one* . . ." He backed out a little, then pushed in again. "*Four . . .*" He pressed in a little deeper than before, accompanying the increase in tremors. "*One . . . Five . . .*" Out and in again, matching penetration to vibration—then a sudden thrust of word and flesh, "*Nine!*"

Siona gasped. Fingers clutching at the bedding, she waited for him to move, to match the intense pleasure buzzing madly through her flesh. She tried lifting her hips into his to encourage him to continue, but he shifted with her, avoiding all but the smallest of frictions. Frustrated, she finally growled, "Move!"

"Move? Like this?" Marc asked, lifting his hand and wriggling his fingers in an aimless flutter.

"*Spike* me!" Siona ordered, not caring if the term was crude and beneath her station. "Spike me *hard*!"

Flashing her a grin, he complied. Vigorously. Even better, he leaned down close enough to tell her what she could only presume were the decimal numbers associated with *pi*, given how randomly they were placed. With each flex of his hips, he matched the strength and depth of his thrusts to the value of each number growled.

Somewhere in there, at a depth of mathematical understanding only a mathemagician would bother to memorize and recite, she shattered in bliss. Thankfully, he gasped out a *zero* between thrusts and shuddered a few strokes later in his own orgasm. Sagging gently onto her, considerate enough to brace some of his weight on his elbows, he pressed soft kisses to her shoulder and collarbone.

As her breathing recovered, a stray thought floated through Siona's sated mind. "So . . . ?"

"Mmm?" he asked, placing another kiss on the upper slope of one breast.

"So . . . what's your *third* favorite number?" she clarified, arching one of her brows.

Her husband laughed, delighted by her query, until she lifted her head from the bedding and claimed his parted lips for a kiss.

"So . . . we're supposed to *say* 'Marquis of Calabas' . . . while *looking* at this Baron Odious . . . and it's *not* going to be a lie?" Errick, the manor's farrier, asked dubiously.

Siona—or rather, Boots, since she was in her cat form—nodded. Marc had remembered to charge her translation amulet earlier that morning, after she had hissed at him and pawed at her throat. But it was working, and it was very handy. Having introduced herself as an "agent of the new marquis" to explain her authority, she was using Errick as a test subject. The farrier was phlegmatic enough to accept a talking cat, but smart and skeptical enough to poke holes in her logic. "Yes. Just think of the real marquis and answer as if you are addressing him, even though you're not actually looking at him."

The farrier rubbed at his chin, though he didn't tug on his ear like her husband did. "I don't know if I *can* . . . Maybe if the real one was right there? Or at least in hearing range?"

Cats could sigh, even if they couldn't shrug. She nodded patiently and *mewed*, letting her necklace translate her words. "I'll see what I can do. But I *am* asking you to indulge the baron in his little whims to spare yourselves further harm. You'll have to decide on your own what that requires doing. Spread word to the others when you can, but do it discreetly. Now, if you'll excuse me, I have to run down to the miller's house and tell Marla about all of this. She'll spread the news of this across the west half of the marque."

"How do you, a mere cat, know so much about Marla and her gossiping habits?" Errick asked

"Magic," she *mrraued*, flicking her tail. He laughed as she scampered away, heading for the edge of the manor grounds. Pausing briefly to look back at the house, Siona fancied she could see Marc through one of the upper windows, but knew it was unlikely. He was stuck inside for the next few days, going through all the estate records.

At least his diligence would have a twofold effect. One, it would allow her to spread the word about *appearing* to call Baron Oger by the title of marquis, even if they might only be able to do it when Marc was alongside the odious, overgrown man. And two, it would be good to have a proper mathemagical analysis of the Calabas accounts and properties. Her family had always done well enough with basic accounting practices, the sort that didn't require a mage to compute, but it wouldn't hurt to have the books gone over by an expert.

An expert who had taught her a deeper appreciation for *mere numbers* just last night . . .

"WHAT are you *doing* in there?" Marc hissed two days later. Scooping her off the threshold of the partially open door, he hurried both of them down the length of the balcony to his suite of rooms. Siona barely had time to paw the air, closing the doorway where he had found her. Shutting the door to his own rooms, he cradled her in one arm while he fished out a scrap of chalk. Marking the panel with a quickly scribbled silencing ward, he glared at the black cat in his arms. "Do you know what he would have *done* to you if he'd found you snooping around in his bedchambers? Or one of his guards?"

Siona flattened her ears and hissed back. The wire and crystal necklace translated her intent. "They aren't *his* quarters! They're my parents' quarters! And he's *gutted* their things! Most of their clothes have been tossed into sacks like they were rags, and I have no clue where my mother's jewelry casket went! That *thief* is ruining *everything* he touches!"

He shook her. Gently, but he shook her. "This is *not* a game! He's pressuring me to find some way to increase the rents off the tenants and hide the extra income in the record books."

She growled wordlessly for a moment, then *mrraowled* in a way that the translator spell could actually use. "I *know* it isn't a game. I also know he went down to the solar to have a few drinks before dinner, so I thought I had plenty of time! Why aren't you down there with him?"

"I had to use the refreshing room. *Don't* go doing things like that while he's actually in the manor house," Marc admonished her. "The risk of being caught is too great!"

"I can't do it when he leaves the manor because he spell-locks his quarters!" she shot back, tail flicking rapidly. "Besides, I *think* I've found evidence against him."

"You have?" he asked. "What? How?"

"He brought a writing desk with him. One of the legs smelled rather strongly of sweat and body oil at about the midpoint, indicating it had been touched a lot more than normal. *Handled* a lot more than normal. It wasn't easy, but I managed to sniff out a couple of other spots along the underside which he's also touched a lot more than would normally be touched. I *think* there's a hidden compartment in his desk." Seeing he was paying attention to her, she calmed the thrashing of her tail and flicked her ears. "I intend to find out.

"My plan is to craft a couple of recording crystals tonight and position them around the room, very small and subtle ones which individually won't record very much, and which won't give off enough of an aura to be detected since they'll be scattered separately. But once they're gathered back up and assembled into an illusion projector, we should be able to re-create how he gets into the desk, without risking an ignorant—and thus potentially dangerous—attempt ourselves."

He considered her suggestion. "All right. But *if* we're going to do this, it'll have to be carefully timed. And I'll want to do a test run of these recording Artifacts, to see if they are indeed as subtle as you claim—you do realize that if you're going to work on crafting them tonight, we're not going to be able to make love?"

His reminder lowered her ears. In just three short nights, she had grown rather fond of his inventive lovemaking. Sighing, Siona flicked her tail. "I guess it's a sacrifice we'll just have to make. At least the artificing can be done in a single night, though I'll have to stay here to catch up on my sleep in the morning."

Marc groaned. "Ugh. I was hoping to have you along. I'm supposed to be taking a tour of the exact extent of the Calabas estate boundaries with His Excellency on the morrow. Several hours of being stuck in a carriage with Baron Odious isn't exactly my idea of fun."

"As you yourself said," Siona *mrrewled*, "this isn't a game. We both have to take some risks and make some sacrifices. At least with you along, he shouldn't have any excuse to flog the oath-bound peasants he runs across."

"Yes, whatever you said to the stable hands, the way they addressed me while looking at *him* cheered him up when we were outside earlier," Marc agreed. Moving away from the door, he set her on the bed, pausing just long enough to stroke her spine a couple of times before heading for the refreshing room. "We'll have to figure out how to get you into that other suite without getting caught. Maybe when the servants clean it?"

"How about when you go in there to make an inventory of the previous owners' wealth?" she *mraowled* after his retreating form, glad he had restored the sound-dampening ward. So long as the door wasn't opened, she could talk to him openly like this. Leaping down to the floor, she trotted over to the refreshing room door, not wanting to *meow* too loudly, since that would stress her shape-shifted throat. "His attention will be on *you*, not on me. He'll be watching your aura to see what magics you cast, if any. If you do nothing but Arithmancy in his presence, but do enough of it, that could mask me placing the crystals."

"Perhaps, but if you do it while the maids are in there," Marc countered through the door, "he won't be *watching* for magic, because he'll be elsewhere."

"But what if he's paranoid enough to do a thorough scrying sweep after each cleaning?" she retorted. "If you're there and he doesn't see you casting any untoward spells, then he'll probably not feel the need to recast any detection spells immediately after. I am a mere cat, after all, and thus hardly noticeable."

"To everyone but me. I'd notice you anywhere." Having washed his hands, Marc emerged after a few more moments, brow pinched in thought. "That *might* work, but we'd have to give him a reason to access his secret compartment before the next thorough cleaning. I suppose I could draw up a contract that, *if* I come up with a way to hide the extra income he wants to squeeze out of the Calabas tenants so that it can't be assessed and taxed by the government, *I* can't be held liable for his illegalities should they be uncovered. A magically binding paper of a nature he'd want to keep hidden from all other prying eyes."

Siona purred. The translator necklace surprised her, for it spoke up in its approximation of her natural voice. "I *knew* you were brilliant . . ."

Smiling, he scooped her off the floor and nuzzled her with his bearded face. "Thank you, my dear, for the lovely compliment."

She squirmed a little in feline instinct, then licked his cheek.

"HURRY!" Siona hissed as Marc worked his fingers into the hole at the back of the drawer slot, trying to find and activate the last puzzle tumbler. "I don't know how much longer the manor servants can keep him occupied with one fiddly little crisis after the next."

"I've got it, I've got . . . there!" Bending his arm sideways in the drawer slot, he pulled out a book, two scrolls, and several papers. He set the papers on the floor for her to read, quickly unbound the scrolls and laid those next to the papers, then pulled out the larger blank book, pen, and jar of ink he had prepared for this moment.

Siona pounced on the scrolls, unrolling them and scanning their contents. She hissed at the contents of the second one. "Here! This one is a missive granting Oger the rights to the Marque of Calabas . . . and it's dated two weeks *before* we were attacked. Is this evidence enough for you?"

"I have even more evidence right here," Marc murmured, flipping page by page through the blank book and the book he had pulled from the niche in the writing desk. He dipped his pen in the inkwell and drew a straight line across the next blank page, his gaze on the text of the Baron's book, then let the copying spell spill that line of ink into a duplicate of the pages he was speed-reading. "Calabas isn't the first crime he's committed, though it's the biggest. This is his . . . his *brag* book, for lack of a better word. Everything from drowning the prized puppies of a rival cousin back near the beginning of this thing," he flipped over the next pair of pages, "to blackmailing a certain marquess into having an affair with him . . . He's a real piece of work."

"Master-crafted in a Netherhell," she agreed. "Make sure you get a copy of this scroll. Once we take down Oger, I want to keep it as evidence to blackmail His Majesty into dropping all further pursuit toward taking over our lands."

Marc smiled, though he didn't stop his rapid spellcopying. "*Our* lands. I like the sound of that. We work rather well together, don't we?"

Sitting on her haunches, Siona curled her tail around her paws.

"Yes, we do. Getting married as quickly as we did was indeed a bit hasty, I'll admit, but I wouldn't say it was a mistake. At least so far." That earned her a sharp look. Siona smirked and added, "I'll have to give it another twenty years before I can be absolutely sure. So . . . what would you think of sticking around for a while, of trying this marriage thing for real, if and when we take out the Odious Oger?"

His smile broadened. "I'm game if you are—why, Boots, are you purring at me?"

She flicked her ears. "No, I'm playing the harp. Of *course* I'm purring!"

"Shh," he admonished. "Unless you can jump up here and wield this pen for me, I'll need to concentrate. As you said, we don't have much time, and you can't do this for me."

Not for the first time in her life, Siona wondered why her ancestress had to have been granted the shape of a four-toed cat, rather than the six- or seven-toed kind that had a sort of awkward opposable thumb. Instead of bothering Marc with more comments, she contemplated a much more important question: How to kill a mage more powerful and dangerous than both of them combined.

By the time he shooed her off of the second scroll so that he could copy it, she was reduced to thinking up wilder and wilder ideas. Most of the plausible ones weren't all that feasible, given the disparity in their power levels. *Even combined, Marc and I could barely take him on in a straightfoward fight. But we can't neutralize his magic with, either; his aura reeks of self-protective spells against all manner of outside forces.*

The only way it would work is if he limited his powers, and then we ambushed him. But even without his magic, he's still physically power-ful—one of those mages who doesn't believe in letting his magic do all of his fighting for him. And I can see why. Magically or physically, he's a tough opponent.

Outside, she could hear birds twittering; their high-pitched chirps were annoying. Not just for the way they made her sensitive, pointed ears twitch, but because they plucked at her feline instincts. Part of her wanted to go outside and stalk those birds, but she couldn't do that just . . . yet.

Oh! "Marc? Can you shift your shape?"

"Not naturally. No grateful gods in *my* family history." His attention was more on his copying efforts still, but he did give her question consideration. "If you mean via a spell . . . I did take the basic course in Anthromancy and I passed it with a reasonable grade. But I didn't pursue it as an elective. I didn't have the aptitude."

"Could you . . . you know . . . steer *him* into a discussion of shape-shifting magics?" she asked.

"There, done," he murmured, quickly rolling up the scroll and retying it. He cast a delayed cleaning spell on the scroll and stooped, tucking it into the niche with the other scroll, the letters—which included his contract of non-liability—and the bragging diary. Having carefully replaced the puzzle locks, he fitted the drawer back into place and packed away his copying materials. "So . . . you want me to engage him in a discourse of applied metamorphism. Why?"

"Because I'm wondering if you could not only get into a discussion of it, but, say, challenge him to a *demonstration*? Flatter his power and abilities, encourage him to try large shapes, that sort of thing?" Siona asked.

She let him scoop her up after he cast another cleaning charm on the floor and the door so that he could carry her back out of her parents' former quarters. Falling silent, she waited with bated breath while he checked to make sure no one could see them entering the upper balcony, and stayed silent until they were back in the guest quarters with a freshly applied silencing rune.

"More to the point, Marc, after challenging him to take on a large form, since that's easy enough for a large man to do . . . could you trick him into taking on a *small* form?" she asked, looking up into his green eyes. "A *very* small form?"

Catching on to her idea, he nodded slowly. "Yes . . . yes, I could. But that would place the burden on you. He'd expect an attack from me, just as he would be checking for untoward magic from me. Could *you* . . . well . . . ? Fast enough that he couldn't . . . ?"

She nodded solemnly. "I'll do my best. I have done it before, though only with actual rodents. It *is* the God-wrought duty of the women in my family to learn how to kill rats, after all. We certainly can't take this to the king. Not when that scroll implicates him, too. All we can do is use it to blackmail him to stay off of Calabas lands. We can't do that to the baron, too, now that he's been formally declared the new marquis. He's too firmly ensconced. But *that* means . . ."

He sighed and rubbed behind her ears. "Yes. Morally repugnant, but I guess there really is only one thing left for us to do."

It wasn't quite as simple as engaging the odious baron in a conversation about magic. Though her husband did manage to confirm Baron Oger knew several shape-shifting spells, he couldn't get the man to actually display any of them. So, as Siona watched from her "pampered pet" position on a chair cushion, Marc decided to get the two of them drunk.

Normally, mages didn't overindulge. Alcohol lowered inhibitions and weakened willpower, which could make a mage lose common sense and self-control—untrained mages were forbidden to drink until they had passed a certain level of control and competency at the very least. But by using the same distract-and-conquer tactics, and by playing the part of an increasingly tiddly court gossipper, Marc egged Oger onward, both in increasingly salacious conversation and in refilling each other's drinks. He was witty, charming, wicked, and over the top.

Listening to the two men getting into a belching contest, Siona flattened her ears against her skull and lowered her chin to her paws. *Men . . . No refinement, no sensibility . . . Wow, that's an impressive burp . . . but . . . ewwww! Oger has now completely earned the title "Odious." I didn't even know it was possible to pass gas simultaneously from both ends, on command! Disgusting!*

Evidently her husband agreed. Marc flapped his hand in front of his bearded face. "Gods . . . I can't even top that . . . S'ppose I'll hafta challenge you to shape-shifting, now."

"You still on 'bout that?" Oger asked. He tipped his glass up to his lips. Marc leaned over and poured more rum into it. "Thanks . . . What is it wi' you an' shpellshifting?"

"I think I've found somthi-*hic*-ink I can beat you at, magicamally. *You're* all talk," Marc added, waving the decanter around before topping off his own glass, "but no acshun. I don' think you *can* . . . you know. Shift-spell . . . shift."

"Course, I can!" He belched and scratched his ribs. "I can shift *sheveral . . . several* animal forms."

"Okay . . . what is your *largest* spellshape?" Marc asked.

Oger tapped his lips with his finger. "Dromid."

"A what-id?"

"Dromid! Dromid! Aren't you educated?" the baron snapped, picking up his glass for another sip. He waved the small goblet around as he gestured, not quite slopping the drink. "One of those . . . desert-y things. Sundaran animal. Looks like a . . . a shaggy overgrown sheep with a really long neck an' a really bad back."

"Ah." Marc frowned in thought. "But . . . if it's a sheeplike thing . . . well, that inn't very fierce, is it?"

"It's *big*. And unusual in these parts. They like deserts, an' we live in a lush foresht. Or something. Good rum."

Marc grunted and offered the decanter again. "Good enough, it's running out—hey!" He paused mid-pour and gestured, tilting the decanter up to keep from spilling the dregs of the amber liquid. "What's your *fiercest* shape? We c'n call in th' maid to fetch up 'nother bottle for the decanter, an' *you* can scare her!"

Siona reminded herself this was an act. If she hadn't been keeping an eye on the difference in how much he refilled each of their cups, she might have thought Marc was indeed inebriated beyond good sense. His tactic worked, though.

Baron Oger laughed heartily at the idea. Setting down his cup, he grabbed for the bell on the small, six-sided table set between their lounging chairs. Ringing it fiercely, Oger stood up, settled his shoulders, muttered the words of the spell, and transformed himself.

A few seconds later, the door to the parlor opened—and the middle-aged woman summoned by the bell screeched at the sight of the huge lion lurking just beyond the door. The lion *roared*, making her scream again, before shifting back into his normal, odious baron-self. Oger laughed heartily at her fright.

"*Rum*, woman!" Marc shouted, waving the decanter. "Rum! Fetch us more rum! And be quick about it!"

Trembling, the woman staggered back out onto the balcony, letting the door swing shut behind her. Still laughing, Oger stumbled back to his chair and plopped down onto it. "Priceless! *That'll* put th' fear a' me into her. Bet you can't do better'n that!"

"Oh, well, *large* forms are easy," Marc dismissed, flipping his free hand airily. "The . . . um, whatsits. The *conversion* rate of magic to matter in the art of Anthromancy is forty to one! Any idiot can make hemshelf . . . himself . . . into something of a . . . a comparable size or even something larger. It takes a *true* spellshifter, an' a great deal of power an' control, to *redushe* your *shize*. If you *really* want to impress me . . . what's the *smallest* animal you c'n shift into?"

Baron Oger scratched and belched, thinking about it.

"A rabbit?" Marc prompted. "A . . . rat?"

Oger smirked. "A *shrew*."

Marc snorted. "Ha! I don't believe you! You're like . . . twice the size of me! All big . . . burly . . . muscles . . ." Having paused to top off both glasses, Marc lifted his to his lips. "Prove it. Prove you c'n turn into a shrew, and . . . and . . . I'll do your taxes! For free! 'Cause *I* don't think you *can*."

"Ha!" Knocking back half his glass, Oger shoved to his feet. Siona tensed, watching and waiting. The baron set his glass on the table with a *thunk*, rubbed his large palms together, shrugged his shoulders, and muttered a new set of spellwords. With his back mostly to her, she quickly rolled from her side to her paws, crouching in anticipation. As soon as his body finished shrinking, his clothes shifting from blues and greens to a mottled gray and his nose lengthening into a long, slender snout, she sprang.

Leaping twice, once from cushion to floor, the second from floor to prey, she slammed into the little creature's back with her paws and clamped her jaws down on his neck and head. A hard, fast shake *snapped* something—and the body swelled abruptly, letting her know she had succeeded. Knocking him unconscious wouldn't have ended the spell; only death could have had that power. Jerking her teeth free, Siona scampered away from the dead baron, jaws gaping and throat yowling. The pendant translated her wordless distress.

"Gods in Heaven! Get it out of my mouuuuth! Disgusting disgusting *disgusting*, I've got his *blood* in my mouth! *Ewwwww! Out! Out! Out!*"

Scrambling out of his chair, Marc grabbed for the water flask on the sideboard and a bowl of nuts near the flask. Dumping the nuts on the sideboard tray, he splashed water into the bowl and tucked it under her distress-wrinkled muzzle when she came near. Disgusted but grateful, Siona buried her head in the liquid, swishing her face. Pulling out, she sneezed twice while he dumped the water on the floor and gave her a fresh bowlful to swish in. The second time she pulled out, her wail of disgust turned to a choking yowl.

The collar translated that, too, projecting her distress as, "Oh, Gods, I'm going to be *sick*—hairball! Hairbaaaall!"

Her husband had the temerity to laugh at her, proving he *was* at least somewhat drunk. Not completely, but somewhat. Recovering enough to stroke her back while she coughed up the contents of her stomach, he offered her a third, fresh round of water to clear the new nasty taste from her mouth.

"There, there, puss . . . You'll have to stay Boots a little while longer, to wait for the baron's magics to fade," he reminded her. "Given how strong he is, or was, that could take up to a week. But it's over. You did it. You were *very* brave and skillful, my dear."

Muzzle wet, gut still cramped, Siona leaned into him as he scooped her up for a post-battle cuddle.

At that moment, the parlor maid returned with the bottle of rum. She opened the door cautiously this time, peering warily around the edge. The moment she spotted the bloodied, mangled body on the floor, she gasped.

Staggering to his feet, Marc stepped over Oger's unmoving form and held out his hand. "Ah, the rum. Thank you! You have perfect timing. I would like to apologize for egging him on like that and thus scaring you. I'm terribly sorry, but I hope you can take some comfort in the fact that it was necessary at the time."

"But . . . the baron . . ." she stammered, glancing between him and the corpse on the floor.

"Ah, yes. It seems he not only insisted upon scaring you as a lion, he foolishly went on to transform himself into a shrew, ignoring the fact that there was a cat in the room," Marc dismissed airily. "And, cats being cats, with their instincts written into their bones by the Gods Themselves, well . . . every mage is cautioned that such things can happen, and warned over and over in their spellshifting classes to be alert for such possible dangers.

"But he went and did it anyway, so only the baron himself is to blame for his timely . . . pardon me, terribly sorry, his *un*timely demise." Patting her on the shoulder, he took the bottle of rum from her. "Be a dear and call up some manservants to carry the body out to the chapel for consecration and preparation, will you? I'm sure Oger's family will want it spell-preserved and transported back to his family plot, too.

"Don't you worry," he added as the woman gave him a doubtful look. "The *rightful* heir to Calabas will be returning shortly, and everything will get back to normal very soon. Or at least a reasonable facsimile of it. Come along, Boots. We're still on our honeymoon, and *I'm* in the mood to celebrate!"

Bottle of rum tucked in the crook of one arm and slightly damp wife-cat cuddled in the other, the Marquis of Calabas strolled out of the downstairs parlor, leaving the poor, befuddled maid behind.

The King
Who Heard a Joke

Author's Note: This is one of those fairy tales that has several variations. Some say it was a king, others a farmer, others a fisherman, so on and so forth. And normally—being a rabid equalist—I would balk at the medieval mind-set prompting the "moral" behind the original tale. But this being the modern world, there is plenty of room for mutually consenting activities of, shall we say, a kinkier than average nature? Plus, in the version I've chosen to tell, there is a message worthy of being gleaned. With all of that in mind, I decided that my own version would make for an acceptably interesting story. Here's hoping you'll enjoy it, too.

JACK King couldn't breathe. As fast as he tried to gasp in air, it spasmed right back out again, until his face was a reddened rictus from being scrunched. If he hadn't been seated on the milking stool, he might have fallen to the ground and injured himself; as it was, he slumped to the ground, wheezing and panting and *heeheehee*-ing as though his very life depended on it.

His wife, coming back for the second milk pail, stopped in the doorway and gaped at her suffering husband. Hitching up her skirts, she rushed the rest of the way into the barn. "Jack! Jack, dearest! Whatever on earth is so funny?"

That sobered him up. Somewhat. Shaking his head quickly, he struggled to breathe instead of guffaw. The sight of one of the barn cats flicking her ear and swishing her tail only made him laugh hard once again. Tears leaking from his eyes, he heard his wife exclaim in disgust. She tried to help him up, and when that failed, she pulled the milk pail out of reach, just in case it got knocked over.

"Jack . . . Jack!" she snapped, giving him a disapproving look. "Stop laughing! Dandelion still needs milking, and you're getting your shirt and breeches all dirty. And what in heaven's name is so terribly hilarious?"

He shook his head, struggling for sobriety. He couldn't tell her; he honestly could *not* tell a single soul. As much as he wanted to, he couldn't. Pushing upright, he dusted himself off, struggling against the occasional stray chuckle.

"Honestly!" Ellen scoffed, dusting off his backside with practical whisks of her palms. She lingered a little over his buttocks before brushing the bits of straw from the backs of his thighs, then whapped off one last bit of chaff. "Now, what was so funny that you couldn't breathe?"

Avoiding even looking in the direction of the barn cat, Jack drew in a deep breath and let it out.

"Nothing. Nothing, my dearest." Turning, he caught her hands and kissed them. Ellen was beautiful, smart, and talented at homemaking. She could have been a governess, but had chosen to marry him and take up her share of the work required to make King's Farm one of the best dairies in western Massachusetts. "Thank you for your help. I shall finish the milking, freshen their feed and water, and be in shortly after that to break my fast. Go on. Go make those drop biscuits I love, and the salt-pork sauce with onions."

"All right—but I expect to hear whatever this jest was," she warned him, waggling her finger.

"It was nothing, my dear. Just a stray thought, long since fled." Judging from the look she gave him, she didn't believe him, but he just kissed her on the cheek and sent her on her way with the freshly filled bucket. Claiming the one she had brought, Jack resettled the stool next to the patiently waiting heifer. A glance over his shoulder reassured him he was alone once more. Turning, he mock-glared at the cat and hissed, "*That* was very dangerous of you! You *should* have waited until she'd brought back the third round of goat-milk pails and gone back in to finish breakfast."

The barn cat flicked her ears and her tail, and *mrrrred*. Whiskers forward, she took a couple steps toward him. Or rather, the milk pail.

"I don't know why I *should*, considering you almost killed me," the farmer muttered. "But . . . a bet is a bet," he sighed, before chuckling to himself. "And that *was* the funniest thing I've ever heard. Come on, then—I know you didn't get it, Dandelion," he added as he carefully squeezed milk from one of her teats into his palm, before lowering his hand and offering the creamy liquid to the cat. "But a cat's sense of humor is quite different from a cow's."

Dandelion *huffed* and returned to chewing her cud. In the pen next to her stall, two of the nanny goats bleated, reminding him he hadn't milked them yet. Nodding, he waited until the cat finished lapping up her treat, then focused on squeeze-pulling the rest of Dandelion's milk into the new pail.

He had five dairy cattle, three with heifer calves—the bull calves having already been sold to a neighbor—six nannies with kids and a billy goat, and the two horses who pulled his plow and his wagon with equal aplomb. The horses and the billy didn't need milking, but they would need feeding. Jack had always made a point of feeding them before himself every morning and evening meal. It was something they appreciated, and something which made it that much easier to manage them. But then there was a reason why King's Farm was the best, if smallest, dairy around, and why he trusted no one but himself to be kind to his animals.

Your family has always been good to us, Jack King, the Wee Man had whispered in his ear twelve years ago. *And so the King of the Tor has chosen to grant you this gift, to help you to prosper as you make your way to the New Land. You will hear and understand the speech of all the animals that walk on the land or fly through the air, which will make you a great farmer . . . up to a point. But to have this gift at all, you must be willing to pay a terrible price.*

You must never *tell a single human being that you can hear and speak with the animals. At that moment, if you should ever give in to the temptation to tell another human soul, the price of this gift will be forfeit. Should you ever do so, Jack King, you shall turn to solid stone the moment your tale is through . . .*

It was a good thing the Wee Man had given him this gift when Jack was one-and-twenty years of age, old enough to understand the value of self-control. And he had kept it all this time, despite the temptations over the years to let others know that he knew far more than a mortal man should. Hardest of all, however, was not telling his beloved wife.

He had met the blue-eyed, black-haired beauty on a trip to Boston shortly after news reached him that the war had ended. Unlike himself, who had been born an Englishman before emigrating to the New World prior to their second war with England, she had been born and raised a colonial. And unlike most women—thanks to the damnable war—she hadn't shunned him just because he had once been "one of *them.*"

Her father hadn't entirely approved, being a schoolmaster and expecting a better match for her than a mere farmer, but Jack had persevered. Ellen was bright, kind, beautiful, and strong-willed, raised with an almost libertine attitude toward her education. Thanks to her father's generosity, she had the wits and the inner fire to match Jack's own. He had learned too much over the years of listening to his animals talk to believe a woman was second-class to anyone, and he had not wanted to see her strength of will and character subdued by some overbearing suitor, the kind who would treat a marriage to her like a business proposal, a transaction, and treat her like a mere commodity. Like an animal.

Jack loved her, and he wanted to be with her for the rest of his life. The happiest day had been the day she told him she loved him deeply, with the second happiest being the day he took her as his wife. Third happiest had been the day her father had finally consented to the match, even if Jack had been born an Englishman. The days of their months-long marriage were a close fourth to all of that, a little slice of Heaven on earth. She was his wife, and she completed him.

He just couldn't *tell* her certain things, for fear it would end their happiness. Namely in a man-shaped monument for his grave.

THE more he told her it was *nothing*, the more his dismissal exasperated Ellen. This wasn't the first time, either. There were other times when she had caught him laughing or smiling unexpectedly, and times when he had gone quite still and intent, his gaze on one of the animals of his farm, before taking some action. Often the action was something that helped those animals; she was proud of his skill as a herdsman, his conscientious care of his animals, but sometimes . . . Well, sometimes he just went about it in a rather strange manner.

Still, he was quite smart, and when all their chores were done each evening, he spared no expense in keeping a few extra candles lit after supper so they could share reading passages with each other from beloved books. It didn't matter the topic, either; he enjoyed discussing the philosophies of the likes of Calvin, and Hobbes, and the fairy tales collected by Michael Alexander Nenasheff, though Jack's French was worse than hers and they sometimes stumbled their way through the tales with a healthy sense of good humor.

With any other husband, she might not have been allowed such a thing. Ellen knew she would have been expected to tend to her husband's needs first and her own desires second. Jack was different, however; he was a man with a liberated mind. Other women might have looked down upon him for being a mere dairy farmer, but he was so much more to her.

Which, I suppose, is why his reticence on certain subjects is so vexing. Glaring at him over the supper table, three days after hearing his shouts and his guffaws, his giggles and wheezes, she could not help but continue to press the matter. "I don't understand, Jack. *Why* can't you tell me what made you laugh? It had to have been the most spectacular jest in the world to have made you laugh so hard. And don't tell me you don't remember it. Everyone remembers what made them laugh the hardest!"

"I *told* you. It was just a passing thought, long since forgotten," he repeated patiently, gesturing with his fork. He used to eat left-handed like an Englishman, but in the effort to seem more American, he had managed to make the switch. The original war for independence was long over, as well as the second war with England, which had ended a few years ago, but it didn't pay to advertise one's foreign origins too closely even now.

She set down her own fork. "Well, I *cannot* believe it. I refuse to! Dearest, as much as I love you, some of the things you do are just . . . utterly inexplicable! And to keep *denying* that you laughed over something so cunningly funny . . . I feel like I'm being ignored. Like I'm being shut out of your life as . . . as someone unimportant."

Jack winced at that. Ellen knew she was pressing hard by putting it so, but she really did feel that way. One of the things he had sworn to her was that he would always take her thoughts and feelings as seriously as his own. She didn't *want* to say it, but she felt like she had to say it.

Reaching across the table toward his hand, she gave him a helpless look. "Jack, my darling . . . I feel as if you're treating me like a silly female, without a thought in my head capable of comprehending whatever made you laugh. You *know* I can!"

"I am not trying to slight your intelligence, darling," he replied, setting down his fork long enough to cover her outstretched hand, "but I *cannot* tell you what made me laugh. So please, for my sake, stop asking."

"No, I shan't stop asking," Ellen pressed as he picked up his fork again. "You are hiding something from me, and you have *always* been hiding something from me. I can see it now." That was a slight exaggeration . . . or it had been, until she saw the faint flash of guilt on his face. The pinkening of his cheeks and the sidling of his gaze which couldn't quite meet hers for a moment. "You *are* hiding something from me!"

"Have done, Ellen! *What* could I possibly be hiding from you?" he demanded. "Think about that! I have shared with you my life, my heart, and my thoughts. And if I should find a funny thought running through my head, if you are there, then I should tell you about it. If it is of a gentlemanly nature, of course. But if you are *not*—and you *were not* there at that time—then once it has passed, why should I share it? Some jests are amusing *only* in the moment in which they occur and cannot be shared once that moment and its context have passed! In this case, that moment has passed for sharing the jest, and we need to move on to other things.

"Now, I intend to go to town tomorrow with the latest of the ripened cheeses. If you will remember, the mayor's wife asked for us to bring her some more of the herbed goat cheese when it was ready. She mentioned something about entertaining relatives visiting from Providence in the next week," he reminded her. "Do you think you could pick out five of the most flavorful cheeses from the well house cellar in the morning? I think she might enjoy some of the ones with the savory and chive, since you have a wonderful hand when it comes to flavoring those."

If her husband thought the subject was dropped, he was mistaken. Ellen allowed him to redirect the conversation for now, but she wouldn't forget it. Nor would she forget that little flash of guilt she had seen. She had not imagined that. Nor would she let him forget that she didn't believe for a moment that *he* had forgotten the source of his laughter.

She would *not* be shut out of his life. She would *not* be treated like a simpleton—or dismissed like a mere girl!

THUNK. "Here's your milk pail! Have you anything to say to me, or have you *forgotten* it?"

Biting back the urge to groan, Jack finished pulling on the nanny's teats with a few more ripples of his fingers and traded the full metal pail for the empty one she had brought. "Enough, woman! It has been a full week. You didn't even rest on the Lord's Day. Must you go on about this forever?"

"You *promised* you would treat me as an equal when we married, Jack King," Ellen retorted, all but sloshing the goat's milk out of the pail as she snatched it up by its handle. "Yet here you are, dismissing the simplest of my requests! What kind of a man have I married, that you would go back on your word to your wife? *What* are you *hiding* from me?"

"Leave it be, Ellen!" he ordered tersely. Not that he had much hope of that; she had nagged him for a solid week now.

"How can I? How can I ever trust you again? You promised you would share your life with me, but you won't share whatever it is you are hiding! How can I live with a man who has lied to me?" she challenged him. "Tell me the truth, Jack King! If you ever loved me, tell me the truth!"

She just would not let it go. These last seven days were rapidly turning into the worst of his life. For the last three nights, she had not responded to his advances in their marriage bed. Not being of a nature to force the issue, Jack had spent each night in restless misery.

"What am I to do, Husband?" Ellen asked him pointedly. "Am I to . . . to have a good reason to stay here, confident that you love and trust me? Or am I to believe—without cause to support otherwise—that you do *not* trust me with your life? And if I cannot have your trust and share with you all the aspects of your life, what then? What then . . . but to go home to my father? *He*, at least, never held back the truth from me!"

Her threat made him pale. *Ellen . . . leaving me?* It was almost inconceivable. He loved her! He could not envision a day of his life without her. *I might as well be dead, than to not have her by my side . . . but . . . God in Heaven and the Wee Folk of the Tor, if I don't tell her, she'll leave me and I'll die . . . but if I do tell her, I'll die anyway! King of the Tor, why did you curse me with this gift?*

He was too far from the Tor to expect an answer, of course, being on the other side of an entire ocean.

His wife took his anguished silence for stubbornness. A soft sniff made him look at her. She stood gazing at him with tear-bright blue eyes and a trembling lower lip, but with her chin lifted high. "Very well, then. I shall pack and leave first thing in the morn."

No! Everything within him clenched at that idea. Broke at that idea. Shaking his head, Jack found his voice. "No! No . . . I'll tell you."

She didn't smile in triumph, but neither did the tears fall from her eyes. Ellen held herself still, almost as if breathing would make him change his mind . . . or make her change hers about staying to listen. There was just one problem with telling her immediately; Jack didn't want his final moments to be spent in the barn, of all places.

"I *will* tell you. Tonight," he promised. "I will tell you everything. *But*," he cautioned, "I want no arguments out of you, and no nagging, and no unpleasantness—and no mention of packing up and going to your father. No fighting, no recriminations . . . just the rest of this day spent as peacefully and lovingly as possible. Will you promise me that?"

She blinked at him, as if unsure she had heard him right, but nodded slowly all the same. "A peaceful, quiet day . . . I suppose. But why can't you tell me right now?"

A glimpse of the barn cat who had started this mess gave him the inspiration he needed. Managing something of a smile, Jack offered, "Well, now, I could hardly tell you what the joke was when both of us are angry and upset. It just wouldn't be the same, would it?

"Come here . . . my love," he offered, struggling to hold back his anguish at those two little words. Thankfully, she accepted his outstretched hand. As much as he wanted to take her into their house to make love to her, he still had two more goats to milk, hay to pitch, and water to draw from the well. He kissed her knuckles, then pressed her palm to his cheek. "Just remember for the rest of this day that I *do* love you. With all the life left in my body, I love you that much . . . and so much more."

She flushed. Only the bleating of the half-milked nanny goat, Parsley, broke their tableau. Taking the full milk pail with her, Ellen retreated from the barn. Once she had gone, Jack was free to bow his head in pain. There was nothing he could do to stop the inevitable, one way or another.

The nanny bleated again, irritating him. Lifting his head, he glared at her. "*No*, I will *not* let her do that! I don't care if it spares me my life to have her return to her father and leave me alone. *She* is my life— Keep your bleating to yourself!" he added as Parsley protested again. "I'll have the rest of this day to make perfect, and I'll *not* have you spoiling it in any way."

Sweeping the other animals a firm look, he finished with a glare at the cat.

"As for *you* . . . I'm beginning to feel like I should have drowned *you* at birth. You have *ruined* my marriage and brought about the *end* of my life. If you want me to be kind to you for the rest of this day, then get out of my sight!"

Wisely, the cat scampered out of the barn.

Turning back to the nanny goat, Jack positioned the emptied pail and began milking the last of the liquid from her udder, careful to keep his rippling strokes firm and purposeful, but not bruising. He would not end his last day on earth by abusing his animals. However much Parsley's suggestion to let his wife leave with her questions unanswered might vex him, he would not hurt her.

TWICE over breakfast, she opened her mouth to ask him to tell her now, because the wait until evening seemed interminable. Each time, he discerned her intention and narrowed his eyes in silent warning. Subsiding each time, Ellen sought for something else to say.

"The weather seems to be quite good; will you be cutting hay in the southwest field today?" she finally asked, adding a dollop of honey to one of her buttermilk-raised biscuits. "I planned to do some weeding in the herb garden, then perhaps collect some wood from the forest this afternoon. I know we have plenty of logs left from the winter to see us through most of the summer, but I was thinking of gathering bits and pieces for tinder and kindling, for which we're running low."

"No. Today . . . I would like us to do something different," Jack stated slowly. His blue eyes looked troubled, though his words were remarkably romantic. Even for him. "I would like to spend the rest of today with you going over every memory we've ever made together. From the very first moment I saw you in Boston, looking so lovely in your bonnet and pelisse, laughing at some jest, to the . . . to the way you look, all flushed and dreamy, yet fiery at the same time when I hold you in my arms at night."

Ellen blushed. She searched again for something to say. A faint noise distracted her. Frowning, she tried to pinpoint it.

"I still remember quite clearly the day we met, my love," Jack continued earnestly. "I thought you—"

"Shh." Lifting her hand, she silenced her husband. Turning her head, she strained to hear. *Yes . . . I think there's some sort of disturbance outside.*

"Ellen?" Jack asked, frowning.

The noise was growing. "Can't you hear that? There's something outside—Jack, I think something is disturbing the animals in the barn!"

He bolted up from his breakfast, and from its place of pride over the mantel he snatched his Springfield musket, which she knew he always kept carefully oiled, loaded and ready out of habit from the days of the second war with England. Never having been of the temperament to cower in a corner, Ellen rose as well, moving to one of the kitchen cupboards and snatching up her wedding gift from an elderly aunt, a solid, marble-carved rolling pin. It was the sort of weapon guaranteed to brain anything that threatened her, whether it stalked on two legs or four.

Hurrying after her husband, she followed him outside, where the bleating and bawling of the goats could now clearly be heard. She almost ran into Jack as she hastened inside, for he had inexplicably stopped just a few feet within the door. Peering around his broadcloth-covered shoulders, she spotted the reason for the commotion.

Their one billy goat was butting and biting and chasing one of the nannies around and around their feeding stall. Cowslip bawled and charged, and Parsley bleated and dodged. When she finally tried to escape out through the open half door into the pasture, he cut her off with a savage whirl and kick which flung her off her hooves. Stunned, the poor nanny lay tumbled on her side, dazed and bleating weakly, her summer-short wool scruffed and slowly reddening from the blood welling out of two scrapes Cowslip had made.

"Jack! Stop them! Cowslip's gone mad!" she begged, tugging on her immobile husband's arm.

Cowslip snorted and bleated, then looked their way. He bleated twice again, snorted, and trotted outside, leaving Parsley huddled shivering in the hay, her head half buried in the stalks.

"Jack! Aren't you going to do something?" Ellen demanded, tugging on his shirtsleeve.

"Yes, I am." Handing her the rifle, he entered the stall and crouched over the cowering goat, checking her wounds. "Just the two scrapes, and some tender bruises," Ellen heard him murmur after a few moments.

He gently prodded the nanny's side. Parsley bleated, then shook her head. Jack sighed roughly.

"Well, you have no broken bones, so you'll heal." Rising, he came out of the stall, taking the rifle back from Ellen. "Find some clean cloths. I'll fetch the bottle of spirits and clean her wound to keep out an infection while you see to the tidying of the breakfast things."

"What about Cowslip, Jack?" Ellen asked, hurrying to keep up with his long strides as he headed for the house.

"What about him?" There was an odd, grim edge to his voice. She wasn't sure what to make of it. He looked handsome, as he always did with his golden brown hair and blue eyes, but there was something rather stern, almost authoritarian about him just now. Ellen wasn't sure if she liked it.

"Well . . . he's mad!" she offered, doing her best to keep up with his long, purposeful strides. "Attacking poor Parsley like that . . . !"

"Mad? Hardly. As for myself . . . I have come to my senses. Go tidy up," he ordered her.

Mystified, Ellen did as he requested. She returned the rolling pin, wiped her hands on her kitchen cloth, then went upstairs to the second bedroom, which until they had children had been left as a sort of library and crafts room. She had to move several books, including an illustrated tome of fairy tales, with its fanciful picture of the Frog Prince embossed on the cover, but at least she knew where to look for what her husband would need. She fetched strips of cloth from the rag bag in the trunk beneath the tome and carried them downstairs to Jack. Then she covered their plates with bowls in case either of them grew hungry again, since their meal had been interrupted.

With nothing else to do but wait for his return, she started tidying the rest of the kitchen. Jack came back when she was wrist-deep in soapy dishwater. Setting the bottle of distilled spirits back in its cupboard, he crossed to her and held out his hand. "Come."

Ellen gave his fingers a bemused look. "Right now? But I'm in the middle of the dishes . . ."

"They can wait. This cannot. Come," he repeated.

Unsure what he was about, since he didn't entirely look angry, but neither did he look romantic, Ellen lifted her hands from the soapy water. She dried them on her apron, then tucked one hand into his. Without a word, he pulled her in his wake, heading for the stairs. A quick glance behind her at the kitchen showed there was nothing on or near the hearth fire that could pose a threat if left untended. The entire floor was paved in bricks, and their dining table and its chairs were set too far away for even the most vigorous spark to reach.

It was a good thing everything was fine as it was, for he marched both of them straight up to their bedroom, brought her inside, and closed the door.

"I want you to know that I love you," Jack stated, though this time his tone was more grim than emotional. "I love you beyond everything in God's Creation. And that I will continue to honor the vows I swore unto you, your father, and to God Himself. That I will love you, cherish you, honor you, and *respect* you as my *equal*."

Ellen flinched at the hard bite in those emphasized words. She found herself towed a second time in his wake, this time to their bed, where he turned and faced her, giving her another stern look. Before she could do more than open her mouth to ask him what was wrong, he sat down on the neatly made bed, disturbing the loft of the feather-stuffed mattress which she had patted into shape just that morning while he was checking for eggs before milking the cows. More than that, he tugged sharply on her wrist, making her stumble into him unexpectedly.

He did catch her, but not to right her. To her startlement, Ellen found herself twisted and dropped stomach-first onto his thighs. "Jack?"

"I have given you *equality* and *respect* in the understanding that these things would be *returned* to me. Equality is all about things being equal on *both* sides of a matter, and respect must be *mutual* for it to have value as well as meaning. You have *not* been respectful to me, Wife."

"Jack! That is not true!" she protested. She struggled to rise, but he pushed her back down, pinning her on his lap. She could feel the wooden strip of the busk in her stays digging into her breastbone and stomach, and knew it was digging into his thighs as well, but he didn't relax the pressure of his left palm between her shoulder blades. "Jack! Let me up!"

"Quiet!" he snapped, alarming her.

He unnerved her further by rucking up the hem of her gown, lifting it up above her rump. He also lifted her waist petticoat, following it with her chemise. Embarrassed, Ellen squirmed, but a firm press from his left hand made her hold still. She gasped in the next moment, for his right hand touched her thigh above her garter, and slid slowly up the back of her leg to the soft, bared curves of her buttocks.

"I promised myself I would never raise a fist to you. But over the last week, you have disrespected me. In fact, you have disrespected me grievously. You have ignored my requests to drop the subject of why I laughed and, in doing so, belittled my wishes as less worthy than your own. You have accused me of lying, without proof of any truth to the contrary, which means you have deliberately chosen to distrust me. You have *nagged* me and bossed me about as if I were a lowly servant and thus *not your equal*."

Jack paused, his hand on her rump. Ellen shivered. Normally, he only touched that part of her anatomy when he was aroused and wanted to be with her, to arouse her as well. She blushed with the naughty memory of how often he had praised her curves, murmuring scandalous things to her in the dark of the night. And while he had seen that part of her by candlelight at night during the months of their marriage, both of them worked too long and too hard on the farm most of the time to bother dallying by day. It was embarrassing to be exposed so, particularly on such a bright, sunny day.

"I love you very, very much," he repeated in a softer murmur. Almost of its own volition, as if prompted by the same memories she was recalling, his fingers moved gently over her bum, stroking the rounded flesh. The contrast between his touch and his words confused her, for it both aroused and alarmed her. He continued quietly, almost reverently at first, slipping his hand to the other globe and feathering his fingertips over the crease in between. "I talk with you, I consult with you, I treat you as my equal because I love, cherish, and respect you. But I also respect myself too much to be treated like a rag-braided carpet. Whatever transgressions you may *think* you have suffered, you have transgressed against me all the worse.

"In short, Wife . . . you have behaved like a spoiled child. In sparing the rod this last week out of my love for you, I have spoiled you. As much as it grieves me to do so, I know that *because* I love you, I must now punish you, for I cannot allow this ill-behavior of yours to continue unchecked, to ruin our marriage."

That was all the warning he gave her. Lifting his hand off her rump, he brought it down with a sharp, painful *smack!* Ellen yelped, shocked that he would do such a thing. Not even her own father had punished her like this, preferring instead to make her do her least-liked chores and to write essays analyzing chapters from exceedingly dull-witted books. Never had any man lifted his hand to her like this, and—*smack!*—she did *not* like it!

"Jack! Let me up at once!" She struggled to get off his lap, but he bowed himself over her, caging her in place with his left arm wrapped around her chest. "How dare you!"

"I *dare*, Wife, because *you* dared!" He spanked her again, stinging her rump painfully, then switched his next blow to her other upturned cheek. He didn't pause between strokes, either, but rained them down with a steady *smacksmacksmack*, sometimes on her left buttock, sometimes on her right one. He spanked her in spite of her protests, her squirmings, and her yelpings as the stinging became a burning.

Finally, his hand feathered down over her skin instead of whapping. Overwrought with pain and humiliation, Ellen shivered at his suddenly gentle touch. Within moments, her cheeks burned for a different reason as his fingers soothed her thrumming skin. While the sting of each slap lingered painfully, there was also a newfound sensitivity to her skin, one which magnified the tenderness of his caress.

It confused her, that she could feel such pleasure from his touch when he had just given her so much pain.

"I *am* sorry I have to spank you, my dearest," Jack murmured. She couldn't look up at him very easily, given her ignominious position, but she could hear the sincere regret in his voice. "But you have given me no choice."

"No *choice*?" she spluttered, craning her neck to look up at him. "You did so have a *choice*!"

Slap!

"I hear *defiance* in your voice, Madam Wife!" Jack scolded her sternly, ignoring her startled yelp. The authority in his voice, deep and commanding, made her shiver anew, for he had never spoken like this before, like a man whose very life depended on her understanding and compliance. "Defiance, which is disrespect! While I will *never* raise my fist to you to beat you bloodied and blue, as Cowslip did to Parsley, should you choose to continue to behave like a spoiled child, you shall be *dealt with* like a spoiled child! And spoiled children are *spanked*!"

With that, he rained his palm down upon her backside once more. His hand fell like a fierce summer storm, lashing her skin with a whipping from his own. Ellen yelped and squirmed, but he kept her in place, paddling her mercilessly. Pain and confusion mingled with the burning in her rump and even down onto the backs of her thighs when her writhing to escape made his aim occasionally slip.

This time, he didn't stop until she was sobbing. Slowing his blows, he finally brought his hand to a standstill atop her burning bum. It hurt so much, she couldn't help but move her hips in the futile attempt to escape the pain . . . and the circling of her hips made his lightly resting fingers shift on her skin. The sensation evoked by the inadvertent caress was so strong, it made her gasp and shift her hips even harder. This time . . . not to escape, but to arch her buttocks further into his touch.

More than that, in the gyrating and the parting of her thighs . . . she could feel how moist her feminine folds had grown. How very, very slick and moist. Normally it took her husband many minutes of kissing her on her lips and her breasts, of playing his hands over the hills and valleys of her femininity, even of rubbing that special spot that felt so good, before she grew so wet that she noticed it. But now all he had done this time was assert his will, tell her he loved her, scold her soundly, and spank her thoroughly. And gently touch her afterward.

I cannot believe how good *this feels! God in Heaven,* how *can this feel so* good?

His hand skimmed over her burning skin; she knew he did love her and that he was trying to soothe the traces of each impact . . . but all it did was further arouse her. A whimper escaped her throat. Unable to lie still, ignoring the stiff wooden busk of her stays still digging into her ribs, the bunching of her skirts over her hips, the fact that it was broad daylight, with untold chores awaiting both them, Ellen circled her hips, trying to get him to touch more of her overwrought, impassioned flesh.

"Are you repentant?" Jack asked her, almost petting her rump. "Will you now give proper weight to my wishes, honoring them and thus respecting me as your equal? As much as I love you, my dearest, if you *ever* treat me like an inferior again, I shall turn the tables on you exactly as I have just done, time and time again. You *will* respect me, as I will respect you. *When* you are worthy of my respect."

She whimpered, stuffing the knuckles of one hand into her mouth. She knew she was supposed to be punished, not pleasured—and she could reluctantly admit to herself that her husband *did* have a point—but those soft strokes on her sensitized skin were inflaming her senses almost as much as the spanking had, if in the opposite direction.

Smack! "Answer me!" *Smack smack slap whap!* "Are you *repentant?*"

With the splaying of her thighs, the raising and circling of her hips, his last blow landed on the folds of her quim. Her naughty, wet, wanting quim. She yelped around her knuckles, then moaned when he left his hand resting right there. Almost as if claiming the territory he had just tamed.

Her body shuddered in pleasure a mere moment later; liquid trickled from her depths, seeping copiously past her nether-lips. Both of them froze as it dampened his fingertips. Mortified yet aroused, Ellen held her breath, wondering what her husband might do next.

❧

WET.

His wife, whom he had just spanked, and spanked thoroughly for what was probably the first time in her life . . . was *wet*. Very, thoroughly wet. Dimly, as the blood rushed first to his face, then promptly reversed course and headed for his loins, Jack realized her whimpers were the sounds no longer of a woman in pain, but rather of a woman in need.

Sensual need, the sort of sounds he normally only heard at night. Sounds which he hadn't heard from her since before this whole mess started, given her angry, cold treatment of him this past week.

A sense of power, heady, primitive, and primal, rushed through his body. His loins, halfheartedly stiffened at the first exposure of her tender, beautiful skin, now tightened and thickened to the point that the fitted front of his breeches pinched his flesh from the strain of being confined. For a moment, he knew how Cowslip felt, dominant and powerful, superior and in control over his mate. Except the billy goat had actually, deliberately hurt his mate with the force of his anger, going well beyond merely refusing to give in to her nagging about getting Jack to save himself by driving his wife away.

Guilt followed on the heels of that rush of feeling. Sliding his fingers out of her folds, he gingerly ran his hand over Ellen's reddened skin. He wasn't completely sure, given the rosy hue of her rump, but he was fairly sure she would only have a few minor bruises at best by the end of this. He didn't *want* to hurt her . . . God, how he didn't want to hurt her . . . but he did need to drive his point home somehow.

She moaned again, hips twitching under his touch. Twitching *upward*, as if offering herself to him. Lust boiled in his blood. Corralling it sharply, Jack stilled his hand on her heated flesh. He *had* to remain in control until she admitted she had done wrong.

"I love you," he repeated firmly, for he couldn't not tell her; he didn't want her to forget *why* he was doing this. "But until you repent your sins against me, you will continue to be punished."

Lifting his hand, he spanked her three times, each one harder than the last, making his palm sting. Letting his hand linger on her flesh after the third one, he deliberately caressed her, hoping she was indeed able to accept that he *could* punish her and still love her at the same time. Two more swift, sharp swats, and he rested his smarting fingers again.

"Until you swear you will *never* again ask me why I laughed, or expect an answer . . . I *must* keep punishing you," he stated as firmly as he could. "Even if this hurts *both* of us."

With that, he steeled himself with a deep breath and swatted her rapidly. After a dozen or so blows, when her whimpers became grunts, he switched to glancing blows, as if vigorously dusting dirt from her rump. Ellen gasped and arched in his lap, her legs flailing at the new sensations being imparted by his swatting attack.

"Swear it," Jack ordered when he paused again. She moaned loudly and clung to his thigh and calf, legs squirming and splayed wide. "Swear you will never bring up these questions again! Swear it!"

"Please . . . oh please!" she groaned.

He swatted her again, whapping the globes of her flesh back and forth with the palm of his hand. "Swear you will respect me, and never again ask why I laughed!"

"Please, Jack! *Please!*" she begged. He heard her voice break and paused in his spanking. Her breath caught in her throat. Jack thought she might be sobbing, but the pins holding her black hair in a bun had come loose, leaving clumps of her dark locks dangling over her face in a concealing ebony curtain.

A wriggling squirm of her hips slipped his fingertips into her cleft.

She was so hot and wet, his manhood strained at the fall of his breeches, striving to get out of the confines of mere cloth and into the confines of her flesh. Pure lust overrode his control for a moment, making him seek out the folds of her femininity, then circle and flick the little peak of her pleasure. His wife cried out, arching her back. He did it again, making her shudder, and thrust two fingers into her depth without warning.

"*Jack!*" she shrieked, bucking up into his touch.

No! No pleasure! Not yet, he warned himself, forcing his hand to withdraw from her. She whimpered and moaned in protest. He struck her rump twice more in emphasis, then left his hand hovering in the air just a thumb-width from her flesh. He knew she could feel the heat of his palm, because she strained up into it, though he didn't let the two connect. However much he longed to stop spanking her and instead plunge into her, to claim his mate in the most primal of ways, she *had* to submit first. Nothing else would spare his life, or keep them together as husband and wife.

"You *know* what I want!" he ordered sharply. "Swear on your life you will never ask me again, or you will continue to be punished over and over. You *will* obey me in this, Ellen. You will never again disrespect my wishes!"

When she didn't swear, he spanked her again. He spanked her until she was sobbing openly and his hand was burning and his rod was throbbing, until she finally cried out the words he needed to hear.

"Yes! Yes, I swear it! I swear I'll never ask it again! Oh, God, Jack—take me! Take me! *Love* me! *Please!*"

Hauling her off his lap, Jack pushed Ellen onto their bed. Ripping at the buttons of his trousers, he unfastened the fall, yanked up his shirt and undershirt, and faced his wife. Impatient, he shoved up the folds of her skirts, which had fallen halfway back down her limbs, only to find her thighs spread wantonly wide. Blatantly waiting to be claimed by him, Ellen moaned his name into the quilt covering their feather-stuffed bed.

Pulling on her hips, he got her to knee up on the edge of the bed. It took only a moment to aim his stiff flesh at her glistening folds, and then—Heaven on earth—he pushed inside. He pushed in so hard and deep, his groin snugged up against her hips, until he could feel the burning heat of her punishment-warmed flanks against his belly.

He could also feel the contracting ripples of her flesh in that special way that signaled his beloved wife was about to climax. Groaning, he pulled back and slammed home, without finesse or care for any spanking-induced bruises. It just felt too good; this felt too primal, too *right*, to slow down or deny. Knowing she was enjoying it—grateful she so clearly enjoyed this—Jack let his self-control go, rutting with the full force of his victory over her while she—his blessed wife—accepted, craved, and even demanded it from him with each sobbing breath, responding just as passionately.

It was primitive and yet primal, and when he spent, he roared like a bull. His wife, clawing at the covers under the force of his claiming, screamed hoarsely herself with the force of her bliss, like one of the mountain lions he had occasionally heard in the distance of the untamed hills to the north and west of his home. Pride surged through him at the sensation of her flesh squeezing him senseless, encouraging him in a few, last, pleasurable thrusts, until fierce pleasure faded, dragging his strength in its wake.

Panting heavily, Jack slumped over his wife. He covered her not only from exhaustion, but to enfold her in his arms. Nuzzling through the tousled locks of her hair, he kissed her tenderly, lovingly on her nape.

"*Now* we can be equals again . . . Mind your promise, my dearest," he breathed, inhaling deeply to restore some energy to his limbs. He heard her sniff, face still pressed to the bedding, and kissed the back of her neck again. "I hope you will. I *never* want to hurt you. I just want to love you and live out the rest of our lives together for a very long time, happily and in harmony."

Carefully, he eased out of her, backing off of her prone body. Unfortunately, he couldn't finish his intent to rise and resume their day, for his limbs threatened to turn into jam preserves. The force of their coupling had drained him just that much. Sagging onto the floor, he rested on his knees and heels, his breeches bunched up over his calves.

The position brought him down to eye-level with her rump. It was strawberry red from the force of his blows. The black hairs dusting the folds of her flesh were matted down with their combined juices. In the clear light of day, he could even see the little tremors of her thigh muscles, still quivering with the intensity of her orgasm.

His own satisfaction still thrumming through his veins, Jack could admit to himself that this portrait of intimacy had to be one of the most beautiful visions of his life.

Leaning forward on impulse, he dusted her reddened flesh with tender, loving kisses, rising up on his knees just enough to circle all around her flesh. With each deep breath, he enjoyed the musk of their coupling, until she whimpered and squirmed, twitching her hips higher into his face. It was wanton, willing, and irresistible. The hay cutting would have to wait, the herb garden would have to keep its weeds for another day, and she was right earlier: They did have enough wood to last them a few more months, even if the tinder and kindling supplies were running low.

All those chores weren't nearly as important as loving his wife for the rest of the day, right here and now. Particularly since he had just guaranteed he would be able to *keep* loving her for the remainder of his hopefully long-lived life. Tugging at the impediments of his clothes, Jack stripped them away between succulent, scandalous, broad daylight tastes of his wife's utterly willing, utterly delicious quim.

She moaned his name in that way that said she wasn't ready to stop. The way she normally did only in the darkest depths of the night.

Their chores could *definitely* wait.

❧

JACK whistled happily as he worked. The early evening was a hot one, so he had stripped off his shirt and foregone an undershirt while he mucked out the stalls. The cows and the nannies were due to return to their byres, udders thick with rich, pasture-fed milk, which meant their shelter had to be tidied and ready. He could do no less for the animals dependent upon his care and aid.

While the hard work did make him sweat, his wife had promised him a cool bath before their evening meal. In fact, she was taking a bath herself right now, having asked him to bring the tin washtub into the kitchen so that she could bathe while their supper cooked. *My life is just about perfect, now*, he thought. *Praise be to God, and to the King of the Tor, it's just about perfect . . .*

"Well, now *that's* a welcoming thought, Jack King. Thank you!"

Whirling, pitchfork in hand, Jack found a very short, redheaded man dressed in blue standing in the open doorway of the barn. A very short, very familiar, Wee Man. Recovering quickly from his shock, Jack glanced toward the house, but couldn't see his wife. Knowing it likely that one of the Wee Folk wouldn't appear if there was the threat of a nonbeliever about, Jack laid the pitchfork aside and swept the little man his most courteous bow.

"Welcome! Please, come in. Would you like me to call in one of the cows for a bit of milk? Something from Dandelion, or perhaps from Buttercup? Are you tired from . . . well, from such a long and incredible journey you must have had?"

The Wee Man chuckled. He rubbed at his clean-shaven chin, then shook his head. "No, I don't need any milk just yet—though I shan't say no if you'll set out a bowl after supper at some point before you retire. And I haven't come such a long ways as you'd think; there are passages, and passages, 'twixt the lands of the King of the Tor to the far east and the Prince of the Lake a short journey to the north. The ways of our kind can make such a great distance seem very short. No, I've been sent to bring greeting to His Majesty's kin, you see . . . and sent again with a short but important missive for *you*."

Approaching the Wee Man, Jack sank to his knees, bringing their heads closer to level. "I'm honored to be remembered by His Majesty. How is he faring, and his lady-wife, and the rest of the Wee Court?"

"Oh, well enough! The Tor will live on and on, as it always has. And your courtesy is appreciated, as always." Hands clasped together in front of his chin, the Wee Man winked at him. "I've good news. We've been keeping an eye upon you, Jack King, and given how carefully you have kept your little gift a proper secret, His Majesty wishes you to know he has granted you a second boon. Not quite so big as the first, but good enough, I think."

Jack tried not to let his fear show. The first one had been bad enough, in its own way. "A . . . *second* boon?"

The Wee Man chuckled, his blue eyes gleaming with mirth. "An easement, if you will. No longer will you be constrained by the threat of death, Jack my boy. In fact, you can even tell your wife, and still live exactly as you have these last few years. But should you ever tell another living, mortal soul—outside of your wife and your children—how you can communicate with the animals of the land and the sky as well as you can with your fellow mortal men . . . the gift shall be taken from you. But *only* the gift, and no longer your life as well. No more turning to stone for you, Jack King! Thus is the King of the Tor's second boon."

Sagging with relief, Jack nodded. "*Thank* you. And thank His Majesty, too, for such deep generosity."

The Wee Man tapped the side of his nose and smiled. "Oh, you'll have cause to thank him again. Just teach your children to respect the Wee Folk . . . and we might have a boon for your firstborn son one day, too." He paused and glanced to the side, then nodded. "Your wife is coming, and I can tell she has an interesting question on her mind.

You'd best attend to her needs—and don't be forgetting that bowl of milk, if you please."

"Every night, for as long as my cattle and my goats give milk," Jack promised, clasping hands with him. "For you, while you visit, and for the court of this Prince of the Lake, for as long as I shall live and milk cows—you may tell him his Wee Folk are most welcome by me. And they would have been welcomed properly all the sooner had I known they were about!"

Chuckling, the Wee Man tipped his hat. "First, they had to be sure what kind of a man they had on their southern doorstep hereabouts. You're a good man, Jack King. A good evening to you!"

"And to you," Jack whispered, watching the Wee Man fade literally from his sight. A few moments later, he broke from his daze, aware that his wife was on her way out. The Wee Folk were never wrong about such things. Rising from the hay, he dusted off the chaff, wondering what question she might have for him.

A moment later, he almost sagged back onto his knees again, for his wife appeared in the barn doorway clad *only* in her shift. A shift which clung in visibly damp patches to her freshly scrubbed skin. Desire gleamed in her eyes, though her cheeks were slightly flushed. "Husband . . ."

"Yes, Wife?" he asked, devouring the sight of her curves through the thin, summer-weight muslin of her shift. Even her feet, bare on the soil at the barn entrance, were gorgeous to him.

"I was wondering . . . why did you laugh so hard the other day?"

Dismay snapped his gaze up to her face. For a moment, he forgot what the Wee Man had just promised, and horror that Ellen would go back on her word so soon churned and clenched in his gut. Then the King of the Tor's promise caught up to him and he relaxed. But only by a little bit. Licking his lips, Jack carefully asked his now pink-faced wife, "Do you not remember what I promised you, Ellen, should you ever in your insolence ask me *that* question again?"

Her blush brightened. Slowly, seductively, she strolled closer, until she stood in front of him. "Oh, I *do* remember. I remember how you swore you would . . . spank me . . . again."

Lifting a hand to his chest, she dragged it down over the sweat-dampened thatch of hair, outlining each of the muscles her fingers passed, until she reached the waistband of his doeskin breeches. Her fingers slipped to one side, toying with the buttons of the fall. The near-caress of his masculine flesh made that flesh twitch and strain in the direction of her hand.

Beyond her, out in the yard between barn and house, he could see a certain barn cat plopping her backside down on the ground, tail curling around her haunches and whiskers perking in smug, self-satisfied humor.

Ellen recaptured his attention with a shift of her hand straight to the bulge of his groin, and a sensual purr of her own. "I remember all of it *very* well . . ."

Love and lust blazed within him hotter than the midsummer sun. Wordlessly, Jack dragged his wife to the nearest pile of freshly strewn hay. The animals could wait just a little longer to be milked, as well as the rest of their chores. He had a deliberately insolent wife begging for penance.

And Jack loved his wife far too much to say no.

JEAN JOHNSON

The best part about being a writer is the joy that comes from entertaining others. Whether it's sad or scary, silly or sexy, I love knowing that one of my stories has given someone a good time. I hope this collection contains one of those stories for you, too. I currently live in the Pacific Northwest, but the easiest way to chat with me is to drop by my website at www.jeanjohnson.net.